The Belly of the Beast

Book II- The Jungle War Series

Kregg P.J. Jorgenson

Print ISBN: 978-1-64719-906-7
Ebook ISBN: 978-1-64719-907-4

Published by BookLocker.com, Inc., Trenton, Georgia.

Printed on acid-free paper.

BookLocker.com, Inc.
2022

First Edition

Library of Congress Cataloguing in Publication Data
Jorgenson, Kregg P.J.
The Belly of the Beast: Book II- The Jungle War Series by Kregg P.J. Jorgenson
Library of Congress Control Number: 2021921818

This book is for my big brother,
former U.S. Army Artillery Captain, Kevin Jorgenson.

Much thanks to Rachel Bodnar, Mike Shintaku, Jon Frantzen, and Kappie Jorgenson for their editing efforts and helpful suggestions. I swear one of these days I'll figure out, how, why, and, where, to, correctly, place, a comma… eh, one of these days. Just not yet.

The Belly of the Beast

“For there is no folly of the beast of the earth which is not infinitely outdone by the madness of men.”

-Herman Melville

Chapter 1

Phuoc Long Province, South Vietnam, 1971-

The U.S. Army helicopter racing in low over the remote stretch of jungle was less than two minutes out.

"GET READY!" Sergeant Ben Carey yelled over his shoulder to the five other Rangers behind him.

The helicopter, carrying the heavily armed and rucksack laden Lurps from Company R- 75th Infantry- Ranger, MAC-V, was heading towards a small, grassland clearing that would serve as the team's start point for the five-day patrol.

That the olive drab colored, giant tadpole looking Bell UH-1H *Iroquois* troop transport helicopter, better known as the Huey, would only set down long enough to off-load Team Nine-One deep inside enemy held territory, along with the loud, pulsating thumps from the helicopter's main rotor blades, had the Lurps' adrenaline racing as well.

Crouching inside the cramped cargo bay and inching towards the open doorways as the shuddering helicopter descended further, the six Lurps were more than ready to leap out once the aircraft touched down. A nod from the Huey's Crew Chief' and a slap on the shoulder and a '*Go*!' from Staff Sergeant Rob Shintaku to Carey that would send he and his team out of the aircraft, three on the left and three on the right.

The Huey had already made two sham touchdowns at several other natural gaps in the rain forest to confuse any enemy units that might be operating nearby. But this would be where Nine-One would actually begin their patrol, or where the helicopter and everyone in it would be shot down in a tumbling ball of flames in the attempt.

"*Come on, come on, come on*!" Carey muttered under his breath, quietly compelling the Huey to land.

Stepping out onto the landing skids of the helicopter the 21-year-old Team Leader was holding onto the doorframe of the Huey with one hand and his CAR-15 Assault Rifle in his other. He thumbed the selector switch of the assault rifle from SAFE to FIRE to AUTO, and then steadied his breathing, or tried to.

Scanning the jungle above the treetops as the helicopter began slowing its air speed, his rifle barrel tracked his line of sight, ready to fire. A thin layer of shimmering morning mist was rising from the clearing, like a ghost-like apparition that drew his eye and aim, but Carey held his fire as the imagined threat quickly dissolved in the sunlight. His stomach tensed, but then it always had just before any insertion behind enemy lines. He used to think it would go away with the more missions he pulled in the bush, but twelve missions on and it hadn't, nor had his habit of muttering to himself.

"*Come on, come on, COME ON*!"

It didn't help that the partially concealed machine gun pits and fortified bunkers and fighting positions of the once hidden enemy encampment were coming into view, as was a well-defined network of sun-dappled paths leading to those defensive positions. The tens of thousands of NVA soldiers who had made their way down the Ho Chi Minh Trail, as well as the Viet Cong battalions campaigning in the region, had carved out many similar camps and staging areas in this far flung part of the province and Carey was now praying the machine gun pits and fighting positions for this particular one were empty.

Lurp Team insertions were the most critical and dangerous times for a five-to-six-man patrol because the helicopter was going in cold.

With larger Infantry platoon or company size insertions, the practice was to prep potential hot Landing Zones with artillery fire or have the helicopter crew chiefs and door gunners firing up the tree line as a line of helicopters made their final approach, but that wasn't the case for a Lurp team drop off. While the mission of a long range reconnaissance patrol relied heavily upon stealth, any sneaking and peeking the six Lurps would do wouldn't begin until the clamoring helicopter that had made the insertion roared away.

An aircraft flying high in the sky might be tracked from the ground below heading towards its destination, but one flying in fast and low over the treetops might instead only be briefly glimpsed and heard, thanks to the near impenetrable jungle, and its ever growing weave of vines, leaves, and branches that would diffuse the bulk of the noise and its exact location.

Still, any enemy patrols nearby would certainly recognize the reduced popping sound of the helicopter's rotor blades for what it was and race towards the nearest landing site to set up a nasty welcoming surprise. That's when the helicopter, and those inside it, would be at their most vulnerable as the Huey slowed its approach to the designated insertion site, flared, and finally set down.

Natural clearings provided the only practical access to these otherwise inaccessible areas. A second similar open clearing several miles away had been selected as the team's pick-up point. Both locations had been chosen the day before on the pre-insertion overflight by Carey and his Assistant Team Leader, his A-T-L, Specialist-4 Luis 'Louie' Hernandez. The overflight look-see from 2,000 feet up found the start point for their patrol as well as a second site the team they would use for their exfiltration just short of one week later.

Views from 2,000 feet up, though, didn't always provide critical intricate detail. More could be gleaned with closer inspection, but that wasn't on the menu. If a helicopter circled an area too long or flew over it too low, then any enemy spotters might get the notion that something was brewing in that location. Make it look like a normal helicopter in flight going from one base to another, though, then all was good, and the team got their designated drop off site and, more importantly, their pick-up location. Those selected sites, those natural grassland open spaces, just needed to be big enough for a helicopter to safely get in and out of the surrounding jungle in the shortest amount of time possible.

This clearing, at best, was forty yards wide and maybe ninety long, and Carey knew that even if the pith helmet of the North Vietnamese Army's worst shot fell over his eyes, the enemy soldier still wouldn't have any problem scoring more than a few direct hits on a target as big and as close as a forty-seven-foot long, fifteen-foot-tall helicopter that was little more than a mechanical sitting duck. Never mind the better shooters, or the calmer one with a carefully aimed, shoulder-fired Rocket Propelled Grenade.

That too was on the Team Leader's mind and very likely on the minds of the other Lurps and air crew as the Huey went from flying to preparing to land.

Much like a galloping horse when the rider yanked back on the bridle and bit, the Huey that had been racing in slowed and flared to a reined stop by the aircraft commander working the bucking machine like a belt buckle winning rodeo champion cowboy. Beneath the helicopter's skids landing gear, Carey briefly glanced at the two inches or so of standing rainwater glistening over the dark ground beneath it before his eyes went back to the enemy fighting positions and the jungle where any real threat would be hiding.

Natural clearings in the rainy season were little more than sumps where the runoff from seasonal rains would collect and pool. With it being the start of the rainy season that accounted for the few inches of water and likely a little inevitable mud that would accompany them out of the clearing. The mud would slow their run from the clearing to the surrounding jungle and leave signs of their passing, too, but that couldn't be helped. It was to be expected. To counter it, Carey would move the team quickly into the rainforest, buttonhook back paralleling their short path, and then *lay dog* to see and hear if they had been compromised or were being tracked. If they were tracked then the buttonhook maneuver would allow for a hasty ambush. That was the game plan, and it was seconds away from being put into play.

Touchdown! Carey couldn't see that Shintaku was locked in an animated conversation with the pilots, but he heard the helicopter's crew chief yell, 'GO!' The crew chief's hands never left his M-60 machine gun that was ready to fire. His eyes were locked on the brush-lined jungle in front of him and the exposed enemy fighting positions, as were those of the door gunner on the opposite side of the shuddering aircraft.

"GO!" the crew chief yelled again, this time waving the Team Leader on.

The Huey would only be on the ground for eight seconds. There would be no time to hesitate or dawdle.

Carey sprang off the helicopter's skids as did the rest of the team out of the bouncing aircraft, which is when it suddenly hit him that the helicopter shouldn't have bounced, The pilot hadn't set the helicopter down, and he was actually only holding a hover. That was confirmed a split-second later as Carey and the five others plunged deep into the bog.

"Sonofabitch!" he grumbled as he sank into the wetlands up to his elbows and the magazine pouches on his web gear.

Even as the helicopter was making its ear-piercing Lycoming turboshaft engine getaway, all six of the Army Rangers were sinking up to their waists in the dirty water and then a foot more into the muck and mud. It didn't help that the rotor wash from the departing Huey sent a parting gift of rippling waves of algae-covered bog water and plant life breaking back into the struggling Lurps.

The '*what can go wrong, will go wrong,*' civilian curse of Murphy's Law had military applications as well and had Carey thinking that one day he'd like to find Murphy and kick his ass.

With the combined weight of his backpacked radio, rucksack, weapon, and what was on his web gear, Specialist-4 Gary Pettit, Nine-One's radioman, had been driven down to his hands and knees beneath the dirty water. Pettit was wildly flaying beneath the surface before being pulled back up by his Team Leader. He came up spitting water and gasping for air.

Carey held him up long enough for Pettit to steady himself, tapped him on his skewered boonie cap, and pointed the way he wanted him and the others to go. Two steps behind him the Team Leader froze as something long and undulating bumped and brushed past his left knee beneath the dark water before slithering on.

"Into the tree line! Move! Move!" said the Team Leader, shoving Pettit forward and away from the direction the snake or whatever it was had taken. "Move!" But the suctioning mud and the weight of all that they were carrying, combined with the stagnant water only hampered their escape, and it now became a twisting, splashing, and pivoting struggle for the Americans to reach solid ground and the cover of the jungle that they desperately needed to get to.

With green, black, and woodland colored grease face paint and camo fatigues the Lurps could easily blend in with the jungle, while in the open clearing, and slogging their way out of the gripping bog, they stood out like much too close, and easy to hit, pop-up targets.

Six mud sucking and water plant dragging yards on Hernandez stumbled over a submerged tree root and momentarily disappeared underwater. The A-T-L too was swearing and gasping for air as he came back to the surface, but the 23-year-old short, rangy Cubano from Hialeah, Florida was swearing for another reason. He'd dropped his M-16 and was now bobbing under the water trying to retrieve it.

"*Chingada madre*! Are you kidding me?" he said, angrily at his first two failed attempts, while on the third try he came out of the water with his missing rifle.

The team medic, Doc Moore, was helping to steady the newest new guy, a second lieutenant tag-along, when the young officer lost his footing under his 80-pound rucksack and started to fall backwards into the bog. Moore had managed to grab onto the L-T's shoulder harness to steady him before he too went underwater.

The only team member seemingly not having any difficulty was Specialist-4 Johnny Blake Bowman, a former FNG who'd proven himself over his last three missions and was no longer considered a dreaded *Fucking New Guy*. There was a certain irony that as the team's rear scout he was the closest to the dry ground Carey had pointed out, and that the 18-year-old was the first to reach it. Coming out of the bog, through the bulrushes, and then just inside the tree line, Bowman took a knee with his rifle up and ready to provide cover fire for the rest of the team that were still struggling to break free of the marsh. His narrowed brown eyes darted to every flickering leaf or creaking sound in the jungle in front him, watching and listening for any sign of the enemy.

Over his shoulder he could hear the five others who were still slogging their way out of the murky mess, laboring with each step to pull their boots from the suctioning mud that didn't seem to want to give up its hold. A quick glance at his field watch showed that what should've taken less than a minute on dry ground for the team to move from the clearing to the jungle, was now going on seven minutes and change. A trail of disturbed algae and dragged water plants showing their direction of movement in their wake. The longer it took to get to the tree line, the more danger they were in. Bowman watched, waited, and then breathed a sigh of relief when the last Lurp in line came out of the bog.

With all six Lurps on solid ground, Carey quickly led them forward into the jungle. Nerves were on edge and teetering and he needed the mission to get back on track without any more fuck ups. Ten yards on he made a buttonhook pivot to his right and then brought the team five yards back paralleling the route they'd just taken. It was time to *lay dog,* and this dog was a mess.

"Commo check," Carey whispered to Pettit as the team set up in a small, three hundred sixty-degree wagon wheel formation, only the team leader didn't really have to give the order as Pettit was already on the radio, wiping the water from the handset, and making the required call.

Now it was just a deadly waiting game of Hide and Seek or, hopefully not, combat TAG.

Fortunately, though, for Team Nine-One there were no enemy soldiers monitoring the jungle clearing, watching on, or even following them, so there was no incoming machine gun fire or whooshing rocket propelled grenades flying their way, either. If there had been, then just before the enemy soldiers opened up on the Americans, the six Lurps likely would've heard a great deal of guffawing laughter from the North Vietnamese soldiers because the team's insertion had been one big ass, comical clusterfuck.

"We got commo," whispered Pettit, handing the radio's handset over to his Team Leader.

"Valhalla relay, Vahalla relay," whispered Carey, reaching for his compass and map. "Longboat Niner-One, over."

"Valhalla relay. Go."

Longboat Nine-One was the team's callsign while Valhalla relay was Ranger Staff Sergeant Shintaku who was aboard the outbound helicopter and served as the immediate link to the team he'd just inserted.

"Niner-One on the oars," Carey said. The '*on the oar's*' response was the code that the team was ready to move. Carey very much wanted to ask why Longboat Nine-One had been torpedoed on the insertion but held his thoughts.

"Roger Niner-One, I copy. Sorry about the diving platform. Not my call," said Valhalla relay. "Valhalla relay, out."

They didn't move and remained in place a few minutes longer until the jungle began to settle back into a more normal and natural state. The cockup drop-off, at least by the enemy, had gone unnoticed. With the helicopter long gone, a slow and steadily pulsating drone of mosquitoes began to fill the morning around them, as even the birds high up in the trees were growing comfortable with the human silence.

"Bowman? Drop your ruck, You're with me." He whispered to the Rear Scout. To Hernandez he said, "Back in a minute."

The two were going to check out some of the nearby enemy bunkers and fighting positions.

Carey crept towards the first fighting position, an L-shaped dirt and log covered bunker with a gun port facing the clearing and a three foot deep trench-like entrance opened in the rear. He steered clear of both the bunker's gun port and the entrance.

With Bowman covering him, the Team Leader carefully slipped down into the trench and then inside the bunker. It was dark, dank, and mercifully empty, as were the next few bunkers in line they'd checked of the many they could see through the underbrush. A few empty bunkers and fighting positions, though, didn't necessarily mean an unoccupied bunker complex. The large bunker complex that appeared to be covering the clearing, had at one time or another, easily housed one hundred Viet Cong or NVA soldiers or more. The few empty bunkers and fighting positions, though, didn't mean that a newly arrived platoon of thirty others, ten to twenty yards on, weren't waiting and buying their time to attack. But with no sight or sound of the enemy, the two Lurps quietly made their way back to the others. Carey was a little more relieved with their findings.

Taking out his compass and map and looking around he began marrying them up with the physical terrain. Leaning over to his Assistant Team Leader, he pointed out the azimuth and direction he wanted Hernandez to take when they did move out. No words were exchanged. The dark-eyed Floridian knew what to do and nodded.

They would move west, away from the fighting positions and interlocking trails in the bunker complex, and head deeper into the bush towards their targeted recon zone. In the near distance something made a muffled grunt that had the tag-along lieutenant nervously turning to see what it was while the others took it as a familiar sound and the good sign it was.

After a few more quiet moments wait, and when he felt it was safe for the team to move, Carey shoulder his rucksack and gave a nod to his A-T-L. Hernandez returned it with a chin up nod of his own, rose from where he was kneeling, and took the lead.

Once the Pointman was three paces ahead of the others the Team Leader pointed to Lieutenant Plantagenet, the tag-along, and tilted his head for him to follow the A-T-L. The mud-covered, wide-eyed second lieutenant nervously nodded, stood, steadied his rucksack, and then slowly started forward in the Ranger file formation.

Following protocol, the Pointman covered what was to his front with each Lurp in line behind him then alternating the cover to the left and right while Bowman, bringing up the rear, occasionally did a slow turn to watch for anyone that might be trying to sneak up behind the team.

As the tag-along officer was looking to his left, covering his assigned sector of responsibility with his eyes locked on the jungle, he didn't see the old bamboo stalk in the dried grass beneath his left boot, but he did hear the loud, menacing crack as he stepped on the bone-dry tube.

The crack, that fell just short of a clap of thunder, but not by much to the other members on the team, sent a nesting bird in a nearby tree to a squawking frightened flight as the jungle suddenly became awkwardly quiet, again.

The team members dropped to a knee and froze, their adrenaline pumping yet one more time as their eyes searched the surrounding trees and heavy wall of brush and leaves for anyone else nearby who might've heard the loud break and was coming to investigate. The tense, few minutes wait came with visible scowls on the faces of the other team members towards the tag-along officer. The resentment also came with some muffled swearing.

When no one showed and no incoming enemy fire came at them, and the jungle once again slowly reverted back to a more natural state, several of those Lurps angrily turned and scowled at the FNG lieutenant who'd shattered their noise discipline.

Hernandez, though, wanted to be certain the tag-along understood his mortal sin, so he quietly backtracked his way to within inches from the lieutenant's face, all the while glaring at the sinner as he went.

"Goddamnit lieutenant, watch where you fucking step!' His voice was barely above a whisper, but that whisper might as well have carried the impact of a shout as Hernandez was looking as though he wanted to shoot the *Fucking New Guy*, officer, or no officer.

The new guy lieutenant was spared any further anger, disdain, or embarrassment when Carey snapped his fingers, pointed to Hernandez, and the direction the team needed to be going, and mouthed the word, "Go!"

The frustrated A-T-L turned and, once more, took the lead.

As the six-man Lurp team disappeared into the jungle, Bowman, the former FNG who was the last man in line, smiled as he made his next slow three hundred and sixty degree turn all the while thinking that it was good to no longer be the FNG on a team.

Very, very good.

Chapter 2

It was a rookie, dumbass mistake to make, and he knew it.

By the time the Team Leader called for a brief halt half an hour on, and as the tag-along lieutenant was facing out of the team's wagon wheel defensive formation covering his assigned sector of fire, he was mentally kicking himself.

The fiasco at the insertion site was a lousy start of the mission, but it was nothing he hadn't encountered before in stateside Ranger training. At Camp Rudder, during the Florida phase of Ranger School, he'd slogged through enough chest-deep, tea-colored, foul-smelling swamp water and mud to understand that Rangers operated in sorry conditions and hazardous places. It sucked, you dealt with it, and you moved on towards the objective. But because he had been so bent on covering his sector of fire as they moved out, he wasn't paying all that much attention to the ground in front of him, and he stepped on that damn tube of bamboo. The *faux* fucking *pas* had potentially compromised the team with that loud, God-awful crack.

It was bad enough being the FNG on the team, but it didn't help any that he was an officer, and they were all enlisted men. They expected more from him, just as he expected more from himself.

Like all hunters, and they were hunters, their going was purposely slow and vigilant because it had to be. Here their prey hunted back, and any hurried or even simple mistakes could get them killed. So far the two mistakes that were hurried and simple, were also avoidable and they'd, no doubt, be addressed afterwards on the mission debriefing and taken as Lessons Learned, but not now. Now they had to concentrate on the task at hand without any more tactical errors.

They patrolled on.

As they went they didn't so much bust brush as they did carefully brush it aside. They used stealth and caution to avoid bullets and bayonets.

Up ahead on point Specialist Hernandez held up an upraised clenched fist as he took a knee. Carey moved forward to see what Hernandez had found and the two huddled up. Murmurs were exchanged before Carey nodded to Hernandez and the team leader turned back and faced the others. Snapping his fingers twice to get all eyes on him, he brought them up and forward as Hernandez started a quiet detour around whatever it was to his front.

Now third in line and taking the same detour, the tag-along lieutenant saw the reason behind both the halt and the detour. Through the sliver-like openings in the jungle brush there was a semi-open stretch of ground dotted with bomb craters and the shattered and scattered trees made from a recent bomb run. Each crater was the size of an ugly pond and scarred the face of the rain forest like troubling acne.

The detour would skirt the bombed out area and have the team remaining inside the cover of the jungle before they got back on their original course. The going was still slow and the jungle, with its layered underbrush, low hanging branches, and clinging wait-a-minute vines, had made it so.

It didn't help that the morning temperature was already in the mid-80s and steadily climbing with little to no breeze. The day was also pushing punishing humidity, so when the first actual rest break came a little over an hour from when they started, it was necessary and appreciated. There was time to adjust loads and tighten loose straps.

By the second rest break an hour after that, dark sweat rings began to appear on their lower backs and arm pits, and by mid-day the trek wasn't just proving to be hot and sticky to the tag-along lieutenant as much as it was feeling more like he was caught up in a steam bath with no shut off valve. He was sweating more than he thought anyone ever could or should. Slow rolling beads of perspiration were dripping down and around his forehead and ears with several droplets pooling on his upper lip. His face was flushed beneath the now smeared camo face paint, and he was wiping away the sweat that had rolled into his eyebrows and had threatened his already stinging eyes.

"How you doing, lieutenant?" asked Doc Moore, checking in on the officer. Moore's voice was barely a whisper.

"Good," breathed Plantagenet, and maybe a little too eagerly added, "I'm good-to-go."

The medic could see that besides looking like the family dog that had been left in a car too long on a hot summer day with the windows rolled up, the lieutenant's once new tiger stripe jungle fatigues were stained not only with patches of mud from the bog, but with deeper, dark blotches of sweat, so Doc Moore wasn't so sure about the self-diagnosis.

"Here," said Moore, handing him a small pill. "Salt tablet."

"Thanks, Doc," Plantagenet said, reaching for one of the two canteens on his web gear.

"Stay hydrated, L-T. Heat stroke can take you out just as fast as an RPG."

Plantagenet nodded as the medic checked in on the others.

Taking the salt pill and a deep gulp of much-needed water from one of his two canteens, he kept his eyes locked on the jungle in front of him for two very good reasons. First, to demonstrate that he could do the job, and, secondly, and perhaps more importantly, so he didn't have to see any of the faces of the other team members that still might be harboring any visible scorn or frustration aimed in on him because of the earlier noise blunder. Since he made the literal misstep, he was now more careful and cognizant of where and how he stepped.

While the rest breaks were appreciated, they were also short lived. Sergeant Carey gave Hernandez the hand signal to move out and the team continued their patrol back in their Ranger file formation. Less than a hundred yards on, Hernandez raised his left hand high up in a closed fist signaling for yet another halt while his right hand had his M-16 leveled at whatever it was in front of him as he slowly took a knee.

Those behind him didn't need to be told to drop to a knee with their weapons ready. Just as they'd been taught in training, they automatically followed the lead of the Lurp in front of them and covered the jungle around them facing out for whatever it was that had caught Hernandez's eye this time, or what they had possibly missed.

Dropping his rucksack, Sergeant Carey brushed by the lieutenant on his way forward to his Assistant Team Leader and took a knee beside Hernandez.

What do we got, Louie?" he whispered to his A-T-L.

"*Mira*! Small trail," Hernandez whispered back, tilting his head forward and down. A few yards on there appeared to be a thin hallway-like opening in the jungle.

Plantagenet couldn't hear what was being whispered or see what they were looking at but saw them exchanging whispers and nods before the Team Leader used hand signals to bring him up to where they were.

"Drop your ruck, L-T," whispered Carey when the tag-along officer knelt directly behind him. "Follow me and stay low."

Lowering his rucksack down he nodded he was ready and the two slowly crept forward for a better look at what Hernandez had spied. As the sergeant then took yet one more knee at the edge of the discovery, the lieutenant moved in beneath an overhanging broad leafed plant that he figured made for good concealment. Taking so many knees had him feeling like a tactical altar boy in a brilliant green cathedral.

From where the two had stopped they could easily make out the open space of the good-sized trail that had been cut through the jungle. Three feet in width and shielded by aerial observation under a roof of double canopied trees, the path had more of an appearance of a sun-spackled green and brown tunnel. Pastoral in color and setting, it was also deadly threatening.

"Cover me," the Team Leader whispered to the officer. Carey, though, didn't wait for a reply as he moved forward and crouched at the near edge of a north-south trail.

Oh, so slowly he leaned his head out of the brush cover and peeked out at the pathway. Slowly turning both his head and rifle to the left and then the right, he was carefully looking to see if there were any expected guests at an unexpected get-together. An eye didn't always pick up slow movement, but any quick movement tended to draw attention.

The trail was empty, so the team leader turned back to a three-foot section of dirt path directly in front of him and studied it. The early morning soil was still damp and showed no sign of recent activity, just several old two-wheeled tire tracks and indentations of heavy foot traffic long since passed. The weathered edges had been rounded and eroded with time and the elements, but the three-foot section of trail held a story.

Carey motioned the lieutenant forward.

"Tell me what you see, L-T?" he whispered, tilting his head towards the trail. The officer looked to Carey and then to the trail in front of him.

As Plantagenet eyed and studied the path the Team Leader kept watch. Teaching moments didn't have to be fatal.

After a moment of skewing his face at what he was looking at, the lieutenant said, "Old boot prints, theirs, not ours, a bunch of them, seven or eight, maybe, a week or so old, judging from the look of it. Don't know what those grooves are?"

"Bicycle tracks. The NVA used them to transport heavy weapons and equipment through the jungle. You see anything else?"

"Nothing more I can make out."

Sergeant Carey nodded.

"Good," he said. "So, we'll keep moving west and see what else we can find. Head back to the others, and..."

"I know, no stepping on dry bamboo or old branches," said Plantagenet, smiling.

Carey shrugged. "That too," he said. "But I was going to say was, 'be careful under some of the overhanging brush.' Besides the snakes that sometimes cling to tree limbs and branches there are a few other nasty things like these Weaver Ants," he added, slapping away a few of the frenzied ants on the lieutenant's left arm.

"Weaver ants?"

"Uh-huh. They're like fire ants, only worse. One bite from one of those suckers will make you feel like you stuck your tongue into a light socket and left it there. There's a few more on your boonie cap. You might want to brush them off before you move back to the team."

Although the lieutenant's eyes showed surprise he didn't panic as he used the back of his left hand to clear away the rest of the ants from his cap and clothing. Once he was sure he'd gotten them all he looked to the Team Leader who tilted his head back towards the rest of the team.

"War isn't always Hell. Sometimes it's just a pain in the ass," said Carey. "Go."

Chapter 3

"Nine-One's on the ground, Captain," said First Sergeant Walter '*The Brick, as in wall, just don't ever fucking call me Walter*' Poplawski coming into the Orderly Room from the TOC, Romeo Company's Tactical Operation Center.

The announcement was accompanied by the straining twangs from the over-stretched spring fastened to the Orderly Room's screen door when Poplawski had pushed it open, and the decided thump when the too taut spring slammed the door back against the wooden doorframe.

"Any problems?" asked Captain Robison, looking up from the paperwork in front of him.

Seated behind his field desk Captain Robison, Romeo Company's Commanding Officer, had been going over the overnight Situation Reports the SITREP summaries of the teams in the field as well as the company's Morning Report. A half-smoked Cuban cigar with a faint orange glow behind a thin layer of pale ash sat in a pressed metal ashtray and was sending up a thin wisp of pungent, aromatic smoke. A mug of coffee rested within easy reach beside the ashtray.

"Sergeant Shintaku says the dry ground on the insertion LZ wasn't. He was trying to get the pilot to land further up the field, but the crew chief told our people to go. Apparently, the team went waist deep into a marsh, but they made it to the tree line without incident."

"The pilot didn't land?"

"Couldn't. There wasn't enough dry ground beneath them to get out of the clearing."

"Hmm? Then that'll make for a memorable start for our new lieutenant and maybe show him just how fast things can go wrong in an instant in combat. Plan for the worst, hope for the best, just don't tread water."

"Yes sir, and good for him to see what the team's actually encounter in the jungle on patrol, given that, depending how well he does on the mission, and if he can cut it, he'll potentially be their new Platoon Leader," said the First Sergeant.

“There’s that,” agreed the Ranger Company Commander with a grunt as he picked up the cigar, and brought it back to life. Blowing out a rising plume of smoke, he said, "I'll want to talk with Nine-One's Team Leader after the mission and see how our new officer did. That's Sergeant Carey, isn't it?"

"Yes, sir, I believe it is."

“Then, the lieutenant’s in good hands. Last night, I reminded him once again that he was only to be an observer on this patrol and that, although his Team Leader might only be a sergeant, he, the sergeant, was in charge of the team, and that his decisions were final. Let's hope he understood it."

Poplawski shrugged. "Well, he's a brand new second lieutenant, sir, so that might be a stretch,” Poplawski said. “However, since there was no report that he was playing Marco Polo in the bog water shows there's hope."

Captain Robison smiled. "There's that, too," he said and moved on to other teams in the field. "What's the updated status of the other two teams on patrol?"

"All’s good. Nine-Two gets extracted tomorrow and Nine-Three is on Day Three of its six-day patrol in Cambodia, north of Katum.

Negative SITREPS from each as of one-zero mikes ago. So, all's copacetic so far."

Robison nodded. "We just got a request from the BIG-TOC's Two-shop to send a team atop the Nui Ba Den for a look-see mission on the mountain."

"They say what they want our people to see while they're looking?"

"No, but we'll get more at a briefing today at 1300 hours," he said. "What team is up?"

"Nine-Four, sir," said Poplawski. "Sergeant Thomas' team, two, which I'm told, are FNGs."

This last bit gave the Company Commander pause which showed on his face.

"That wise?" he asked, sharing his concern.

The First Sergeant shrugged. "Not much choice, really. We're short on people, sir."

"I see that from the Morning Report."

"Yes sir, one of our people is in the Third Field Hospital in Saigon with malaria, another just went to the Aid Station with Jungle Rot on both feet, two on R&R, one stateside on Emergency Leave, one with an early out of the Army who leaves next week, and one at the dispensary with a sprained ankle from yesterday's rappelling class. If it's any consolation, Sergeant Thomas has Specialists Li and Daley with him on the team. They're both solid in the field, so the New Guys will have some good mentors to learn from. Bottom line, Captain, we gotta break them in sometime."

Poplawski's take showed both the crux of the matter as well as the working solution. After a moment the captain gave a slow and reluctant nod.

"True," he said, thinking that you were only new until you weren't. "Once we hear more of what BIG-TOC wants, we'll put together a Warning Order for Nine-Four."

"Yes, sir."

BIG-TOC was Camp Mackie's Command Center from whence all wisdom flowed or at least where the Lurp mission requests came from on Camp Mackie. While the Ranger Company was officially under the auspices of the Military Assistance Command-Vietnam Headquarters in Saigon, referred to by the acronym MAC-V, Romeo Company was, in fact, assigned to the local Command, who requested Lurp patrols and assigned them in support of ground unit operations within the Camp's area of operations.

The Lurp patrols were used in the incremental pile-on strategy by the command. Send in a small ground force Lurp team for a look-see and if they found a larger enemy force or an occupied hidden jungle basecamp, then send in a larger force, say a Recon platoon with the support of gunships and artillery to solve the problem, or, if need be, a larger Grunt Company, or even larger Battalion, if things escalated.

Turning his attention back to the Company's Morning Report that he'd been going over before the First Sergeant came through the doorway, Captain Robison frowned as his eyes dropped to the synopsis Poplawski had prepared earlier that morning.

"I also see that two of our people got arrested by the MPs overnight for stealing a jeep and crashing it," he said, setting down the cigar and thumping the report with his index finger. Robison was none too pleased with what he'd read, and his dark scowl confirmed it.

"Yes, sir. Specialist Redmond and PFC Wexler. The charges are Disorderly Conduct and more."

"Drunk and disorderly, I take it?"

"Yes sir, very on both counts. The Provost Marshal told me Redmond also fled the scene and resisted arrest when he was apprehended, so he's up on charges for that as well."

The captain's face couldn't mask his anger at that last bit of news. "And Wexler?"

"Mostly passed out drunk, before, during, and after. They had to wake him to put him in cuffs and then he promptly passed out again. Oh, and in the crash, he did a header into the windshield frame and suffered a cut over his left eye."

“Bad?”

Poplawski shook his head. “No sir. He'll live. The MPs brought in a medic from the Aid Station to check him out. The medic stitched up and bandaged the cut, and said that Wexler's hangover will probably be the bigger headache, judging by the near empty pint of whisky he was holding at the time. Hopefully, though, the header knocked some sense into him.”

"And the '*more*' you just said but didn't mention in the summary report?"

Poplawski started to smile but caught himself at the last moment. "The jeep they took for their joy ride and crashed into a deuce and a half when the MPs gave chase..."

"Uh-huh?"

"Is, ...well, was... Colonel Becker's."

"Colonel Becker's?" echoed the Company Commander, lowering his head with an audible sigh as he rubbed his eyes at the news.

"Yes, sir. I'm told the jeep's radiator was totaled, along with the left headlight, left front tire, and wheel well. No real damage to the truck, they say. Redmond and Wexler were banged up some, but drunk as they were neither sustained serious injury. The MPs said I could take custody of them, but I thought I'd wait for your input after you've had your morning coffee, sir."

Robison sighed, again. "They stole Camp Mackie's Assistant Commander's jeep?"

It wasn't so much a question as it was a frustrated understanding of the inevitable ass chewing he'd receive from the top brass that inevitably would follow.

"Yes, sir. The one with the Lincoln Continental looking spare tire cover on the back with the big full bird eagle rank insignia that had..."

"...CHESSMASTER 6 X-Ray painted on it in bold, block print."

"Yes, sir. And it gets better."

"You're enjoying this, aren't you?"

"A bit, Captain, yes. The Humpty-Dumpty looking Colonel doesn't like us all that much. Thinks we're prima donnas who use up too many of his precious assets with not too much bang for the buck is his take."

"Where did you hear that?"

"The Command Sergeant Major. He likes us. Says General Reese does too. Did you know that the General served with the Alamo Scouts in the Philippines in the War?"

The War to Poplawski was World War Two. His view was Vietnam was a war as well, and something else entirely.

"I did. We studied the Cabanatuan POW rescue at West Point. The Alamo Scouts did the reconnaissance on that raid, as I recall."

"Yes sir, then he's our kind of people. Our Humpty-Dumpty Colonel, I heard, served on Eisenhower's support staff in London."

"*Humpty-Dumpty'* Colonel? Seriously, is that how you speak about your superior officers behind their backs, First Sergeant?"

"Some, sir, especially the arrogant ones, but only when they're not within hearing distance," said Poplawski, still smiling.

The Captain stared at his First Sergeant for a moment and then slowly shook his head.

"Okay then, so what's the '*better*' about this? Spill it."

"As I said, Wexler, who was passed out in the passenger's seat and, who I'm told, doesn't remember getting into the jeep, let alone pissing himself."

"No, no, no! Tell me he didn't?"

"Oh, yes sir, he did."

"On the seat?"

"Yes, sir. And all over the Colonel's big and spiffy looking sheepskin wool passenger's seat cover that he'd special ordered from Australia," he said. "The Colonel wants to meet with you later this morning."

"I'm sure he does. He say when?"

“0-900 hours at the BIG-TOC.”

Robison checked his watch, It was 0-750. There was time.

"Any way we can't get that seat cover cleaned?"

"Already on it, Captain," said Poplawski. "I spoke to a buddy of mine in Flight Line Maintenance. He said their pressure washer is down, but they'll have it working by later this afternoon. Said he'll get his people on it, ASAP. We should know soon after that if that'll work."

"Good."

"I promised them a case of beer for cleaning it."

"That shouldn't be an out-of-pocket expense for you."

"No sir, it won't be. I’ll make sure that Butch Assholery and The Some Dunce Kid foot the bill. You want me to get those two out of lockup?”

"No, not yet First Sergeant. Let's give them time to consider the pending consequences of their actions. Then, depending upon the Colonel's wrath, they'll either receive Article-15s or be shot at sunrise tomorrow."

"I'd be happy to arrange a firing squad, sir."

Robison sighed. "Wouldn't we all," he said. "So, Redmond was the one driving?"

"Roger that, sir," said the First Sergeant.

"And he resisted arrest?"

The First Sergeant nodded. "After the MP Sergeant chased him down and tackled him. Redmond said he'd go quietly, only as the MP was putting on a handcuff on one wrist, Redmond turned, and sucker punched the Sergeant with his free hand."

"Sucker punched the MP?"

Poplawski nodded, again. "That's affirmative, sir, but I'm told the MP Sergeant who was on the Fort Gordon Boxing Team, shook it off, smiled, and then decked Redmond soundly before slapping on the other cuff and hauling his ass back to the jeep."

"What's your assessment of him as a Lurp? Redmond?"

Poplawski shrugged and gave a hand-wavering gesture. "So-so, I'm told, when he's in the field and more of a first-rate asshole when he isn't. My personal issue with him, the one that pisses me off the most, is that he ran off and left his teammate bleeding in the jeep after the crash."

"Left him?"

"He did and didn't bother to check to see if his buddy was okay, even though Wexler was bleeding from a cut over his left eye."

"And you say Wexler's okay?"

Poplawski nodded. "Yes sir. God truly loves drunks and babies," he said.

"What's your take on him?"

"Worth salvaging. He's only 19 and prior to this incident, Sergeant Shintaku, said he shows some good potential. Also, prior to this I was thinking of promoting him to E-4, but maybe not so much now."

“We’ll put that on hold,” replied Robison.

“And Redmond?”

It didn't take long for the captain to render his judgment on him.

"He's gone," Robison said. "We'll send him packing and let him deal with the assault charges on the MPs. As for Wexler, well, besides the Article 15 we'll give him that'll take away a little of his pay for the next month for the joy ride, I want him on the shit burning detail for the next two weeks, when he's not in the field. Oh, and when the sheepskin seat cover comes back, have him fluff it up pretty and I don't care if he has to use his own toothbrush to make it happen."

"Yes, sir, I'll have SFC Kozak overseeing that."

"Kozak? Ah, yes! That's right, because your R&R is, what, one day and a wake up away?" he asked, staring up at his First Sergeant.

"Yes, sir, it is," said Poplawski, beaming like an alligator at an all you can eat Chihuahua buffet.

When the R&R slot came open six weeks earlier, he jumped at the opportunity, and put his name on the bid list. When a week had gone by and no one else in the unit had put their name in to go, the Bangkok slot was his. He'd been looking forward to the R&R since he received the official approval. It would be his first leave in seven months, which might've explained his good mood and his wide and persistent grin.

Robison stared up at the still grinning senior NCO as he began tapping at the Morning Report and the Duty Roster beneath it with the eraser end of a bright yellow #2 pencil. He liked Poplawski. He was a solid soldier. Steadfast, loyal, and in the military vernacular, he knew his shit. He was also someone you wanted at your side in a fight, even if he was also the human embodiment of the bull in a Southeast Asian China shop. Charge an ambush, Hell! He’d lead it! That being said, or thought of by the Ranger Company Commander, what his First Sergeant lacked were some serious typing skills.

"I'm thinking we could use a company clerk. You think you can find me someone that could handle the job before you go on your R&R. Call me picky, but perhaps someone who knows how to type would be nice? And, oh, I don't know, someone who uses erasers and makes less type-overs on reports. I'd try for a hat trick and ask for someone who makes better coffee, but that might be pushing my luck."

Poplawski snorted and the snort turned into a chuckle. "I'd be hurt by your words, sir, if I wasn't already in a great mood knowing as you've correctly stated, I only have one day and a wake up before my R&R."

They could've used the days of the week, but every day in Vietnam was like the previous and the next, and it was only the descending number count that primarily mattered to many. Most GIs kept their remaining tour of duty day count on their personal short timer calendars, checking off the days until they finally could go home. Poplawski's short timer calendar was focused on his R&R.

"Bangkok, is it?"

"Roger that, sir, for five whole glorious days of fine food, a nice warm shower or two, a steam bath maybe, and a good-looking woman telling me how pretty I am."

“A blind one, is it?”

“The best kind for love or even, R&R pretend love.”

"Well, I'm sure you'll enjoy the time off, First Sergeant," said Robison, "especially in Thailand. You know it's nicknamed, *The Land of Smiles.*"

"I do now, sir, and I intend to smile. I've been putting money aside for this for a while now, so I intend to make it joyfully epic!"

Poplawski was smiling all the while he was talking. The war, at least for him, would be placed on hold for a week. For the Ranger Company and their operational long-range reconnaissance patrols, though, the war would go on.

"What about you, sir? Don't you have an R&R or seven-day leave coming up soon?"

"I do," said the Captain, wistfully. "I'm meeting my wife in Hawaii next month. Her mother will be watching the kids, which will give us some alone time together to reconnect. Army life is tough on families. I know you're divorced but do you have any kids, First Sergeant?"

Poplawski shook his head. "No, but with two Exes, I'm pretty sure I can claim my divorce lawyers as whiny little needy dependents. Semi-true love is expensive, sir. But who knows? Maybe I'll find my future ex-wife in Bangkok while I'm there?"

The Ranger Company Commander smiled and slowly shook his head at his First Sergeant before he turned to matters closer to the war and the compound they called, '*home*.'

"Have you briefed Sergeant Kozak yet on the morning report responsibilities and other Orderly Room tasks while you're gone?"

"Yes, sir. He's good to go."

"Good,. Oh, and have him sit in on Nine-Four's OP Order team briefings in the TOC with you and Lieutenant Marquardt tomorrow. It wouldn't hurt to have those in the TOC and on the teams that are going out to see him in the new acting First Sergeant's role, either."

"Will do, sir."

Sergeant Kozak was Sergeant First Class Mikhail 'Mike' Kozak, who'd been brought in to oversee Romeo Company's fledgling Second Platoon, of Lurps, all twelve of them. Just five weeks on the job he was already proving to be a good fit.

With the Company's operational strength hovering at fifty, and with five functioning teams, and the necessary training and support personnel, Kozak had been recruited from the 1st Cavalry Division's Third Brigade to take on the task. A former Platoon Sergeant for one of the First of the Ninth CAV's 'Blues' Air Crew Rescue and Recon Platoons posted to Camp Mackie, he was more than competent enough to handle the job. That he had a slight alcohol problem, which some said, may have been a little more than slight, was the elephant in the room when Robison initially saw his name as a possible candidate for the position on the list the First Sergeant had drawn up for consideration.

Poplawski knew that when sober, Kozak was one tough and competent NCO. When half-drunk, he could still keep up with the best of them half his age. However, full tilt, blind ass drunk, he was useless.

He hadn't been Robison's first choice for the job when the short list came out for the position, especially when the Ranger Company Commander spoke with Kozak's former Platoon Leader, at Camp Mackie's small, but well-stocked Officers club, to get his take on the senior NCO. Later, when he shared the negative comments of what he'd learned with First Sergeant Poplawski, '*The Brick*' chuffed and offered his own take.

"Actually, I think the *Mad Cossack* is exactly who we need, Captain."

"*Mad Cossack*?"

"His nickname when we were in Ranger School, back in the day. His Grandfather was Russian royalty, a Duke or some such before the

Revolution, and his Grandmother's Ukrainian family lineage stretches back to with some old country Cossack warrior line, so he didn't mind the nickname, and it stuck. Ran into him again at the NCO Club at Bragg when he was in the 82nd and leading a platoon of hard chargers, so I was happy to see him here at Camp Mackie.

"Okay, so what else do you know about him that I should know?"

"I know that he has no quit in him, sir, and that when you give him a task, he'll get it done with no bitching or whining. Maybe more importantly, and even more recently to prove my point, I know that he was the one who led the Quick Reaction Force when Team Nine-Three got compromised and got caught in that nasty firefight when they couldn't E&E."

"He led the QRF?"

"Yes sir, he did," said Poplawski. "That happened at the same time their Blue platoon was recovering a downed Huey in the same area of operations. They'd already rescued the injured crew members, secured the crash site, and were waiting for a Chinook to come in and sling load out the downed bird when the call came in to help our people. If you recall, sir, their TOC said the QRF platoon wasn't available."

"That's right and left us scrambling to try to come up with something until the 'Blues' sorted it out with their own working plan."

"Yes sir, they did, and it was Kozak who found the solution. He suggested to his L-T, well, pleaded actually, to get the Troop Commander's approval to keep half of the Blue platoon to guard the crash site and wait for the Chinook while he'd personally lead the other half, along with the downed Huey's two recovered M-60 machine guns, to fly in, and get our people out. The L-T couldn't make up his mind, so Kozak got on the horn and made the request to his commander himself."

"And you know this how?"

"I play poker with a few other senior NCOs once a week at the Engineer Battalion, including with his unit's First Sergeant. Word gets around and spreads about who actually did what and when, and more importantly, who didn't."

"Okay. Anything else?"

"He's what we need, Captain."

"And the drinking? I'm told he hits the bottle a little too frequently."

Poplawski shrugged. "Probably no more than any other senior NCO I've ever known. His problem, though, is that when he does drink a little too much, he tends to tell those who fuck up on a regular basis his thoughts on the matter, eh, and never mind the rank. He doesn't discriminate and, I suspect, told his Platoon Leader one too many times to either lead, follow, or get the hell out of the way."

"Always sound advice in combat."

"Yes, sir."

"And you'll vouch for him?"

Poplawski gave the question some scrunched up eyebrow thought, weighing his decision and response. When he spoke again it came with a confirmation nod.

"I don't know about the others on the list, but I do know that he stepped up when we needed him, so yes sir, I'll vouch for him just on that alone."

"Good enough, First Sergeant," said the Company Commander, settling the matter. "I'll put the request in."

Shortly after the transfer assignment was approved Poplawski drove over to Kozak's unit to give him a ride to Romeo Company. On the drive he told the *Mad Russian* that he was going to be the Platoon Sergeant for the company's fledgling Second Platoon. Poplawski told him too that he'd have to clean up his act a bit when it came to the drinking.

"Copy that," said Kozak, a little embarrassed but appreciating the opportunity to be in the Lurps.

“And no chewing out the Company Commander, especially the Company Commander. I served with Robison back in the day on his A-Team. He was a good leader then, and a better one now. I trust him completely with his decisions in and out of the field. You copy?"

"I copy."

"Good, however, the two lieutenants we have in the company are another matter. Well, one, at least, who shows promise, our X.O. and West Point grad, Lieutenant Marquardt. The other is an ROTC Second Lieutenant, who just graduated from Ranger School and should be showing up here in-country after his thirty-day leave. I'm told by some of the cadre I know at Benning that he did well, so the more you work with the two of them, the better they'll both be to the enlisted men who'll be counting on them to lead them when they rotate out to line units six months from now. Understood?"

"Understood," echoed Kozak.

"That's good, too. Because we sure as hell can use you, Mike," Poplawski said and reached into the right cargo pocket of his jungle fatigues, pulled out a black Ranger beret and handed it to him.

"Ditch the ball cap. Welcome to Romeo Company!"

After the transfer and after taking on the job as the Platoon Sergeant for the second platoon, the *Mad Russian* showed that he could soldier and Rangered up better than most. Not much on small talk, but a whole lot when it came to doing what needed to be done, he soon whipped the young Lurps in his platoon in place, with ready reaction drills while schooling the young NCOs on leadership training.

Wanting to prove himself, and with permission from Captain Robison, he took over and led the Company's daily PT and later set up volleyball games in the company area in the late afternoons. During Airborne Training at Fort Benning there had been Boxing Matches to help burn off some of the pent-up frustration and macho steam from being in an all-male, aggressive environment. The matches had helped platoons build better cohesion amongst the platoons and helped them foster team spirit, give, or take a few bent noses.

Well aware that team activities could also benefit the two Ranger platoons, Kozak also knew that volleyball matches could do that without as many broken noses. At six-three and surprisingly athletic, he hugged the net, could spike the ball hard and fast, and soon became the sought after go-to team player for whichever side of the net needed him the most. Afterwards, while the players went for a beer at the small club that Captain Robison and the First Sergeant had had constructed for the enlisted men in the company area during their downtime, Kozak returned to his hootch. There he kept a few bottles of Vodka in his foot locker that he thought the Company Commander and First Sergeant didn't know about, but did. Robison and Poplawski, though, gave it a pass as the off-duty drinking hadn't affected the new Senior NCO's job performance.

The two were also pleased that Kozak took it upon himself to oversee uniform and grooming standards in the company, so that the young Lurps looked like the Rangers they were supposed to be. Young

Rangers in their berets didn't need to look like walking black capped thumbtacks or Poppin' Fresh Doughboys.

Captain Robison wasn't worried about SFC Kozak taking on the First Sergeant responsibilities while his First Sergeant was on R&R. A career soldier of the better kind, the *Mad Russian* was slated for higher rank, regardless, if he could keep his drinking under control. So far, he had and so far, with the exception of the stolen jeep incident, all was relatively good, and all was smooth running with Romeo Company.

Team Nine-Three was mid-way through their mission up near Loc Ninh, Nine-Two was on day four of their patrol just north of Cu Chi, and Nine-One was just doing swimmingly.

The captain checked his watch. "Let's go retrieve our jeep thieves from the Provost Marshal, First Sergeant, so we can get that problem out of the way before I get my heels locked by Colonel Becker while you continue to grin at your upcoming R&R to Bangkok."

"Yes sir, and don't you just love a city that's named after it's favorite activity," he said with a wicked grin.

"I do worry about you a little from time to time, First Sergeant," Robison said, slowly shaking his head.

"If it's any consolation, Captain. I worry about me a little from time to time, too."

Chapter 4

"It's a four-day walk-off mission from the Radio Relay Station atop the Nui Ba Den. Well, technically, a walk *down* mission with air support from gravity," Lieutenant Marquardt said, chuckling at his play on words during the briefing he was giving to Team Nine-Four's Team Leader and Assistant Team Leader regarding their upcoming patrol. The Lieutenant who was standing in front of a wall map in the company TOC paused with a grin and a nod to his small audience for what he thought was his good, if not, clever quip.

His front row audience, seated on empty ammo boxes in the Romeo Company TOC, consisted of Buck Sergeant Darrell Thomas and Specialist-4 Harold 'Harry' Li, who gave the officer obligatory amused half-smiles with chin up nods. However, those standing in the back of the recently expanded underground bunker, First Sergeant Poplawski and SFC Kozak, only stared at the lieutenant questionably at the lame pun.

Besides the Ranger Company's Executive Officer who was conducting the briefing, and the First Sergeant and the *Mad Russian* who were assisting him, Sergeant Cantu, the TOC's NCO was seated at a small table in front of a bank of radios on the shelf of the right side of the bunker monitoring the teams in the field.

SFC Kozak, who had taken his first sip of the coffee the First Sergeant had poured from his Italian Alfonso Bialetti coffee maker, was staring into the mug wondering if maybe he needed a knife to cut through it. He looked to Poplawski who seemed to be enjoying his cup of what he called his 'strong Earthy-flavored Columbian coffee' while Kozak was wondering if, perhaps, some of the beans had come out of Juan Valdez's ass.

"We're reconning the mountain, sir?" asked Nine-Four's Team Leader, Sergeant Thomas.

Any Cajun flavor to Thomas' East Texan accent was likely due to the close proximity to neighboring Louisiana and its own brand of steamed shrimp with a tangy hot sauce, and a side order of deep-fried pickles with a cold Pearl beer or two; something he was so looking forward to enjoying when he finally made it home from the war.

"A section of it, anyway," replied Marquardt, turning back to the wall map. "Over the course of the patrol, you and your team will work your way from the rocky summit, *here*, down to about the 1,500 level, *here*, where we want you to concentrate the focus of your patrol."

Marquardt was using a three-foot long wooden pointer with a rubber tip to point and tap at an enlarged section of the mountain that he'd tacked up next to a wall map while slowly dragging it from the summit of the 3,200-foot, high peak down to the mid-way mark, and thumping those locations every time he said the word, '*here*.' As it was the only actual mountain in the otherwise flatland Province, the start point, and targeted recon area weren't hard to miss. The enlarged section of the map face showed the cartographer's fine detail of the dormant, inverted cone-shaped volcano.

Both the Texan Team Leader and his Chinese/Hawaiian Assistant Team Leader leaned in for a better look at the map section and were studying a few of the brown lines that were printed close together that had their concern. The many brown lines that were close together had indicated steep terrain with cliffs that looked to be one to two hundred feet drop offs close to where they'd be working.

A second enlarged section of the map showed that the top of the mountain had the outline and look of a poorly defined boot print with the bulk of the Nui Ba Den jutting out of a vast sea of green rainforest.

In English, *Nui Ba Den* translated to the Black Lady or Black Virgin Mountain, with its name and historical significance reaching far back into the folklore and history of the Khmers, Chams, Chinese, and the Vietnamese who previously, or presently, claimed it as their own. An ancient shrine carved into the mountain on the eastern slope paid homage and respect to the old myth and legend while the deep pockmarks and bomb and shell craters to the north, south, west, and on and around the summit told of the many and more recent and vicious fights. Unhappily wedded to generational wars, the Black Lady was scarred, battered, and brooding over the troubled relationship.

"Why halfway down, sir?"

"Ah, good question, Sergeant! Somewhere near the mid-mountain range, and primarily on the western and southern sides of the mountain, the BIG-TOC Higher-highers say elements of the 95-C VC Regiment and 7th NVA Division have hidden and fortified enemy heavy machine gun positions in what they suspect is an elaborate tunnel system. The BIG-TOC's intel team wants you to concentrate your focus on those areas. Specifically, to locate the hidden heavy machine gun positions, observation posts, and any and all cave and tunnel openings you happen across, and mark them on your map for better targeting."

Thomas was using a red grease pencil to mark the locations on the clear acetate sheet covering the small map he'd be carrying on the mission as the lieutenant passed along three, eight-by-ten black and white photos of the targeted recon area to Li for the two of them to peruse and scrutinize.

"Higher-highers, sir?"

"The brass, Specialist Li, those with considerably more rank and clout than we mere mortals. You copy, Specialist?"

“Copy, sir,” said Li.

"Good. Now, as you can see from the photos, the mountain is a beast, but it ain’t Everest, so four days will give you enough time to semi-circumnavigate it while remaining unobserved during your patrol. In that regard, keep in mind it is an active enemy area. Think hornet’s nest."

"Will there be an over flight to get a better look at the recon zone you want us to check out, lieutenant?"

Marquardt shook his head. "That's a negative," he said. "We can't get a helicopter in close enough to those areas on the mountain for a better look without drawing attention and some serious anti-aircraft fire, hence the photos from the telephoto lens... and before you ask, these three photos are the best ones of the bunch that were taken the day before yesterday. The helicopter took some serious enemy fire getting these photos, so here's to the pilots and crew and the Army photographer who took these shots and several near miss gunshots. The photographer and the air crew are fine, by the way."

"Good to hear, lieutenant," admitted Thomas. "But..."

"But you're wondering why it wouldn't be easier to send him back up in another Huey to pinpoint those troubling areas with his camera rather than sending a Lurp team to estimate it, is that what a good Lurp Team leader might be thinking?"

"Yes, sir," agreed Thomas, suppressing a smile. "That might've crossed my mind."

"Then you'll be happy to know that our ever tactically inquisitive Company Commander asked that very same question of the fine minds at the BIG-TOC command, which they dismissed and ordered the mission to go-ahead anyway. Could be, too, they likely asked themselves why risk a million-dollar aircraft and their highly trained pilots and crew, not to mention the talented combat photographer and his expensive Nikon and its Carl Zeiss telephoto lens when we can send in $3 a day Lurps?"

"We're, like, seriously underpaid, sir," lamented Specialist Li.

"Yes, Specialist Li, we are, and thank you for adding your two cents worth. I stand corrected, but that doesn't change the fact that the mission stands as well."

Thomas and Li went back to studying the photos, and then with a not quite convincing nod, the Sergeant asked perhaps the more obvious question.

"Sir, wouldn't it save some time and trouble to have the Higher-highers call in air strikes or artillery on those general areas and turn them into, oh, I dunno, gravel?"

"They have at some locations," said Marquardt. "But the east side of the mountain is a combat No-Go zone because of the shrine. It's a sacred place to the true believers, Buddhists, and Cao Dai religions, and maybe a few others as well. The VC and NVA know this and use it to their advantage. It's no secret that we occupy the top of the mountain and that the Viet Cong and NVA occupy everything else in between, including, we suspect, the shrine area, which gets a pass from bomb runs or artillery."

"Does that also mean no small arms fire, sir?"

"Rules of engagement preclude military action on the eastside of the mountain or anywhere near the shrine. Well, at least the ones we play by. As for similar positions of interest adjacent to the areas you'll be monitoring, last week several Air Force jets played a few rounds of Whack-a-mole near the areas with a few 500-pound bombs. That was followed up a few days later by a Cobra gunship run with rockets and mini-gun fire hammering more of it into rubble, so count on running into some fields of scree..."

"Scree, sir?" asked Li who was unfamiliar with the word.

"A large field of loose rocks, shale, and broken stones. Think landslide-like."

"Ah!" exclaimed Li, taking in the word and meaning while the Texan nodded along, thoughtfully. Turning to Thomas he asked, "Did you, like, know what scree was?"

"No, I did not, but I thought I pulled off looking worldly and wise quite well, didn't you?"

"Avoid them, not just because they're open areas," added the lieutenant, bringing the focus back to the briefing, "but also because they are potential ankle breakers."

Both the Team Leader and Li gave a nod and credence to the warning. Breaking an ankle on an enemy occupied mountain didn't appeal to either of them, not when they might have to make a run for it, if they got compromised by the North Vietnamese who'd be fast on their heels chasing after them in a running gun battle.

"Outwardly, all of the pounding that the military ordnance did to the general area over the years, shut down some enemy gun positions, but apparently, not all as Mister Victor Charles and his northern NVA cousins are still firing at passing friendly aircraft flying into the Tay Ninh Basecamp as of 0-900 this morning.

"Field Force II's latest Intel is that there is a labyrinth of fortified and protected caves and interconnected tunnels throughout the mountain. The Intel analysts concluded Uncle Ho's ancient ancestors started digging when they were fighting the Chinese 1,000 years ago, back when both sides were still using swords and spears and getting

Dear John letters sent to them on terracotta tablets with '*It's not Yu, it's Mi.*' excuses."

He chuckled, but when no one else did, he coughed and went on.

"As I said, your mission is to sneak and peek and locate and mark any enemy gun positions you come across. You're to note any caves and old or new tunnel openings you find on those sides of the mountain as well, and then come back for a two-day stand-down. You copy?"

"Yes, sir. But do we check any of them out? The tunnels and caves, I mean, if we happen to stumble across any?"

"With discretion, sure. But your primary task is to pinpoint their locations, mark them on your map for artillery or air strikes, and move on. If you spot a DShK heavy machine gun position and can take it out with a LAW or small arms fire, then again, that's at your discretion. Just keep in mind that the Relay Station on top of the mountain has reported increased enemy sightings and activities over the past few weeks. Their outposts have observed what they believe are NVA units coming in from the north and west at night and disappearing somewhere near the base of the mountain. The latest suggested estimate is that each one the enemy sightings has been a platoon size or larger."

"Larger?"

"Roger that, judging from the number of flashlights that have been observed over the last week the Intel people believe it to be part of an on-going build up, which means firing a LAW into an opening might just stir up some trouble for you and your team," said Lieutenant Marquardt. He added, "If they don't know you're sneaking around and watching them, then, I suggest that reconnaissance would be your better option, if you catch my drift."

They did. With only five men on their team, caution had to be more than just a watchword.

"Like, why do, like, the Intel people think it's a build up?" asked Specialist-4 Li. "Why are they worrying, dude? I mean, sir. Sorry."

Li, who was born in Taiwan and whose family had immigrated to Haleiwa, Hawaii in the mid 50s, had more than acclimated to his new home. He thrived. Hawaiian style. Although his parents were hoping that their only son, Harold, would become an architect, or better yet, a doctor, young Harry's dream was to own his own North Shore Surf Shop, like the one where he'd worked before he was Drafted. When he wasn't renting surfboards to tourists, fixing dings, or sweeping out the shop, the teenager was kicking back with a blueberry/mango syrup flavored shaved ice or trying to get comfortable with the bar chords playing *Walk, Don't Run* on his battered six-string Epiphone guitar. An avid surfer since he was twelve, terms like; *dude, man, braw, bummer, whoa, bitchin,' stoked* or other beach related slang were a key part of his everyday vernacular; something that even the Army and Lurp training cadre had tried and failed to eliminate from the young Draftee.

That the five-foot, five inch tall, 125-pound Chinese American who looked all of 15 but would turn 20 in six weeks, was a standout Lurp and well on his way to becoming a team leader gave him something of a pass.

"Last night the Relay Station reported seeing a long line of flashlights winding up through the jungle on the southeastern approach to the Nui Ba Den that disappeared somewhere around here," he said, thumping the map again with the pointer.

"You may or may not know it, but back in 1968 the Viet Cong attacked and overran the Relay Station." Marquardt paused to let that news sink in and then added more weight to the story. "Two-dozen GIs were killed, many others wounded, and several were even captured and taken prisoner. The Viet Cong lost a few dozen of their people, too, and heavy blood trails showed they took some severe hits. Since then, there have been the usual mortar and rocket attacks and sniper shots, but more troubling are the recent ground probes on the Station's perimeter."

"Which means they'll also have Observation Posts keeping a close eye on the Station?" asked Sergeant Thomas.

"That's affirmative, as the BIG-TOC's take on it is that the NVA who've moved into the A-O are preparing to attack the Relay Station again once they have their numbers in place, which they also estimate may not be all that far away. So, I say again, you find and mark the active tunnels and caves, and the Air Force and artillery will try again with better targets to stall and stifle any serious attack on the Relay Station. However, if you happen to stumble across a lone NVA soldier on your patrol before the completion of your mission and can bring him back able to walk and talk, then that will constitute as being a successful mission. Capture a POW early on and the Intel people will want you off the mountain A-SAP."

Both the Team Leader and Assistant Team Leader brightened at the possibility of a shortened mission as they went back to studying the photographs.

"Oh, and Captain Robison says that if you do grab up and bring back a live POW two members from your team will receive a three day, in-country R&R to Vung Tau."

Vung Tau was a port city on the South China Sea and a popular in-country beach area R&R site with its many bars, massage parlors, and outdoor cafes. That bit of incentive was well received by both Thomas and Li, as it would be by the other members of the team, later when the T-L and A-T-L passed it along. The two to go to Vung Tau would be chosen by straws. Thomas would excuse himself from the draw as he didn't think it was right for a Team Leader to compete against his teammates, not to mention he didn't want to catch the clap.

"Some pretty gnarly looking boulders here, sir," Li said, studying the photographs, again. His eyes went from the eight-by-tens to the lieutenant, and then back to the photographs again.

"If, by gnarly, you mean dump truck-sized boulders, then yes. And also, steep inclines and dense vegetation, well, once you get past where the Engineers have pushed back the brush and jungle from the Relay Station's perimeter. The Air Force defoliated some of the jungle leading up to the station, but not all, so you'll need to move quickly across the open area unobserved to find better cover and concealment in the jungle below it. Like I said, it's not Mount Everest, but it'll still be a butt kicker."

"Quick reaction Force?" asked Thomas, wanting to know what help would be coming for them, if they needed it.

"A platoon of South Vietnamese paratroopers out of the Tay Ninh Basecamp will be on stand-by, if you hit the shit and cannot escape and evade."

Thomas looked to Li and they both looked to the lieutenant. The former 25th Infantry Division's Tay Ninh base camp was a fifteen-minute helicopter ride away, but fifteen minutes when a Lurp team was in contact and surrounded by the VC or NVA that were closing in could be a lifetime away, and for some Lurp teams in the war, had been.

It was the First Sergeant who spoke next.

"In addition, we'll have a heavy team from the company, our company, on location A-SAP. SFC Kozak here will lead it. I would accompany him, but as of tomorrow I will be on one week of glorious

R&R leave in Bangkok," said First Sergeant Poplawski, offering an answer that quelled any doubt about the size or type of QRF.

Poplawski, with his coffee cup in hand, took a sip of his coffee. "Your QRF will be ready, if and when you need it."

"Whoa dude, Bangkok!" grinned Li. "Cool!"

"When do we go in, sir?" Thomas asked the lieutenant, getting back to the mission.

"Late tomorrow afternoon."

"Our Extraction Point?"

"Rather than heading back up to the relay station you'll make your way down the northwest side of the mountain to this location," Marquardt said, showing the location on the wall map and whacking it with the pointer once again. "Here you'll be picked up by a unit from the 11th Armored CAV out of Di An. They're heavily armored 113 personnel carriers and, I suspect, a few Sheridan's accompanying a convoy to the Tay Ninh Basecamp."

The two leaned back in for a closer look at the exfil site and Thomas marked the coordinates on the mission map.

"Tanks?" asked Li.

"You're welcome," said the First Sergeant, holding up his coffee cup and offering a brief nod.

Li started to nod, caught himself, and then slowly shook his head and chuckled.

"Dude, that was bad," he said.

"That's First Sergeant Dude to you, Specialist Li, because if I hear you fail to acknowledge proper military rank one more time then you'll have wished you wiped out at the Pipeline and your ass got shredded by that very ugly canyon of razor-sharp coral instead, if you catch my winter offshore drift?"

"Yes, First Sergeant," said the chastened soldier.

"Then there you go, young Lurp!" said Poplawski.

"If you are compromised and have to E&E, chances are better than good that the NVA will think you're heading back up to the Relay Station and try to cut you off," said the lieutenant. "In that regard, by Day two, the 11th ACR people will move into position be ready to provide any firepower to anyone chasing after you on your extraction. You can thank our good CO, Captain Robison, for getting the 11th ACR and their considerable protective fire power to bring you out."

"What about the NVA spotters watching the Relay Station, asked Thomas. "Won't they report our team coming in on the chopper?"

"No," said Lieutenant Marquardt. "You'll go in via a closed-door helicopter when it makes its usual mail run to the Relay Station. Since yesterday we've had the helicopters close their doors before going up to the mountain top, so it won't be anything out of the ordinary when you and your team go in, either."

"Do we remain at the Station overnight, sir, or go out at last light?"

"You'll over-night at the Relay Station and go outside the wire just prior to sunrise and slowly start working your way down the mountain. Much like the area around it, the mountain is covered with some pretty thick jungle and massive boulders that you can use to your advantage. The primary objective here is sneak and peek, which even if you have trouble remembering that there are two n's and two s's in the word, *reconnaissance* like I do, then you at least know how to define it and carry out the mission. You copy?"

Thomas and Li nodded. "Yes, sir," they said in unison. "Sneak and peek."

"Outstanding!" said the First Sergeant, using the Army's go-to compliment of the day. "Any questions?"

Thomas and Li shook their heads as Poplawski and Kozak joined the lieutenant at the wall map.

"Good!" said the lieutenant. "Then brief your team, draw your ammo load and rations, clean your weapons, and get your gear ready for inspection by either the First Sergeant or me by 1600 hours tomorrow. First Sergeant?"

"You heard the lieutenant," said Poplawski. "Oh, and before we conduct the weapons and equipment check, make sure that any and everything that can rattle or make noise is taped down and secure. Knowing SFC Kozak as I do, I'm sure he'll also have you run a few Immediate Action drills, both with and without rucksacks. Isn't that right, Sergeant Kozak?"

"Count on it," said Kozak.

"You two copy?" said Poplawski to Thomas and Li.

"Yes, First Sergeant," said Thomas while Li nodded and said he did as well.

"Good, then you're dismissed."

Stopping in the TOC doorway on his way out, Specialist Li turned back to the First Sergeant.

"Like, how do you know about all of the sharp coral, like, at the Pipeline, First Sergeant?" he asked, genuinely puzzled. The First Sergeant was hardly the surfer type, unless of course gorillas could hang ten.

"Like, I am your First Sergeant, Specialist Li. It is my job, like, to know everything, like, also when to actually use the word, *like*, and maybe not saying like every other word or two in a sentence. It is properly used as a preposition, a conjunction, noun, adjective, or an adverb, but not like buckshot. You use it too frequently then you might be mistaken for a second lieutenant. You, like, copy, specialist?"

"Eh... yes, First Sergeant."

"Good. Now go and sin no more."

Chapter 5

When twenty-two-year-old, Second Lieutenant Richard Henry Plantagenet had stepped off the back ramp of the bulky looking Chinook helicopter with a just as bulky-looking duffle bag on his left shoulder and a large manila envelope of travel and assignment orders in his right hand one month earlier, he was met by two R-Company Rangers standing beside a jeep at the edge of the camp's flight line.

Their spit-shined jungle boots, starched jungle fatigues, and black berets canted at the prescribed, *'we're studs, and you ain't'* angles, weren't hard to miss. The two enlisted Rangers were there to escort him to the Ranger Company.

One was a young and smiling Asian-looking Staff Sergeant while the other was a stern-faced, early thirty-something Senior NCO who could've easily doubled as a bouncer at a bar on a bad side of town or an outlaw biker Sergeant-at-Arms. The Staff Sergeant appeared pleasant enough, the Senior NCO not so much so. Brand new second lieutenants seldom brightened any senior NCO's day, let alone immediately improved their dispositions when they reported for duty.

As he approached the jeep the Senior NCO and Staff Sergeant saluted, and the young officer set his duffle bag down and returned the required military courtesy.

"Lieutenant Plantagenet?" said the Senior NCO, using the French pronunciation of name as *Plan-taz-ja-nay*, which surprised the officer as most others during his limited time in the Army had not.

Plantagenet nodded. "Yes, Sergeant."

"Sir, I am First Sergeant Poplawski," said the senior NCO, bluntly. "This is Romeo Company's Training NCO, Staff Sergeant Shintaku. Welcome to Camp Mackie, lieutenant."

Nods were exchanged, but not first names or handshakes. Shintaku offered to take the officer's duffle bag, but Plantagenet shook his head and declined.

"No, that's all right, I got it, but thank you, " he said to the Staff Sergeant, appreciating the gesture.

"Then right this way, lieutenant," said the First Sergeant, already turning back towards the jeep without waiting for a response.

From the flight line the First Sergeant turned onto the camp's perimeter road, the defensive *Green line* that ringed the large camp. On the drive, the wide-eyed lieutenant wasn't so much taking in the camp as much as he was gawking at what all he saw along the way on the dust-filled, bumpy ride. This was a Forward Operating Base seated along a north-south dirt road that was surrounded by jungle that up until now he'd only seen from the air.

The drive took them by a series of fortified bunkers and manned guard towers that were strategically placed along the Base perimeter and protected the base from ground attacks. Plantagenet took in the No-Man's Land that led from the multiple rows and strands of barbed wire, ankle high tanglefoot, and rolled concertina razor wire in front of the fighting positions to the jungle 100 yards beyond. Intermixed into the barbed wire he could see trip flares, dangling empty beer and pop cans likely filled with pebbles as make-shift noise makers, Claymore anti-personnel mines, and several innocuous looking, but deadly 55-gallon drums planted into the packed ground and leaning outward at a 30-degree angle. The large drums that were filled with Fugas were ready to unleash a breaking wave of napalm-like Hell on any unfortunate attackers trying to overrun the camp anywhere near the blast radius of the 55-gallon drums when detonated.

On the flight into Camp Mackie, he noticed that, unlike the huge Air base at Bien Hoa where he'd arrived in-country two days earlier, here there were no snack bars, flush toilets, or anything remotely civilized looking. Nor were there any nearby cities, villages, or hamlets. Camp Mackie appeared to be smack dab in the middle of nowhere adjacent to a dirt road that ran through the hinterlands and jungle of Warzone C. An island-like encampment surrounded by a sea of green. Exchange the jungle for a desert then it might as well have been something out of *Beau Geste*.

A hundred yards along on the perimeter road, Poplawski downshifted a second gear turn into a dirt road that led into the camp proper. As the jeep turned, Shintaku, who was riding in the back of the jeep and leaning into the turn, caught the new lieutenant checking out the right sleeve of First Sergeant's jungle fatigues showing Poplawski's arrowhead patch and rocker of his previous combat tour of duty with the Special Forces. The officer was taking in the many tabs and combat patches that adorned the front of the sun-faded jungle fatigue shirt.

When the lieutenant realized the Staff Sergeant was watching, Plantagenet turned away and made a point of taking in some of the less than scenic sights and sounds in the basecamp, of which there were many. To him, and likely anyone else who'd toured the base, Camp Mackie was little more than a military Boomtown centering around its main runway and flight line, where C-130 fixed wing aircraft, Chinook helicopters, Cobra gunships, Huey lift ships or smaller *Loach* scout birds were taking off, landing, or were parked in fortified L-shaped revetments.

The occupants of this jungle outpost were housed in heavily sandbagged Quonset huts, large tents, or tin roofed wooden hootches. The less than Grand Tour took them by an armor unit, where soldiers in grubby, sweat and grease-stained tee shirts were pulling maintenance checks on vehicle engines and tracks, or cleaning gun tubes, and .50 caliber machine guns on several tanks and M-113 troop carriers.

One left turn later and further on they passed an artillery battery where one of the three howitzer cannon crews appeared to be on stand-by awaiting a fire mission. Beyond that there were more Quonset huts and tin roofed hootches with stand-alone outhouses and shower points, piss tubes sites, fighting positions, mortar emplacements, ammo dumps, tents, and every so often a large, heavily fortified bunker covered with layers of sandbags and sprouting multiple antennas.

Loud diesel-powered generators spewing blue/white smoke fed electricity to the various concerns and were kept running by adjacent 55-gallon drums of fuel. Plantagenet wasn't surprised to see that a large number of the barrels had been emptied, scrubbed out, and repurposed to hold water. Those designated water barrels had been set over small outbuildings in groups of four to serve as shower areas. The drums were marked in bold print reading: NON-POTABLE WATER reminding the GIs that the water wasn't safe to drink, something the young officer would keep in mind.

He also noticed that some of the empty drums had been turned into modified grills where Mess Sergeants and cooks squinted through rising smoke readying meat for nearby Mess Tent meals. Still more barrels that had been cut in half were used in the various outhouses as evident by several sullen-looking GIs that were stirring rising flame and black smoke-filled tubs on shit burning details that the jeep had passed on their way to Romeo Company.

Plantagenet was startled by a sudden series of loud, reverberating booms behind them from the howitzer artillery battery they'd passed earlier that was now carrying out a fire support mission. Surprised as he was, the lieutenant was sinking down in his seat and flinching with each blast. The First Sergeant who was driving, and the Staff Sergeant in the back of the jeep hadn't seemed bothered by the outbound artillery fire and the second lieutenant felt a little foolish for his reaction.

Somewhat embarrassed he sat up straight again and turned his attention to a flight of three Huey helicopters taking off from the Camp and heading out high above the jungle. Their loud whop-whop-whopping blades chopped the morning sky like teams of woodcutters and soon lost their volume, diminished by distance.

The jeep bounced by an Engineer compound, a maintenance hangar and shop of some kind, a small but busy base exchange, and several open motor pools where jeeps, trucks, and trailers sat parked in line.

The less than scenic forward operating base, the outbound cannon fire, and the many ruts and potholes on the dirt road the jeep was bobbing along on had the new lieutenant thinking that the term, '*Boomtown*' was a more accurate definition for Camp Mackie than a Base. Everything about it screamed makeshift and temporary, and told him that once the war had moved on, the camp would shut down, and a new one would spring up somewhere else.

"Turn your head to the right, lieutenant!" shouted Poplawski to the young officer.

"What?" said the lieutenant turning to the left and the First Sergeant only to be hit with a face full of heavy, black, acrid smoke and a disgusting, stomach-turning smell from another of the shit burning details just to the side of the road. The wind had momentarily shifted as they were driving by, and the dark cloud engulfed the jeep.

Plantagenet's eyes were stinging, his nose was burning, and he began hacking and coughing, and thinking that he might even vomit before the air quickly cleared as the jeep outran the swirling dark cloud and horrible stench. He had just finished coughing as the ride took a final turn into the Ranger Company Compound and came to a jerking stop in front of the unit's Orderly Room that was the front half of a sand bagged fortified Quonset hut. The First Sergeant switched off the jeep, set the handbrake, and jumped out. Staff Sergeant Shintaku hopped out of the back seat, retrieved the new lieutenant's duffle bag, and handed it to the officer. Shintaku then jumped into the driver's seat, started it up, and drove off towards the unit's small motor pool, such as it was, twenty yards away.

It wasn't much of a motor pool as Romeo Company only had one other jeep, a deuce-and-a-half truck, a more practical three-quarter ton utility truck, and two M-274 flatbed mechanical mules. The mules, that looked like somebody's grown-up notion of 4 X 4 flatbed Go-Karts, were the most used vehicles the company. The new lieutenant would soon learn that the mules were practical necessities for the Lurp unit, especially during the rainy season. They could easily carry a half-ton of supplies and equipment, and often ferried rucksack-laden teams to and from the helicopter flight line before and after their patrols. The one jeep, deuce-and-a-half, and two mechanical mules were authorized equipment, while a second jeep and a quarter-ton truck were '*borrowed.*' The truck's original unit identification information had been painted over and now showed R Company-MAC-V subdued shoulder patch markings on the truck's bumper. The patch showed a sword through the opening of a walled fortification.

The Ranger Company compound, in reality, was just three Quonset huts, one large platoon-size tent, and a few smaller out-buildings that he correctly guessed were a latrine and a shower point. A volleyball net was set up in the open ground in front of one of the platoon-size hootches and beside the large green canvas tent that was surrounded by a three-foot wall of sandbags. At a nearby weapons cleaning table, a handful of GIs were stripping down several AK-47 assault rifles and putting them back together. Several of the young soldiers were staring at the new lieutenant before their team leader turned their attention back to the weapons familiarization class.

"Right this way, lieutenant," said the First Sergeant leading Plantagenet into the unit's Orderly Room.

"Sir," First Sergeant Poplawski said, coming through the screen door of the Quonset hut and finding the Company Commander standing behind his gunmetal gray government issued desk, holding a cup of coffee. "The new lieutenant's here."

Captain Robison looked up, stood tall, and waited for the new lieutenant to report in.

"Sir!" barked the Second Lieutenant, setting his duffle bag down, coming to attention, and saluting. Plantagenet was initially taken aback that the Company Commander was black, and then even more so, by the Special Forces combat patch and tab, U.S. and Vietnamese jump wings, and Ranger scroll that decorated his uniform. To the University of Georgia's ROTC graduate, the West Point ring the captain wore made him all the more intimidating. Plantagenet handed his assignment orders to the senior officer.

"Stand at ease, lieutenant," said Captain Robison, giving the new arrival the order to stand somewhat relaxed as he briefly went over the orders. "So, is it Dick or Richard?

"Dick, sir."

Robison nodded, offered his hand, and the new lieutenant shook it.

"Plantagenet's an old family name, I take it?"

The lieutenant's face reddened. He wasn't totally embarrassed, just the usual amount.

"Yes, sir," he said, lowering his eyes.

"I had a hunch."

And there it was! The hunchback reference of Richard III. The third of three sons, it didn't help that one of his oldest brother's name was John and everyone, even the family, called him *Gaunt.* Whether there was a genuine connection to the historical personages or simply wishful thinking family lore, the two brothers bore the brunt of the curiosity, ridicule, and puns that came with the family's surname and those provided by his parents. His next oldest brother, Tony, at least, had escaped the ribbings. It didn't help that, unfortunately, the lieutenant was also the third son. The captain's first remark was at least subtle, the next one wasn't.

"I'm assigning you to a platoon of young Rangers, lieutenant so don't be a dick to them. That being said, welcome to Romeo Company. As one of my two Platoon Leaders, I expect you to lead by example and take care of the people I'm putting under your charge."

"Yes, sir."

"Make no mistake about it, they are yours. Any issues or problems they have then I'll be looking to you to explain to me why they exist, and what you did about them prior to bringing them to my attention. Understood?"

"Yes, sir."

"Good, and that likewise will apply to any of the good, and even spectacular things they do, which I'll attribute to your fine leadership style and top-notched performance."

"I'll do my best, captain."

"No lieutenant, you will do your best and then you will do better."

"Yes...yes, sir."

"Take that mantra to heart and you'll fit in well here."

The carrot and stick welcome talk from the Ranger Company Commander was to have the second lieutenant understand what would be expected of him as a Platoon Leader with the Lurp Company.

“Single? Married?”

“Married, captain. We will, well, *were* going celebrate our second anniversary next month until I got my deployment orders.”

Robison nodded, grunted. “Sorry to hear about the poor timing on the Army’s part, but you’ll be home with something more to celebrate next year. Kids?”

“Baby girl.”

“How old?”

“Ten months, a wobbly toddler.”

Robison smiled, nodded again, and got back to business.

"Ranger School, I see," he said, giving a nod to the gold and black tab on Plantagenet's left shoulder.

"Yes, sir," said the junior officer with a proud nod in return.

"Good," said Robison. "Then you have an idea of what the nature of the job is for the people you'll be leading. 95% of those young Lurps we have in the company are not Fort Benning trained Rangers, but they are combat Rangers, and the 75th Infantry scroll they wear is every bit as valued and impressive as the one you've earned, some might argue, more so."

Although Plantagenet nodded again, he wasn't so sure about the captain’s comparison, but wisely kept his thoughts to himself on the matter. The eight-week school he’d recently graduated from in

Georgia and in the fetid, gator-filled swamps of Northern Florida was no cakewalk.

"While you won't be expected to complete our in-country Lurp/Ranger training, you will be expected to go out on at least one mission to better comprehend the difficult job we are doing here and those who volunteer to be combat Rangers. Some of our people came to us from safe and comfortable rear area bases and cushy MOS jobs because they wanted to be combat Rangers. First Sergeant?"

"Sir?"

"Who's that former Image Interpreter Intelligence Specialist we have that volunteered for a secondary Infantry MOS to be here?"

"That would be Specialist Pettit, sir."

“And what exactly is an Image Interpreter? Enlighten us if you will.”

“Someone who probably sits in a clean and comfortable air-conditioned office in Bien Hoa or Long Binh looking at aerial photos before calling it a day and heading over to the Enlisted Men’s Club for a cold pitcher of beer to listen to a halfway decent civilian rock band while smiling at dancing Go-Go Girls dressed in skimpy outfits.”

"And didn't his Platoon Sergeant tell you that he tried to talk him out of volunteering to be a Lurp?"

"That he did, Captain, as did his wise and venerable First Sergeant who informed him that he wouldn't be spending his time wearing a Smokey the Bear hat and pointing visitors towards geysers and picnic tables! I suspect he might've even asked him what the fuck he was thinking, but Pettit volunteered anyway for our unit and graduated in the top of our Lurp/Ranger selection training class a few cycles ago.

We also have another Lurp in the company that used to be a warehouse forklift driver in Long Binh," said the First Sergeant.

"See! There you go, lieutenant," said the captain. "That's the kind of people we have here in Romeo Company. Bottom line, they all volunteered to be here, graduated from our training course, and have earned a right to be here. They're young, loud, and proud and share the 75th Infantry-Ranger combat legacy. They're the ones you'll be in charge of, the ones you'll be leading."

The second lieutenant perked up at the mention of leading a Ranger patrol in combat and nodded like a determined teetering toddler looking for a chance to open the refrigerator freezer to get to the ice cream.

"Yes sir, I'm looking forward to leading a patrol."

The First Sergeant snickered, and the captain shot him a shaming glance. Poplawski got the message and covered it with an unconvincing cough.

"You won't be leading patrols," said Captain Robison, turning back to Plantagenet.

"Sir?" asked the confused lieutenant.

"You will be the Platoon Leader for the Second platoon once we actually have enough people to fill a second platoon. However, you will not be a Lurp Team Leader, unless the task calls for a heavy team or Quick Reaction Force. Then I'll make that call and expect you to step up and lead, if, in fact, I deem you are ready to lead."

The Second Lieutenant's face registered more hurt than surprise. He seemed to shrink a bit, his shoulders slumped, and the tone of his voice that followed was just as telling.

"Yes, sir," he said, quietly.

"To that end, one of the tasks I'll also be assigning you will be to assist Staff Sergeant Shintaku on the next training cycle for those looking to become part of Romeo Company. As I said, because you recently attended Ranger School at Benning, you won't be expected to go through the two and half weeks of our own training program, however, I will expect you to monitor the training classes and do the daily PT with the trainees."

"Yes sir."

"Good. After assisting in that training cycle, where you will see and appreciate how Ranger Lurp operations are done here in our little corner of the war, you'll be assigned to a team where you'll pull your very first Lurp patrol."

The new lieutenant's face and spirits rose with this last bit of news.

"Yes, sir!"

However, the Company Commander's next comment would temper it considerably.

"Keep in mind your Team Leader will be in charge of the team on patrol. More than likely, it'll be an E-4 or E-5. As a Ranger School graduate, you should be familiar with patrols at times being led by Enlisted Men, as no one during the training wore rank as I recall, so rank wasn't an issue. If the team you'll be assigned to has an E-4 or E-5 Team Leader, then that means that I, along with my senior cadre, believe that Specialist or Buck Sergeant, is qualified to lead a Lurp team, do you copy?"

"Yes, sir."

"That's good, too, because like it or not, on your first patrol you'll be viewed as an FNG, you understand what that acronym means and all the contempt it carries and conveys?"

"Yes, sir, I do."

"And just to be clear on this, as of this moment that is what you are and exactly how you will be perceived by the team that you'll be assigned to. That also means you will follow the Team Leader's or Assistant Team Leader's orders on patrol in the field to the letter."

"Yes, sir."

"You will watch, listen, and learn," added the captain. "And more than that you will experience what members of a Lurp team experience in the jungle on patrol. That experience is gold, and it will help you to better understand and more importantly, value the Rangers in your platoon, and in our company."

“Yes, sir.”

“They, in turn, will see that you can also do the job. Word spreads quickly in our small company, so if you do screw up, everyone will know it. And if you do screw up badly and can't cut it, then I'll have you out of my Company faster than a rifle round goes down range. You copy?"

"Yes, sir," said the lieutenant, knowing his role in the conversation.

"Outstanding," said the captain. "Then the First Sergeant will show you to your quarters, and once you're settled, we will give you a familiarization tour of the Company and Camp Mackie. Any questions?"

"No, sir."

"Outstanding! I want you back here in two-zero minutes for our Camp Mackie Show-and-Tell. You're dismissed. Oh, one more thing…"

The Ranger Captain reached inside the right drawer of his desk and pulled out a handful of red, white, and black R Company- 75th Infantry Ranger scrolls and MAC-V patches and handed them to the new lieutenant.

"Have the scroll sewn over the MAC-V patch on the left shoulder of your uniforms."

"Yes, sir."

Once the new arrival was out the door First Sergeant Poplawski paused in the doorway, turned, and quietly said, "What say we replace our motto to what you just said about doing your best, and then doing better? It has a nice ring to it."

"What? You don't like *Audentis Fortuna Luvat- Fortune Favors the Brave*?"

"Huh? So that's what that means. As a lapsed Catholic I thought it meant, *Fortune Favors Bingo*. The Nuns should've beaten me more."

"I imagine they tried," laughed Robison. "Okay, then find someone with decent penmanship to paint it on our unit sign."

"Roger that, sir."

Nineteen minutes later when Plantagenet returned to the Orderly Room, he found the Company Commander and a First Lieutenant waiting for him.

"Dick, this is Ryan Marquardt, my Executive Officer," said the Company Commander. "He'll give you a tour of the company, Camp

Mackie, and show you where we eat chow. We share a mess hall with the Engineers down the road and while they don't assign any of our people KP duty, we share their perimeter guard responsibilities, which means you'll also be assigned as the Officer of the Guard, from time to time."

"Yes, sir."

To Marquardt he said, "Ryan, while you two are out and about, swing by the PX so Lieutenant Plantagenet can pick up a few odds and ends to make his quarters a little more comfortable."

To Plantagenet he added, "The PX we have here isn't much. It's about the size of a two-car garage but more like a corner store in a lousy neighborhood. If they have a rotating fan at the PX, I suggest you pick one up."

"Yes, sir."

"Okay then. Ryan, he's all yours."

"Sir," said Plantagenet, holding out his hand to Marquardt.

"Where are you from?" the XO, asked, shaking the offered hand.

"Savannah, Georgia, in the last move. My father is in the Coast Guard and Savannah was his last duty assignment before he retired. He was the Acting Shipping Commissioner there. Now he's acting at playing Golf."

"Coast Guard, huh?"

"Yes sir, for the last twenty-four years, and when someone asks me where I'm from, I generally respond, *which year*?"

Listening in Robison chuckled. Such was the life of military brats, his own included.

"Ryan, before you hit the PX take him by the BIG-TOC. Introduce him and show him around," said Captain Robison.

"BIG-TOC?" echoed Plantagenet.

"The nickname we use for the Camp's command Tactical Operations Center," explained the Captain. "It's the nerve center that sometimes gets on our nerves. Lots of brass, lots of Intel people, and lots of taskings for us, lately. Oh, and when you get back, I'm going to have you shadow Ryan in our TOC tonight so that you can get an idea of how it functions as the lifeline for our teams in the field."

Plantagenet nodded again. A lot was being thrown at him and he wanted to impress the CO and XO that he was eager to take it on.

"When's the next training class scheduled to start?" Robison asked his X.O.

"Day after tomorrow, sir," said Marquardt. "We have thirty or so volunteers ready to go."

"Good. If we can get seven or eight to graduate the course, then that'll be enough to supplement the teams we already have. In the morning after the morning formation, I want you to introduce him to Staff Sergeant Shintaku, our Training NCO."

"Roger that, captain."

"I've already met the Sergeant," said the new lieutenant, speaking up. "He was with the First Sergeant when they picked me up from the chopper."

Robison nodded. To Marquardt he said, "Do it anyway."

To anyone watching it was beginning to look like a bad tennis match between the captain and his two junior officers with the conversation quickly going back and forth as Robison laid down the proverbial law to the new arrival. That he tag-teamed lieutenant Marquardt in on it, better moved the play along. It was the Company Commander's turn again.

"Lieutenant, as I've said you'll be in charge of our next in-country Lurp training cycle, and by in charge, I mean, you'll stand behind Staff Sergeant Shintaku looking strong and wise, and occasionally give some thoughtful nodding to the wisdom he is passing along. Shintaku would give any of the Ranger Instructors at Benning a run for their money, so if he believes you're competent enough to teach one of the various mandatory courses during the training cycle, then you will do so under his guidance and tutelage. How are your map reading skills?"

"They're good to go, sir."

"Outstanding. Then that'll be a good place for you to jump in and assist. Map reading and land navigation, in my opinion, are two of the most underrated skills every Ranger needs to have down pat, especially here in III Corps. The jungle here is vast and uncompromising, and knowing your location, knowing where you are in it, and how to reach your extraction site, or where to accurately direct artillery, is critical. You copy?"

"Yes, sir."

"Outstanding! Now, go forth and multiply your skill sets because there is no rest for the wicked, nor for a second lieutenant in a combat Ranger Company."

"Roger that, sir."

"Oh, and don't fuck up because lives are going to depend on you and the decisions you make. Any mistakes you make from those decisions can prove fatal for our people in the field, not to mention yourself as well on your patrol. So, what's the key point here, lieutenant? What's the main take away from all that I'm trying to pass along to you?"

"Don't fuck up."

"There you go. Carry on.

Chapter 6

First Sergeant Poplawski's R&R journey began at zero-dark-thirty with two helicopter hops from Camp Mackie to Cu Chi, Cu Chi to Bien Hoa, one bouncing jeep ride from Bien Hoa to Saigon over potholed roads, and a military bus ride to the Tan Son Nhut airport where he checked in at the R&R processing counter.

After checking in at the R&R desk he was pointed towards a waiting area. Twenty minutes later an NCO addressing the vacation-bound GIs announced that the plane to Bangkok they were scheduled to take at 1215 hours would now depart at 1500 hours in the afternoon. Three o'clock.

The NCO drowned out the disappointed grumbling and groans from the soldiers with a somewhat droned rehearsed speech about hotel vouchers, a reminder not to break the law while on leave in Thailand, and the importance of using condoms should the need or anything else arise. He finished his announcements with a slightly louder cautionary statement for emphasis.

"ALL RIGHT, PEOPLE! LISTEN UP!" he bellowed to ensure that all heads turned in his direction. "You need to stay in the immediate area. Do not miss your scheduled flights to and from Bangkok. *I say again*, do not miss your scheduled flights. Your allocation slot is a one-time deal that is set in stone. If you miss the flight today, you will not be allowed on another. Your R&R will be cancelled, and you'll have to go back to your unit, and put in a bid for another R&R slot at a future date. No amount of pleading, whining, or crying will change that. Also, if you miss your return flight you will be considered AWOL, Absent Without Leave, and will be dealt with accordingly. I say again, remain in the immediate area and do not miss your flights, to or from."

Heads nodded in understanding, even Poplawski's, as those heading to the Thai Capitol on the afternoon flight acknowledged the importance of what was being said. That was when the Romeo Company's First Sergeant walked outside, ostensibly for a smoke break, and then made his way over to the airport's front gate where he flagged down a Pedi-cab on Republic Street. His new destination was the former CIA safe house that had been reassigned to the Special Forces much misnamed, Studies and Observation Group.

There was time to visit. Besides, technically he was on his smoke break. Pulling out his Zippo lighter and pack of Marlboros he lipped out a cigarette and fired it up. The kamikaze Pedi-cab ride through Saigon wasn't for the weak of heart, given the busy and hectic flow of mostly old French Simcas, Renaults, and Peugeots, delivery trucks, sputtering Lambrettas, scooters, and motorbikes, push carts, and military sedans and jeeps all crowding the already crowded streets.

The address Poplawski gave the Pedi-cab driver took them to a sprawling old, colonial villa compound on a tree-lined street in Saigon's District #1. The villa that had once served as a CIA Safe House now had a new, and some said, a *better class* of occupants. With its walled perimeter and guarded gate, it was still safe, but Poplawski wasn't going there for security reasons. He had another purpose in mind. Because the house was being utilized by a unit of the U.S. Army's Special Forces that meant that it quite likely had a decent bar and grille where he could at least have a cold beer and something to eat before he headed back to the airport. Hopefully too, he'd maybe bump into a few old friends, if they weren't out doing their sneaky SOG shit.

After being cleared by the security guard manning the villa's wrought iron front gate, he ambled up the walkway, climbed the porch stairs, and after putting out his cigarette, stepped inside the villa. From the foyer he followed the music into the small, near empty bar just off to his right and paused in the doorway. Glancing at who was there all he found were a bunch of young faces. *That's the trouble with being in my 30s, he thought. Everybody else looks so damn young these days!*

A soft and soulful Brazilian jazz ballad from Joao Gilberto and Stan Getz was playing over a TEAC reel-to-reel tape recorder and two Pioneer box speakers but even the Brazilian guitar and the American's tenor saxophone couldn't quite block out the noise of a loud game of pool by two preppy looking college types in their button-down, short-sleeve shirts, khaki slacks, and penny loafers.

"Five ball, left corner pocket!" called one of the pool players pointing with his pool cue. Lining up behind the cue ball and eyeing it and the bright orange ball like he was trying to decipher some obscure code, he took the shot and missed. The hard, hit ball caught the edge of the pocket, careened off the rail, and then harmlessly rolled back to the center of the table.

"Oooooh, so close...NOT!" laughed the second player, stepping up for his turn at the table. "You choked!"

"Choke on this!" said the shooter running his fist up and down the pool cue.

The two weren't military. When questioned about who they were and what they were doing in Vietnam the pool players would probably say they were government clerks or low-level paper pushers at the Embassy, or perhaps, analysts with USAID, but Poplawski immediately had them pegged. Their haircuts defied military standards and they were too smug looking and too cleanly dressed to be on the Operational side of the CIA, so they were likely newly arrived, lowly agency '*Twats Without Borders, Company types.*' Young as they were, he reckoned they were newly minted intel analysts as well, and like their military FNG counterparts, they would have much to learn before they became of any real value to the agency or those operating in the field on that intelligence. Perhaps one of the first things they should've learned was not to be so loud and obnoxious in the Special Forces bar.

Loud cracks from the hard hit and poorly aimed pool balls grated on the otherwise relaxed ambiance of the bar, as did their loud whoops and hoots for the occasional shots made. The whoops and hoots drew more than a few annoyed frowns from at least two of the other patrons in the bar; one, a black man, who was quietly contemplating something or other over his drink, and a short, stocky Guamanian two tables away who was finishing up what little was left of a plate of steak and eggs and a partially eaten slice of fresh watermelon. For combat soldiers, and especially those in SOG, peace and quiet over a good drink or meal was often prized and very much appreciated in between their secret missions. And SOG missions were secret, as their small patrols took them deep into Cambodia, Laos, and North Viet Nam.

Poplawski suspected that until the two pool players placed a little higher on the learning curve and acquired a better job proficiency level, they would have a way to go before they actually became useful. Until then they would be the kind who nodded and took copious notes during team debriefings and staff meetings, pored over captured maps and other enemy documents, correlated and compiled reports and records of Soviet and Chinese weapons shipments, pondered large scale enemy movements, tactical trends, weather, and terrain, and then would misinterpret it all and screw it up for the next SOG team on the ground.

In time they would get better at their jobs and maybe even be appreciated, but for now the brash new arrivals were little more than strangers in an often confusingly strange land.

A short and stocky bartender, wearing what Poplawski thought was one incredibly ugly maroon Hawaiian shirt with giant yellow flowers and bright green leaves, came out of a backroom storage area hefting two wooden cases of bottled beer that he began loading into an ice filled metal tub beneath the bar. There was little doubt that the bartender and the two customers at the tables were SOG, even in their mismatched civilian clothes.

The two CIA '*company types*' at the pool table were easy to separate from the SOG people. The SOG soldiers were very much at ease with themselves while two other 'civilians' were behind the eight ball in more ways than one.

"Hey, Barkeep! Hey, you!" said one of the pool players to the bartender. "How about putting on some better music?"

The bartender paused what he was doing, turned to the pool player making the request, and shot him an annoyed look.

"No," he said, sourly, and went back to stocking the beer cooler.

"Don't suppose you'd want to play a game of Nine Ball, say $20 against one of those gook flags or helmets you have hanging on the wall?"

The loud pool player's accent was just across the Charles River from Boston, somewhere deep in frat boy Cambridge where the bartender, a Special Forces Master Sergeant, figured the Agency must have been doing their recruiting at MIT, Harvard, Lesley, or somewhere else they needed more smug little fucks who could confuse the Vietnamese when they tried to pronounce their R's. He also was thinking that Southy, Dorchester, or Lowell might've been a better choice to find a more suitable and sturdier class of assets to pick from, but for some reason he could never quite fathom, the CIA was very much Ivy League with Yale being in the lead.

The bartender frowned again at the cocky young man who was chalking his pool cue awaiting an answer.

"Eh, that's another no," said the bartender. "By the way, it's not a 'gook' anything, they're North Vietnamese Army flags and helmets, PAVN to be more precise. Bet you didn't know the word *gook* came from the Spanish/American War in the Philippines in the late 1890s and referred to prostitutes? It's also derogatory to a lot of good people

I know, like, and have served with, not to mention my Korean wife and son, so I'd appreciate it if you didn't use it in my fucking bar."

Any further exchange was interrupted by what came from Poplawski.

"Why, I do believe that is Master Sergeant Billy Mezza in all of his fine sartorial splendor!" Poplawski said loud enough to get the bartender's attention, and apparently the attention of most others in the small bar as well.

Mezza turned his focus from the pool players and gave a coat-hangar sized grin when he saw *'Walter, the Brick, as in wall, just don't ever fucking call me Walter,'* Poplawski walking towards the bar carrying his PX purchased, black, ubiquitous AWOL bag. Mezza's Sicilian face was swallowed up by his smile.

"BRICK!" he yelled, genuinely happy to see his old friend. "I heard you were back at Bragg after you got Medevaced from a bayonet wound in the derriere."

"Volunteered to come back so I could be a pain in everybody's ass."

"And, what? Obviously on loan from Group to a Lurp Company, hence your cute and Beatnik looking black beret," Mezza said, coming around the long bar, shaking Poplawski's out-stretched hand, and joyfully pulling him into a bear hug and slapping him on the back. "I heard you were on loan to another unit and hey, as a First Sergeant, they say!"

"Acting First Sergeant for a Ranger/Lurp Company, hence I'm still an E-7 but in a more manly black beret," Poplawski said. "How about you, Billy? I figured you'd be running a whore house in Cholon by now."

"Sounds promising, but these days I'm only running occasional team insertions and extractions, and tending bar in the interim."

More whoops and hoots from the pool table brought on a sidelong glance and another sour look from Billy Mezza.

"I'm also trying my best not to thump a few of the loud little pissants that Langley keeps sending us and who insist on trying to tell us how to better run our Ops because they've read Cliff Notes on Sun Tzu or Von Clausewitz. They all seem to think they're budding James Bonds, rather than a bunch of pussies galore they inevitably turn out to be."

This last and loud response was aimed at the duo at the pool players that bristled at the comment and glared at the Special Forces bartender.

"Oops, my mistake," said Mezza, raising both hands up in a *wait a minute* apologetic gesture to momentarily lower their hackles. "I shouldn't have said pissants. I meant to say, assholes."

"Why don't you kiss my ass, beanie boy!" said the one who'd wanted to play for the captured NVA military items.

The music didn't stop, nor was it suddenly quiet enough to hear a pin drop, but the comment carried a prolonged pause as Mezza, the *Brick*, and the two other Green Berets in the bar turned towards the civilian that had just insulted them all.

Less analytical than he should've been, the loudmouth hadn't considered his audience. His next mistake only compounded the situation when his youthful bluster assessed that the bartender was older, shorter, and appeared to be out of shape, but Master Sergeant Billy Mezza smiled the smile of a junkyard dog that had slipped its choke chain at someone who was climbing over a locked gate with a posted, DO NOT ENTER sign.

"Seriously?" Mezza said, turning towards the pool table and facing off on the young CIA officer. "We do some shit jobs for you, and this is how you treat us in our own bar?"

"I...I have a brown belt in Karate," said the loudmouth.

The second, and obviously smarter associate was looking for the nearest exit when Poplawski started laughing at the mention of the Japanese Martial Art. Poplawski removed his black Ranger beret, tucked it under his belt, and joined Mezza, as did the two other military patrons who came out of their seats and closed in behind the bartender and the Ranger NCO for more than just moral support.

It was Poplawski who spoke next.

"It's nice that you've had some empty hand training as does Sergeant Mezza here who was one of the top Hand-to-Hand Instructors we had at Fort Bragg, and who along with another younger and more handsome NCO taught improvised weapons and gutter fighting to our fellow *beanie boys*."

"I'm not sure about the handsome part but I do believe that other NCO was you, First Sergeant," replied Mezza. "Well, that was until you got invited by the Agency to go up to Virginia to better enhance the real world, nasty Asian fighting techniques and principles for their recruits at the Farm, as I recall. What was the motto you taught them? '*If you find yourself in a fair fight, then your strategy sucks*.'"

"A win's a win."

"True, and I do believe Director Colby thanked you personally for your efforts."

"Hmm? Must've slipped my mind, me being so scared shitless by this Karate black belt and all."

"I think he said he was only a brown belt."

"Ah, my mistake! But hey, aren't brown belts generally trying to prove they're just as good as black belts?"

"That they do, and painfully so, at times. However, these two also have pool cues."

"True," said Poplawski with a thoughtful nod as though he was recalculating the outcome.

"On the other hand, that'll make it easier to shove them up their asses once we take them away."

"That is true as well," agreed Poplawski, brightening at the prospect. He smiled as he tilted his head to the left and right until several vertebrae in his neck loosened and popped, ready for whatever came next.

Billy Mezza's smile, though, vanished and what took its place was frightening.

To the pool players, he said, "I get it. Your Station Chief probably told you that this is a good and even safe place to get something to eat and drink without worrying that you might get shot by some ill-informed Viet Cong assassin at an outdoor cafe on Tu-Do Street who might mistake you for being critical intelligence assets. But you've just worn out your welcome. So, finish your drinks and leave, or we *beanie boys* may just toss your arrogant asses through the fucking window. Not to worry, though, as we have the phone numbers of some talented local glaziers in our Rolodex."

"They do quality work at reasonable prices, I hear," said Poplawski.

"Buy one, get one free," replied Mezza. To the pool players, he said, "So, your call or ours?"

The two pool players wisely set down their drinks, placed the pool cues on the table, and made their way out of the bar, but not before the snarky one slammed the front door of the villa, stomped down the front steps, and fussed his way through the gate like a petulant child badly in need of a nap. With peace in the bar restored, Poplawski turned back to Mezza with a puzzled expression.

"You know, Billy, I remember we did teach Hand-to-Hand at Bragg, but I don't recall me ever being invited up to the Farm to teach or meeting Director Colby," he said. "You either, for that matter."

"Come to think of it, I do believe you're right. But hey, I also believe it was Sun Tzu who said that *the supreme art of war is to subdue your enemy without fighting*."

Poplawski was impressed and said as much. "Wow! You actually can quote Sun Tzu?"

"Well sure, from Cliff Notes."

"And Von Clausewitz?"

"*Great things alone can make a great mind,* and something or other he said about not eating a badly tainted Bratwurst, although I might be confusing him with Julia fucking Child."

"Yeah well, there's that, too, I suppose."

"Buy you a beer?"

Poplawski nodded. "I see your bar has a kitchen."

"It does."

"Your cook any good?"

"Better than good, actually."

"Then, what say if you can get that cook of yours to make me a tasty breakfast or lunch, I'll buy you a drink?

"Can do," said Mezza. "Bacon cheese omelet, okay?"

"That'd be outstanding!"

As Mezza was calling out the breakfast order to the one-armed 40-something-year-old Vietnamese cook in the kitchen, Poplawski turned to the two Special Forces soldiers who'd backed them up and asked if he could buy them a drink as well.

Both nodded, thanked him, and after the drinks were served, he left them to their downtime and turned his focus back on Billy Mezza and his own drink glass.

The beer was Ba Muoi Ba- number '33' brand Vietnamese beer, served chilled in tall glass Schooners. With the tantalizing aroma and sound of bacon sizzling on the griddle and his omelet being prepared, there was time to talk.

"Judging from what just happened with the Langley boys, I take it you're not overly fond of the agency these days?"

"I'm not," Mezza said, quite frankly. "One too many of our CCN Teams have been getting compromised up North, no thanks to some of the Vietnamese double agents these college boy Agency types keep mistakenly recruiting. Their vetting process leaves a lot to be desired. So, what are you doing here in Saigon looking all clean and spiffy and carrying an AWOL bag? Heading home?"

"Naw, R&R to Bangkok!"

"Ah, Yul Brenner's own! I take it you're going to be happily humming, *Getting to Know You* to a few lovely ladies in a soapy bathhouse or two?"

"All in the interest of cleanliness and furthering better international relations, yes."

"Yeah, I bet," laughed Mezza. "In that case, let me recommend a place in Bangkok that I think you'll like. It's in the Patpong District, but it's upscale and classier than what else you may find there, let alone anywhere else in the city."

"I'm all ears."

"It's called The Bangkok Social Center, and trust me, it is very, *very* social. I've heard there's a steep cover charge, though."

"How steep?"

"Steep enough to be well worth the admittance," they say. The ladies there are very innovative."

"Innovative?"

"Legendary, or so I'm told."

"What? *You've heard, they say*, but no first-hand knowledge?"

"No, not from me. In case you've forgotten, my wife's Korean. She'd cut my balls off and then beat me black and blue with the sack, if I ever stray like a butterfly. Nope, but some of our guys here swear by the Center and come back from Bangkok with some very big grins on their faces. But you're married, too. Aren't you?"

"Was."

"Was?"

Poplawski nodded. Shrugged. "You might find this difficult to believe but my latest Ex thought I was an asshole," he said, taking a drink of his beer and letting out a small belch.

"Actually, that Ex of yours sounds like quite the astute woman. How many starter wives does that make for you, two, three?"

"Two."

"Any kids?"

Poplawski shook his head. "Just the ones in my Ranger Company and apparently you have one or two in here from the looks of it. Jesus Billy, when did we get old?"

Mezza's chuckle turned into a sigh. "One or two wars and a few conflicts ago, I suspect," he said, doing the mental math. "But hey, speaking of those young fire breathers you got in that Lurp Company of yours, are any good candidates for the Q-Course?"

"A few, actually. You remember Captain Robison?"

"The white or black one?"

"Black," replied Poplawski.

"West Point, right?"

Poplawski nodded. "That's him. He's our Commanding Officer. Romeo Company's in good hands."

"Romeo? I thought the Ranger Companies only went from A to P? I didn't realize they added a Quebec Company before yours?"

"They didn't! Someone somewhere forgot their alphabet or maybe didn't like their last visit to Montreal, so they skipped over it. Anyway, between the captain and our small cadre, we put together a pretty good in-country training and selection course. For every thirty volunteers we have, we only get five to seven that graduate and earn the scroll."

"Scrolls, not tabs, and a dainty looking black French artist beret too, I see, or am I getting the wrong impression, Monsieur Monet."

"Well, we Rangers can always use a live nude model to help brush up on our strokes...so tell me, is your mother still charging fifty cents an hour?"

Mezza howled laughing.

"Damn, Brick! I missed you," he said, reaching under the bar, pushing aside the warmer beers he'd brought in from the storeroom, and pulling out two more cold ones from the ice-filled tub. "Why don't you come back to we merry band of brothers? We sure as hell could use you."

"Maybe after this assignment," he said. "This gig's only temporary. MAC-V has us on a short shelf life. Eight months more, they say, and then done. A shame too, because those young, stud Lurps are doing some pretty good recon work. We've got Spec-4's and Buck Sergeants leading teams and bringing some serious mayhem to some of Uncle Ho's best, although it's been quiet up near Camp Mackie lately."

"The quiet won't last."

Mezza popped the top of the beer bottle on the wall mounted opener behind him and slid the bottle over to his friend.

"Nope," said Poplawski. "Never does."

"Especially with this whole Vietnamization Peace with Honor thing and Nixon's draw down. It smells like we're getting ready to bug out and leave them hanging."

"Yeah, and when they pull out all U.S. forces, I suspect the North will push a lot harder to take the south."

"They'll certainly try."

Both soldiers took long, and slow contemplative pulls from their drinks, momentarily lost in thought of the political theater that dictated their service. However, the muddled dark turned light when the one-armed Vietnamese cook brought out Poplawski's breakfast order. The omelet came with golden brown hash browns and several slices of mango on the side.

"Eat! Don't let it get cold."

Mezza passed over a knife and fork.

"You sure?"

Mezza patted his not quite paunch. "I've already had lunch."

"A few, apparently."

"Kiss my ass, beanie boy," laughed Mezza and Poplawski laughed along with him as the Special Forces Senior NCO handed him a cloth napkin. "Salt? Pepper?"

"Salt's fine."

"Can do," Mezza reached under the counter and handed him a plastic salt shaker and a half-filled catchup bottle.

After adding what Mezza watching on thought was a little too much salt Poplawski dug into the dish and could barely contain his surprise after he took the first, hefty bite. He chewed the omelet with delight and rolled his eyes in culinary ecstasy on the second bite.

The cook had done something magical with the eggs. There was a hint of fresh garlic, a blend of cheeses, sweet cream butter, red peppers, green onions, and cilantro in the eggs, a spice or two Poplawski couldn't quite place, and with generous cuts of thick, deliciously crisp pork belly bacon. Two slices of buttered toast from the oven fresh bread soon turned up on a separate dish and Poplawski picked up one and took a bite. The toast melted in his mouth like fine pastry and the first slice of toast was gone with two more bites.

“Good, isn't it?” Mezza said, already knowing the answer.

“Wow, seriously, just wow!”

Mezza turned back to the small kitchen with a nod to the Vietnamese cook.

“Sergeant Tran is likely the best cook this side of Cholon.”

Mezza nodded to Tran and Tran grinned and nodded back.

“He’s one of your former ARVN counterparts, I take it?”

“Was,” said Mezza, lowering his voice. “Lost his arm in Cambodia and got medically discharged, and when he could no longer feed his mother, wife, and family on what little the South Vietnamese government gave him, he came looking to see if maybe we had something, anything, for him to do. We didn’t, but he brought him on anyway, and we’re glad to have him. We all chip in an pay him a halfway decent salary and the tip jar money is all his too, by the way.”

Poplawski took the hint. “Great food, Sergeant Tran!” Poplawski said, and reached into his wallet and dropped in a five dollar U.S. note.

The cook looked up through the small open window to the kitchen at the mention of his name and Poplawski held up a forkful of the omelet and gave the former NCO a smiling nod.

“If Congress does pull the plug on the war and you guys are still here when they give the order to bug out, then make sure you take Tran and his family with you! Michelin would rate your kitchen six stars, if the French ever decide to make Vietnam a colony again."

"Won't happen. The Vietnamese are too independent."

"Think the South will be able to hold out after we're gone?"

Mezza thought about it for a moment. It was a good question, so he provided it with a just as good answer.

"If Nixon and Congress don't abandon them, they will, but I think the writing is on the wall. This whole Vietnamization thing, I suspect, is the first part of the political penmanship. Hate to see our country just throw up our hands and bug out."

"Be a damn shame," agreed Poplawski. "A lot of good people here put a lot of trust in us."

"*Us* sure," Mezza said. "But our politicians, maybe not so much." As an afterthought he leaned in, lowered his voice again, and added, "You know, some of the old timers think we should've backed Ho."

"I heard something about that. Not sure what to make of it, though. What do you think?"

Mezza took another pull on the beer and shrugged as Poplawski finished up the omelet and attacked the second piece of toast.

“Colonel Bank…”

“The first commander of the Army’s Special Forces!”

“The very same. Anyway, he once told me Ho would've been a better choice to side with. Said most all of the Vietnamese, north and south, liked or respected him."

“That when you were escorting him around Camp McCall on a VIP visit?”

“Uh-huh, and when you’re out making the potential selectee’s lives Hell.”

"Can’t forge steel without bringing some heat, but hey, did the Colonel maybe forget that Ho was a commie?"

Mezza shook his head. "No. You know he knew him, right?”

“I didn’t. I thought the Colonel was one of those OSS guys that worked behind the lines in France or Germany against the Nazis?”

“He did, and after the war ended in Europe, he was sent to Vietnam to work with Ho against the Japanese. He stayed on for a while too after Japan surrendered. Said Ho was more of a Vietnamese Nationalist than anything else and just wanted the French out for good and thought the Russians would maybe help keep the Chinese from invading them again. I know Archimedes Patti feels the same way."

"Patti? The CIA guy?”

“Yes sir, that too was back when the CIA called itself the OSS and he was all properly sanctioned and approved by the government for working with Ho and the Viet Minh. Had a briefing from him once on the politics of Southeast Asia in D.C. before he fell out of favor with the agency and the powers that be for saying the same thing. The thing is both the Colonel, who the Army seems to have forgotten is the Founder of our Special Forces, and Patti who is one of the agency's brighter minds, and were and are, both of the same mind on the matter. Did you know Ho drafted the Declaration of Vietnam's Independence after ours?"

"I did not."

"Yep, and I think it was Patti who said Ho even had a photo of Abe Lincoln hanging up somewhere in his office too."

"Lincoln, huh? Whad'ya know?"

"Jefferson too, I believe, or maybe both. I also know that Bank likely never got to be a General because of it and that Patti was and is still trying to convince the Pentagon and the State Department that we shouldn't be here in Vietnam. And because they were ignored, our game here and now seems to be Five Card-No Draw poker..."

"Which means we players are stuck with the hand we've been dealt."

"Yep."

"*Ours is not to reason why...*" said Poplawski, placing the knife and fork back on the near empty plate.

"And preferably do and not die each time we ante up," said Mezza. He shrugged again and took another swig of beer.

"Speaking of the why, or more like the how, so, I'm wondering...." Poplawski said, changing the subject.

"Wondering what?"

"How did a second-generation Italian from Staten Island, New York ever get a name like William Tecumseh Mezza? Tecumseh Sicilian, is it?"

Mezza scowled. "This from a Detroit Pollock who prefers to be called by masonry! After my folks got off the boat and settled in to start a family my father and mother wanted their kids to be proud Americans. I got a Civil War hero and my sister got Betsy Ross. She can't sew worth a lick and took a lot of needling for it in Junior High. Anyway, when does your flight to Bangkok leave?"

"A few hours from now," Poplawski said, taking a look at his watch. There was time. "Just thought I'd stop by to say hello and see if the food lived up to its reputation."

"And does it?"

"Like I said, if you people here suddenly get the order to *di di mau* then make sure Sergeant Tran gets on the helicopter with you! Also, if there's no room on the bird then you can always kick off one of those Pool playing Langley boys."

"Well, one for sure. Might not be a bad idea for him to see some of the fighting up close and personal."

"It might mess up his loafers a bit."

Mezza smiled. "Better still."

Chapter 7

Team Nine-Four left the Relay Station at the mountain's summit shortly after four in the morning and well before the sun ever began to show itself over the horizon.

They left through one of the perimeter's heavy chain locked access gates under a light rain and swirling low fog. The darkness, weather, and cloud cover helped hide their movement from any spotters that the NVA had monitoring the Relay Station and the open ground beyond the barbed wire perimeter.

"Good luck," whispered the MP sergeant, securing the gate behind them.

The fifth and last Lurp in line, the team's rear scout, acknowledged the MP sergeant with a small chin up nod and quietly kept walking.

Chain-locking the gate behind him and reattaching several trip flares, the MP sergeant returned to the fortified machine gun position he and two others were assigned to, and all three watched on through the open gun port as the Lurp team was making their way across the No-Man's Land in the darkness. One of the MPs, a tall, skinny Spec-4 who had his right arm draped over an M-60 machine gun, was slowly shaking his head.

"That's nuts," he said, watching them go.

"What? Those guys?"

"Yeah."

"No kidding," agreed the MP sergeant checking the tripod swivel on the night vision Starlight scope and then following the five-man team under its pale green glow. The Lurps, who appeared as black silhouettes in the scope's green haze, moved quickly and quietly in single file across the open ground and started down the crest of the mountain. The two in the lead dropped out of sight and soon they were all gone from view through the scope as well.

"You ever think about doing that, Sarge?" asked the machine gunner to the NCO.

"What? That Ranger shit?"

"Yeah."

The MP sergeant turned to the machine gunner, stuck out his bottom lip, and nodded.

"Yeah, I did," he admitted. "But that's as far as it went. My momma didn't raise no fool. Plug the Claymores back in and stay alert. I get the feeling that those boys are gonna cause us some trouble."

Nine-Four was well down into the cover of the jungle when Thomas called for a halt and had his team set up a defensive posture. They would *lay dog* and begin their wait.

Thankfully, the light rain had stopped, and the fog around the summit was lifting. The route they'd taken from the Relay Station in the dark had been slippery in places and precarious. At times, they had even found themselves sliding and having to grab at any branches and vines to keep from slipping further or falling. Their focus was torn between watching the dark and seemingly impenetrable jungle where the enemy might only be a few feet away, to occasionally watching their footing as they moved downhill. One wrong step might send a team member tumbling ten yards into large boulders, thick tree trunks, or even over a ledge with a deadly drop like they had seen in the photos during their briefing. Waiting in place until light was a better strategic option, so Thomas took it.

Too dark to find a good hide he set the team down in what appeared to be thick brush and behind a good sized boulder that at least would make for good cover.

“Stay alert!” he whispered back over his shoulder. It probably didn’t need to be said to the two other veterans on the team, and frightened as they were, the two FNGs had been on high alert since the team left the Relay Station as well as on the helicopter ride in.

In their hide site they waited and watched as the sun slowly rose over the flatland below with an initial array of muted colors. The blue/black night bled into a washed out purple, and finally into a thin line of orange. The orange line soon turned to an expansive yellow wash as the sun slowly began to spread across the province, climb its way up the eastern slope of the mountain, and filter down through the trees revealing what all was around them. Like a staged play’s spotlight opening up a performance in a theater in the round, the five-man Lurp actors found themselves surrounded by rich, dense vegetation and an array of large, truck-sized boulders that dotted the surroundings like intimidating sentinels.

The rocky slope wasn't as steep as Thomas had first thought, but there were distinct ledges, and some sharp drop offs they would need to avoid. The morning light would help accomplish that and more.

Because of the angle of their descent and the surrounding jungle, the only sign of the Relay Station, or the top of the mountain now were the tips of the Station's tall radio antennas that came in partial, occasional glimpses through the trees.

Given the contour and curve of the mountaintop with its many boulders and masking jungles, Army Engineers, driving heavy shovel loaders, cleared away much of the rock and foliage surrounding the Relay Station's perimeter for better security. A few rounds of Agent Orange defoliation spray from helicopters or fixed wing aircraft had killed more of the jungle brush cover beyond the scraped away No-

Man's Land, but not all. Nature was slowly staging a struggling comeback.

At the far end of the open ground and on the edge of the jungle that had somehow refused to die under chemical spraying, NVA spotters, sneaking into position, often kept track of the comings and goings of those on the mountaintop outpost. The edge of the jungle with its heavy brush and foliage also veiled the occasional enemy sniper who'd picked out selected targets of opportunity on the Relay Station.

Thomas had counted on the early start and weather to cover the team's exit from the Relay Station by any of the NVA spotters or snipers in the tactical ruse. That no one on the team had been injured in the dark, given the natural hazards, was also a plus.

So far, all was good, or as good as could be expected. With the rain-soaked ground, and in Charlie's high rise playground, the Texan opted to keep the team in place awhile longer to see if any of the enemy spotters, or snipers were up, and either moving into, or out of position for the next go at the Relay Station. If they could catch one this close to the Relay Station then all the better since it would be a short walk back to the wire, but he knew that was just wishful thinking. Still, it remained a possibility, so he kept his team ready in case the opportunity presented itself.

This was his third time leading a team and Harry Li's second as his A-T-L. A third veteran on the team, Sergeant Gus Daley, was a transfer from a 1st CAV line unit, while the two remaining team members on Nine-Four, Privates-First-Class Norse and Sanchez were FNGs. Everything about Vietnam and the war was still new, fascinating, and terrifying to them, even if, perhaps, their macho wouldn't allow them to admit it.

Daley, the team's designated radioman, was carrying the team's backpacked PRC-25 radio. The Miles City, Montanan only had forty-two days remaining on his tour of duty and less than six months left in the Army. A happy *Short timer*, he was looking forward to getting back to the *world*, or at least, as he said, 'his better part of it.' The married father of two young boys longed to be a civilian again.

The *world* was anywhere else but the war to the GIs in country, but mostly it meant their families and homes back in the states. The home origins, family members, and even the first names of the two FNGs were unknown to the three veteran Lurps because they were still new, and nobody had bothered or had cared to ask. It was the general plight of most, if not, all FNGs in Vietnam. They didn't have value to the team until they'd proved their value, and the verdict was still out on that decision from the three veteran Lurps on the team who'd serve as their jury.

Daley had been with Thomas and Li on their last patrol and the 1st CAV trooper proved to be a good fit. An easy going, life-long hunter, he was comfortable in the field. To him the jungle was just a different kind of field, so he wasn't intimidated by the environment. He didn't rattle easily, either, and, if he extended his tour of duty, then he was slated to become an A-T-L on the next team to be designated or when a Team leader or Assistant Team Leader rotated home. But Thomas and Li both knew that Daley wasn't going to extend his service. He was ETS-ing out of the Army and they didn't blame him. In truth they actually envied him because neither of them were career soldiers. They too were Draftees. The Army and the war were a one-time gig for each of them. Darrell Thomas had sixty-three days left to go on his *Short timer's* calendar while Harry Li had a little over one hundred days remaining. Both were counting down the days till their own Estimated Time of Separation from the military the way some kids eagerly looked forward to opening presents on Christmas morning.

For new guys Norse and Sanchez, less than one month in Vietnam and on their first mission on the Nui Ba Den, any notion of going home anytime soon was still too distant a thought to even wrap their heads around. Other than looking a little nervous at any, and nearly every natural sound around them, let alone the mortar or machine gun fire far off in the distance that came to them in faint thumps and rips, they were doing what was expected of them. All things considered, they seemed to be handling it all okay.

Thomas would keep an eye on the two, mentally noting how each man was doing, how they reacted, and if they were actually worth a hoot in the field as Lurps. He was reasonably content with *okay,* but also knew any real test would come when they would be confronted with a difficult situation, or worse, a firefight. That's when the true test of their mettle would be revealed; not that Thomas wanted things to get that bad. A picnic mission would be fine by him. Do the job undetected, find and mark any cave openings or prominent gun positions, and then quietly move down the mountain for extraction. That would be testing a portion of their mettle as well in his book.

The Texan smiled to himself remembering when Harry once said he thought the word was *metal* because of the whole strength thing when Li brought it up after the team briefing.

"Naw, I'm pretty sure it's mettle," said Thomas. "M-e-t-t-le."

"What? Like when you mettle in somebody's business?"

"I think that's m-e-d-d-le."

"Seriously, Dude?"

"I think so. My Momma's a schoolteacher and one of the judges for the annual Sam Houston Junior High Spelling Bee and was, and probably still is, embarrassed that her only child somehow could never get past the first round in the competition."

"So, what couldn't you spell?"

"Mettle," laughed Thomas. "I went with m-e-d-a-l."

"Like the award?" grinned Li.

"So, they told me," said the Texan. "Never got one for spelling and not even close enough for a shiny pretty ribbon, either!"

The rain had moved on and a glorious morning sun was beginning to wrap the Black Lady in a warm, golden blanket. The sunlight that had taken its time filtering its way down through the trees left the cloak with several dark patches and still troubling shadows.

Once Thomas had called for a halt and as their small wagon wheel perimeter was setting up, Gus Daley had already established commo with the Romeo TOC. This new wait began and there would be no patrolling or settling in until enough time had quietly passed to know the team wasn't compromised.

So, they watched and waited, and when enough time had passed without incident and with the rain letting up, Thomas gave the word to get some morning chow. They would eat in shifts. Daley and the two New Guys would eat first while Thomas and Li kept watch.

Unlike some missions where the radio reception was spotty, here there were no problems. The Radio Relay Station and the summit of the mountain may not have been within shouting distance, but close. Even so, Daley had the radio's handset clipped to the shoulder harness close to his left ear for any radio traffic coming their way as he pulled out a dehydrated Lurp ration from his rucksack and one of the two quart canteens he carried on his web gear. Slowly mixing the water into the food pouch, the Montanan stirred the contents of the pouch with a plastic spoon and took a bite. Unheated the Beef and Rice might as well have been an odd tasting breakfast cereal given the crunch. Still, it served its nutritional purpose.

When the three were done eating they took up the protective watch while Thomas and Li ate. A short time after they all had finished chowing down, as 'eating' only applied to actual better meals rather than something cold or greasy from an olive-drab colored pouch or can, Thomas gave the order to *saddle up.* It was time to move. Any garbage or litter they created, they carried out or buried.

Once all was ready, when rucksack straps and loads were adjusted so the straps wouldn't rub shoulders and lower backs raw from the shifting weight as they patrolled, the Texan slowly led them further down the mountain in a serpentine diagonal route. Twenty minutes on he held them up with a raised closed fist when he came upon a small footpath. The footpath, or what he could see of the thin track, was leading up towards the Relay Station from somewhere down the below and there was fresh sign. Several enemy boot prints with sharp and distinct edges and a few scuffs showed the one-way traffic of a lone soldier that had very recently tramped by. Rainwater was still seeping into the soil from the heel print.

"We'll set up here," whispered Thomas back down the line of Lurps deciding that where they were would not only make for a good hide site but a good ambush location too, if it came to that.

Li, his A-T-L, got busy and set up several Claymore anti-personnel mines to cover their position, while Thomas positioned the rest of the team.

Once again, they waited, this time, though, to see who would show. Given the individual boot prints, most likely it was a sniper or spotter. Several questions immediately came to the Texan's mind.

'Judging from the fresh sign, the sniper or spotter likely wasn't in place when the team left the Relay Station, but had he seen or heard us, and is he close by and maybe biding his time?'

“One man. Whad’ya think?” whispered Li, sidling up beside Thomas as the team leader shared some of the nagging questions with him.

“Could be a Pointman,” said Li. “Maybe monitor the path to see what the traffic looks like?”

Thomas nodded and the latest wait began. As the sun rose over the province so too did the heat and humidity. After an hour had passed and after a second hour had ticked away on his watch, and when no other NVA soldiers came up the path, Thomas devised another plan with Li.

“What goes up must come down,” he said. “I’m thinking when the NVA solder is done with his shift we should give him a warm welcome. We tackle him.”

Li grinned. “You go high, I’ll go low. Let’s get us a POW.”

The plan was that when the NVA or Viet Cong soldier made the return trip down the mountain, Thomas, would jump out and tackle him while Li would jump in, grab the soldier’s legs, and use his McGuire Rig rope to quickly tie up the prisoner and then gag the man with an arm sling bandage tied tight around his mouth and head. Filling the others in on the plan, the team waited for their soon to be arriving POW. This close to the mountain’s summit, and if all worked out then they’d make their way back to the Relay Station with their prisoner in short time and celebrate their success. It was a good plan, now all they had to do was carry it out. With their Claymore anti-personnel mines in place, decent cover, and good concealment, their actual Day One of the patrol was looking promising.

"We'll make this our RON as well," Thomas whispered to Li. "Let's see if our little friend or any of his buddies with flashlights show up after dark."

Their time as Lurps had schooled them that the Viet Cong and NVA tended to use the jungle trails and paths in the dark to their advantage, so their plan had merit.

As *RON* was recon speak for Rest-Overnight, this would also be their night halt position. A two-hour guard shift schedule would be set up beginning at sunset for each member of the team to get them through the long night to first light the following morning.

The day-long wait was uneventful and as the sun began to set, the muted light beneath the tree cover once again began to shift and change. The clockwork metamorphosis that brought on a dark and ominous presence was stark and profound. Pockets of shadows grew and expanded as dusk and then nightfall slowly inched its way up the mountain. The once defined leaves, vines, trees, and boulders, and even the trail in front of them that was only a handful of yards away, began to disappear entirely. The one and seemingly only constant was the buzzing drone from inbound and hovering mosquitoes, and, perhaps, the one and seemingly only advantage of being this high up on the mountain and away from the flatland jungle below was that there were fewer mosquitoes. Fewer, though, didn't mean none and the minute-by-minute battle against the bloodsuckers began.

For the most part, the night too proved uneventful. However, that changed a little after three in the morning when a parachute flare lit up the sky over the southeastern side of the mountain. The burning magnesium that was spitting and sputtering its glaring white light slowly sing-songed its way back down under a small white parachute canopy and burned out before it touched down in the tops of the trees.

Li squeezed Thomas' arm to wake him when the flare was fired from the Relay Station, but Thomas' eyes were already open. The whooshing sound from the flare going skyward and the distinct pop when it ignited brought him out of a light sleep. A second flare brought the rest of the team awake and on alert.

"Anything?" Thomas whispered to Li.

"Maybe," came the quiet reply. "Could be connected to that. Look at my eleven o'clock."

Thomas strained to see what Li was looking at over the A-T-L's right shoulder and through a break between the trees, and finally saw it, too.

Far below the mountain, and well below the temple shrine a line of flashlights was snaking its way through the jungle towards the Nui Ba Den. The flashlights flickered through the heavy vegetation making it appear as though those holding the flashlights were turning them off and on.

"Charlie's on the move," said Li.

They watched as the line of flashlights bounced closer to the southern base of the mountain only to suddenly go out when they reached it which indicated yet another possible cave, or hidden tunnel entrance.

"They all either ran out of batteries at the same time or went inside the mountain to party."

"Yep. Give me the radio and get some sleep. I'll keep watch," said Thomas. His guard shift started at four a.m. and there would be no way he'd be getting any sleep for a while, anyway.

"You sure, dude?" said Li.

"Yeah, I'm good."

"Cool," said Li. Setting his rifle down beside him, he pulled out a small section of camo blanket and, like the others, used it to cover his face against the mosquitoes. Then he settled back against his rucksack to find whatever sleep there was.

Other than the constant buzzing from mosquitoes and the occasional snort or grunt from a small animal moving down the mountain, all was relatively quiet for the next few hours until the muted whumps of incoming mortar rounds could be heard impacting on the Tay Ninh Basecamp in the distance. That brought three of the other four Lurps out of their slumber, leaving one of the New Guys still fast asleep. There was no need to wake him as there wasn't any immediate danger.

The hidden enemy launch site, somewhere far down in jungle below, where the six rounds from the medium weight 82mm mortar were fired was soon met by return artillery fire. The outbound revenge was swift and overpowering, but off-target as the NVA mortar team familiar with the routine had quickly moved on. Trees were being splintered and ground was being blown open as the jungle was once again paying the price.

"Another day in paradise," muttered Daley dryly, as he laid back down and covered his head. "Fun, travel, and adventure."

There was still time to sleep.

At dawn Thomas woke the others with a nudge. After rubbing the sleep from their eyes, and stretching out a few kinks, the Lurps took care of their necessary bodily functions and readied their ambush as they continued the wait for the lone enemy soldier to show. Thomas gave the ambush site another two hours before he called it quits.

"Looks like he's a no-show or he took another way down," the frustrated Texan whispered to Daley and Li who nodded. "We move out in ten mikes."

Li quietly gathered in the two anti-personnel mines he'd set out the day before, packed them away in his rucksack, and with a nod to Thomas, Team Nine-Four was once more ready to move.

From the hide site they crossed over the small path before starting their next descent. Three hundred yards on they reached the age-old trail and main route up and down the mountain. The trail that the religious faithful visiting the temple and shrines had used for centuries was so beaten down and well defined that it had been added to the tactical map the French had used back when they too were scouting the mountain in search of the Viet Minh in the previous war. A brief, but closer inspection showed no fresh signs of current use.

In past, more peaceful times, and at just over 3,000 feet, the Nui Ba Den, was a steep, but moderate climb for the worshippers that would use the well-defined trail to make their pilgrimages. But peace wasn't something associated with the mountain in this latest war, so the once busy trail that was highlighted on the map would be well zeroed-in and subject to targeted mortar and artillery fire by all sides in the conflict.

Nine-Four wouldn't be taking this main trail, let alone any other trails they'd happened upon. Instead, they would keep making their way slowly down and across the mountain towards their target site through the tangled jungle while trying to make as little noise as possible. Staying off the trails would also help in avoiding the possibility of running into boobytraps or sudden face-to-face encounters with enemy soldiers. No one wasted ordnance on sites others would never use, especially the NVA or Viet Cong.

While the rain forest offered concealment and good cover for the enemy and the Lurps, it sometimes allowed the accidental run-in with snakes or other wildlife, most of which tended to avoid humans even as opposing enemy forces tended to seek each other out. Today, though, any snakes or animals that had heard or felt them coming had moved on.

Patrolling the mountain left at least the three veterans on the team appreciating being higher up where the temperature was cooler than on the flatland below. Instead of the almost 100-degree plus heat and sweltering humidity, it was a more comfortable temperature in the low to mid 90s with some low cloud cover and a slight breeze that somehow found its way through the tangled weave of tree limbs, vines, and leaves. The mountain jungle may not have been the living sauna they were used to on other patrols in the lowlands, but the tropical heat on the Nui Ba Den was still penalizing enough to leave them spent from the effort, stress, and the overburdens they carried.

One after another the five crossed the old trail and disappeared back into the layered foliage in a lateral move. They were no more than fifty to seventy yards across the far side of the pilgrimage trail when the Texan came to an abrupt stop at a steep and precarious looking drop off. A weathered, dust-covered, ledge, no more than a foot in width ran across the face and length of an exposed rock wall from where he stood to the direction where the team needed to go. At one time the ledge might've been an easy and efficient way to cross the rock wall but in its present condition it might take a rock climber or a circus acrobat with a better sense of balance to traverse it. For soldiers carrying weapons and heavy rucksacks the odds of them all making it across without a serious mishap were slim. One slip would send a team member hurtling twenty to thirty feet down into a pile of broken rock and other rubble below. Although the fall might not kill someone, the risk of breaking a bone or two was considerable. The crossing would also take them out into the open for the four to five yards on the face of the wall needed to get to the other side, exposure would be problematic and potentially costly as well for another reason. They didn't need to be slow moving ducks in a row. Any enemy soldier that might spot them attempting the crossing would want to go for an easy prize.

Thomas turned and began searching the surrounding area for another route that wouldn't result in someone getting injured or killed crossing over to the other side.

"Plan A sucks, boss. What's Plan B?" Li said, after coming up behind him and eyeing the old route.

"Something, anything better," replied Thomas, which was why he made the decision to skirt the ledge.

Plan B, his *better* option, was to climb up and around the open rock wall. The ground below had too many ankle breakers and the ground above them would at least keep them hidden in the jungle as they moved across to the other side. Up it was maybe a 15 foot climb. It was steep, sure and the short climb wouldn't be easy, but thankfully, there were enough rope-like vines and sturdy branches to grab at and assist them in the effort.

Thomas took the lead on the detour and the climb and traversing the rock wall took more time and effort than he had anticipated. It was climb seven feet up and slip back three as old vines broke or they struggled to find good hand and foot holds. It didn't help any that the soil was loose and crumbling. On the other side they dropped back down to a more moderate slope where Thomas called for the next rest break.

"We rest here," he whispered to his RTO behind him who passed the word along. They eased into their 360-degree defensive team perimeter glad for the brief stop.

Li joined Thomas as the Team Leader was pulling out his map from the right cargo pocket of his jungle fatigue trousers and looking around to try to get his bearings.

"What you thinking, *Brah*?"

Thomas shrugged. They hadn't yet found any tunnel openings or caves, let alone fighting positions. So far, the patrol was proving to be a lousy nature walk.

"I put us about here," he said as he removed his boonie cap, wiped his brow, and put the cap back on his sweat drenched scalp before pointing on the map to Li to where he believed they were on the mountain.

Li stared at where the Team Leader was pointing on the map and then began looking around for some visual confirmation, although there wasn't much in the way of identifiable landmarks in the rain forest to say for certain. The marked position of the old main trail on the mountain had helped, as did the compass heading, and modified pace-count they had taken, but the Nui Ba Den was good at hiding her secrets. It was still a best guess scenario, plus or minus fifty yards.

"Yeah, that looks right," said Li, checking the map coordinates.

"I'm thinking that if Charlie is keeping an eye on the Relay Station, then we'll probably bump into one of their snipers or OPs around here where they'd most likely be doing it. I'm going to take Daley with me and look around and see what we can find. Keep the team tight, Harry. We'll be back in a few."

Li nodded.

To Daley, Thomas added, "Drop your ruck and radio, Gus. You're with me."

Without their rucksacks and only their weapons and LBE harness that held a lethal amount of rifle magazines and grenades, the two Lurps moved more easily across the side of the mountain. Forty yards on through the tropical brush and trees Thomas's attention was drawn to several temple pillar-like granite boulders drunkenly leaning into each other in the near distance. The leaning boulders looked to be a good location to monitor both the main commo bunker and the helicopter pad at the summit. The tops of the twelve-foot-high twin monoliths were partially covered with a latticework of vines and creeper plants that hid the view from the Relay Station from above while offering a good vantage point for anyone thinking of using them as an Observation Post. Leaning together as they were, the solid-looking boulders left an open space below near its base that looked like it would require closer inspection.

It might be something or it might be nothing, thought Thomas but he pointed it out to Daley, anyway.

"Could be an O-P," whispered Thomas. "What do you think?"

Daley took a look at where Thomas had pointed and gave a slow nod to the potential tunnel opening or Observation Post.

"Yep, worth taking a closer look-see," he said.

Moving in tandem, the two Lurps slowly crept through the jungle towards the twin boulders. While one moved, the other covered the cautious go. Ten yards on Thomas came to a sudden stop when he discovered a small, but well-used path leading to the opening between the giant rocks. The path showed fresh and plentiful boot print activity. And there was more.

"Well now," Thomas whispered, dropping down on his stomach. Clearing away a few stones beneath him for a better and more comfortable firing position he brought up his M-16 and aimed it in on what else had caught his attention.

Daley, who was two yards to his right, couldn't see what Thomas was seeing, but wisely followed his play. Using hand signals the Team Leader pointed to his eyes and then to the base of several large boulders. Scooting over and finding a better vantage point, Daley too now took in the woven bamboo mat cover over the four-foot-high entrance. This close there was no mistaking what it was. He dropped down behind his rifle sights.

The mat was covering the four-foot-tall opening at the base of the boulders. A small wooden bucket, covered with some dark green netting, sat just to the right side of the mat covered entrance. A wooden ladle was tethered to the side of the bucket. A small section of old mosquito netting had even been placed over the bucket to keep bugs out. The two Rangers had indeed found a tunnel opening or the entrance to an Observation Post. Either was a bingo.

"Front porch," whispered Daley, leaning into Thomas. "Think we maybe should go knock on that bamboo mat and see if they'd be interested in subscribing to Better Guns & Gardens?"

Thomas chuckled. "Naw, I think we wait to see how many people are home first. Wouldn't want to crash their party only to find they have a big, ugly dog."

Looking around Thomas liked and even appreciated what he saw of the surroundings. The site was well-concealed from any aerial observation by the overhead canopy in the tall trees, and it was well protected by the heavy boulders that enclosed it. Unless you were physically boots-on-the-ground close to it, then you'd easily dismiss it until you saw the thin, but well-worn path traversing the side of the mountain and leading to the entrance. The NVA had chosen the site wisely and had worked it into the jungle setting to their advantage.

Of course, they had, thought Thomas, and the thought was confirmed seconds later when a lone and unarmed NVA soldier, hunched over and bent at the waist, casually pushed aside the bamboo mat cover, stepped out, stood, and walked a few feet over to the left of O-P. Unbuttoning his trousers, he was readying to take a piss.

As the soldier started out of the outpost both Thomas and Daley were lowering themselves down on their chests and stomachs even further as the man began urinating.

The NVA soldier finished his makeshift bathroom break with two flex knee bounces, buttoned up his trousers, and started to head back inside the observation post only to pause at the opening. Reaching down, he pulled aside the netting that was covering the small bucket, dipped in the wooden ladle, and took a drink of water. When he finished quenching his thirst the enemy soldier covered the bucket with the netting and stepped back inside the opening behind the woven bamboo mat.

Thomas waited to be certain the NVA soldier was settled back inside before turning to Daley and pointing back the way they came.

"Go!" he whispered and the two scurried their way back across the mountain side towards the rest of the team.

Rejoining the others, Thomas shared what he and Daley had found.

"No talk. Just listen and nod," he said in a low voice as the others huddled around. "It looks to be a one-man O-P, fifty to sixty yards out. We're going to move on it."

"O-P?" asked one of the new guys, the blond guy whose ears stuck out of his boonie cap like side mirrors on a Chevy.

"Observation Post," said Li, staring at him like he was an idiot. "And what part of 'no talk, just listen and nod,' didn't you understand, Dude?"

Chastened, the new guy stared at his boot tops and quietly listened.

To Daley, Thomas said, "Call it into Valhalla."

To the others, he added, "Saddle up! No noise, and I mean ninja library fucking quiet."

Heads nodded but he went from face to face anyway to make sure they had gotten the message. When Daley had finished making the call, he signaled the Team Leader he was ready.

"Harry, take drag and cover our six."

Li nodded, took a knee, and faced back the way the team had moved earlier. When he was set, he gave the Okay hand signal to Thomas.

"Okay," he said to the others. "Follow me."

They moved on the enemy O-P with considerably more stealth and caution. They needed the stealth and caution it would take to make it work. Each team member was well aware that it could all turn to mayhem if they weren't careful. Even if it was a one-man Observation Post and not a tunnel opening, then a larger force wouldn't be all that far away.

When Thomas figured they were where they needed to be in relation to the occupied enemy site for good surveillance, away from the small path leading to it from below, he had his team move into this new hide site. There were enough smaller boulders and brush in and around the hide site to adequately cover them and they would use it to their advantage.

When the team was in place Thomas and Li went to work setting out a series of Claymore anti-personnel mines. They placed one facing the enemy outpost, a second covering the path from below, and a third back the way they had taken. Satisfied with the additional level of protection, the two made their way back to the new hide site and hunkered down with the others.

Then the familiar wait and surveillance began. They watched on through the rest of the day, until dusk, when a thin sliver of flickering light at the edge of the bamboo mat covering showed that the soldier had lit a candle. From time to time, they could hear the NVA soldier inside moving around. Metal bumped against metal, and later when the soldier began humming softly, it was enough to tell Thomas and the others that he was alone since no one else was telling him to shut the fuck up.

There was no way in hell a North Vietnamese NCO or Officer would let the soldier make any undue noise, let alone hum on guard duty. Eventually the humming stopped and a faint scent of burning tobacco began wafting from the O-P and across the jungle on the thin air currents. That told Thomas and the team members that the NVA soldier wasn't concerned about any airborne odors.

The Lurps watched throughout the night in individual two-hour guard shifts. As dawn broke, their modified morning rituals were interrupted when Li heard the sound of someone coming up the mountain from below.

Li gave two quick finger snaps that caught the others' attention as he pointed to his ear and then in the direction of the man-made noise. The Lurps lowered themselves down behind cover and waited to see who or what came with the noise.

Their adrenaline went from zero to sixty as they watched on with weapons ready in the direction Li had indicated, but also as they focused the surrounding jungle-covered mountainside in the event they'd somehow missed something and had been found out, or in Lurp terms, *compromised.*

Repeated small ticks and thumps of metal against metal were coming from back down the mountain and were growing louder. After a few drawn-out, butt clenching minutes, two enemy soldiers came up from the jungle below on a section of the trail the Lurps hadn't seen and were heading towards the Observation Post. The soldier in the lead wore red collar tabs on his uniform blouse and had a holstered pistol at his side showing that he was an officer. Judging from the sun-faded uniform that was devoid of rank and the SKS rifle slung over his right shoulder and bouncing against his hip causing the rifle's swivel to tap against the rifle barrel, the soldier trailing the officer was a lower enlisted man. These weren't Viet Cong. Both were PAVN, soldiers of the People's Army of Viet Nam. Hardcore NVA.

From their relaxed gait and casual demeanor, the two seemed unaware that they were being watched. At the entrance to the Observation Post the NVA officer came to a halt and called out something to the NVA soldier inside. A moment went by before the lone guard came out of the entrance carrying a Mosin-Nagent rifle, a cooking pot, and a small cloth shoulder bag of likely personal items. Salutes and small talk were exchanged, and the new replacement guard took up his post inside the O-P as the once lone guard disappeared back down the mountain with the officer.

Thomas now realized this was little more than a shift change and that the new guard could very well be on his own until he was relieved the following day.

"New plan, same objective as yesterday," whispered Thomas to Li. "POW snatch mission. We take this guard and make for the Relay Station."

"Roger that," Li said, smiling at the change of plan. There were smiles all around from the other team members too as the mission would be both cut short and deemed a rousing success.

A live and scared POW was an intelligence coup and a better win for the team. Under interrogation by an experienced Military Intelligence team, an enemy soldier stationed on, and in the mountain, might willingly, or inadvertently, give up critical Intel and information. The average soldier in any army had a basic working knowledge of their organizations; the number and size of the unit he was in, the weapons they carried, routes taken to and from the mountain, and any bunker complexes or hidden base camps they stopped at along the way. The more attuned soldier might even know the locations of various hidden gun positions, tunnel openings, weapons caches, and something more of the command structure of the units occupying the mountain. Men talked. They boasted and bragged of their conquests.

Like all women of mystery, the Black Lady held her secrets close, and Thomas and Li were both working out how they might learn a few of her mysteries from someone who had a little more intimate knowledge.

Chapter 8

Lieutenant Plantagenet, by his own estimation, had a miserable fucking night.

At daybreak, in that frail first light, when the last Lurp on the overnight guard duty shift woke the others, Plantagenet sat up, rubbed his eyes, and gave a blank stare. His eyes were not fixed on any one thing in particular except for his assessment. He was tired, stiff-muscled sore, and way more than willing to argue the point that trying to find a more civil, genteel, or socially acceptable way to describe what he had endured throughout the excruciatingly long night wouldn't adequately or accurately convey just how much it had sucked.

Oh sure, maybe when he completed his tour of duty and got back home, and, say, if his father, mother, or wife at the dinner table asked what the war was '*really*' like, he might choose his words a little more diplomatically. But sharing a pitcher or two of beer with his brothers and civilian buddies who might ask the same thing, he'd begin with what it was like on his first night of sleeping in the jungle and fall back on this morning's take on the evening's events.

Either way, if they were genuinely curious and honestly wanted to know more, and asked about this or that, then he'd first consider his audience and offer several edited takes. Each, though, would start with the elongated hours in the dark that seemed to defy any sense of actual time on his watch. He'd follow that with the difficulty of trying to get comfortable on wet or damp ground that was covered in rotting leaves, twigs, and bug-infested mulch, and that the ground had the same comfort, appeal, and stench as a broken bag of week-old food scraps.

He knew there would be questions aimed at him in the retelling. He was sure of it and the previous day and night would provide many of the answers to what they had on their minds or from any confused or quizzical looks they had on their faces.

"But you had, like what, a folding cot and tent or something, right?" he knew one of them would ask.

"No, no cot, and no tent or shelter. No camp or campfires, either. Nothing that would give away where we were hiding."

"But wouldn't your sleeping bag get wet?"

"Uh-uh, no sleeping bags or air mattresses either, just the ground."

He'd explain how after pulling his two-hour shift of guard duty, when he tried to stretch out to sleep, how small rocks, exposed roots, and a whole host of insects played havoc in the trying. He'd tell them how annoying it was, too, having to sleep, if you could call it that, with his LBE web gear on and how everything that was attached to it around his waist dug into his kidneys, lower back, and hips and made something as simple as rolling over an Olympic trial event.

"What's an LBE?"

"Army speak for Load Bearing Equipment, really just a wide pistol belt with a shoulder harness that had all of our ammo pouches, two canteens, First Aid pouch, bayonet, smoke grenades, a separate canteen pouch that held three or four grenades, and a D-ring carabiner and rope clipped to one shoulder clip and bayonet, or knife attached to the clip on the opposite side."

"On your pack?"

"No, our rucksacks were separate, heavy too, so those we set down to maybe lean against, but the LBE and weapon you kept close in case you got in a running gun battle and had to Di-Di Mau."

"Di-Di Mau?"

"Run."

“Ah!”

He knew he'd shake his head from time to time in any retelling, and maybe with a resigned laugh too when they listened to him say how the 90-to-100-degree heat of the day and the ridiculously high humidity lingered and hung around long after the temperature had dropped down into the mid-80s after the sun had set, and how he was still dripping sweat well after midnight.

"Think August in a heat wave with no breeze, thick air, and a broken fan. That kind of heat."

If he pulled out the photo of him posing all cocky and macho and smiling in the team picture before the mission, the one with his nice and clean tiger stripe jungle fatigues, then he'd also tell them how after just a day or so afterwards, he looked like an off-leash Golden Retriever who'd romped around in the mud, and how later that night his shirt stuck to his lower back and how every so often, when he'd shift his weight to try to find a brief moment of comfort, how the wet and filthy cotton fabric would slowly peel away from his back until he once again leaned back and started the ridiculous process all over again.

Over the beer, he’d tell them about how he'd caught the back pocket of his trousers on a sharp branch moving through the jungle and how the branch had tugged and tore away part of the seat to his pants and left the left cheek of his ass dangling and exposed for all the world to see, and how apparently, every insect in the surrounding jungle to target.

They might even chuckle or laugh at that, too, until he added that the only good thing about the rip in the trousers was that it took away some of the pressure in his crotch where the wet fabric had rubbed the inside of his thighs raw to almost bleeding.

"See, the thing is the Tiger stripe jungle fatigues were hard to come by in Vietnam. They weren't always standard army-issue, so I had to buy my own set from a Vietnamese vendor in Bien Hoa before I reported to the Ranger Company."

More than likely, they wouldn't know what Tiger stripe jungle fatigues were either, or why it was an out-of-pocket expense for him. "But hey," he'd say, "they looked John Wayne Green Beret movie good!"

"No shit? You had to buy your own uniforms?"

"If you wanted Tigers because they weren't standard army issue, yeah."

Would he tell them how badly he wanted to look the part of a combat Ranger, and how the Tigers were the way he did it for his first combat patrol? Maybe not. However, he would say that because the Tigers were locally made, that meant thinner cotton material that didn't hold up well in the jungle, something he soon discovered on patrol with the first rip and tear.

"The company issued us '*flowers,*' camouflage jungle fatigues that had better durability, only they hadn't fared much better, either. Sharp or broken branches, and nail-sized thorns were always grabbing and tugging at us. Rips and tears were the norm, the commonplace, so were lost buttons, stains from fat bugs or banana sized slugs that squashed and popped like rotting fruit when we accidentally sat on them."

"Oh man, that's gross!"

"Uh-huh. And the cheap cotton material covering our kneecaps were also scraped and frayed from taking a knee when a closed fist went up because someone spotted someone or something out of the ordinary, or when a team leader needed to look at his map to try to figure out where the hell we were. Sometimes you'd kneel on a small rock or hard root and maybe rip a hole in cloth at the knee, while any rips or tears in your back pocket area were quite literally a pain in the ass!"

With a little more beer he'd loosen up, laugh, and admit that it was also a little embarrassing, but there was nothing he could really do about it as the Lurps wore the one uniform for the duration of the mission.

"Just the one uniform?" one his pals would certainly ask.

"Yeah, just the one."

"For the entire time you were out there?"

"Five to six days, but yeah."

Like any good war story, he'd move on the things that went bump in the night and the noises that played havoc and fucked with his imagination, especially during that first night in the pitch-black dark. He'd maybe tell them how, all the while, he just knew someone, or something was going to jump out and scream a Vietnamese or snarling animal version of '*Boo!*'

If they asked what kind of noises, he'd lean in and describe how the low croaks, screeches, growls and groans, or the sound of something slithering through the underbrush nearby that instantly brought him up wide eyed and straining to see and hear what it was when it was so dark he could barely make out his own hand.

"Snakes?"

"Oh yeah, apparently they like to hunt at night and some of them like the King Cobra, for instance, were eighteen feet long!"

"Eighteen feet long! You saw them?"

"No, never close up and not like in the movies reared back with a flared hood, staring you in the face, eye-to-eye, ready to strike. Uh-uh. Most of the snakes I saw close up were the ones somebody else had shot outside the outhouse latrine or a bunker at Camp Mackie. In the jungle, though, sometimes all we ever saw was a glimpse of their backs or tails as they slithered away through the underbrush."

He might even go on and admit how he'd been scared shitless a time or two, as well, twisting and turning in place, this way and that, coming out of a fitful sleep or every so often, startled and trying to figure out where the slithering was coming from, and what, if whatever it was, was moving closer. By daybreak the muscles in his neck and shoulders would be pinched, aching, and sore from all that canting, twisting, and turning from only his first night in the jungle. Never mind that his nerves were frayed, as his imagination took over any rational thought because of the noises the nocturnal animals made in the dark.

“Half the time you just knew it was a Viet Cong or NVA soldier sneaking towards the team looking to cut our throats or bayonet us, or worse, maybe even a tiger or crocodile looking to gut us and drag us off to eat later?”

And in case they didn't know it he'd tell them how Vietnam had tigers, crocodiles, six- foot-long monitor lizards with spikes for teeth, and rock apes too, for that matter, along with a host of other angry animals, vipers and other deadly snakes better left in zoos behind moats, bars, or protective glass than coming in to say hello. But in the jungle, there were no protective moats, no bars, or reinforced glass. And if that didn't bring on a '*Holy shit*!' or two from his audience, then he'd mention the scorpions, the eight-inch and longer stinging centipedes, blood sucking leeches, and biting ants, all in their natural habitat, "while we," he'd say, "were the unwanted trespassers that were just passing through and that they and the jungle wanted gone."

He'd explain how long before the real threats he faced on patrol there were the imagined ones that also had been burned into his psyche and soul, kindled, and stoked by the war stories he'd heard before he ever set foot on Vietnam. The various cadres during every phase of his training all had their war stories and tales of the rice paddies, swamps, and jungles that they'd share piece-meal.

“Charlie did this, or Charlie did that…”

“He also knew that someone would ask the inevitable. “Who’s Charlie?”

“Victor Charlie, Mister Charles, the VC, Viet Cong, and anyway how the dumbass FNGs who'd screwed up had paid horribly.”

In those early war stories someone, he’d say, generally an FNG, was always getting their balls blown off by a Bouncing Betty landmine, choking after swallowing broken glass in Coke bottles that local kids had sold them, or triggering a boobytrap that ripped off an arm or leg.

"Oh, and when you arrive in Vietnam, you are that FNG, that know nothing, fucking new guy, and everyone lets you know it."

The cadre during his Officer's training at the University of Georgia, had more war stories, as did the Black Hat cadre in Jump School, and the RI's- the Ranger Instructors, in Ranger School at Fort Benning. Every combat veteran seemed to have his own take on a dozen ugly ways a GI could die in Vietnam by screwing up, somebody else screwing up, or simply from bad luck.

"By the way, there's no such thing as luck, good or bad. There are only better decisions and outcomes or painful dumbass mistakes when you fuck up, so pay attention to what we're trying to teach you!" one Instructor said to his training company after a long day and a night land navigation course was about to begin. "And no dozing off, because if you're dead ass tired here and you doze off in the bleachers now during the instructional phase, then you'll doze off over there, and your literal dead ass will be dumped into a body bag and tossed on the floor of an outbound helicopter sent like a dead letter home!"

The closer it came to completing the stateside training and the closer it came to receiving orders sending he and the others to Vietnam, the more those stories held the spellbound attention of those slated to go to war. Every combat veteran had a war story, and whether they would share it or keep it to themselves, those individual pieces would be part of an overall complex puzzle.

Each new day in the country and on patrol would only contribute more to Plantagenet's own war stories and personal playback in the retelling once he made it home, with each following day and accompanying miserable night adding to the tale of the shit show.

If he was being honest, he might tell his pals how the scary noises kept him awake and anxious that first night while they didn't seem to have an effect or even bother the Lurp on guard duty, or the other members of the team that were sleeping. He was still new to it all, and he knew that he was new, and was aware that with time, he too would be able to tell the difference, and if there was an actual problem or serious threat. He just didn't have enough time in combat yet, so maybe he'd admit that much and say, "Yeah, I was a little scared."

Depending on who he was telling, he'd keep it light, shrug it off, and only stick to the simple lessons, like the one that had to do with mosquitoes and how to deal with them when they swarmed in and targeted any open and uncovered piece of flesh they could find.

"There were swarms and swarms of the little suckers! I'm talking clouds of them! You'd slap a dozen or more away and another dozen or two took their place. At least once or twice a night a mosquito would make its way up my left or right nostril, bump around in there, and have me panicking and blowing them out. One time, though, I snorted one in and then spent the next few seconds blowing out snot and bits and pieces of the damn thing."

"Aaarrrgh! That's disgusting!"

"Yeah, it was, and I squashed a bunch with my little finger trying to get inside my ears, too! It was a constant fight with the mosquitoes."

Anything more to keep them leaning in and listening, though, would take a little more schooling. The morning of Day Two on the mission would provide him with that more to tell those back home. All he had to do now was survive in order to tell those stories.

At sunrise, worn out, disarrayed, and feeling physically frayed from little to no real sleep, and with what he estimated to be a million mosquito bites dotting his face, ears, neck, and hands, the new lieutenant looked and felt a mess. His left eyelid was a bright scarlet, swollen lump that was threatening to close over the eye.

It was Hernandez that first noticed the damage on the tag-along lieutenant's face from the insects as he checked on the team.

"Jesus, L-T, didn't you use bug juice?"

Bug juice was DEET insect repellent that the military issued to ward off mosquitoes and most other insects, most, but never all of what the Southeast Asian fetid bogs, wetlands, and steaming jungle had to offer.

Plantagenet shook his head. "Somewhere near the bottom of my ruck. Couldn't find it in the dark. Didn't want to make any noise."

Hernandez stared at the tortured looking officer as he deliberated something for a brief moment before he dug into the top pocket of his camo fatigues and pulled out a small clear plastic squeeze bottle.

"Here you go, sir," he said, handing it to Plantagenet. "I have an extra. Slather it on and keep the bottle close. You right handed?"

"I am."

"Then, the top left pocket works best."

The A-T-L pointed to the lieutenant's ripped trousers.

"With that tear you might want to check for leeches. If you find any, don't pull them off. They have hundreds of teeth that latch onto you. If you try to pull one off some of their teeth will break off under your skin. If that happens, the bite mark will get infected, so instead use your bug juice to get them to release their hold. Pour some on any you find, and they'll curl up. Then, when they do, you can easily pick or flick them off."

"Thank you," Plantagenet said, genuinely appreciating the gesture.

"No problem, L-T. When you're done, get something to eat, and check over your weapon and gear. We've got another long day ahead of us."

The lieutenant nodded. Hernandez returned the nod, and then made his way over to Carey as Plantagenet loosened his belt, unbuttoned his trousers, and checked for any of the smarmy predators.

He found a dark brown, wet lump beneath his left testicle, and briefly panicked. The engorged leech was the size of a cigar stub! Following Hernandez's advice, he took the bug juice, and squeezed out enough on the dark lump to get the leech to release its hold. It took a few seconds before the agitated leech began to wiggle and squirm and give up on its bite. When it did, the lieutenant pinched it between his thumb and index finger and tossed it away. There was trickling blood residue, his blood, from the slimy little vampire on both his thumb and trigger finger that he wiped off on his right pant leg.

High above him and intermingled in the vine covered trees was a beautiful white and maroon display of wild orchids while just three feet over from where he was sitting a column of thousands of army ants were assaulting a two-foot high, dried mud mound. The ants were in a life and death struggle with an army of termites occupying the dirt mound. Exotic beauty and primordial battles- all showing the sharp and conflicting contrasts found in the rainforest that was often at odds with itself.

Buttoning up his trousers and adjusting his belt, he chuckled to himself, only there was not much humor in it. If you wanted to be a Ranger, then this was one aspect of it.

The eight weeks of Ranger School training in Georgia and the swamps of Florida had taught him a lot about working through difficult situations, challenging him mentally and physically with little to no sleep. It didn't polish off any rough edges but hardened them more, so that a Ranger School graduate came away leaner, meaner, and with a better understanding of himself and an appreciation for the small gold and black rocker tab that read: RANGER.

He was proud of the Ranger tab and what it took to earn it, just as he would be proud to finally earn Romeo Company's 75th Infantry red, black, and white Ranger scroll after successfully completing this patrol. He'd been handed several scrolls and subdued MAC-V shoulder patches when he reported to the company and had sewn on his rear area fatigues as he'd been instructed to do, but he hadn't felt he'd earned the scroll yet. Having one wasn't the same thing as earning one. This patrol would hopefully change that. All he had to do now was just prove he had a right to wear it. Getting pin cushioned by flights of disease carrying mosquitoes, latched onto by a few blood-sucking leeches, and whatever else came next would carry some supportive weight towards that right.

The tabs and scrolls came at an additional cost for any 11-Bravo Infantryman, and it occurred to him that the price difference for the combat Ranger school was significantly higher than the Ranger school tab. In Ranger school and all of his previous training, you only felt like you were dying at times. Here, though, there were many that were actively plotting and working hard to make that happen.

After chow the team moved out on patrol with a handful of brief rest breaks in between the distance they would cover that day. By the end of another daylong patrol and not finding squat, the team settled in for the night in this new hide site. This time they plopped down inside a clump of bamboo off yet another old trail. The thick stalks they squeezed through to find a site were well hidden in cover of the living screen of bamboo leaves.

The lieutenant fared a little better during the second night. Smearing himself with bug juice, he made it through the early evening of buzzing around his face, ears, and the back of his neck with fewer bites. Another generously applied round of the insect repellant when it was his turn on guard duty to monitor the radio and watch over the sleeping team, got him through till morning.

Unfortunately, the ground wasn't any more comfortable this time around and the eerie sounds of the jungle at night still disturbed the bulk of his sleep, but he had survived the second night with slightly less agitation. He figured it was all baby steps and a whole lot of combat teetering, knowing that with time and familiarity he'd soon be walking and then be up and running.

"With time," he said to himself, checking his groin area for more leeches and finding another one on his left inner thigh. "Just not yet."

After the morning rituals of shit, no shower, no shave, and scarfing down cold dehydrated rations, and checking weapons and equipment, it was time to move out, again.

"Saddle up!" Carey said in a low tone to the team as he rose, shouldered his rucksack, and then bent over at the waist to adjust the straps and load before he righted himself.

It was the same with the other team members who secured their rucks and gear as best they could. The weight of the rucksack and the things they carried was bad enough and it didn't need to be compounded with loose straps. Shifting loads were brutal on shoulders, backs and knees.

Sergeant Carey took the lead on point, and he moved out at a slow and careful pace. He was in no hurry. He and his team had five days to check out their assigned Recon zone. Recon meant reconnaissance and that meant quietly observing and recording undocumented trails, hidden bunkers and basecamps, or enemy activity without being observed in return. While they could ambush small enemy patrols, they weren't equipped or well-suited to take on larger units without sustaining heavy casualties of their own. They could hit and run, with running being referred to in Army speak as ‘E and E,’ which meant trying to Escape and Evade from the enemy immediately afterwards. Escaping and Evading also meant hauling ass as fast as they could go to keep from getting shot, captured, or killed.

Today, the morning was quickly heating up and a thermometer somewhere back at Camp Mackie would reach into the high 90s. It would be another hot day. Their first rest break for the day came in late morning, where once again, they each took a knee in their protective perimeter. By their second break a little over fifty minutes later, a few went to their canteens, and by early afternoon all of their faces were flushed with beads of slow rolling sweat trickling down their foreheads and ears. Several members of the team were showing signs of dehydration, though, it wasn't just the profuse sweating and dry mouth. Muscle fatigue was setting in and that would be followed by dizziness that could lead to a dazed state of awareness.

Doc Moore caught Carey's attention by shaking a near empty canteen and the Team Leader got the message. Carey waved both Hernandez and the medic over for a quick word.

"Louie, I want you to take Doc and find a water source," he said. "Fan out, but don't go too far. We need water before we reach the defoliated area. We may have to scoot through it pretty quickly to get to adequate cover on the other side. Best to not get caught short on water. See what you can find."

"Roger that," said the A-T-L while the medic nodded.

Carey didn't like separating the team like that, but two traveling light would beat six with their heavy rucksacks struggling in the ridiculous heat, with one or more going down with heat stroke or heat exhaustion. It wasn't the best choice, but it was a working one. As the rest of the team dropped down to set up a defensive position the two team members began their search.

The Lurps wouldn't move towards the defoliated area until they had the water they needed, and they needed to cross the defoliated area in order to get to the primary target area that the Intel people back at the BIG-TOC in Camp Mackie wanted checked out. Solve the first problem and then deal with the next one that turned up.

The defoliated area was a huge, barren swath of jungle that the Air Force C-123 airplane tankers, with specially fitted nozzles, had sprayed thousands of gallons of the nasty cocktail mix of Agents Blue and Orange. The toxic blend of the caustic chemicals had killed nearly all of the trees, leaves, vines, and other greenery in its path. Poisoned and denuded, the swath of jungle was a quite literal dead zone.

The sprayed area was too big to go around. That would take time the team didn't have and would put them behind schedule, so the site Carey chose to cross that he had marked on his map during the pre-mission overflight was a desolate, fifty to sixty-yard strip. From the air the thin strip looked like the bar between heavy dumb bells. That the defoliated area provided no concealment presented a serious tactical problem. The Viet Cong and NVA soldiers wouldn't use it during daylight hours for that very same reason because it presented too much of an open killing ground for roving teams of low bird Scout helicopters and Cobra gunships or anyone else watching on.

Because the enemy avoided using the defoliated areas that didn't necessarily mean they might not be monitoring them, especially if they thought any of the American '*Ghost soldiers*' were patrolling in the vicinity. '*Ghosts Soldiers'* and the '*Men with the painted faces'* were some of the ways the Viet Cong and NVA used to describe those small reconnaissance teams because of the streaks or stripes of green, black, and sand colored face paint and camouflaged uniforms they wore and how they moved through the jungle like deadly apparitions. There were other derogatory terms the VC and NVA sometimes uttered under their breaths about the origins of the Lurp's mothers or other aspects of their lineage as well.

However, the deadly apparitions on Team Nine-One were now dead-ass tired and close to dehydration from patrolling in the hothouse jungle, and weighed down by the heavy rucksacks, weapons, and gear that each man carried. Compounded by the weight of an Aid Bag and the backpacked Radio, the additional weight of what the team's acting medic and RTO were humping was pushing them to their limits.

Each man carried two, one-quart canteens. At the start of the patrol the two canteens held a combined total of 64-ounces of water that was now running dangerously low. With the high heat and with what each Lurp was schlepping, several on the team were inching dangerously close towards heat exhaustion.

A while back in the Company area Doc Moore gave a refresher course on basic First Aid and when the subject of hydration came up, the medic explained that the average person needed two to three liters of water a day in normal weather and activity to properly function. "Here, in Southeast Asia, and especially in the field, and with temperatures pushing up and over 100-degrees, you need more than that to stay hydrated. This is no joke. I'm serious."

Heads nodded and then someone asked the obvious next question.

"So, how much in ounces is in a liter, Doc?"

"A liter is basically 33-ounces, so times that by three. You can function on less, but you may find yourself fighting your body before you ever fight the enemy. Stay hydrated."

As the Assistant Team Leader and team medic dropped off their rucksacks and started off in their search for a water source, Carey repeated something else Doc had said during the refresher course and showed Moore that at least someone had been listening.

"Any flowing creek or stream you can find will do," said Carey. "Just no bomb crater or standing water."

Moore smiled, nodded, and was pleased that he'd remembered the warning regarding stagnant water. The two soon returned saying they'd found some good water. It was a thin, slow flowing creek off twenty, maybe thirty yards to the east and down a slight ravine. The water trickling through it was reasonably clear, and it would meet their needs.

Carey and the others followed Hernandez and Moore to the lip of the small ravine and stared down the crumbling bank at the creek.

"Two fill their canteens at a time, four will cover," Carey whispered to the others and then at the medic and lieutenant. "Doc, you and the L-T go first. Bowman and Pettit, you'll be next. Louie and I will follow. Do it! Get it done."

Doc Moore and Lieutenant Plantagenet made their way to the creek, knelt in the mud at the water line, and pulled out their near empty canteens as the four remaining team members kept lookout.

That the water had a distinct orange tint to it came as something of a disappointment to the lieutenant; a disappointment that he tried not to let show.

Slow to dip in his first empty canteen, Moore offered him some useful advice along with several Iodine water purification tablets as the officer began filling the heavy plastic quarter container.

"Toss one of these into each of your canteens as you fill them, sir, shake it up well and good, and then let it sit for a bit before you take a drink," he said. "The tablet needs time to do its thing and the sediment needs time to settle."

Plantagenet nodded, held the first hard green plastic canteen at an angle and let the water from the stream flow into it. He used his left hand to brush away some of the waterborne insects, a few curious mosquitoes, and leaves and twigs from going into the spout and was reasonably satisfied with the effort. When the water level reached near the top of the canteen, he dropped one of the tablets into the canteen, twisted the cap back on, and then shook it briskly. He did the same with his second canteen.

With his canteens refilled, and following the medic's lead, the lieutenant palmed two handfuls of the water from the creak and splashed it over his face and neck. The water was cool, pleasing, and very much appreciated. The lieutenant felt a small sense of relief as he got to his feet and started back to the others in the over watch. That the canteen water would now taste like an untreated swimming pool wasn't the problem that dehydration could be on patrol. It just became something to the growing list of things that sucked on the mission.

On his way back from the creek he passed Specialist Bowman who was readying his canteens. The young-looking soldier looked up, smiled, and gave a nod to the officer. The officer nodded back thinking that maybe not everyone on the team thought he was useless.

With their water supply replenished, Nine-One was once again ready to move on the defoliated area towards the recon zone just beyond it. Taking a new compass heading, Carey married it up to his map, shot a line-of-sight azimuth, and then followed it through the jungle towards the defoliate area. Even with a compass heading there was never a straight line to anywhere through the jungle, so it was always an indirect route and relying on a pace count and compass needle. Not that it mattered as the defoliated area was easy enough to find. Coming to it was like coming out of a dark tunnel into bright sunlight as the jungle soon gave way to a vast and a too bright block of emptiness under harsh sunlight. The Team Leader took a knee just inside the tree line at the demarcation edge of the surviving bush.

The contrast in the surrounding coloring was startling. On one side was a wall of vibrant, living green and brown vegetation, with opulent and brilliant foliage and flowers while what was in front of them was a decayed dead zone half the length of a football field.

The defoliated area wasn't just empty of living trees and brush, it was devoid of any sign of life. There were no birds, monkeys, or any sight or sound of wildlife or insects, not even any buzzing from the ubiquitous mosquitoes. The chemical spraying from low flying Air Force transports had killed acres and acres of the once lush rainforest and drove who or whatever was in it away. The withered trunks of tall, dead, sun-bleached white trees that had refused to fall, stood facing the sky in askance. Three-to-four-foot high, windblown, and weathered termite mounds showed abandoned kingdoms. With no trail or game path the ground was little more than an ugly carpet of faded brown, long dead vines, and leaves.

To the team members awaiting word, the Team Leader who was intently studying the dead zone, finally said, "I go first, then Pettit, followed by the L-T, Bowman, and Doc. Louie, you bring up the rear. I want everyone to keep at least three to four yards apart until we reach the other side. Move fast because dressed in camo we're going to stand out like green Gumbies in a Marshmallow fucking Forest."

Carey took off at a quick pace, not running, but definitely moving with a new purpose. Hernandez sent the lieutenant out next, followed by Pettit, Bowman, and Moore. As the last man in line, Hernandez was doing a slow and cautious 360-degree security turn as he moved because he knew that the NVA or Viet Cong didn't always hit you from the front.

They were three quarters of the way across the contaminated area when Hernandez, doing another slow turn, stepped on a landmine. The triggered explosion shattered the silence and sent him tumbling. He was on his back and moaning even as the rising dust and torn, dead leaves rose, fluttered briefly, and then slowly fell like bad confetti. Frightened birds in the still living jungle to their front squawked and took flight as several once quiet and curious monkeys screeched and excitedly sprang through trees fleeing from this latest man-made danger. Hernandez was slowly rolling back and forth on the ground while holding his left ankle and boot, writhing in pain, and swearing under his breath. The swearing was an angry mix of Spanish and English.

All of the remaining team members immediately went down on one knee except for Doc Moore who had started to turn back to help him when Carey barked out a command.

"DOC, STOP! EVERYBODY HALT!"

Considering the explosion, his adamant order for the medic to stay where he was didn't give up much in the way of volume, let alone their position.

"Don't move!" Carey said in a calmer tone to the others. "Landmines."

All eyes shifted from Hernandez and Carey to the ground around them as the team members desperately searched for small prongs, exposed pressure plates, or tripwires.

It was Pettit who identified the threat for what it was.

"Button mines," he said, his eyes settling on what looked to be several clumps of dead leaves.

"What?" asked Carey as all eyes turned to the radioman.

"Button mines," Petite said, again. "They look like dried out, old leaves."

"Soviet?" asked Carey.

Pettit frowned and shook his head. "Uh-uh," he said. "Ours. The Air Force drops them in clusters. Dozens of them in one breakaway bomb canister."

Scanning the ground around him he reached over and carefully brushed away some of the leaves and picked up what appeared to be a small, flat, light brown, wedged shaped pouch that was no bigger than a coin purse. Holding it up between his right thumb and ring finger he nodded in confirmation.

"Yeah, Button mines," he said. "I saw these once in a demonstration briefing in Bien Hoa. They also call them Gravel Mines. They're pressure detonated, no fuse or trip wires, just some sort of chemical mix crap that explodes when you put enough pressure on them. Not enough to kill you, but enough to injure you so that it'll take one or two other soldiers to carry you. I don't think they'll go off if you move them aside."

"Don't think or don't know?"

Pettit shrugged. "Don't know. The ones the Air Force Rescue people showed us said they take more than a few pounds of pressure to set them off. These ones look like they've been here a while. Could be they're deteriorating. This one's in bad shape."

Behind them Hernandez was slowly getting to his feet, stomping his numbed foot, and swearing. The heel of his left jungle boot had been partially blown off. His foot and ankle were sore, but other than that he wasn't bleeding and didn't appear to be wounded or have broken any bones.

"Louie?" Carey called to his A-T-L. "You okay? Can you move?"

The Assistant Team Leader turned to the team leader, frowned, and reluctantly nodded.

"Yeah, and we all should!" he said, angrily.

Hernandez was right. They needed to keep moving, now more than ever. The noise from the explosion carried. It would draw the attention of anyone within hearing distance. The jungle might dampen some of the noise and perhaps shield the direction it came from, but it would still bring on the curious, and the curious in this part of the land weren't friendly.

"Doc, you and Bowman use your knives or bayonets to scrape away the leaves and any of those Button mines in front and behind you as far as you can safely reach. Do it and be careful when you do! Get working. Slowly."

The medic and rear scout attached their bayonets to the mounting lugs of their M-16 rifles, locked them in place, and were ready to do some cautious raking.

"L-T? Pettit? Cover us," Carey said to the remaining two on the team as both he and Hernandez, who were carrying civilian hunting knives, shouldered their rifles, went down on all fours, and ever so carefully began clearing a thin path in front of them. When they'd finished with the front, they turned around and did the same behind them. With the rucksacks on it wasn't easy and they occasionally wobbled and struggled to keep their balance. Hernandez was muttering something in rapid Cuban Spanish beneath his breath again as he was scraping away the dead leaves and several more of the Button Mines like the one that had brought him down. The lieutenant's Spanish was good, but he couldn't keep up with the mile-a-minute pace of Hernandez's comments. There were a few *hijo de putas*, one or two *cono's*, and at least one *motherfucker*.

It wasn't long before the four Lurps had the makings of a working path through the minefield. Provided none of the Button Mines had been buried over time, they'd scraped away enough of the ground cover and hopefully the explosive pouches to safely keep moving forward and get them out of this mess.

"We good?" Carey called to Hernandez and looked to the two others. Hernandez nodded, as did the medic while Bowman gave him a thumb's up. The Team Leader then told the lieutenant and the Radioman to do the same as they had done.

"Carefully, and I mean *carefully* scrape away the ground cover to reach the man in front and behind you," he said and the two remaining Lurps went to work while the four others scanned the surrounding jungle for any sign of the enemy.

Still down on his hands and knees, Carey slowly began crawling forward, clearing away the rest of the way in front of him. He kept up the work until he reached the far side of the defoliated area and turned back to cover the others still out in the open.

The minutes ticked by like hours but when they were reasonably sure they had done as much as they could, Carey gave the order to move.

"Stay in the cleared away spaces. What you can't walk, you Hop-Scotch! Got it?"

Heads nodded and one by one they started forward again but this time as though it was a high wire act. At times and at several places, they awkwardly leapt from one cleared space to the next one in front of them until they were all out of the dead zone. Hernandez being the last one out, limped and sneered as he walked.

Back into the cover of the jungle Carey shepherded them into a makeshift perimeter to be ready for what or whoever came next. When they were all in place and had adequate security, Doc Moore checked on the A-T-L's foot injury. Hernandez had eased off his boot and as Doc began the exam it took a moment for the medic to determine if what he was seeing were bruises or just dirt and grime on the size 10 foot. Hernandez wasn't wearing socks, and with the exception of the tag-along lieutenant, no one else on the team was wearing socks, either, let alone underwear. Dry socks and army boxer shorts may have been a staple in the Rear Area bases, but in the jungle when they got wet, they only became a detriment and hazard. They didn't need a case of festering jungle rot on their toes, feet, or crotches.

Other than a nasty looking bruise on his ankle and calf, some redness around the heel, and the damaged boot, Hernandez wasn't all that bad off for what had happened. He wasn't bleeding and no bones appeared to be broken. If anything, he looked more pissed off and annoyed from the ordeal.

"You're bruised, but I don't think anything's broken," Doc Moore said as he applied a wraparound compression bandage. "You good to go or do we call in a Medevac?"

"I'm good."

"You sure?"

"Yeah Doc, I'm sore, and pissed off, but I'm good to go."

"When we get back, I want you to get that leg X-rayed, you copy?"

The A-T-L nodded.

Carey moved over to Hernandez. "Seriously? You good to go, Louie?"

Hernandez nodded. "Might've been nice, though, for those Intel *cabrones* at the BIG-TOC to let us know that the Air Force had dumped a boatload of these antipersonnel mines in our patrol area," he said, more than a little dismayed.

"Yeah, no kidding," agreed Carey as he circled the area they'd just crossed with a grease pencil over his plastic-covered map. He would damn well let them know when the team got back and they were being debriefed, and like his injured A-T-L, he too might be a little angry when he did. But that was later. There was another more immediate and pressing concern.

"Let's set out some Claymores," Carey said, turning back to the defoliated area and then the jungle around them. To the tag-along lieutenant he said, "L-T, grab two Claymores. You're with me."

The Team Leader was giving him his first opportunity to deploy the anti-personnel mines in an actual combat environment.

During the Lurp training Lieutenant Plantagenet had overseen with the latest class of trainees, he had watched with some concern as Staff Sergeant Shintaku demonstrated Romeo Company's preferred method, which was exactly what Carey had him doing now.

"Angle it back towards the way we came and away from the team, and then daisy-chain it to the next one," he said to the officer.

The officer gave a quick nod and got busy setting up the first anti-personnel mine in what he personally considered was way too close to the team's new hide site. As Sergeant Carey directed, Plantagenet angled the back of the first Claymore away from the team to avoid the brunt of the backblast, knowing full well that when detonated, the concussive force would still be a problem. But, as Staff Shintaku had explained to the Ranger trainees during a Claymore demonstration, the mines had to be set reasonably close by to keep an eye on them so that Charlie or the NVA wouldn't turn them back around on the team.

Besides, Sergeant Carey was the Team Leader and he had picked the spot, and like it or not, he followed the order. Captain Robison's order to him had been adamant and direct. The Team leader was in charge. "You follow his orders. Period."

Given that he'd heard that both Captain Robison and First Sergeant Poplawski had five to six combat tours of duty between them and that the two had designed the unit's Lurp training program, he did as the Team leader had directed.

With the first mine in place, he went to work on the second Claymore, this one facing what looked to be an animal path and the wall of jungle to their front. The Team Leader used hand signals to have him shift the mine a little and gave the lieutenant a thumbs up once it was better in place.

Plantagenet slid the first blasting cap into the molded plastic locking screw and then screwed them in place into the Claymore's detonation well and linked it together with a detonation cord to the second anti-personnel mine.

Satisfied that the L-T had done a good job, the Team Leader gave him an approving nod before he had him unwind and lead the charging wire back to the team's defensive position and then attach it to the clacker, the Claymore's hand-held squeeze detonator. Making sure the flip-bar safeties were on, he set the clacker down.

"Nice job, L-T," Carey said loud enough for the others to hear. "Now go settle in and cover your area of responsibility."

The much-relieved young officer nodded and scurried to the left of the Team Leader and returned to his rucksack where he left it. Carey turned his attention to his injured Assistant Team Leader.

“Button Mines," said a frustrated Hernandez to Carey as he pulled out his knife and cut away the damaged section of the boot heel. Once done he eased the newly bandaged foot back into the boot.

“You sure you’re okay?”

The tough Cuban shrugged and finally nodded. “I’m sure,” he said. “I’m just wondering what other nasty little surprises our side set out that we'll find that nobody told us about?"

"I can call in a Medevac."

Hernandez, who had carefully slipped the boot on and was tying up the laces, frowned and shook his head. "No need, *hermano*. It's no worse than a bad PLF," he said. "It just fucked up my boot is all."

Carey nodded. He wasn't Airborne, which meant that he wasn't parachute qualified, so he wasn't really sure what a bad PLF- parachute landing fall felt like, but if it was anything like stepping on a Button

Mine and getting tossed up in the air and dumped on your ass, then he had the general idea.

Motioning to Pettit for the radio's handset, Carey called in his SITREP to the Romeo Company TOC. The situation report call got a '*wait one*' response from the TOC that Carey figured had Lieutenant Marquardt, and maybe the C.O., mulling over a few working options since he wasn't calling for a Quick Reaction Force or a Medevac bird.

A few moments later he got his reply. Carey listened and nodded but already had a working idea of their decision.

"Roger that, Longboat Niner-One. Out," he said, handing the radio handset back to Pettit.

"Charlie Mike," he said to the others. *Charlie Mike-* Army speak for, Continue the Mission.

Team Nine-One would continue the mission, which for now, was waiting where they were to see who'd show and how the team would greet any curious enemy soldiers that came looking.

Had any nearby Viet Cong or North Vietnamese Army element heard the Button mine explosion, then they would've certainly sent someone to investigate. And, if those doing the investigating found any sign of the team's passing in the area then they would've fired signal shots to let others know the whereabouts of who they were targeting. But hearing a muffled blast through the dense jungle didn't always provide an accurate location of where it had originated.

No visitors showed and there were no signal shots.

Thirty minutes later when, again, no curious onlookers showed, Carey huddled up with Hernandez to plot their next play. It was time they concluded for the team to move on.

"Pull in the Claymores, L-T," he said to the lieutenant, who nodded. “Pettit, cover him.”

The RTO nodded and handed the backpacked radio over to Carey and followed the tag-along officer out of the defensive posture. As soon as the anti-personnel mines were retrieved, the charging lines, blasting caps, and det cord were brought in, and safely stored, Carey gave the order once again to, '*Saddle Up.*'

The mission continued.

Chapter 9

Back up on the Nui Ba Den, Sergeant Thomas was using hand signals to deploy his team into better tactical positions as they moved on the enemy Observation Post for the take down and grab.

He wanted to be sure that the Observation Post's entrance, any likely exit points, and also the trails leading to and from it were covered before they put the plan in play. With only five people the manpower was limited, so placement was critical.

He had his people down behind what he thought was effective concealment and cover before making his way over to Li.

"I'll take him with me to make the grab."

The *him* was one of the new guys. Morse, Norris, Norse, maybe. Something like that.

"You have the others keep an eye on the lower trail and cover us," Thomas whispered to Li as the Team Leader then motioned the Private First Class to join him.

"You!" he whispered and pointed to the blonde, big eared, gap-toothed PFC. "Drop your ruck. Ammo and weapon only. You follow and cover me, but you don't fire unless I fire. You copy, eh…"

"Norse," said the FNG with a few bobble-head nods as he lowered his rucksack, grabbed his secondary weapon, and looked up to show that he was ready.

The two were up in a low crouch and just about to move when excited finger snaps behind them got their attention. When they turned, they saw Li pointing to his ears and back down the trail before he lowered himself down. Thomas and Norse, the FNG, dropped down behind heavy brush cover as the same NVA officer as before came up from the lower trail leading yet, one more soldier to the Observation post. The two traipsed by the five unseen Americans and at the Observation Post the unexpected change of guard was taking a slightly different twist. The guard on duty came out of the entrance painfully bent at the waist and holding onto his stomach and ass. He was obviously ill which explained the unexpected change of guard and that also told Carey there was a radio inside the O-P and the sick guard had called for the replacement.

There was more. Neither the NVA officer nor the replacement guard looked all that worn out or tired from the hike up to the Observation Post from wherever their base of operations was, which suggested to Thomas that there was a likely tunnel opening or an NVA stronghold nearby. Li, who had a better view of the two departing PAVN soldiers from his vantage point, crept after them and confirmed it as they made their way back down the path and disappeared behind another series of boulders less than fifty yards down the mountain.

Li's *All Clear* hand gesture came with his left thumb and index finger in a circle and three fingers held up high to show it was okay to continue. If the snatch mission was going to happen then it needed to be as soon as possible before any more changes of guard or visits took place. This would be Nine-Four's better window of opportunity for the POW grab if they also were to make a good getaway.

"Now," he whispered to the new guy and the two slowly rose up and crept like thieves towards the mat covered entrance for the takedown. They weren't using the small path but were paralleling it through the brush to keep out of the direct line of fire of the entrance.

The FNG was armed with an M-79 grenade launcher, the *blooper*, for the sound it made when it was fired, and Private-First-Class Norse was gritting his teeth and nervously squeezing the weapon's grip and stock as he followed after his Team Leader. The expression on his face was a mix of, '*I'm ready to kill anyone who comes charging out at me, and please, oh please, dear God, don't let anyone come charging out at me!*'

The short, blunt looking grenade launcher fired a variety of shells; everything from high explosive short and long-distance rounds, smoke rounds, buckshot, and even a *flechette* canister shell, which was what Norse had loaded into the M-79 ready to fire. The round, when fired, would send hundreds of nail-like projectiles into a target. That Norse had it loaded with buckshot made it a Blunderbuss on steroids.

Thomas and Norse, the New Guy were within a few yards of the mat-covered entrance when a hand began casually pushing aside the cover from the inside. The hand was followed by an arm, shoulder, and the top of the dark-haired head of the new guard who was coming out of the O-P. The Texan froze as did the PFC and when the unarmed NVA guard lifted his head, he froze as well and stared with open-mouthed stunned at the two camouflaged covered faces of the two Lurps.

"*Dung lai! Dung di chuyen!*" yelled Thomas, telling the enemy soldier in Vietnamese to stop and not to move.

The terrified soldier was visibly trembling at the two camouflaged Lurps but more by the one that had the short, squat grenade launcher aimed squarely in on his thin chest that would shred it in an instant.

The frightened soldier's eyes darted from the Lurps to the bamboo mat covering behind him and towards the rifle he had left inside.

"No! Don't even think about it!" said Thomas, waving the index finger on his non-shooting hand slowly back and forth.

Even if he didn't understand the words, he understood the tone and gesture, so he did what he probably thought was the next best thing.

He took off running back down the path, and when he did it was Norse that had the best, clear shot at him.

"Don't shoot! Don't shoot! I want him alive!" Thomas shouted to the New Guy as he chased after the enemy soldier and yelled after the enemy soldier, "*STOP! Dung lai! Dung lai!*"

The trail leading back down the mountain was blocked by another American *Ghost soldier* that rose up out of nowhere on one knee with a well-aimed rifle, so the fleeing guard quickly pivoted and raced across the slope of the mountain on yet another small, almost indiscernible path towards a brush covered, small mound of rock and dirt landslide spill. With Norse only a few steps behind Thomas, the two chased after the fleeing soldier. Li had the rest of the team up and following with the others in an almost cartoonish looking foot race.

The unarmed NVA soldier went up and over the small landslide and dropped down to hide behind the brush. Only the closer Thomas got to the dirt mound he could see that the soldier wasn't hiding at all. He had disappeared into the entrance of a well-concealed tunnel. The landslide spill was man-made and along with the brush hid the tunnel that was built for the Vietnamese or what Thomas figured was tall enough for all of Snow White's roommates. Old wooden beams and dirt filled bamboo stalks framed the entrance and blended in with the surrounding mountainside. From the air or even at a close distance it was easy to miss.

The enemy soldier had a few seconds, and a few steps lead on Thomas, so the Texan quickly dropped down at the entrance, set aside his rifle, and scrambled in after him in a crouching run. Thomas was on him within a few yards with a touchdown saving tackle. Grabbing him by his left foot, he yanked him back as hard as he could. The enemy soldier was dragged back a foot or so but didn't stay down. He cried out in anger and fear and wildly began kicking back at the American's hands. The third hard kick caught the Texan's left thumb, loosened the grip, while the next kick that followed freed the foot. The frightened NVA soldier scurried on.

"Damn it!" yelled the Texan shaking the pain from the thumb and charging on.

The tunnel ahead was dark and getting darker, but with the light of day coming through the opening behind him, Thomas could see that the walls were braced by heavy wooden beams and thick stalks of bamboo filled with dirt as supports. He knew better than to grab onto or accidentally bump up against one of the support beams. Charlie had often Booby-trapped tunnel entrances as a fail-safe measure. A careless grab or bump could set off an explosion and bring down the mountain around them.

Four, maybe five yards on and Thomas was quickly closing the gap on the runner when he heard the excited PFC following him into the tunnel and clawing and pulling his way forward.

"NO, NEW GUY! STAY BACK! DON'T FOLLOW AND DON'T TOUCH ANY OF..." was as far as Thomas' warning got when the new guy grabbed at one of the bamboo supports to pull himself forward and triggered a boobytrap.

The deafening explosion behind the Texan came a split-second after a rush of heated air, flying rock, dirt, and other debris blew at, into, and over him in a tsunami-like wave. Something slammed into the back of his head and knocked him face first into the hard packed dirt floor. Dizzy and reeling, he lay there as the ground beneath him began violently bucking and the low ceiling overhead showered him with crumbling dirt and rubble.

The explosive device was designed to block the tunnel's entrance when detonated; only the amount of Semtex explosive used to do it was more than sufficient to accomplish the task. The one, and perhaps, only saving grace for him and the others in the tunnel was that the

Semtex had been positioned a little too far above the tunnel's entrance so that when it detonated, it would only cause a landslide and seal it shut. In theory there would be minimal damage, that is, except to those triggering the boobytrap. Had the Semtex been set closer to the actual entrance then those inside the small tunnel would've been ripped apart in an instant by the thermal heat and concussive force of the blast.

The walls and ceiling of the tunnel around and above Thomas that had shook, buckled, and threatened to collapse, somehow had held. If the plan was to block the entrance and save the bulk of the small tunnel, then the explosive charge had accomplished what it was designed to do and then some. Not that it mattered to Thomas who was still reeling in mind-numbing, dizzying pain in the dust-filled dark. He was circling the proverbial drain, and in one last slow spiral, he went down and out. Then there was nothing.

The nothing had proved to be a small blessing because later, when he finally came to, when his dirt and dust-covered eyes stutter-blinked before they finally opened, he violently began hacking up what felt like an acre or two of the mountain. He felt like he'd been caught inside a tube of a Howitzer cannon the moment after someone had pulled the lanyard. He didn't know how long he had been unconscious, and in the dark void, with more than a few pulsating aches, bruises, and pains radiating throughout his body, he wasn't all that certain he was happy to be awake. Still, he was alive and the painful groan he was making said as much.

That he'd been well away from the entrance when the boobytrap exploded had been in his favor. Although there had only been a partial collapse around him the size of the tunnel had been dramatically reduced to little more than a crawlway. Both of his hands and arms were trapped up to his elbows under a mound of compacted dirt and rock. His head, shoulders, butt, and back had been pelted with bits of flying rock, clumps of clay, and debris and the back of his head felt like someone had swung a Louisville Slugger aiming for the center field cheap seats and connected with the pitch. He was addled, his ears ached, his eyes and nose burned, and he was struggling to breathe. Pulling his arms free he propped himself up on his elbows and as he did his body convulsed in a series of several more painful, hacking coughs. When the coughing subsided, he began blowing out a dust-filled spray from his nose and spitting out dirt and phlegm. As his head began clearing he remembered something more.

Jesus! The new guy! What was his name? Oh yeah...

"NORSE? HEY NORSE! CAN YOU HEAR ME?" he yelled behind him, hoping for a response, but there was only silence or what passed for it given the ringing going on in his ears. To him his words sounded like it was coming from the inside of an empty stairwell. Things echoed.

He called out again, all the while conducting an inventory of his own injuries. There were small cuts and a whole lot of bruises and when he reached behind his head his hand came away sticky and wet. Fortunately, or unfortunately, a dirt clog had stopped the bleeding, but left untreated would likely infect the small head wound. But that would be later and not now. There were more immediate concerns. Bigger priorities.

"GODDAMN IT, NEW GUY! ANSWER ME!" yelled the Texan, still hoping for a response.

The swearing was more from frustration and despair than anger and when no reply came, Thomas only hoped that Norse hadn't been killed in the blast or crushed to death, and that maybe the others had managed or would manage to somehow pull him back out. Doubt, though, soon crept in and lingered. That doubt had his thoughts turning dark because he knew that the New Guy had been closer to the explosion. Any pain the Texan was feeling from being caught up in the blast was compounded by festering Survivor's Guilt knowing that one of his people, one of the team members he was responsible for, was very likely seriously injured or dead under the collapse and cave-in behind him. *And for what, following me for the glory of bringing back a POW.* The weight of that realization drove him into a place much darker than this mountain crypt.

The guilt-laden worry and blame, though, was for another time and place because, like it or not, there was no time to waste on it now. He was still alive, and he needed to act like it.

Darrell Thomas had been a Junior in High school when he lost his father. A drunk driver barreling down a road just off U.S. 20 outside of Tyler, Texas lost control of his pickup truck and T-boned his father's Chevy Chevelle. The crash shoved the Chevelle into the path of an on-coming 18-wheeler. His father might've survived the first crash but not the second. The loss hit the boy hard, and after the funeral, he was plunged into a deep funk until his mother's brother, his Uncle Dave, sat down with him on the back porch with a long neck bottle of beer and some advice.

"Won't lie," Uncle Dave said, matter of fact. "Life done dumped a load of horse manure on you and your Momma just now. Ain't saying you're gonna find a unicorn underneath it, neither, but you gotta dig to find your way out of the mess and find some better light. Your daddy woulda told you the same thing if it was me or another family member, and you know it, 'cept for maybe he might not have given you a beer. You keep digging and keep going, and you'll find that light. I promise you."

It was good advice then and practical now. Reaching under his chest, he fished out the flashlight he carried on his LBE shoulder harness. With his rifle outside of the tunnel, he pulled his bayonet from the scabbard on his shoulder to have a weapon handy, and to at least to have something he could also dig with.

Thumbing the ON switch of the flashlight, the beam from the attached red lens sent a muted glow to his limited surroundings. There was a good size mound of dirt and rock in front of him that had trapped his arms, but there was open space beyond it, too. Room to move.

"Okay, there's that," he said to himself, taking a deep breath of relief before he rolled over to have a better look at what was behind him.

The flashlight's beam bounced off a large slab of granite that had blocked off any chance of escape back towards the entrance. Scooting and slowly inching back, he kicked at it, but it was like kicking the Great Pyramid and expecting it to tumble. There was no give to the massive stone and no going back. The next kick brought down more dirt that spilled over his boots but fortunately slowed well before his heart did to something more normal.

Okay, okay, okay, I get it! No more kicking!

Rolling over on his stomach with more than a little grunting effort, he aimed the flashlight at the pile of dirt in front of him and the open space beyond it. He was going forward. It was his only option, so he went to work.

"Never mind the unicorn," he muttered, "I'll settle for better light hiding under this mess."

With the flashlight facing the mound of dirt and using the flat side of his knife as a trowel, he slowly started clearing away the blockage while being overly cautious not to hit or bump any of the surviving support beams. Two of the now compacted supports closest to him on his left were still in place but were skewed, creaking, and struggling to remain upright. Whether they too were boobytrapped, or ready to fall, he didn't know, but he wasn't taking any chances. A closer look and inspection of another support beam just to his right showed that it looked to be a lot older than perhaps what would've been recently constructed in this American version of Vietnam's forever wars. He doubted it was booby-trapped, but given the angle it was at, it could still be a problem if it was nudged.

He made a point to steer clear of it and kept up the trowel work on the loose dirt and rock in front of him. When the knife struck stone or large clumps of dirt, he used the flat part of the blade and his forearm to pull some of the larger rocks and dirt behind him and then used his boots to kick and push it further back. Once there was room to move, he scooted forward a foot or two at a time, and then dug some more. He figured he maybe had cleared away two to three yards before he took a much-needed break.

It was slow going, and with the tunnel blocked behind him, and with no air coming in from the outside, he soon found himself sweating from the expended effort. With no fresh air coming into the entrance the oxygen level had thinned, making it harder to breathe and take in anything more than dusty, stale breaths. Maybe it was his imagination but there seemed to be cooler air ahead of him, and that gave him hope. So, he went back to digging and clearing away the dirt and rubble. Three more yards on, though, the beam from the flashlight picked up a sizable obstruction just ahead of him.

"Well now, ain't that just dandy?" he muttered, frustrated at the thought of this latest hurdle he needed to get beyond.

Crawling closer, the bouncing beam from his flashlight found and settled on a blood-covered, rubber-soled boot and the broken right ankle of the North Vietnamese soldier he'd been chasing. The boot was sticking out of the pile of dirt and debris. A sharp shard of bone was jutting out of the side of the boot. Inching forward he realized that what had looked to be blockage from the cave-in was actually the lifeless body of the enemy soldier covered in a mess of dirt and broken stone.

"Shouldn't have run," he said to the dead soldier.

In the space beyond the body the flashlight picked up a section of the tunnel that hadn't been damaged and was reasonably still intact. With the dirt spilling down behind him he realized the urgent need to reach the better part of the tunnel. If he were to reach it, though, he'd have to be squeezed by the dead man.

It would be a tight and more than likely messy move but there was no choice, no other option. Clearing away some of the dirt on the NVA soldier's pant leg, he grabbed the leg well above the splintered and exposed bone, ready to pull on it to try to roll the body into the wall to find more room. He was pulling on the soldier's ankle above the break when another boot shot out of the dirt and began kicking at his hands. The kicking was followed by a muffled low and pain-filled moan. The enemy soldier that had taken a few harder hits in the explosion than he had was still alive. That he hadn't tried crawling his way out, even though there was more open space in front of him to do so, told Thomas that the soldier had a few more serious injuries than just the bone sticking out of his boot.

Brushing away dirt, rock, and clumps of clay from the badly injured man, the light from the flashlight revealed why he hadn't crawled on. His lower back and left hip were encased in clay, and besides the compound fracture of his foot, his left shoulder and his left elbow were sitting at unnatural angles. There was no useful way for him to lift the arm. His right shoulder and arm looked to be fine until the flashlight revealed that the back of his right hand was covered in blood, dirt, and splintered rock.

Thomas rolled him on his left as best he could to squeeze by and crawl on. As he did, the soldier groaned under the weight and pressure in the confined space, and then went quiet again after the Lurp had passed. This new section of the tunnel had been largely spared in the explosion. There still wasn't room to stand but he was no longer low crawling either. He was hot, sweaty, and dirty but there was cooler air coming at him, along with the faint sound of trickling water just up ahead that kept him going.

He crawled forward on all fours and kept crawling until he could no longer feel the damaged tunnel walls bumping at his elbows and shoulders. Turning the flashlight side to side and then up and down the walls were gone as was the low ceiling. Warily, he waved his hands left and right and then above him just to be sure and was happy to find only open space.

Rising up on his knees, he twisted both his body and the flashlight around to see if there was room to stand. There was. The light showed that the ceiling was a good ten to twelve feet high. Pushing himself up, he stood, wobbled briefly, and then steadied himself as best he could. Like a drunk man rising out of a bar stool any going forward would involve a few curves.

Slowly he began inspecting the empty space he was in to try to get a better idea of what more was there. It wasn't a cave as much as it was a natural cavern that had been worked on and carved out over the millennia. Checking it out he took five swaying strides forward and reached the back of the chamber before turning around and retracing his steps. He then did the same to his left and right and with some quick math, estimated the chamber to be no more than twelve to fifteen feet in length and maybe the same in width, give or take a few chiseled edges. There were no side tunnels or passageways out of it and no openings in the stone ceiling. However, what was in its center was a carefully hollowed out, large, rock cistern with two rock steps in its center to allow better access to the water inside. Moving to it he settled the beam of the flashlight briefly on a piece of dried dirt embedded with small squares perched on the top step. He then moved the light up and over the rim of the cistern. The water tank that took up the bulk of the space in the chamber had likely served as the fresh water source for the enemy soldiers on the mountain.

The Texan leaned over for a closer look at the water inside the giant tub. Brushing away a thin layer of dust from the surface of the water that had blown into the chamber from the explosion, he stared into the pool of water in the dark and deep basin. Under the red glow of the flashlight the water took on the troubling color of blood.

Hoping it was the red filtered lens of the flashlight coloring the water, he set the flashlight down and then did a quick wash of his filthy face and hands, happily splashing it over his face, head, and neck. When his hands were reasonably clean and his mouth and nose free of dust, he cupped the hands and filled them with water.

He gargled with the first sip, spit out the grime, and then took a long, slow, and satisfied drink. He took another drink and smiled.

"Well, at least I ain't gonna die of thirst," he said, picking up his flashlight he used it to locate the source of the trickling water, following the noise with the light beam back to its origin. The steady stream of water that was feeding the large cistern was coming out of a small channel in the ceiling. An overflow drain had been carved into the left side of the cistern to keep the water level at a constant level and from flooding the chamber. The overflow drain itself was little more than a small trough that ran down the right side of the cistern and along the back wall. Thomas followed the open drainage system to the right corner of the chamber where it emptied into a foot-long opening carved through the wall.

"Yeah well, I ain't that skinny, Twiggy."

Inspecting the chamber a second time he was still hoping to find another way out, but there wasn't. The crawlway was the only way in and out, and it was blocked. More out of habit than necessity he checked his Seiko wristwatch and found a cracked crystal and a detached hour hand rolling around inside of the face of the watch. He had no idea how much time had passed or would pass.

"Now, ain't that a kick in the nut sack?" he muttered to himself with a half laugh since he still had three more payments to make on it. Seeing how he'd purchased the watch on time at the small PX on Camp

Mackie he mused that at least the watch still had some value to Uncle Sam's Department of Defense.

"I'd be more than a little happy if you sonsofbitches would come along and repossess it right about now. Yep, that'd be nice, thank you," he said with a sad laugh that just as sadly echoed back to him. "Any moment now would be good," he said, chuckling to keep from swearing again or maybe even crying.

When no one showed up to repossess the watch, he sat with his back against the front of the cistern and considered his next move.

He was lost in thought when a low moan, coming from the crawlway, began growing and reverberating through the tunnel before engulfing the chamber. The injured NVA soldier apparently had come to and had maybe realized his condition and possible fate. The pathetic moans grew louder and more frequent.

"Oh Hell," Thomas muttered, readying the flashlight and knife as he turned back to the small tunnel and slowly began to make his way back to the enemy soldier. The Texan knew what he had to do.

Even before he reached him, Thomas could hear the injured man's labored breathing. Maybe both of the man's lungs weren't bruised, but one certainly was. The NVA soldier was barely conscious, and his tormented face cringed even more when he saw the menacing, camo painted visage that was splattered in dirt and blood glowing red directly in front of him. He cried out in panic at the demon coming at him and tried fighting Thomas with his badly cut right hand only to have it slapped away.

"You could've at least tried to kill me, you little shit," said the Texan, raising the bayonet up and then bringing it down hard and fast.

The red light suddenly went out and the NVA soldier could hear the knife digging into the hard-packed dirt and debris round him.

When the digging stopped and he no longer felt trapped, he found himself being dragged forward by the canvas magazine pouch he wore on his chest. The demon was dragging him deeper into the darkness. After a few painful and difficult minutes later, the badly injured soldier found himself in a larger open space and being pushed up into a sitting position against a rock wall by strong, unseen hands. The red light came back on, and he was staring at the American who was crouching down in front of him and going through his pockets.

When the injured NVA soldier tried to stop him, Thomas slapped the hand away.

"Uh-uh! No!" he said. "Stop it!"

Thomas was checking to make sure the soldier didn't have any party favors hidden on him. There were no weapons, knives, or grenades, just a few small personal items; including a well-used toothbrush, a pencil and small notebook, and a wallet with a picture of who he guessed was the soldier and his father, mother, and little sister in better times.

The notebook was a third of the way filled with what the Texan guessed was a diary of some kind and a few rough drawings showing steep mountains and nicely drawn flowers. Maybe it was all just personal notes, observations, or thoughts, or maybe it had some genuine Intel value, but since his Vietnamese was limited to a handful few phrases, he'd hold onto it and pass it along to the TOC when he got back to Romeo Company, who would then figure out where it better needed to go.

Satisfied that the injured NVA soldier wasn't a threat he gave back the wallet and all that was in it but kept the pencil and notebook.

"I'll hold onto these," he said, stuffing the confiscated items in his top left pocket and then reached back and retrieved one of his two canteens. "But I'll give you this instead. Lean your head back. Drink!"

Thomas tilted the canteen's spout towards the NVA soldier's mouth.

The injured soldier hesitated, but then took a much-needed sip of water. He coughed out some wet dust and then spit out some more before he took an actual drink.

"Thank...thank you," he said in heavily accented, but surprisingly good English. That surprised the Texan.

"Wow! You speak English! *Ban noi... ban co tieng Anh...*" Thomas said, struggling to remember what few Vietnamese phrases he knew.

"Some," said the enemy soldier.

"Same-same with my *tieng Viet*."

The NVA soldier started to pass the canteen back to Thomas, but the American shook his head.

"Naw, you hold onto it."

Then the injured enemy soldier surprised him further.

"Thank you. You will have an opportunity to learn more Vietnamese," he said, matter of fact. "You my prisoner."

The Texan smiled at the irony of the situation. They were trapped in a crypt-like vault inside the mountain, and the only way out had crashed down behind them.

"Yeah well, you ain't exactly up for a tussle, pardner, and in case you hadn't noticed you don't have a weapon, and, oh, lookie here, I have a knife," he said and then the injured enemy soldier did something Thomas wasn't expecting. He smiled.

Chapter 10

Li was the furthest away from the tunnel, but the first to reach the heavily damaged entrance.

The brush that hid the entrance behind the dirt mound had been stripped of its foliage in the blast. A quick look inside the entrance had Li swearing under his breath. The explosion had all but collapsed the tunnel with heavy rock, packed clay, and was slowly bleeding dirt. There was room to crawl but not much and not all that far in. There was also no sign of the New Guy or Darrell. Li didn't have the tools to attempt a rescue but he, at least, was going to try.

"Call it in and set up a perimeter as best you can!" he said to Daley. "I'm going in."

Taking in a deep breath he crawled up and over the mess as far as he could go, and then wildly began digging out the broken rock and piles of dirt trying to reach the two trapped Lurps. Loose dirt was spilling down from the ceiling and the few support beams that remained were creaking and threatening to give.

Even so, the Assistant Team Leader managed to clear away enough of the debris to find the FNG that had followed Thomas inside. The New Guy's right leg was twitching where a good size chunk of splintered wood from one of the support beams had speared the hamstring. More splintered wood and bamboo spears were sticking out of his back and shoulders. He was face down in the dirt, so Li turned it to the side to give him room to breathe. He was badly injured, wheezing and groaning, but he was still alive.

"I found one!" he yelled back over his shoulder to the others outside the small tunnel. Li tried pulling the New Guy free by his LBE harness, only the injured Lurp didn't budge. He was trapped under heavier debris.

"You're gonna be fine, Dude," lied Li. "Hang in there. We'll get you out of here."

The New Guy's eyes were open, but nothing registered. He was out of it but not out of danger. Li brushed and scraped away more rock and dirt from the New Guy's outstretched left arm, and soon found the reason why he couldn't free him. The arm was trapped beneath a giant slab of stone.

The only thing that had kept the hand and arm from being severed was the grenade launcher the New Guy was carrying. When the boobytrap exploded well above him and the ceiling collapsed, the *Thumper's* thick barrel and stock bought the hand and wrist some crucial space when a large slab of heavy stone came crashing down. The weapon was crushed, but not the New Guy's hand. Using his bayonet, Li dug beneath the damaged M-79 to free the trapped hand. The *Thumper* was a write off. It couldn't be salvaged. Broken as it was, it would never fire another round, let alone make for a good club, so he left it.

"Hey you! New Guy!" Li yelled over his shoulder again to the other FNG who was sticking his head inside the crawlway. "Gimme a hand!"

"It's Sanchez," said the other FNG making his way inside the tunnel to help.

Li nodded. "Yeah well, grab his ankles, Sanchez. I'll grab his LBE. On three, we pull!"

Li did a quick countdown and together the two hauled out the injured team member from the triggered cave-in..

"We got'cha, New Guy!" Li said as the two Lurps pulled him over behind the small dirt berm.

"Norse," whispered Sanchez, tilting his head towards the injured Lurp.

Li nodded, again. He got it. "Norse? Listen to me! Listen to me! You're going to be fine. You hear me, dude. You're gonna be okay."

Only the Private First Class who'd only been in Vietnam for less than a month didn't look or feel okay. His back and thighs were peppered with splintered wood and bamboo from the support beams. There were countless small cuts and bruises, and he was bleeding from his mouth, nose, and ears that suggested possible internal injuries. Still, he bought the lie. He had to.

"Roll him on his left side," Li said, shifting Norse over just enough to check for more wounds and fortunately finding none. The back of the new guy bore the brunt of the damage from the explosion and the cave in.

To the second FNG on the team who now was a name to him, he said, "Sanchez? You got the Aid Bag?"

"Yes, Sergeant."

"It's Specialist, *Braw*," said Li. "Get it and bandage anything that's bleeding on him." Leaning in closer to Sanchez so Norse couldn't hear what more he was saying, added, "Leave in any of the big pieces of rock or wood splinters. We don't need him bleeding out on the mountain."

"You call in contact and bounce our QRF and a Medevac?" he said to Daley as he began removing his LBE web gear.

"Done," said Daley.

"Alright then. I'm going back in to look for Darrell."

Daley almost said, '*you think that's a good idea?*' but caught himself and nodded instead. It was an unwritten rule. Rangers don't leave other Rangers behind. It was a noble sentiment but rules like that in combat weren't always do-able. Still, it was the trying that made all the difference.

"Roger that," he said and handed the radio over to Sanchez as he dug into his rucksack and brought out a Claymore.

"Monitor the radio and cover me!" he said, before scrambling out to set up another anti-personnel mine while rolling out more wire from the one he had set near the path the NVA had taken up to the O-P. He placed the additional Claymore just to the left, but ten yards back from the top lip of the path.

The three mines made for a good defense from the front and sides where the bulk of the threat would come from. In theory, a Claymore covered a sixty-degree area for one hundred yards, fifty being the more reliable number, given the big rocks and surrounding jungle. The anti-personnel mines would take care of the trail head and anything immediately to the left and right of it. When the last anti-personnel mine was set, he quickly covered it in bunchgrass and leaves to hide it from view. Then he slowly started unwinding the charging line back to where Sanchez and the wounded Ranger were down behind the cover of the dirt berm. He passed the charging line of the Claymore over to Sanchez who was surprised he was given the task.

"Plug it in and stay ready," he said to Sanchez. "How's he doing?" Daley tilted his head towards Norse who was moaning on the ground.

Leaning into Li he whispered so the injured soldier wouldn't hear him. "Not good."

Daley nodded and noticed the empty Syrette of morphine pinned to Norse's boot.

"You gave him morphine?"

Sanchez nodded. "One shot. Pinned the empty to his collar."

"Good," he said and then patted Norse on the left leg. "Hang in there, Norse. The medevac's on the way. We're going to get you out of here."

Turning his attention to the makeshift perimeter he was satisfied with both the cover the rocks provided as well as the placement of the Claymores. Looking around he nodded at the steep drop off to their left. Unless the NVA had their own mountain goat squad then there was little to no worry about an attack coming from that direction. No, it would come from the trailhead, back the way they came, or worse; from what he didn't like when he looked above them. Twenty, maybe thirty feet up was an awning-like overhang of trees and rocks. If anyone came at them from above, then they were fucked, even if Sanchez, the frightened looking FNG, hadn't realized it yet.

Sanchez had good reason to be frightened. If worse came to worse, their only option, if help didn't arrive before the NVA did, would be to abandon the dirt berm and move inside the tunnel to fight it out. There they would hold off any attack while being trapped in what Daley thought would be a very small Alamo.

"The QRF's on the way," Daley said, maybe to reassure Sanchez and maybe just to reassure himself.

As all this was happening Li was back in the tunnel as far as he could go, probing and pushing on the solid block of stone that had trapped Norse's hand and had blocked the way. There was no give to the heavy stone and no moving it aside. More loose dirt was spilling down above him and threatening a second cave in. In the limited enclosed space, the surfer could feel both a rush and a sense of panic coming on. It wasn't claustrophobia as much as it was an understanding that like being in a tube, it all could collapse and wipe him out at any moment. Still, he kept digging around the massive stone with his knife to find Thomas only when he dug the knife deep into the rubble several new clumps of dirt began falling on his back and head.

"*Ta ma de*!" he said, swearing in Chinese, covering his head until the falling dirt had settled. It was fucking shit because with the cave in and the threat of more collapse he knew there would be no getting further into the crawlway without heavy tools and equipment.

Frustrated and concerned by the steady flow of dirt spilling down and with no room to turn around he inched his way back out.

Daley was there to help him out while Sanchez was seeing to Norse.

"Anything?" Daley asked Li, hopefully.

Li didn't have to answer or shake his head; his crestfallen face said it all.

"What's the status on the QRF and the Medevac?"

"A Medevac is in-bound out of Cu Chi," he said. "They say they're 15-20 mikes out. A QRF from Tay Ninh is on its way as well. They're closer."

"Let's set another Claymore out," said Li. "We may need it."

"We're good. I already took care of it," pointing to where he'd placed the additional anti-personnel mine and then added, "Well, every direction except for what's above us."

He pointed just above them to where the jungle awning was jutting out and over the rock wall. The overhang looked to Li like yet one more wave about to close out over them in what would be the real problem if the NVA took the high ground. They wouldn't have to worry about shooting the Americans. They could simply lob down grenades. There was little that Li and the others could do to cover that except maybe to find a better angle to deal with it, if, before it happened.

"Let's move to some better cover out there and use this as our fallback," he said looking around and finding what looked to be a better defensive position a few yards away or at least one that wouldn't leave them vulnerable to an attack from either the path or from above. The move gave them a little more protection, but not much.

Li took up his rifle and stared down the thin trail that led to the tunnel's entrance. Just over the lip of the path and out of sight, but not out of hearing range, he and the others could hear the enemy soldiers charging up from below.

Li took up the clacker for the Claymore facing the center of the pathway, took in a slow, deep breath, and whispered to Daley and Sanchez, "Get ready!"

Chapter 11

Minutes after Sergeant Cantu in the Romeo TOC was bouncing a Medevac and QRF for team Nine-Four on the Nui Ba Den, the frantic call from a second team in contact came in over the bank of radios on the shelf in front of him. Team Nine-Three was in a firefight and the radio call that Specialist Taras fielded was punctuated with heavy small arms fire and repeated explosions.

"Valhalla, Valhalla. Longboat Niner-Three in contact! I say again, Longboat Niner-Three in contact, over!"

The desperate voice was that of Nine-Three's Team Leader, Staff Sergeant Tommy Wade. Wade had transferred into the Company with Shintaku and Cantu early on. They were the first three volunteers. Like them he was on his second tour of duty, well versed in patrolling, and considered by most to be Romeo Company's top team leader.

"Roger, Niner-Three. I copy you are in contact," said Taras. "What is your status, over?"

When there was no immediate response, Taras tried again as Lieutenant Marquardt hurried to his side, staring at the radio speaker box for the scene it would describe.

"Longboat Niner-Three, this is Valhalla. I say again, what is your status, over?"

The white static noise from the small speaker broke with the reply.

"One Line-One and two Line-Twos! Bounce a Medevac and a Quebec Romeo Foxtrot, A-SAP!"

'Contact' was the term Romeo Company used to denote a firefight with the enemy, and the term *Line-One* was Romeo Company's commo code that a team member was dead. A *Line-Two* meant that a team member was wounded. KIA or WIA over an open radio frequency would give too much away.

"Roger Niner-Three. I copy one *Line-One* and two *Line-Twos*. Bouncing a Medevac and a Quebec Romeo Foxtrot to your location, over," Taras said loud enough over his shoulder so that both Lieutenant Marquardt and Sergeant Cantu would know as much as he did.

"Get on it!" the lieutenant said to Taras. Taras wasted no time calling Camp Mackie's BIG-TOC on a separate radio frequency to get yet one more Medevac helicopter and Quick Reaction Force in motion for the second time that afternoon.

Marquardt located the last known position for the struggling team on the TOC's wall map and passed over the coordinates to Taras, who then passed Nine-Three's location in Cambodia along to BIG-TOC.

Once that call went out by Specialist Taras, the lieutenant held his hand out for the radio's handset. "I'll take over for you. Find the Old Man, and let him know what's happening," he said to the young ranger as he covered the radio's handset with his hand, "And get us one of the trainees too. We'll need a runner! GO!"

"Yes, sir," Taras said and hurried from the TOC across the company's compound to the unit Orderly Room.

The next transmission that came in from Wade through the radio's speaker box was clear, concise, and a punch to the gut. His Assistant Team Leader, Specialist Jonas Warren was dead and both he and Specialist Leon Hagar, the team's RTO, were wounded. No names were given, but the terms, *Niner-Three Actual, Niner-Three X-Ray,* and team position number *three* told those in the TOC who they were.

There wasn't time to get the full story then, but what would later be learned was that Warren had been walking point and had just brushed aside a curtain of broad leaves the size of elephant ears from a seven foot high plant when he came face-to-face with a ten-man Viet Cong team resting on the side of an unmarked trail. The Viet Cong soldiers that had been hauling an 82mm mortar tube, plate, and rounds on bicycles, modified to carry the heavy loads, had leaned the bikes against several trees on the far side of the trail and were taking a rest break.

In a split-second understanding of what was all about to go down, Warren stiff-armed Wade behind him, knocking him on his ass. The Team Leader stumbled back and fell hard on his back against his rucksack as the Assistant Team Leader opened up on the enemy soldiers that were scrambling for their weapons. The exchange of gunfire was immediate and ridiculously close.

Warren sent a three-round burst into the soldier closest to him who was reaching for his AK-47 when a thick-bladed machete sliced deep into the side of his right knee by an enemy soldier he hadn't seen.

"MOTHERFUCKER!" cried the A-T-L as the leg buckled, and his body twisted in agony as he fell. The Viet Cong fighter, wielding the machete that had been hammered out of an old truck spring, was trying to wrench the thick blade from the American's leg where it was stuck in meat and bone as a grimacing Warren turned, and shot the attacker through his snarling face.

Struggling to get to his feet and falling again with the machete stuck in his leg, he shot and wounded two more of the VC from the ground and then turned his rifle on a fourth VC a few yards away who was readying to fire off an RPG round. The fighter was aiming the Rocket Propelled Grenade in the direction of the team when Warren pulled the trigger on an empty magazine. Frightened, the enemy soldier hurried the bazooka-like shot, and the flying projectile flew off target, and the nose cone shaped rocket exploded well behind the Lurps and high into the trees.

Warren dumped the empty magazine and was about to slam another into his M-16 to shoot the soldier reloading another rocket and warhead round in the RPG when he took a three round burst of automatic rifle fire from a Viet Cong soldier on his left.

The big man fell back hard, gasping and spitting blood-drenched air and bubbles. The AK fire, the impact from the three rounds, fired at close distance, shattered his rib cage and lungs. The shooter then turned his assault rifle on where the American came out of the jungle and emptied the magazine into the screen of leaves.

Wade was still down and struggling like a turtle on its back from the weight of his rucksack to right himself while Specialist Leon Hagar, who'd been standing just behind and to the right of Wade took a burst to the left thigh from the in-coming fire. The force and impact of the AK-47 rounds at the close range flung Hagar back and down like a rag doll upon impact. His right femur was shattered and what was left of the thigh and leg were barely hanging on by bloodied ribbons and torn threads of both tendons and fabric. He was screaming in nightmarish agony.

Finally freeing himself from his rucksack that was holding him down, Wade quickly got up on his feet and back into the fight. Firing through the brush in the direction where the heaviest enemy fire was coming from, the Team Leader reached down and grabbed Warren by his LBE and dragged him back.

With more enemy fire raking the jungle in front of him he grabbed a grenade, pulled the pin, and lobbed it in the direction where the RPG fire had originated. That would be where the next serious threat would come from. A second grenade toss immediately followed, this time he threw it like a hardball at the Viet Cong fighter who'd shot Warren and

Hagar. The baseball grenade thumped into the man's chest and bounced a few feet away.

"FIRE IN THE HOLE! FIRE IN THE HOLE!" Wade yelled to the team members behind him telling them to get down.

The two, near simultaneous explosions that sent a spray of burning shrapnel across the trail, was followed by Wade racing forward again to the trail where he took out two more of the enemy soldiers with better-aimed rifle fire before searching for other targets. Unsure of exactly how many Americans there were or where they were, the confusion and panic that ensued had the Viet Cong firing in all directions and running from what they believed was an ambush. That provided the Lurp team with a momentary advantage they desperately needed to exploit the situation. Had the foliage not hid the damage to the five-man team, the remaining VC would've pressed their attack.

It also helped that the first fragmentation grenade Wade had tossed had wounded the enemy soldier with the RPG who now was struggling to reload the weapon. The Team Leader jumped up, shot him dead, and then emptied his 20-round magazine at several others that had taken off running back down the trail and disappearing around a bend in the jungle trail. He wasn't sure if he'd hit either of them but was happy to see them fleeing. He quickly reloaded another magazine into his M-16 to face another problem.

The team was still taking sporadic enemy small arms fire from the two-wounded and stubborn VC fighters who'd crawled behind cover and were staying in the fight. As he turned to take them on one incoming round caught Wade high on his right upper chest and shoulder and bowled him over. His clavicle was broken, and he was spilling blood as he found himself being dragged back to cover by one of the two surviving team members that were carrying on the fight.

"My rifle! My rifle!" yelled Wade and reaching for his M-16 with his good arm as one of the two uninjured Lurps, PFC Lionel Fontenac, was pulling him back. Fontenac retrieved the rifle and handed it to the Team Leader.

Specialist Leo Angeles, the second veteran on the team, was providing cover fire. Fontenac, French/Canadian from Montreal was on his very first mission and while Angeles, a wiry Filipino, who had transferred in from a grunt company's Recon platoon, was now shifting his rifle fire to his left through the brush to where they were taking fire from the two VC holdouts.

The return fire from this new direction the Viet Cong hadn't expected was enough. The fight soon subsided as the wounded Viet Cong fighters retreated back into the jungle. The two Rangers left standing remained ready for the counterattack that never materialized. After a few tense minutes, Angeles had the PFC tend to the wounded as he went out to the trail to better assess the situation. The trail was quiet for the moment so he quickly began searching the pockets of the dead enemy soldiers and retrieving as many of the documents, maps, and functioning weapons as he could. Lurps only carried so much ammo, most of which would be used up in a prolonged firefight, so Angeles knew that the enemy weapons; the AKs, RPG, and SKS rifles would add to their own defense, if worse came to worst.

"Get the Medic Bag!" Wade yelled to Fontenac.

The pain in his arm and chest had him closing his eyes, wincing back tears, and had him fighting the urge to roll up into a ball, cry '*Fuck it*!' and just quit. But quitting was a luxury he couldn't afford.

The sudden encounter had been costly for both sides. There were enemy dead scattered amongst the mortar tube, rounds, tipped over bicycles, and other hastily dropped equipment from the Viet Cong. Blood trails told of further injuries to the VC.

Of Team Nine-Three casualties, Warren was dead, Hagar's leg was hanging by splintered bones and sinewy threads, and Tommy

Wade, the Team Leader, was trying to put up a good front pretending that his wound wasn't as bad as it was. The Staff Sergeant would never make it as an actor.

As the Team's designated medic, Fontenac wasn't actually a medic, but like the others on the team had been taught the rudimentary combat life-saving skills. He was assigned the position since he was new, and because the Medic bag added extra weight to his rucksack. Fontenac dug the medic bag out of his rucksack. Opening it he took out several large gauze pads and tape. He was starting to bandage the shoulder wound only to have Wade take the bandage from him and wave him away.

"No! I'm good. I'll do it! I'm good!" he said, pointing to Hagar and Warren. "Help them! Help them!"

Fontenac handed him a roll of tape and a large bandage and crab-crawled over to the radioman. The French-Canadian pulled off Hagar's belt and used it as a tourniquet on what was left of the upper part of Hagar's thigh. He followed that up with a shot of morphine before he applied a bandage and pressure on the wound to try to stop the bleeding. When the bleeding slowed, Fontenac moved on to Warren only to discover that there was nothing he, or anyone else, could do. Warren was gone. The big man was dead. He dragged the body further back into their shaky perimeter and then went back to check on Wade as Angeles returned with his arms filled with enemy weapons and documents. Dropping it all next to the team's radio he went back out to the trail for anything else he could find that could be used against the team. He was back within minutes.

"Five enemy K-I-A, two, maybe three blood trails," Angeles reported to his Team Leader. "Four bicycles, a mortar tube and rounds scattered out there, too."

His face contorted in pain; Wade nodded. "I need you to set up security, you copy?"

Angeles nodded and went to work securing what he figured would be likely lines of attack.

Wounded as he was, Wade had his map on his lap ready to call in the contact and their location as best he could. Once the Medevac and QRF were close enough, he'd have Angeles or Fontenac pop a smoke to better help guide them in, or switch on his strobe light.

"How's Warren?" Wade asked Fontenac, already suspecting the answer.

The New Guy shook his head as he had a morphine Syrette ready to inject it into Wade's good arm when the Team Leader waved him away a second time.

"No!" he said, adamant in his response. "Let's wait until the QRF shows up. I need all my senses working for a bit longer. Set out Claymores covering both directions of the trail and then another back the way we came. You got that? You copy?"

"Yes, Sergeant."

"Good. Okay," said Wade. "Then get to it, but keep that Syrette handy. I'm going to fucking need it!"

Wade's attention turned back to the radio and his follow up SITREP. The pain from his wound was beginning to overwhelm him and he was rushing the conversation.

“We have one *Line-One* and two *Line-Twos*," he said, closing his eyes and rushing the words. "I say again, one *Line-One* and two *Line-Twos*."

"Longboat Niner-Three, Valhalla X-Ray, a Quebec Romeo Foxtrot is on the way, as is a Medevac, over," said Marquardt.

Scouring the wall map again, the lieutenant was looking for the nearest clearing in the jungle that could serve as a makeshift LZ for both the Quick Reaction Force and the Medevac helicopter. There were three possible with the closest one being fifty to seventy meters away. He'd split the difference.

"Can you move to your sierra whisky six-zero mikes, over?"

"That's a negative, X-Ray, the Longboat is pretty banged up and on the rocks and leaking."

Wade's response through the radio's small box speaker was pain-wracked and fixed.

"Roger that, Niner-three. Hunker down. I say again, hunker down. The Cavalry's coming."

"Be advised we have a Victor Charlie eight-deuce mortar rounds, transport bicycles, and other weapons that'll need to be retrieved. Five confirmed enemy Kilo India Alphas. You copy?"

"I copy, Niner-Three. Secure your location," said the lieutenant. "Also, be advised the Quebec Romeo Foxtrot will be coming in from your sierra whisky."

"Roger that, X-Ray. Copy sierra whisky on the Quebec Romeo Foxtrot. Advise both the Dust-Off and Quebec Romeo Foxtrot of a possible hot Lima Zulu. Nine-Three out."

Marquardt's attention was glued to the radio speaker and on the radio traffic between the BIG-TOC and the two Medevac helicopters and the QRFs that were being set in motion as a harried looking Captain Robison came through the canvas-covered doorway of the company TOC. Sergeant Kozak and Specialist Taras were close on his heels.

"What do we got?" said the Captain to his X.O.

"Two teams in contact, sir," said the junior officer handing the radio's handset back to Taras.

Marquardt filled him in on the status of all that was in play and all that was being done to aid them. As he did and as Robison listened, the Captain's face took on a troubled scowl. The news on the losses of the two teams was hard to hear. These were his people, his rangers.

"Contact the BIG-TOC and have a helicopter standing by for me and Sergeant Kozak," Robison said, turning to Specialist Taras.

"Roger that, sir," said Taras and got on the radio and made the request as Robison and Kozak were at the wall map staring intently at the approximate locations of the two beleaguered teams.

"Sir?" Taras said to the Company Commander.

"What is it, ranger?"

"BIG-TOC says there isn't a helicopter immediately available, but there's an in-bound Huey from Di An fifteen-mikes out. They say once it's refueled, it'll be on stand-by for us."

"Then that'll be our Command and Control bird once we're airborne and on our way to the Nui Ba Den."

Robison knew that any turnaround time, plus the additional flight time north wouldn't be of any help or practical assistance to Nine-Three given the further distance away. They'd have to rely on the QRF out of Loc Ninh, but there still might be something he could do to help Nine-Four on the mountain.

To SFC Kozak he said, "Find me an Engineer Officer and one of their best tunnel or mining people and get them over to the flight line, A-SAP! Advise them they're going to the mountain with us."

"Roger that, Captain," said Kozak and was out the doorway of the TOC and racing across the Ranger compound.

"Lieutenant Marquardt, hold down the fort while I search for volunteers."

"Yes, sir," said Marquardt.

"Count me in, Captain," said Cantu, itching to go. "I'll help get our guys off the mountain."

Robison turned to the TOC NCO and was about to turn him down when Lieutenant Marquardt spoke up.

"Sir, Specialist Taras and I can handle it here," he said.

"Fine," said the Captain, happy to have the former team leader. "Grab your rifle and LBE, Sergeant, and round me up another good volunteer."

"On it, sir!" said Cantu. Cantu gave a quick nod to the lieutenant and was out the doorway in an instant.

"Ryan, what's the radio freq for Nine-Four?" Captain Robison said to his Executive Officer as he grabbed a PRC-25 from the corner of the TOC.

Marquardt gave the captain the radio frequency and the captain began turning the knobs on top of the radio to locate it. There were over 900 possible channels on the backpacked radio and Robison made quick work of finding the right one. Each turn of the knob made a distinctive click and when he had it locked in, he grabbed the radio and started towards the doorway.

"Keep me apprised of Nine-Three's situation while I'm on the Command and Control bird. I want to know exactly when they're lifted out, and which hospital they're taking them to. You copy?"

"Yes, sir. Will do."

Robison nodded and turned towards the doorway. "Back soon with our people," he said and exited the TOC. Outside, he said a quick prayer for the wounded and dead Lurp as he ran to his quarters to grab his M-16 and web gear.

Romeo Company had just suffered its first significant casualties, it's first hard hits, and the blows were staggering. The cost of wearing the Ranger beret, shoulder scroll, and of being a Lurp in combat just rose to a much higher price.

Chapter 12

The rescue platoon, the Quick Reaction Force, out of Tay Ninh may have only been fifteen minutes away by helicopter from the mountain, but the NVA were well ahead of them and leading the race.

As Daley had anticipated, the NVA came up towards the tunnel from the lower trail. The first cluster of enemy soldiers that rushed up to see what had caused the explosion were taken out with small arms fire from the three Lurps. A second larger force that had charged up to take out the small group of defenders were met with the full impact of the two detonated Claymores. The detonation of the anti-personnel mines with a combined total of three pounds of C-4 sent 1,400-ball bearings encased in the book-size mine into the enemy line and sent their dead and wounded tumbling back down the side of the mountain.

The next group to show came up with considerably more caution, as well as with a belt fed Soviet RPD machine gun just to the left of the trailhead. With the return fire from the Lurps, the two-man crew firing the RPD, though, couldn't get the gun better seated on the lip of the lower trail. While the machine gun sent burst after burst of automatic fire in the direction of the Lurps, the rounds had little to no effect. The angle of the machine gun was off, just as it was for the AK-47s from the other NVA soldiers coming up into the fight. The bulk of their rounds were only hitting dirt and rocks well above the Americans. Several of the enemy soldiers had taken cover inside the vacant Observation Post and while the massive boulders had provided excellent protection against small arms fire, it didn't provide a working angle to target their aim. The attack was floundering.

The NVA commander in charge soon remedied the setback by maneuvering a squad of his soldiers around to the left of the lower trail and had them working their way up through the steep jungle-covered slope to flank the Americans near the tunnel opening. Gunfire erupted from the team's right, but it wasn't hitting anywhere near the team. Leery of facing another Claymore, the flankers stayed down behind cover and instead began firing on potential locations where they believed other anti-personnel mines were placed. Knock it over and the bulk of the blast would go into the ground or harmlessly be sent skyward.

That tactic initially baffled Li until he realized what the NVA soldiers were up to. Grabbing the firing device for the Claymore facing the flankers, he squeezed the detonator three times with both hands as fast as he could, which only elicited a small pop instead of an explosion. The flankers' gambit had paid off. The repeated bursts from their AKs had found the hidden Claymore, and a lucky shot blew away a chunk of the mine with the blasting cap still inside.

"Fuckers!" cried Li, rising up and returning fire until he emptied his magazine towards the flankers only to have the now concentrated incoming rounds force him back down.

The flanking maneuver was keeping the Americans' heads down and buying time for the RPD machine gun crew near the trailhead to move into better positioning and aim. Still, the machine gun aim was off, but it was enough to keep the Americans' heads down, and if the NVA brought up an RPG the four Lurps would be toast.

With only three long guns between them and one remaining Claymore in place to use as a last resort if the NVA charged their position from the Observation post, Li was thinking that it had all of the earmarks of a losing battle until a Pink Team returning from a mission in Cambodia and returning along the northwest roadway leading back towards Tay Ninh detoured to see what the commotion was about and joined in the fight. Low on fuel, they would stay on station as long as they could. Shooting an azimuth from his compass to give them a heading to aim at, he popped a smoke grenade to show the team's location and then radioed the direction and distance to the gunship. With several passes the targeted M-60 machine gun fire from the low bird and the hammering of minigun and rocket fire from the Cobra gunship ended the NVA's assault on the Americans' position. Within minutes the only gunfire that remained was sporadic so as not to be met with quick retribution from the two helicopters.

In the near distance the sounds of more in-bound helicopters were growing louder. The Quick Reaction Force from the Tay Ninh Basecamp was just minutes out. Three Hueys were ferrying in a platoon of ARVN Airborne Infantry and the helicopters' door gunners on the birds were laying down heavy suppressing fire as they came.

Because of the slant of the rugged slope and with nowhere to land, the first Huey settled in a low hover above an open section of trees and underbrush the exploding Claymores had cleared away. The ARVN paratroopers on board stepped to the skids and jumped ten to twelve feet down. Several of the soldiers landed on their feet, some rolled a bit on the incline, and some went down hard on all fours, but all were quickly up and finding cover to set up a working perimeter. The perimeter would provide the much-needed protection for the two remaining helicopters. Led by a first lieutenant who knew what he was doing, the officer snapped an order to one of his NCOs who immediately went to work positioning his soldiers. The ARVN officer then had a quick word with the Lurp Team's Acting Team Leader to better understand the situation and what more was required.

After Li had filled him in on the situation the ARVN officer barked out a command to his NCOs, and the paratroopers wasted no time in setting up a more viable defensive perimeter to protect the Medevac helicopter that was only a few minutes out. With more boots on the ground the site was soon better secured, but better didn't mean safe. The Medevac helicopter came into a mountainside hover under sporadic fire but held its hover as it lowered down a metal basket-like stretcher to retrieve the critically injured New Guy. Li and Sanchez loaded Norse into the metal basket and came under enemy fire for their effort. Neither were hit but the incoming rounds were close.

"Find some cover," Li said to PFC Sanchez as he turned his head skyward and gave the signal to the Crew Chief on the Medevac to take the basket up.

The rescue basket was pulled into the helicopter and the Medevac helicopter, with a few new holes, soon roared away from the mountain heading towards a Field Hospital.

With the gunship rolling in on the heaviest pockets of NVA soldiers, the main force of the enemy momentarily pulled further back. There would be no show of bluster or strength from the Viet Cong and PAVN fighters. They'd bide their time and patiently wait to pick and choose their targets of opportunity, again. Time was on their side. A thousand years and more of fighting off invaders had demonstrated that it always had been. The Vietnamese had well-learned the art of patience against a multitude of larger and stronger foreign enemies.

Roughly twenty minutes and a few sniper shots later, another Huey brought in a smaller and unexpected QRF from Romeo Company. Li was surprised, but then maybe not, to see that the first one out of the helicopter was their Ranger Company Commander, Captain Robison. Trailing him were SFC Kozak, Staff Sergeant Shintaku, Sergeant Cantu, and two soldiers that Li hadn't recognized. Whoever they were, they weren't from Romeo Company. One of the two soldiers was a stocky looking captain who wore a sun-faded Combat Engineer unit patch cast on the left shoulder of his jungle fatigues as did an older, shorter, and much thinner NCO accompanying him.

They'd arrived just in time as the Cobra gunship and low bird, now low on fuel, broke station and flew off. Shortly afterwards, without air support, new gunfire erupted from the trailhead while those NVA soldiers on the right flank and those in the Observation Post resumed their fight.

In a crouching run the ARVN first lieutenant made his way over to the Ranger Captain, saluted, and broke into English asking for orders. Robison returned the salute but answered him in Vietnamese. The ARVN officer was initially taken aback, but maybe not as much as SFC Kozak, Specialist Li, and a few others watching on.

When the brief conversation had ended the Vietnamese lieutenant nodded, saluted again, gave a loud, "AIRBORNE!" and raced back to where his people were taking the brunt of the enemy fire. Meanwhile, Shintaku and Cantu had made their way over to assist a squad of ARVN that were dangerously close to where the remaining flankers and those holdouts in the O-P had launched a new attack. Shintaku was carrying an M-14 sniper rifle while Cantu had an M-60 machine gun with belted rounds draped over the weapon and hundreds of rounds more crossing his chest like a Jungle version of Pancho Villa. The machine gun fire Cantu had laid down and Shintaku's targeted sniper fire helped quell the incoming fire from the right flank while the Vietnamese officer leading the remaining paratroopers drove back the enemy from the trailhead. The counterattack restored more unnerving calm. It was a lull in the fighting, and everyone knew that like the eye of a hurricane, the lull wouldn't last. But there was the critical task at hand to attend to, so they turned their focus on it.

"What do we got, Specialist?" asked Captain Robison making his way over to the once beleaguered Lurp team with Kozak and the two Engineers in tow.

Li quickly briefed the CO as the Engineer captain and his enlisted counterpart listened on and then went to work inspecting the damaged crawlway.

All the while Li was talking, his Company Commander's eyes went from the small A-T-L to the tunnel and then back again.

"...And after the explosion brought down most of the tunnel, PFC Sanchez and I managed to dig out Norse while Specialist Daley covered us. Norse is pretty banged up, sir, but we got him out and on the Medevac. I ... I went back in to try to find Darrell, I mean, Sergeant Thomas, but couldn't reach him. A big ass rock, like, is blocking the way. I tried digging around it with my knife but couldn't do it. I'm sorry, captain. I couldn't do it."

"That's why we brought the Engineers, Ranger, " he said, patting Li on the shoulder for reassurance. "We got it from here, now go look after the rest of your team."

The Engineer officer who'd been checking out what remained of the crawlway made his way back out of the mess on his hands and knees. Getting to his feet he wiped his hands on his pant legs and then wiped away the sheen of sweat dulled by dust from his forehead and neck. The Engineer sergeant, who'd conducted an outside evaluation on the steep ground above the tunnel, then crawled inside to have a look for himself. When he came back out a short time later the former coal miner's furrowed brow and grave concern gave away what he was thinking. The two Engineers huddled up and exchanged what they each had found before offering their assessment to the Ranger Company Commander.

The look didn't go unnoticed when Captain Robison turned to the Engineer officer for their evaluation.

"Looks like an explosive charge was rigged to collapse the tunnel entrance when it was triggered," said the Engineer officer. "Whoever did it, knew what they were doing. The blast bought down a heavy layer of granite and a ton of dirt and clay blocking the way three to four yards in. No telling how big that rock slab is but it's substantial. And there's no getting through or around it without jackhammers or blasting. It's some serious hard mineral stone."

There was more and the Engineer officer was reluctant to say it, but he did.

"The trouble is, sir, either one we attempt would likely bring down more of the mountain on your guy with it, *if* he's not under the granite slab, and *if* he somehow managed to survive by finding a pocket of air."

The two *ifs* and the Engineer captain's face said it all.

Robison handed his rifle to SFC Kozak, took off his LBE web gear, and set it down at his feet. Retrieving his bayonet and asking if he could borrow the Engineer captain's flashlight, he knelt at the tunnel entrance. He had to have a look for himself.

"Captain," said the Engineer officer, handing him the flashlight and cautioning him on what he was about to do. "The tunnel, what's left of it, is pretty unstable, so if you're going in, then try not to bump any of the old beams or bamboo supports. My guess is the Viet Cong triggered one to explode. Could be a backup triggering device still in play."

Robison nodded, thumbed on the flashlight, and slowly began low crawling inside the heavily damaged passageway. Several of some very old and perilous looking wooden beams were badly splintered and cracked in places, with several leaning at unforgiving angles. Piles of jagged, broken rock and clumps of dirt made it a slow go. Heeding the advice, the Engineer officer had given him, Robison took his time and carefully skirted the wooden beams and bamboo supports and crawled on.

The confined space reeked of freshly churned earth, and the small, but steady flow of falling dirt like sand in an upturned hourglass tended to bring on a heightened sense of urgency, as well as an unnerving sense of dread. He'd been in tunnels before but not one that had suffered a collapse like this or hinted at caving in completely. That the tunnel was unstable and could still come crashing down on him, or that he might trigger a second possible boobytrap, only added to any urgency and his growing angst.

The few minutes that ticked away on his military watch seemed more like hours before he finally reached the heavy stone slab that was the stop point. The Engineer captain was right. The stone slab was massive. Using his bayonet, he tapped on the thick slab using Morse code hoping to hear a response from the other side. When no return taps came back, he tried again.

"Come on, Sergeant Thomas! Talk to me! Say something."

Still nothing.

Blowing some air out between his teeth, he then tried digging around the granite slab as Li and the Engineer captain had previously done, and like them, achieved the same depressing result. It was a no-go. When he tried digging beneath it, he only found more of the giant block of stone below. Trying another approach, he rolled over on his back, and using two hands on the knife for a better go, he worked at loosening the blockage at what he'd hoped was the top of the stone slab. As he was jabbing at the dirt above him his left foot accidentally nudged one of the bamboo supports and the nudge triggered a small landslide. The slight bump, and that was all it had been, brought down a slow, but ever-increasing flow of loose dirt and rubble on top of him threatening to trap him in the tunnel if he didn't back out and back out fast.

Rolling over on his stomach, he propped himself up on his elbows, and used his hands and arms to protect his neck and head. The dirt and rock that was spilling down rapidly began filling in the once empty spaces around him. He needed to move.

Before he too became trapped inside the tunnel the Ranger captain pushed himself back and kept pushing until he was free from the small slide. The mound of dirt in front of him was steadily growing and the creaking sound from the trembling support beams had him frantically scooting his way back the way he came. He was still crawling backwards when he felt a pair of hands dragging him the rest of the way out of the tunnel and away from the opening. The help came just in time, as there was a loud crack from one of the damaged support beams followed by low rumbling as more of the mountain fell and filled in most of what was left of the tunnel. A plume of dust blew out of the few remaining feet of the tunnel and the entrance like smoke from a dirty exhaust pipe. The crawlway entrance was now little more than a scooped-out grotto on the side of the mountain. The Engineer officer and his skinny NCO began brushing dirt away from the captain's head, neck, and jungle fatigues.

"That was close," said the Engineer captain.

"Too close," agreed Robison, as he took over brushing off the rest of the dirt. Handing the flashlight back to the Engineer captain, he stood, picked up his LBE and weapon, and reluctantly realized what next had to be done.

It was growing late in the day and their position on the side of the mountain was tenuous, at best. He didn't like it, but calling the ARVN officer over, he gave the order to withdraw. They, the two QRF teams, the Engineers, and what was left of the Lurp team, would need to be extracted before the NVA mounted their next attack.

"Sergeant Kozak? "

"Sir?"

"Call in our extraction ships. You get our people back to Camp Mackie."

"What about you, Captain?"

"I'll go out with the ARVNs back to Tay Ninh and then hop a flight down to the Field Hospital and check in on our wounded. Tell Lieutenant Marquardt I'll be back by morning, provided I can catch a ride to Mackie later."

"Yes sir," said Kozak and the Platoon Sergeant turned to the task. "Romeo Rangers!" he bellowed. "On me!"

As Captain Robison made his way over to join the Vietnamese paratroopers his mind was already dreading the heavy task that he'd have waiting for him back at Camp Mackie. The condolence letters he'd have to write to the families of Warren and Thomas accompanied him with each step he took towards the ARVNs, each seemed heavier than the last. Both letters would be difficult to write, but one more so than the other.

Losing a son, brother, father, husband, or uncle Killed in Action would be a terrible blow to any family receiving the news. But being informed that one was Missing in Action might be even worse for them to hear as it kept alive the remote possibility of hope; hope that could and would only fester with time the longer it played out to the inevitable conclusion.

Writing the letters to the families of those killed in the war was all part and parcel of the job as the Company Commander. He'd written condolence letters to families eleven times in his combat career, and it was never an easy task. The weight of each pending letter plagued his thoughts well before a pen ever touched paper. The letter to Warren's young wife would be difficult as no amount of sincere, heartfelt sentiment would cushion the devastating blow. The letter, like the previous condolence letters, would haunt him as well.

Without a recovered body, there would always be a lingering doubt that their loved one had actually died in the tunnel, and that perhaps had somehow managed to survive and was still alive. That would play havoc with their thoughts, and his as well, for a long time to come because of the uncertainty.

After the two letters were written, he would write another to his wife. It wouldn't be a long letter home, just enough to let her know he was fine, a little more tired than usual, but that he was okay, and that she shouldn't worry. In it he would tell her how much he loved and missed her, and to hug the babies for him.

He would believe the letter would comfort her, but what he hadn't yet caught on was that women were good at reading between the lines and that the tenor and tone of his words would reveal the hidden meaning he didn't know he was writing. Fifteen years of marriage had provided her with an acute understanding of the man she'd married, and by using the word 'okay' she knew that something, in fact, wasn't okay. Something was troubling him so she would worry regardless.

Even at a distance, wars exacted their tolls.

Chapter 13

The fate of the two teams in contact was soon learned by the remaining teams in the field. As the radio traffic was coming in Pettit held his right hand up in a closed fist signaling for a halt as he went down on one knee. He snapped his fingers twice to get Sergeant Carey's attention. Carey, who was walking point a yard or two ahead of his radioman, turned around to see what Pettit wanted. Pettit was pointing to his left ear that was locked on and leaning into the radio's handset as he took in more of`the frenzied radio clatter.

As Carey was making his way back to the RTO, he wondered what was up. Pettit was wearing a pained expression which had the Team Leader twirling a finger to signal the others to set up a defensive posture. The Ranger file soon became a tight 360-degree circle with guns out.

"The TOC is calling for all teams to hold in place. Nine-Three and Nine-Four are in contact," said the RTO as Carey drew in close. Those closest to Pettit and who had heard what he said turned towards him. "One dead and two wounded on Nine-Three. The NVA broke contact. The QRF is on their way."

Carey nodded. "And Darrell's team?"

"One wounded, and one M-I-A on Nui Ba Den."

Pettit held out the radio's handset and the Team Leader listened in on the buzz of activity coming over the radio.

As Carey listened in, Pettit passed along the grim news to the other members of the team who were wondering what the hold-up was about.

"Two teams got hit. One dead, one missing. Three others wounded," whispered the RTO to his teammates.

It was difficult news to take. Most of them knew some or everyone on both teams, so they swore under their breaths, gritted their teeth, or angrily gripped the stocks of their rifles at the news, including the tag-along lieutenant. Being new, he wasn't all that familiar with many of the men in the company, and maybe could only put a few names to a handful of faces. He didn't even know where or what the Nui Ba Den was either, but that the name now had grave new meaning.

"Who's dead?" asked Hernandez.

"Warren on Nine-Three. Wade and Hagar were wounded and are being Medevaced out. Same-same with one of the new guys on Thomas' team."

"They say who, Specialist?" asked Plantagenet. Two of the recent graduates of the Company's Lurp training that he oversaw were on Sergeant Wade's team.

"No, sir," said Pettit.

"Who's missing?" asked Hernandez, knowing the implication the word carried but not wanting to say it.

"Nine-Four Actual... Darrell. Sergeant Thomas."

The teams hadn't been extracted so until the QRFs went in and pulled them out, then the casualty counts could rise. The order for the remaining teams in the field to halt in place was a cautionary one. Carey acknowledged the command before he handed the handset back to Pettit.

There was nothing he and those on Nine-One could do to help the other teams, but there was something he could do to help his people, only the hold in place order scrapped what he had in mind.

He wanted to move and keep the team moving and focused on the patrol because he knew from the looks on their faces, the longer they stayed in place, the more the news of what had happened to the other teams would mess with their minds. The decision, though, was no longer his to make.

"Valhalla wants us to hunker down in place," he said, pulling out his mission map. Back to Hernandez he said, "Louie?"

"Yeah?"

"Find us a good hide site."

"On it."

It didn't take long for Hernandez to find what the team needed. The jungle was one huge hide site, but the one he'd scouted had both good cover and concealment. One was good, both were better. They moved to the spot Hernandez had picked out and waited to hear what came next. There would be extra vigilance now, some seething anger, and the inevitable angst that went along with it. Perhaps too, there would be a quiet confirmation for each of them that when you were on a five-or-six-man team, deep in well-established enemy territory, shit like this was painfully possible. Each long-range patrol was a roll of the proverbial dice.

Carey had hoped to find a trail system to set up for their rest overnight position, but the bad news changed the plan.

"We overnight here," he whispered to the others as he called in the position site to the Romeo Company TOC.

No one spoke. They dropped their rucksacks and went to set up a working defensive perimeter. Claymores were set out, fields of fire established, and then their attention turned to trying to find some sort of measure of comfort on the hard jungle ground for the night.

There were few dark and broken looking clouds in the sky coming in from the South China Sea that might produce a shower or two, but hopefully nothing that would bring on heavy rain. The night, when it came, would be, at best, under a quarter moon. It wouldn't be total dark beneath the surrounding canopied covered trees, but something very much akin to it.

Then it would begin, not just the noises of the jungle at night, but the dark thoughts would begin to creep in along with a troubling understanding that what happened to the others could very well happen to them.

Chapter 14

"Hey you, G.I.!" said the injured enemy soldier to the Texan startling him out of a light sleep. "You! American G.I.! Hello?"

When Thomas didn't immediately respond, the NVA soldier tried one more time to get his attention.

The NVA soldier coughed and tried again. "Hey, G.I.," he said, "Hello?"

"Yeah, what?" Thomas said angrily, turning on his flashlight and then aiming the light on the face of the man that was calling for his attention. The little sleep he'd managed to find wasn't enough. The back of his head was aching, and he was in a prickly mood.

From how Thomas was holding the flashlight, half of his face was on the peripheral glow of the red filtered light. The dirt and dust spackled, partially revealed face, combined with the smeared streaks of green, sand, and black camouflage paint on it, and framed by the pitch-black chamber made him appear to be eerily floating in mid-air and otherworldly. The visage brought on an audible gasp from the North Vietnamese soldier and made him now wish he hadn't called out. Still, he found the nerve to keep talking.

"Why...why you here?"

Thomas gave a slight chuckle. "Well, I sure as hell wouldn't be if you hadn't taken off running for the tunnel like you did, Flash."

"No. Why you in my country?"

"You from the South or the North?" replied the American with a question of his own as he rubbed the sleep and some dust from his red and tired eyes. *Jesus, how long had I been sleeping?*

"I am from Ha noi."

"Is that right?"

"Yes. It is correct."

"Then correct me if I'm wrong if I suspect some people here in the South might just ask you the same thing and maybe even wonder why you're here pissing in their backyard? I seem to recall someone telling me something about your whole north-south thing and that whole Trinh and Nguyen War that lasted what, 30 to 40 years?"

As he spoke Thomas, now more awake and aware, did a quick check and inventory of what all he had on him. *There are twenty-five full M-16 magazines in my web gear, but no rifle because like a dumbass, I left it outside of the crawlway chasing after this little shit. There are three grenades in a canteen pouch, a flashlight, my knife, a First Aid pouch, an eight-foot section of nylon rope with a D-ring, and one of two canteens. My strobe light's gone, dropped, and lost in the explosion and cave in, not that it mattered much since it wouldn't be of much use to me now in the chamber other than to make for a lousy lightshow.*

"We are Vietnamese. This is our country, not yours!" countered the injured soldier drawing Thomas out of his mental inventory. "You are the foreign invader!"

Thomas chuckled as his hands went to the pockets of his jungle fatigues. "You know, I also seem to recall hearing something too about this mountain and much of the province belonging to the Kingdom of Cambodia not all that long ago. So, did the Cambodians give it to you, or did you folks invade their country and just take it from them? As for me, personally, why I'm here, well, the thing is, I was Drafted. You know, conscripted?"

"You did not join your cause?"

"Naw, I didn't join. Unlike a whole bunch of others who avoided the Draft by parking themselves in college, I couldn't afford it, and unlike some who found other creative ways of lying to fail the physical exam, I must've turned my head and coughed correctly, which means, like you, I'm serving my country, too. Well, at least for the next three and half months and then I'm going home."

"Yes, but you are still one of criminal Nixon's puppets!"

"Oh Hell, Howdy Doody, we're all somebody's puppets at one time or another, but I am not a crook," Thomas said, chuckling. "And if you don't get that punchline now, you will later, and I suspect you'll laugh your ass off."

A small plastic squeeze bottle of bug spray, a packet of toilet paper, a small can of crackers and some putter butter, my P-38 can opener, and a chocolate bar that could double as a jawbreaker. There's a small C-ration can of Turkey Loaf, my compass in my top right pocket with the idiot cord looped through a buttonhole, my team map in my right cargo pocket, a newly acquired pencil and small notebook in my top left pocket, a crap load of small cuts and bruises, and, oh yeah, a bloodied lump on the back of my head made from something the size of a badly shanked golf ball.

"By the way, has anyone ever told you that your English is pretty good?" Thomas said, complimenting the man on the achievement. "You learn it in school?"

"*Dai Hoc Ha Noi*," the soldier said proudly. "Viet Nam National University."

Thomas noticed that when the Vietnamese said Vietnam, they separated it into two words, Viet Nam, much the way the soldier did when he said he was from Ha noi instead of Hanoi.

"A college boy, huh?" nodded Thomas. "Far out, man."

"No, it is in the city."

Thomas chuckled, again. "No, not in distance. Far out is a saying. Slang. You know, slang? It means, alright or that's cool."

"Ah!" said the soldier comprehending the expression. "Perhaps as my prisoner you will teach me more American slang."

That brought a belly laugh from the American that echoed in the chamber and bounced off the rock walls like a small chorus.

"Well, you are one persistent little fella. I'll give you that. But has it maybe occurred to you that maybe you're *my* prisoner? So how about you teach me the Vietnamese phrase for, *Fuck off*!"

"You are my prisoner," said the Vietnamese soldier. "You will see."

"Well then, you won't," Thomas said and turned off the flashlight.

Part of his reasoning for turning it off had to do with conserving the flashlight's battery life. There was no telling how long they'd be trapped inside the chamber until they were rescued, let alone who'd be doing the rescuing. Maybe too, the other part of his reasoning was because he wanted to mess with the NVA soldier's mind a bit. Total darkness frightened most people, me too, thought the Lurp, but hey, I have the flashlight!

"Hello, American?" came a new question through the dark a short time later.

"Yeah?"

"Where are you from? New York? Hollywood?"

"Not hardly, *compadre*," he said. "I'm from Texas."

"Then you are cowboy?"

Thomas laughed and turned the flashlight back on. "Nope," he said, casually slapping away some dust off the knees of his jungle fatigues. "I'm from East Texas where we've been known to wear the boots even when we don't own a horse. That being said, we're still pretty good at recognizing a horse's ass when we see one, and bullshit when we smell or hear it. So, how you doing, Amigo? You good?"

"Good?"

"Your injuries," said Thomas. "You holding up?"

"Yes, I am in pain, but I will live," said the injured NVA soldier. "If that is what you are asking."

"I am, and it is," said Thomas. "That's good, too, because we're gonna get you fixed up fine and dandy in one of our field hospitals when we get you out of here. You're gonna get clean sheets, a comfy pillow, and some wobbly Lime Jell-O that some damn fool kitchen helper will put a piece of pineapple in it and have the nerve to call it tasty. Considering that you'll likely be handcuffed to the hospital bed, maybe it will still seem like a treat, anyway."

"We will see who the captive is and who is the captor."

"Like I said, my friend, we Texans tend to know bullshit when we hear it better than most."

And that got Thomas to thinking and wondering why the injured enemy soldier, hurting as he was, didn't seem all that rattled or worried by the crypt-like confinement or the darkness, or why he wasn't giving up the notion about him being his prisoner.

Why is he so fixed on that? What does he know that I don't?

And then it hit him! *He knows another way out of here! Could be, too, that maybe some of his people inside the mountain are already on their way to see what in the hell was going on because of the explosion. The real question is how will they get inside the blocked chamber? A secret Open Sesame wall, maybe?*

"Your home team on their way to play ball, are they?" he asked, but didn't get a response from the soldier. "Your friends coming to rescue you?"

Thomas took the soldier's shocked look and silence as a yes, which had him back up and inspecting the walls in the chamber more closely than he had earlier searching the hidden passageway. As he was doing it, he was also cleaning out an annoying piece of dirt from his left ear, which is when he found the answer on the tip of his little finger.

"And there it is!" he shouted, startling the injured Vietnamese soldier.

Making his way over to the large cistern he turned the light on the top lip of the stone basin searching for the small, dirt clump he spotted earlier. When he found it again, he leaned in and studied it with new interest. The piece of dried dirt that was no bigger than a dime and stamped with the faint, square imprint, had distinct ridges that were too uniform to be natural. It wasn't like the dust layer he'd scraped away from his clothing or from the water's surface. This was different and telling.

Shining the light on the steps he found a second, smaller, but similar clump of dirt that had the same pressed indentations.

He turned the light back on the next step and then began searching the floor leading up to it. There were no other small pieces of dirt like it on or anywhere near the cistern, just dust from the explosion in the tunnel.

He smiled because he now had a pretty good idea why the dirt was there and who, and what, had caused it. When he was going through Advanced Infantry Training back at Fort Polk's *Tigerland,* he and the other 98 or so of soon to be Grunts in his Training Company were given a training exercise at a mock-up of a Viet Cong village. The purpose of the exercise was to show the Infantry trainees how to do a better and more systematic search of an enemy village. The mock-up village was similar to the ones they might be finding in Vietnam. The training also taught them about what kind of boobytraps they might encounter while conducting a search. In place of explosives the boobytraps in training held flash/bang devices or other noise makers, all set in place with easy to miss tripwires or pressure devices.

One of the training NCOs that had served in the First Infantry Division in the war explained how Charlie sometimes used wells and waterways to get in and out of hidden tunnel systems beneath a village.

Never mind that Camp Mackie was nowhere near any kind of civilization or that Romeo Company ever searched a hamlet, let alone a village, the value of that stateside training was, hopefully, now paying off.

With no other visible way out of the chamber and not much to lose, it was worth a try. He turned off the flashlight and wondered just how waterproof it was as he climbed to the lip of the large basin. The square imprints in the clumps of dirt were made from a boot, an NVA soldier's boot. If he were wrong about it, then he'd at least be a little cleaner.

"I can't hang around for the company you're expecting so here's another bit of slang for you from my buddy, Harry," Thomas said over his shoulder to the injured enemy soldier. "Say it."

"Say, what?" came the reply in the dark.

"Catch you later, dude!"

"What is 'catch you later, dude?'"

"This!" replied Thomas and with a firm grip on the flashlight and the knife he took a leap of faith and jumped into the cistern.

Chapter 15

The water was deeper than he'd expected and a whole lot colder. The shock to his system momentarily stifled his breathing control and had him gasping for air as he quickly resurfaced. It also had him thinking that his just as shocked pecker might never talk to him again.

Taking in a second, deeper breath, and under the weight of his uniform, boots, LBE harness and web gear, and all that was in or attached to it, Thomas slid underwater until he reached the bottom of the cistern eight feet down seconds later.

If he raised his arms and wiggled his fingertips they would be dancing just above the surface of the water, and if he sprang back up from the bottom then he could easily reach the top lip of the cistern again, only he wasn't going up. He believed what he was after was down and forward.

The dark opening was a little lower than where he thought it would be, and a little thinner than he'd hoped. He swam and pulled his way forward. It was a struggle with his web gear, and his heart began racing when one of the magazine pouches got wedged and caught against the tube-like rocky passage. With a little anxious twisting and turning he finally managed to free himself with enough air left in his lungs to swim on and pull his way through to the other side where he slowly, and oh so quietly resurfaced.

Rising slowly out of the water like an alligator eying unfamiliar ground, he found himself in a second, almost identical cistern in another almost identical chamber on the other side of the natural rock wall. Someone, or a few someones, had gone through a lot of time and effort to construct the cisterns and the secret channel linking the two. Given the mountain's long history, the many wars over the last thousand years, and the generations of determined structural engineers, they had plenty of time and talent to do it. The pagoda and accompanying temple was at least 300 years old and the myths and legends had monks and warriors on the mountain untold centuries before so perhaps there was a passageway leading to one or the other. And if there was, then it was highly probable that the local Viet Cong or even the NVA knew of it and we're using it.

Because it had been a short swim, and because he wasn't underwater for very long, he came out of the water without making too many undue gasps or splashes. Not knowing if anyone would be waiting for him once he rose up in an identical cistern on the other side, the Texan had his knife in hand ready to fight if it came to it. Peeking over the top lip of the large stone tank he was relieved to discover that no one was waiting for him.

This new chamber was empty. It also had better lighting. A pale, yellow glow from a bare, low watt light bulb dangling from the ceiling illuminated a large tunnel complex beyond this new chamber. It also left just enough shadows in and around the cistern for him to carefully climb out without being seen by anyone outside the chamber. The tunnel leading to the cistern was like a miner's tunnel where a tall man could easily navigate it without fear of smacking his head on the stone ceiling above him.

Thankfully, the large tunnel, too, was empty. However, somewhere further back into the mountain labyrinth he could hear the distant hum and drone of a generator that powered the lightbulb and likely others with it. Power and commo lines were affixed high on the walls of the tunnel and that told him that if there was a generator, then there had to be a way to ventilate the exhaust that he wasn't smelling and that meant an opening somewhere and a possible way out of the mountain.

Clipping the flashlight back on his shoulder harness he crept towards the large tunnel in a slow crouch with his knife hand ready as he watched and listened for any other movement or sounds other than his own.

Nothing, and that was good, too. He'd only taken a few steps towards the well-lighted tunnel when he suddenly stopped and quickly stepped back out and away from the opening as the steady drone of the distant generator gave way to heated Vietnamese voices and the sound of metal rattling against metal coming towards him. The voices and noise of rifle swivels and gear banging against their hips and chests were growing louder with each passing second. Enemy soldiers were moving his way, a bunch of them.

As his eyes better adjusted to the dim light in the surrounding cavern, he looked around for somewhere to hide, and found a second tunnel hidden deeper in the shadows at the far wall. Hurrying to it, he stepped inside, and leaned back as far as he could against the near wall so as not to make an easy target. He was ready to jab, cut, and slash at whoever came at him. He didn't want this fight, dreaded it even, but he wasn't surrendering, either.

The voices grew louder in the well-lit tunnel as orders were being barked at the soldiers that now had them moving faster. Thomas tensed. His adrenaline was pushing its limits and he was ready to spring off the wall, stab the first enemy soldier who showed himself and wrestle away an assault rifle. If he didn't get shot by the others doing it, he'd at least have a better fighting chance, brief, as it was likely to be. Only the line of enemy soldiers never entered the cistern chamber. Instead, they turned down another unseen tunnel and raced on.

A second squad of soldiers followed the first and somewhere off in the muffled distance he could hear the sound of machine gun fire, the short, staccato-like bursts echoing through the rock walls like a marching band's snare drum solo.

The Texan breathed a sigh of relief and then chided himself for holding the knife. He had three grenades he could've used and realized he'd likely be one of those geezers who'd spend time searching for his reading glasses that would be perched on top of his head. That is, if he lived long enough to become old.

He needed to move and since he wasn't going into the tunnel that had the soldiers, he settled on the tactically better option. Turning back to the second tunnel he listened for sounds of anything other than his own breathing in the dark. When none came, he grabbed his flashlight and thumbed the ON switch. As he started forward, he realized his jungle fatigues were dripping water and his boots were squishing with each step. Uncomfortable as that was, what else was uncomfortable was the realization that anyone searching for him might not have to be a Sherlock Ho-Holmes to figure out which way he went.

"*Methinks perhaps we should maybe follow this slime trail*?" he figured the sly little sleuth might suggest to his fellow NVA Watsons and set the game afoot.

But with no yelling and screaming and with no sirens or intruder alarms going off, at least for the moment, he'd keep moving.

The glowing radius from the beam of the red filtered light was minimal, but then it was designed to be. Still, it was enough to show the way a few feet in front of him at a time. Ten hesitant steps in he came to a spiral stone stairway that led down into the belly of the mountain. The steps were worn, mostly uneven, and lacked a handrail or support.

"Okay," he said to himself and then leaned his left shoulder into the rock wall and cautiously made his way down the staircase. The dripping water and wet boots only made it more of a test and challenge not to slip and fall on the smooth surface of the stone steps. That caution gave him time to count the steps as he went while considering what the possibilities of his future would be if tumbled and broke a leg.

At exactly twenty-two steps down the staircase gave way to a portico and a small landing in a modified storage chamber chiseled out of a natural cavern. On closer inspection he could see that the storage chamber was stacked chest high with dozens of fifty-pound burlap and cloth sacks of rice and open wooden crates filled with an assortment of various cooking pans, plastic and wooden bowls, and wooden scoops. As Thomas was working his way around the heavy bags to check a few more boxes, he patted one, and spooked a fat rat that darted out of one of the other sacks in panic just below him and scurried off into the dark. A little spooked himself, Thomas retreated out of the storage area and made his way to the far end of the landing to another portico and a second stairway.

Twenty-two more steps down he found a similar landing and another storage chamber carved out from another natural cavern. This one, though, was filled with stretchers, metal trays, and boxes and cartons of medical supplies. Prying open a few of the boxes, the beam of his flashlight found plasma bottles, and smaller cardboard cartons of bandages, tape, and gauze, all with Soviet or Eastern European markings and numbers with printed directions and drawings for their specific use. More boxes were stamped with Chinese characters indicating their country of origin. Grabbing a few of the gauze bandages along with a roll of tape, he figured he could bandage the cut on the back of his head later. He shoved the pilfered items deep down inside his cargo pants pockets before moving on.

The second landing and storage area too gave way to a third and fourth set of steps and landings with even more, well stocked storage areas. Inside the fourth storage chamber were a number of open boxes showing musty-smelling mosquito netting, old North Vietnamese Army pith helmets, new uniforms, and worn boots and sandals. To his disappointment there were no pistols, rifles, or weapons of any kind.

On the plus side his jungle fatigues were no longer dripping water. However, his jungle boots were still squeaking and squishing with each step and that presented another very real problem. His wet feet needed to be dried and aired out from his boots before jungle rot set in. While the small drainage holes in the sides of jungle boots let some of the water out, they hadn't drained it all. His feet were feeling mushy, they were beginning to sting, and that wasn't a good sign.

Determining that it was as good a time as any, he took a rest break. He was cut, bruised, sore and more than a little tired and stressed. Before he would take a seat and check on his feet, though, he steadied his breathing and strained his eyes and ears for anything that might tell him he wasn't alone. After what he estimated as being a one minute wait, and when he didn't see or hear anything other than what his flashlight showed and his own raspy breathing, he slipped in behind a tall stack of boxes and crates and sat with his back against the rock wall. Bringing his knees to his chest, he untied his boots, pulled them off, and inspected his feet. The muted red glow of the filtered flashlight lens couldn't hide that his feet were red on their own and raw in places, and badly wrinkled from too long in the wet boots. Pulling one of the uniform shirts out from a nearby box he used it to dry his feet and toes, rubbing them briskly to bring them back to life.

Better, he thought, as he took out his canteen and took a few sips of water and then shook it. The hard plastic canteen with its twist-off top was only half-filled and he instantly regretted not refilling it from the freshwater cistern when he had the chance, especially after giving the other one to the injured NVA soldier.

"*Should've, would've, and could've*, he said to himself, and then shrugged it off. "Yeah well, too late now, Einstein."

He wasn't worried because he suspected there would be more cisterns. There had to be. The trough that emptied the water from the cistern in the first chamber sent it down through a carefully constructed piping system somewhere inside the mountain. Fresh water in the field on patrol, let alone inside a military operational cave and tunnel complex system wasn't something any army would take for granted or waste. Right now, he was thankful to be alive and even more thankful that he hadn't been captured. He was still in the game and that counted for something, he told himself, and then suddenly brightened remembering another count.

There were what, four stairways and a tunnel system linking carefully carved out caves into workable chambers and God knew what else? Each of the stairways too had the same-twenty-two steps, making it eighty-eight steps in total. That mystery was soon solved when he remembered something that Li had once told him about the number eighty-eight when he saw it tattooed under a breaking wave on Li's left forearm.

"It's a lucky number in Buddhism," Li had explained. "It represents joy and happiness."

The Taiwanese born, Hawaiian surfer went on to say that it was also a number that his Grandmother back in Taipei played every week in the lotto, and a number a million or more Taiwanese, and maybe a half a billion Chinese from Hong Kong to Mainland China thought was lucky as well.

"They believe a lot in *fu,* which means luck," he added. "And all that goes with it and with their Chinese Zodiac sign."

"So, what's your Chinese Zodiac sign, Harry?"

"I thought it was an Earth Ox but after getting drafted and ending up here, I'd say it's more like whatever animal that's closely associated with the Year of the Fu, as really being one big F-U."

Eighty-eight steps for luck and hope. Given the well-stocked storage areas in the mountain, the Viet Cong and North Vietnamese soldiers occupying the ancient tunnels, chambers, and caves had much to feel hopeful about, too.

That the steps, landings, and storage areas were all painstakingly hand-hewn, well-used, and linked other natural caverns, the Texan believed it showed that the construction of it all wasn't a rushed job and that the Khmers and Vietnamese had been improving on the inner workings of the mountain tunnel complex for quite some time.

With dozens of uprisings and wars over the last 1,500 years they had the time and patience to calculate and prepare for whoever they would next be fighting. The latest round of stored goods and equipment that they had stashed away in the storage areas would sustain them for a good while in this latest fight.

Still hoping to find a weapon, and from where he was hiding, Thomas dug through a few more crates and boxes, but didn't find anything more than a box of small scissors. However, he also found several boxes of East German army ponchos and another box of truck tire-soled sandals. He sampled one of the pith helmets and ponchos and sifted through the sandals until he found a pair that might fit him. The sandals, that GIs called, '*Ho Chi Minh's,*' fit comfortably enough, and the straps made from old inner tubes held them securely in place. The sandals felt like they might provide a better grip on the stone floor, and they certainly would make less noise than his spongy, wet boots, so he'd wear them. Better still, they allowed his toes and feet to breathe, so he kept them on.

"These are the soles that try men's times," he said and then reached over an open box of old pith helmets he tried one on for size and to his delight, it fit as well! Trying on his new wardrobe, he smiled, and then sat back down.

"Ho Chi Me!" he said with a small chuckle as his thoughts then turned back to his present predicament.

He wasn't sure how long he'd been unconscious in the collapsed tunnel way after the explosion, let alone how long it took to dig his way forward and out. Add in the time in the cistern chamber with the injured NVA soldier before he dozed off for a bit, the swim through the cistern's escape route, the tense trek down the stairways, plus the time it took to check out the storage chambers, then it could've been 24-hours or more. Without a working watch he couldn't be certain.

Since he also didn't know how long he'd still be stuck inside the belly of the mountain before he found a way out, and he knew that he was, quite literally, in the dark, he opted to rest in place a bit longer.

He didn't want to be worn out or physically drained when he finally found an exit from the mountain maze. He didn't want to die because he was too tired or slow to outrun or fight anyone chasing after him.

Down behind the stacked crates and boxes, with his back leaning against the rock wall, he was hidden from view by anyone who might casually pass by the storage area. Reasonably comfortable and using the poncho as a tarp to hide him further, he pulled out a can of C-ration crackers and the small tin of peanut butter spread, if only to keep his growling stomach from giving him away.

With no luck finding any NVA or Viet Cong rations, other than the fifty-pound sacks of rice and one fat and happy rat three flights up, he'd ration what food he had with him. He'd eat several of the crackers, half of the peanut butter, and save the rest for later. The tuna can size of Turkey Loaf and the hard as nails chocolate bar he'd celebrate with later after he found his way out of this not-so-fun house.

Using his P-38 can opener that he attached to Paracord around his neck, he opened both cans and dug in. He ate as quietly as he could, finished the snack, and then stuffed the opened C-ration cans of crackers and peanut butter back in the left cargo pocket of his trousers. With his tongue and his right index finger he worked out the few small clumps of the peanut butter that had stuck to the roof of his mouth, all the while listening for any sound of movement in the stairways or on the landing. The large, round, dry crackers and peanut butter apparently were enough to calm his growling stomach and take away any nagging or immediate hunger pangs.

He didn't think the NVA had found their injured comrade, yet, but he was certain that sooner or later, they would because the injured soldier was certain they would. He damn near said as much. Once they did reach him, if he was conscious, then he'd tell them of the American '*Ghost Soldier*' who was now inside their secret tunnel system. An alarm would go out and a frenzied search would begin. He was keenly aware that he'd have to find a way out and put some more distance between him and the searchers if he was to outrun them.

For the time being, the ever changing now, he was reasonably safe and well hidden, so he'd stay where he was for just a little while longer before he'd set out again. Pulling out the NVA soldier's diary notebook from his top left pocket and finding a blank page, he used the pencil to jot down what he'd found, beginning with the collapsed tunnel. He was doing his best to try to recall the exact number of tunnels, chambers, the stairways and steps, the watery escape route and everything else under the red filtered light as he wrote. When words weren't enough, he tried sketching out the route. Distances and direction were best guesses and maybe it wouldn't amount to much when it came to accuracy, but he wrote it all down or drew it as best he could, anyway, if only to keep his mind on something he could control in his current situation.

When he was satisfied with the entries, he pocketed the notebook and pencil and turned off the flashlight. Leaning his head against one of the boxes on his right, he closed his eyes and rubbed them and his forehead while taking in several slow and steady breaths. He was tired, so he'd take a moment, and needed to. Maybe it was from all that had happened prior to entering the crawlway and the blast that followed? Maybe too, it was from all of the spent adrenaline, or even the stale, warm air of the storage chamber he found himself in, or the peanut butter and crackers he'd just eaten that kept his eyes closed for a little longer than he had planned. And maybe all of it combined was why, without meaning or wanting to, he dozed off, again.

It was the explosion above him that had his eyes spread wide in terror and had his head tilted up towards the dark ceiling just as it collapsed and crashed down on top of him. A cut slab of heavy stone, like the broken lid of a sarcophagus, had narrowly missed his head but had crushed his chest. Blood was seeping out his nose and mouth and he was struggling to breathe. Both Li and Norse were digging through the mess to get to him. And when his two teammates had somehow managed to raise the heavy stone block up high enough, and the New Guy was using every bit of straining muscle and strength he had to temporarily hold it in place, Li slid his mangled body out from under the bloodied rock. Laying him gently down on the landing, Li began telling him the bullshit lie that everyone gave a gravely injured buddy who wasn't going to make it.

'You're going to be okay, Darrell! Hey, listen to me! You're going to be fine,' Li said, right before he pulled a poncho over Thomas' face and loaded him into a body bag.

"No! I'm not dead!" cried the Texan, wildly flailing his arms in the body bag and collapsing the East German poncho on top of him instead as he came awake in the dark storage chamber.

His heart wasn't just racing, it was pounding, and his whole body was chilled and shaking. He wasn't sure how long he'd been sleeping when he was jarred out of the nightmare, but he was greatly relieved and thankful his body hadn't been crushed and he wasn't staring into the zipper of a body bag. He was also feeling more than a little foolish from the trick his mind had just played on him.

The good and bad news is that I'm still inside the mountain and still seated with my back to the wall, literally and figuratively, he thought as he took in a few deep breaths to steady his nerves and calm himself.

Turning on his flashlight, he got to his feet, now more than ever anxious and wanting to move on. Going back was out of the question and staying in place where he was wasn't a working option, either. He wasn't sure where this new opening at the far end of the landing would lead, but at least the ceiling wasn't collapsing, and he didn't hear any NVA soldiers running towards him with spike-like bayonets looking to Shish kabob him either.

Draping the East German camouflage poncho around his neck, shoulder, and back he retrieved the NVA pith helmet he'd knocked off coming out of the nightmare and put it on. Now he was ready to go, reckoning that in the poor light, if any of the NVA or VC glimpsed him in passing, they might dismiss him as one of their own and ignore him.

Side stepping and squeezing out from behind the stacked crates and boxes he started towards the next portico and down this latest rabbit hole. Four stone steps gave way to a long tunnel on a slight decline. The blueprint for the floorplan had changed. Twenty yards on by his pace count, he came to a vertical half-wall barrier that went from the floor to the ceiling. He briefly examined the half-wall trying to decipher its purpose and placing, and in frustration and with a nagging unresolved question or two, he moved on. When he came to a second half-wall on the opposite side of the tunnel twenty more yards on the mystery still hadn't been solved. However, after his third half-wall encounter, he realized that, like the circular stone staircases, the half walls were designed as defensive barriers to slow and hinder anyone trying to take a straight run on this section of the tunnel system. With the half-wall jutting out there was only enough room for one person to move through at a time.

"Why, you tricky little shits," he said to himself, smiling in appreciation. "Nice!"

The series of half-walls weren't all when it came to the tunnel's network defenses. A 180-degree turn into the next stretch of tunnel found a series of three stone steps every fifty or so paces for what his questionable pace count said was fifty yards. Given his short, careful steps, it was probably a great deal less than fifty. *"Fine. I'll ballpark it and call it forty."*

At the end of the fourth set of three stone steps he found a small alcove carved into the left side of the tunnel. Further down the incline he found another one of the empty alcoves. Stepping inside and peering out he found there was just enough room for a fighter to hide and make a stand to protect the open stretch of tunnel. Fortunately for one lost Lurp, the alcoves were empty. Maybe in the time of bows and arrows a fighter in one of the alcoves could hold off anyone advancing on the tunnel, but in the time of grenades the alcoves would only be death traps.

Thirty more doubtful yards down, the inclined tunnel route took a ninety-degree turn where it intersected with two additional tunnels. One was open and looked good-to-go while the other was blocked off with rope and what looked to be a warning sign of some kind hanging from the center of the rope. Peering inside with his flashlight the Texan could see this other tunnel was badly damaged from a cave-in. Heavy rock and dirt covered three-quarters of the way and his flashlight also showed serious cracks in the ceiling. Even if he didn't understand Vietnamese, he understood the universal skull and crossbones *don't be a dumbshit* warning sign. No work had been done to clear the mess to repair the tunnel as the war took on a higher priority.

He was still leaning over the rope and checking out what he could see of the other side when he heard the sound of movement from down the open tunnel. Turning back, he saw a faint glow of a bobbing flashlight coming at him from below. He wasn't going back the way he came, and he wasn't going forward to say, 'Howdy,' so he slipped under the rope of the damaged tunnel, scrambled up and over the heavy rock and dirt mound, and hugged the dirt on the far side. Turning off his flashlight the total darkness soon gave way to the bouncing glow of a flashlight growing ever brighter by the moment.

The sounds accompanying the light too grew louder as the two combined and stopped at the rope blocking the damaged tunnel. After a cursory inspection the soldier holding the flashlight and the others behind him moved on. They weren't looking for him. The brief stop was more from curiosity than anything else.

Thomas waited and when the light bounced on and the sound of the NVA soldiers passing had faded, and he was sure the gawkers were gone, he started to rise up from behind his cover only to immediately drop back down. A second party of NVA soldiers were following the others. Unlike the first group, the second round of bobbing flashlights bypassed the closed-off tunnel and moved on without stopping. He waited until they too were gone before he sat up contemplating his next move.

He couldn't take the good tunnel. It was looking more and more like a one way street at rush hour. If he took it, then sooner than later he knew he'd be that proverbial deer caught in the bobbing flashlight traffic. Since there was no going back either, the only way down was through the questionable tunnel he was in. Closed off roads back home didn't always mean the bridge was out or that you couldn't go forward. Most of the time the warning sign only meant that there were going to be some troubled spots or hazards up ahead to navigate. And that was what he was banking on.

Thumbing the red filtered flashlight back to life he aimed the diminished beam further down the badly damaged route that even the enemy army officials had warned against. "Yeah, well, fun, travel, and adventure..." he said, sighed, and carefully trekked on. The trek, though, quickly turned into more climbing and crawling over or around blockages until he found some better room to stand on the other side. That too didn't have him up and running as the cave-in had also opened up several deep fissures and pits that he initially mistook for shadows until he was almost on them. These he carefully edged his way around or leapt across.

That the way forward was still carefully leading down, he took as a good sign, just as a better stretch of the tunnel opened up allowing for a steady pace. With the thin red beam aimed in on the floor scanning for more pits and fissures, he hadn't seen the spider web spread across the top half of the tunnel. However, he did feel it when the sticky, silk-like web pressed deep into his helmet and face and the four-inch Huntsman Spider scampered down his neck and shoulder, flitted across his chest and left arm trying to get away.

"No,no,no,no,fuckingfuckityfuckme,no!" he cried, and feverishly began slapping away at the clinging web and at the elusive spider that was already long gone. In the one-sided melee, the pith helmet he was wearing went flying and he dropped the flashlight, and in the dark knew that there had to be an army of the giant spiders crawling all over him, trying to bite, wrap him up in their webs, and haul him back to snack on.

There weren't, but the sticky and pliant cobwebs made it feel that way. When he was reasonably certain he'd managed to wipe away the web that was sticking to him and any and all of the spiders, he picked up the helmet and flashlight, blew out a frustrated breath between his teeth, and cautiously moved on. Only now his pace slowed once again as he began alternating the red beam of light from the ceiling to the tunnel floor to keep from running into any more unexpected surprises. Maybe it was partially his fear, the over excitement, or that the oxygen level had dropped and there was less breathable air, that each new step he was taking was taking more out of him. He was sweating like a sprinkler, and he was pitting out.

His droplets of sweat only added to the droplets of water he found that were dripping down from the ceiling, the walls, and across the stone floor in this new section of tunnel in front of him. A thin and flimsy glaze of algae covered the wet surface of the floor and was now making for an even slower and more slippery go. The water and algae wasn't part of the NVA's prepared defensive strategy, just Mother Nature adding her own little twist, and perhaps a twisted ankle or knee for anyone not watching their footing.

Taking a few baby steps without a problem and finding some footing, he took four more tentative steps when his left foot slipped and skidded slightly further than his left hamstring would allow. The clumsy slide sent him awkwardly skating into a half spin with windmilling arms, and although he somehow managed to remain on his feet, his left elbow slammed hard against the wall in the flailing. That sent a bolt of lightning shooting down the arm and through his hand and fingers. He muttered another choice obscenity that didn't have the power to bounce or echo down the empty tunnel walls. The rude insult dissipated long before the radiating pain in his arm did.

Shaking out the needles and pins and massaging the elbow, he chided himself over his lack of noise discipline and, once again, quietly moved on. After a second slip and skid where he'd almost fell again, but somehow managed to brace himself against the rock walls without banging an elbow or falling, it was back to baby steps and quiet grumbling.

The baby steps helped but didn't stop a third skid that sent him into a James Brown dancing split that nearly pulled a muscle. Rolling over on all fours, he crawled on his hands and knees across the rest of the wet area aiming for another half wall barrier.

"I'm good! No, no! I'm good!" he said to himself, laughing nervously. "I'm good, but hey, I knew that I would be..." and started humming the soul brother hit only to stop as he slowly stood and steadied himself.

At the next half-wall barrier, he sat and took another rest break. The algae laced water on the stone floor had seeped through his trousers. His ass was wet again but at least he wasn't falling or smacking his elbows or knees. With his knees to his chest, his forearms on the knees, he lowered his head and quietly chuckled at the tunnel's take on Slip n' Slide.

"It's a man's world, alright, James," he chuckled to himself, "because a woman wouldn't be stupid enough to duck under a skull and cross bone warning sign thinking, hey! What could fucking possibly go wrong?"

Using the half wall barrier to brace himself he got back on his feet and continued on. The wet floor gave way to more large piles of fallen rock and dirt mounds at the far end of the precarious tunnel. Climbing up and over the last of the blockage he encountered a second rope with a warning sign, and two new tunnels. The two tunnels offered two new ways to go. However, there was no way of knowing which of the two would take him deeper into the mountain or out, so his decision became little more than a coin toss. No eenie, no meenie, no miney, just go, so he took the one to his right where the beam from his flashlight caught black commo wire fastened high up on the rock wall. The wire ran the length of the tunnel to where he was hoping it would lead to another Observation Post, or maybe an unguarded exit, but hopefully no more bobbing flashlights.

Taking out his knife again, he crept on. Further on he came to yet one more offshoot tunnel with a slight incline to his right. For some reason he couldn't quite pin down, he knew it was the way to go.

Seconds later he froze and knew exactly why he was heading in that direction. He was hungry and he was following the smell of oil fried garlic, wild onions, and dried chili peppers. Someone up ahead was cooking.

It could've been ten yards or maybe even less, but it was close and as he stood still he could also make out the murmurs of two people talking. The cooking and the conversation were carrying down the tunnel. The NVA soldiers were readying their dinner and the casual talk told him that he wasn't part of their conversation, let alone would be invited to sit down and share a meal, which also told him it was time to quietly retreat back the way he came.

Poke a hornet's nest and the hornets will swarm out and target the fool holding the stick, or in his case, a red-filtered flashlight.

Thomas slowly backed out and took the tunnel to the left with new urgency and a growling stomach that he thought would give him away.

Chapter 16

Lieutenant Plantagenet wasn't sure just where or when he picked up the pencil-tip sized splinter that was just below his left thumb joint, or even how and why it had gotten so infected so soon, but there it was, dark, deeply embedded, and proximity aside, something that was proving to be a pain in the ass.

The thumb was red and swollen just below the nail with an ugly little pus pocket that marked the splinter's location. Through the small bubble-like sack of opaque fluid, he could make out the dark sliver of wood, and would deal with it sooner rather than, *'Uh-oh'* later. Shortly after the team had set out their Claymores, set up in their defensive night posture, and were settling in, he decided it was time to remove the splinter while there was still light.

Using his right thumb and index finger as tweezers, he gritted his teeth, squeezed the pus pocket until it popped, and then wiped the spillage against his pant leg. It wasn't the best hygienic move, but any sense of personal hygiene was a moot point anyway. A second, more concentrated squeeze, brought the tip of the splinter to the surface. When he couldn't dig it out with his finger and thumb, he dug it out with his front teeth, and spit away the small, invasive piece of wood.

After removing the splinter, he turned to the two other remaining annoyances on his mental checklist. With the late afternoon bleeding into the evening, he started on the fix for his second nagging problem, which had to do with the swarms of mosquitoes. Retrieving the bottle of bug juice from his top left pocket, he slathered it on as much exposed skin as he could to his face, the back of his neck and ears, and on the back of his hands. Like the others on the team readying for the long night ahead, he adjusted his rucksack to find a portion that would make for something pillow-like and had his small, olive drab colored towel out and ready to place over his face once he took care of the last, little problem.

The last one, that is until something else took its place, had to do with the hard ground and trying to find or create some small aspect of comfort with it. Using his bayonet, he dug out a round hole big enough for his hips to take some of the pressure off his back and spine. Scooting in he tried it on for size. Nope, not quite. Shifting out of the butt size divot, he scooped away a little more ground and tried again. With a satisfied grunt and nod, he leaned back against his rucksack, and placed the towel over his face and head and closed his eyes. Better, he thought, and gave himself a mental pat on the back.

Three annoyances on his personal checklist up, three annoyances on his personal checklist down. Check, check, check!

The individual guard rotation would begin at sunset, and since he had the third shift, he had four hours to try to find some sleep. It might be another long night, but this night started off less miserably than the previous one and he managed to drift off into sleep thinking about his wife and their warm bed back home. Later, when it was his turn to stand watch and monitor the team radio, Doc Moore woke him up by gently shaking his shoulder. Without a word, Moore handed the team's radio handset to the lieutenant who sat up with his rifle in his lap and began wiping some sleep from his eyes. He yawned and checked his watch. The luminescent numbers showed that it was a few minutes into his shift with an hour and fifty-eight minutes to go. He took a slow look around him before settling in to monitor to the radio. The dark and ominous jungle was less intimidating to him, now. Well, he said, chuckling to himself, maybe a little less intimidating, anyway.

He was coming to understand what the experienced Lurps already knew, which was that the jungle had its own alarm system. Startled birds taking flight, dry branches snapping or breaking under someone's or something's weight. There were the annoyed snorts, panicked grunts, or quick slithering as the bothered animal and snakes moved on, or worse, the metallic sounds of rifle sling swivels banging as they moved, rifle safeties going from SAFE to FIRE with an audible 'click,' talking, laughter, cigarette smoke, and other indicators all gave warning of very real imminent danger. Somebody was nearby.

This night, though, the jungle was quiet with the exception of the in and out buzzing of the usual incoming raid from the swarm of mosquitoes and the croaking, distant cry of his very first '*Fuck You*' lizard. He'd heard the stories about the sounds the Tokay Gecko lizard made and thought it was a joke until now. The lizard's cry wasn't quite '*Fuck you*!' but close enough.

"Yeah well, get in line," he muttered to himself.

The bug juice he had applied hours earlier was still working and after touching it up with another generous application, he only had to slap away a few dozen of the persistent pests. The guard shift passed without incident, and he woke Specialist Bowman, who was the next one up on guard duty. The lieutenant handed Bowman the radio handset, turned back to his rucksack, and once again placed the small towel over his face and head as he leaned back to sleep. Dead ass tired, he slept the rest of the night.

At dawn as the jungle and Team Nine-Four was slowly coming awake, the six Rangers prepared to meet the day and all that came with it.

Carey and Hernandez were going over their map, locking in the new day's route and strategies before the team moved out.

"Saddle up! We leave in ten," whispered Hernandez, over his shoulder to the others before huddling back with Carey.

Heads nodded, rations, the freeze-dried packets supplemented with a few C-ration canned goods were quickly eaten, and each Lurp then checked their weapons and web gear.

Plantagenet smiled at the term that they used: *Saddle Up*. But then thought that, perhaps, it was appropriate for these modern-day cowboys riding their whop-whop-whopping and air pocket bouncing mechanical steeds. The *these*, he mused, also meant *me*.

So far, the war was not like he'd imagined it would be. Before he arrived in Vietnam, he thought he would be slogging through rice paddies, searching hamlets, staring down belligerent water buffaloes, eye-to-eye, and/or caught up in intense open field firefights. But there were no rice paddies, villages, or water buffaloes anywhere near their patrol area, no open ground to patrol, just Tarzan-thick jungle, with no sign of the elusive enemy that very well might be hiding only a few feet away.

He'd heard about the ridiculous excessive heat long before he ever arrived in-country. That was part of the litany of stateside war stories as well.

"You'll sweat your ass off!" some combat veteran would say during training, while another vet would counter it with something about the Monsoons. "And with all of the flooding rain and mud you're gonna get jungle rot! I mean it! Your feet are going to look like raw hamburger!"

The warnings came with slow headshakes and swearing long before a GI found himself smack dab in the mix of this Southeast Asian warzone. Some of it proved true enough, especially about the ridiculous heat that felt like it was trying to drain every last drop of fluid via sweat from his body and had turned his pee darker than amber. In all of the warnings during the stateside training no one had ever mentioned the orange dust that tended to find its way into every opening, crack, or crevice on his body, and into everything they carried, so that many of the teams, after the patrols, looked like an exhausted SWAT Team of Oompa-loompas.

With the heat came the plague of mosquitoes and a host of other nasty insects, and leeches that were out to bite, sting, or drain away some of his blood. There were the long and difficult daily treks spent fighting wait-a-minute vines or thick underbrush when he or the others weren't actually fighting a human enemy. Their meals were in cold ration pouches or cans with food that often didn't look or taste anything like what the labeling purported to represent, and worse still, there was even something as simple and commonplace as trying to take a dump and then burying it without worrying that someone might shoot them in the ass in the process, not to mention the festering cuts or infected thumbs from something as innocuous and commonplace as a tiny splinter!

Ah, but that wasn't all. Because as he was reaching down to grab the shoulder straps of his rucksack, he caught a whiff of something so odorous and disgusting that had him looking around to see if he or one of the other members of the team nearby had maybe stepped or sat in something he or they shouldn't have. They hadn't, and he hadn't either. Momentarily confused, he sniffed again. The stench was still there. Lifting an arm, he sniffed at his armpit, and then winced with a profound understanding that the rancid odor was coming from him.

"Lovely," he said to himself, shaking his head in disgusted resignation. "Just lovely."

He didn't simply smell, he stank. The sweat that had oozed from his body smelled like what he ate and drank, the meats, the beers, whiskies, chemically treated water, or Mess tent Kool-Aid back at Camp Mackie before the mission. He smelled of the soap or shampoo he had used, smelled like his deodorant, and whatever detergent his fatigues had been washed in. He smelled of camo grease paint, of bug juice, and rifle cleaning oil, and of the jungle's wet mulch and rotting leaves, and of bum-squashed insects, and the dried muddy ooze on his boots and uniform.

He wasn't alone in that regard. He was just new to it all in his one set of filthy, sweat-drenched, slept-in jungle fatigues that had splatters of dried muck and mud, pieces and corpses of dead mosquitoes, and a hole in his once new and spiffy looking trousers.

The war was a learning experience for the young officer and for any and everyone else that found themselves in combat trying to make some civilized sense of it. That is, if he and the others involved lived long enough to absorb the lessons.

What was it he'd heard one of the veterans in the outbound line of GIs that were waiting to leave Vietnam say when he and the other new arrivals had walked off the airplane in Bien Hoa that, once refueled, would take them home?

"*Oooh, lookie here, FNGs! Brand new pop-up targets! Good luck, gentlemen, you're gonna need it!*"

Plantagenet didn't generally swear, or tried not to, but now, at least, he better understood why some soldiers had. He knew it was a physiological venting response to a psychological overload, and that, at times, some GIs turned it into a creative art form. He knew there were some hard truths in their remarks, and that those who felt the off-color or brutal descriptions were too harsh or abrasive might need to rethink their own firsthand understanding of war once they'd experienced it. Terms like *gosh, shucks,* or *Oh my* just didn't carry the true weight of the physical or emotional burden.

"I'll take point," Carey said in hushed tones to Hernandez. To the lieutenant and the others, he added, "L-T, you're behind me. All right, Let's move out."

They were now well into the targeted recon zone that the Intel people back at Camp Mackie wanted a closer, boots-on-the-ground look at, so the search by Team Nine-One began in earnest for any high-speed trail system, hidden base camps, or active enemy staging areas.

The discovery was not long in coming. Fifty minutes on through the brush they found a heavily used trail that was protected from aerial observation by the screen of double-canopied jungle overhead. The trail was basically a living green and brown tunnel, tactically fashioned and trimmed for repeated use. Fresh boot prints and tire tracks told them that much and judging from the many and deep indentations moving to the southwest, it was a busy corridor. The center of the dirt path was covered with overlapping boot prints with the edges showing distinct deep, rounded gutters of heavily laden bicycles. Bicycles were the primary vehicles of choice that the Viet Cong and NVA used to move massive amounts of weapons and military supplies through the jungle. Modified as they were, the bikes could carry hundreds of pounds of war materials each and kept the war rolling.

"We set up here!" whispered Carey to the others as he was looking around for a good hide site.

Given the find the team now needed a place to hide, but at a distance close enough to be able to adequately observe who was using the trail without being seen in return. Some cover would be a plus. Both would work better.

Carey hadn't found the better, but Hernandez had. It was on the far side of the trail. The hide site, ten yards away, would be behind a fallen, vine-covered tree that had a large, exposed root system that rose up a foot or so above the ground and was spread out on their flanks like the arms of a drunken octopus. There was just enough space and natural thin windows through the brush to monitor the trail and that it rested behind just enough heavy foliage to mask the position made it even more desirable. The heavy foliage and broad-leafed plants provided concealment while the dead tree and exposed roots offered some protection against incoming small arms fire but wouldn't do squat against RPGs. Still, in jungle warfare you took what you could get, and the getting here was good enough.

Now all that the six Lurps had to do was to move across the trail to the site without leaving sign or disturbance of their passing. Sign or disturbance in this case meant bent or broken branches, turned up leaves, pulled vines, depressed grass, or ground from their boots, or the transference when a boot kicked up a rock and sent it tumbling. It also meant that something as little as a vine pulled from one area and into another with a stretched-out V showed a line of travel.

You didn't have to be Daniel Boone to read the sign either. Sometimes you just had to spot something that was out of place for its surroundings. If you were tracking someone, you reveled in the small finds, except if you were being tracked. Then, the signs and little disturbances could prove ruinous.

With Hernandez providing security the rest of the team moved across the trail one after another, with Bowman and Carey taking their time behind them erasing any sign they might've left behind in the direction of their new hide and ambush site.

On the other side Carey and Hernandez began positioning the other team members behind the fallen tree where he felt they'd be better able to cover the trail and everything else around them. The A-T-L had the lieutenant take cover near the end of the log with Pettit to his right and Doc Moore on the officer's left. After they too dropped their rucksacks, Carey had Bowman digging through his rucksack to bring out a Claymore and then sent him out ten meters to the right of the team to set it up.

"Louie, you and the L-T daisy-chain two Claymores near the trail," whispered Carey. "Make sure the charging line is capped and the safety latch on the clacker is on."

This last reminder was more for the tag-along officer, Carey knew Hernandez didn't need it.

"On it," said Hernandez in a quiet voice and then motioned for the officer to follow him. "Grab a Claymore, L-T and follow me, " he said to Plantagenet. "Let's get them set up."

The lieutenant was pleased that he'd been selected for the task, it was a sign that maybe he was an actual team member and no longer just a tag-along.

This was proving to be his first good day of the patrol as he pulled the two anti-personnel mines from his rucksack and followed the Assistant Team Leader back out towards trail while the others provided security.

The two were no more than a few yards from the trail when they all heard the distinct and rhythmic mechanical squeaks. Both Lurps froze. The noise was coming from the straining spokes of more than a few bicycle wheels hauling overburdened loads, and they were close, too close. Hernandez knew that the bicycle porters would be preceded by a Pointman; a Pointman that would be moving more quietly and cautiously than those that were following.

There was no time to set up the Claymores or risk crawling back to the hide site without attracting attention. Hernandez motioned for the lieutenant to lower himself down. Both were hugging the ground, seeking cover behind whatever leaves, branches, or brush they could find, while hoping the others had done a good job covering their tracks when they'd crossed the trail.

Hope came with sweaty palms and eyes darting at what they could see of the empty trail, as the grating noise from the squeaking bicycle wheels grew louder with each nerve racking, drawn-out second. To the lieutenant it was as though the squeaks had been plugged into an amplifier and someone kept gradually cranking up the volume knob. Setting the Claymore aside, he slowly inched his rifle ahead of him until he had his hand on the grip of the stock. Slipping his right index finger inside the trigger guard he used his thumb to turn the safety switch from SAFE to FIRE as quietly as he could.

Hernandez had the blasting caps for the Claymores, so the anti-personnel mines Plantagenet had brought out with him were basically useless, unless the A-T-L handed him one and he inserted it into one of the Claymores, the line was charged, and the Team Leader back at the hide site decided to make them both ground-level ground round!

Thankfully, no blasting cap came, and the A-T-L kept his hands on his own rifle with his eyes glued on what they could make out on the trail through the thin brush.

No one on the six-man Lurp team moved, especially not the two closest to the trail. The standard operating procedure for ambushes was that no one would open fire until the Team Leader did, but the team wasn't in an ambush posture yet. If it came to a hasty ambush, then Hernandez and Plantagenet would trigger it. If discovered, if they were spotted and compromised, they would be the first to fight, and they would also take the brunt of the NVA's return fire. With no cover, they would die quickly or, worse, horribly slow.

Necessity would dictate the action. During his Officer's Candidate Training, Plantagenet was taught that fortitude, resolve, and proper training would determine a successful outcome in battle while Hernandez, the combat veteran, knew it would also take a shitload of luck.

Chapter 17

Thomas was talking to himself again but took it as a reasonably good sign that at least he wasn't arguing.

The average Vietnamese is what? Five feet four or five? Which might explain the height of the tunnels and why me being a little over six feet tall made for the occasional head knocker. Adapt and overcome, or at least duck, damn it.

He was happy he wasn't wearing his boonie cap. After smacking the NVA pith helmet he was wearing against this latest tunnel's low ceiling, yet one more time, he was now concentrating on trying to keep his head bowed as he moved through the Nui Ba Den's elaborate tunnel system. He didn't need another lump on his already sore head. The pith helmet bore the brunt of the bumps and scrapes and that was fine by him.

Because of the earlier slips and slides he was considerably more careful with his footing, and at what lay ahead a few feet in front of him in the bouncing dance of the red filtered flashlight. He'd given up trying to keep a pace count. The slick and uneven rock floor had him moving like a nervous new diver edging towards the end of a wet, high dive platform with each new step.

The downward sloping tunnels seemed to run in a zigzag pattern, a continuous gradual descent made for an easier go. The pattern made sense too as it made for a somewhat easier climb for those going up the mountain.

His compass might've confirmed the pattern, but the iron ore in the surrounding rock walls made the needle useless and unreliable, so he went with his gut feeling. Same-same with the time this journey was taking. This too, he put down in the notebook on his rest breaks.

With its hands intact a broken watch might be right twice a day, but with what was wobbling around inside of the face of his watch, there was no telling when the broken watch was on the mark or even near it.

He took a seat and a breather at the corner of one of the turns so he could keep an eye and ear out on both dark stretches of tunnel way.

Satisfied all was quiet, he pulled out his canteen and took another much-needed drink before making the next entry in the notebook. This time he'd take the tunnel on the left that would hopefully lead to an exit at the other end. There was some worry that maybe it wouldn't or that it would and that someone might be waiting for him once he got there. Given the importance and the number of supplies and equipment stored in the upper chambers, the entrance he was searching for very well might be one of the main ones that was closely guarded. He'd worry about that later. Now, this new now, still had him searching for an exit, any exit. That was his first priority. Anything more he'd deal with as it presented itself.

Putting the canteen away and shoving the notebook diary back into his uniform blouse pocket, he got to his feet, and with the help of the flashlight's subdued beam started scanning for any more spider webs or wet and slippery spots as he continued his search. Two more changes in direction later he came to a sudden stop and his head went straight up and he smiled when he got a whiff of what was coming at him.

It was fresh air, an actual breeze, and the unmistakable scent of verdant, living and breathing jungle!

After the many hours stuck in the crawlway, chambers, and dark and dank tunnel system, the scent of the rain forest was unmistakable, as was the welcome subtle cooler shift in temperature. There was still no light, let alone daylight or moon light, but the fresh air gave him renewed energy and drive. He stepped up his pace.

One final turn in the tunnel system brought him to one last storage chamber on his right that was partially revealed by his filtered red light, but more so by the golden wash of sunset coming through the other end of the tunnel less than twenty yards away. The green and blue panorama in the golden sky beyond the tunnel was a true joy to behold.

Darrell Thomas wanted to happily whoop, holler, and yell that he'd finally found a way out of the mountain maze but stifled the urge out of tactical necessity. Still, he felt like a kid who got a second-hand Stingray bike with the high handlebars and a well-worn long seat at Christmas. It wasn't new, but it was still something good.

Just say 'Thank you' anyway, you little snot! He said to himself, lightheaded with excitement, but tempered with caution. Still, it was enough to bolster his shaky confidence. How long had he been inside the belly of this beast and how many steps had he taken? How many levels, drops in elevation, and how many storage chambers? How much paranoia and worry about being found out made him lose his count? He'd maybe try to work it all out later, when he was safely out of the mountain, back at Camp Mackie, where and when he could sit down and try to make some better sense of it.

He was glad to be closer to that *later* in finding the tunnel entrance. Turning off the flashlight he stared down the long tunnel towards the golden opening, grinning.

It took a moment or two for his eyes to adjust to the natural amber glow and the comfort it lent, but any warm feeling or joy he had was quashed by flickering shadows and the growing noise of someone entering the tunnel from the outside. Judging from the movement and clamor, it was a few someones.

"No, no, no!" he muttered low and in panic mode.

There was no going forward or back, so Darrell Thomas did the only thing he could do, he slipped inside the storage chamber, flicked on the flashlight, and looked for somewhere to hide. The trouble was this particular chamber was much smaller than the previous supply chambers higher up in the mountain. Worse still, it was half-filled with boxed crates of Soviet 7.62 X 54r ammunition and bulky *'Spam cans'* of AK-47 rounds, but still no weapons.

One of the opened crates showed the contents to be two 'Spam cans' with each of the unopened containers filled with over four hundred rounds. The numbers and Cyrillic coding of the crate showed it was rifle ammunition with the weight labeled in kilograms that he translated roughly to being forty pounds. The crates were stacked against the back wall while ten to twelve *'Spam cans'* were haphazardly positioned in front of the crates. That was it. There was nothing more, and no place to hide.

At best he maybe had a minute or less before the line of enemy soldiers reached him.

The knife wouldn't do him much good, and maybe the three grenades he carried might, but for how long? Three pin pulls, tosses, booms, and then what? He'd still be trapped inside the small chamber with no way out. In the short fight that would follow, and it would be short, he had no doubt that he'd either be seriously wounded or killed outright, and neither appealed to him.

"*Okay*," he thought, "*so when Plan A fails, go to Plan B, then C, D, or as many as it takes! THINK! THINK! THINK!*"

In what came as an epiphany, he remembered something his uncle had once said to him about how some passers-by with better places to be often viewed someone else that was doing dreary, mindless, and mundane labor.

It was two weeks before he'd received his Draft notice. His Uncle Dave had gotten him some part-time, day work as a helper on a construction site on the east edge of town. The foundation for a new restaurant had already been poured and set and the framework was just beginning.

At the end of the long and blistering workday the job boss had called it a day. While the rest of the crew began packing up their tools, lunch pails and water coolers, and were heading towards their pickup trucks and cars, Darrell took it upon himself to start cleaning up the job site. He went to work picking up all of the loose scraps of lumber and stacking them all into a neat pile to make it easier for the others to haul away the next day.

"You can do that tomorrow morning, son, when it's a little cooler," said the job boss while Darrell nodded. "You done good work today."

"Thank you, sir," he said. "I'll just get some of the loose stuff out of the way and finish it tomorrow if that's okay. It'll only take me a few minutes."

"No overtime, but you're welcome to finish out the week, too."

Thomas grinned and went back to cleaning up the work site.

The job boss looked to his Uncle Dave, who chuckled and shook his head. The job boss smiled, nodded, and headed towards his Ford F-100. It was 93-degrees and since the crew hadn't yet put up the roof, there was no real shade.

His Uncle reluctantly joined him on the clean-up, but because it wasn't in his or anyone's job description on the crew to clean up the worksite, yet, and given that it had been a long and hot workday, and this was off the clock labor, no one else gave a second thought to helping out. From the corners of his eyes Darrell watched as the last of the crew drove off with little more than a glance back or a small wave over his shoulder at him and his Uncle.

"Looks like you got yourself another few days of work," said his Uncle. "It ain't the best job, but it's a paycheck. The thing is, most folks don't really want to do any of the scut work, if they don't have to," he added, tossing a few split pieces of two by fours into his nephew's growing scrap pile. "That means they probably won't help, especially if it looks like you ain't struggling. Good on you, you dumbass. You impressed the boss. But as he said, you can finish this up tomorrow. By the way, since you're too young to buy the beer when we're done here, you're at least going to pay for it."

With the pith helmet on his head and in the East German poncho, and Ho Chi Minh sandals, especially from behind and in the dim light, someone stacking crates might not take on much notice or be bothered while doing the universal and everyday scut work. The whole premise heavily hinged on the word, *might,* and a little slouching to hide his actual height.

With his back to the tunnel, he lifted the first crate of ammunition. The wooden box had some heft to it, but it wasn't anything he couldn't handle, nothing out of the ordinary for any soldier in any army performing a mundane task.

Slowly and methodically, he began moving the wooden crates from the back wall over to the left and darker side of the storage chamber.

Soon the U.S. Army Sergeant E-5, Darrell Thomas, Lurp Team Leader for Longboat Nine-Four, of Company R, 75th Infantry-Ranger, had a nice, neat new row of ammo crates stacked for the North Vietnamese Army. He was still shifting and stacking the wooden crates when the NVA soldier in the lead stopped the line of soldiers behind him at the small chamber, glanced at the chore that was being done in the red filtered shadows, and then moved on.

Thomas didn't turn around to see if anyone was watching him work, let alone how many were passing by the opening in the process. Ten? Twenty? More? Less? It didn't matter. He was too afraid to look and was still praying the ruse would see him through.

To his giddy, and much muffled delight, the stunt worked. The line of NVA soldiers did move on and kept moving on. Only when he was sure they were well passed did he turn around to peek out of the storage chamber to catch a glimpse of the last enemy soldier in the line disappearing deeper inside the Nui Ba Den. A look the other way now showed a clear run towards the tunnel's entrance.

There was no time to waste so with his knife back in hand and his flashlight hooked back up on his LBE harness, he crept towards the entrance to the tunnel.

Up ahead the stretch of jungle beyond the tunnel loomed large in the opening in the distance and grew larger with each step. The various greens and browns of the jungle were draped in the subdued and slanting light of sunset, and it never looked better. The day was quickly disappearing and would soon be gone. There had been a quarter moon the night before, so he was satisfied knowing there'd be enough light in the evening sky this night to navigate once he was out of the mountain.

Making the climb back up to the Radio Relay Station atop the mountain was certainly the logical and best bet. Maybe after an hour or two he would reach the station's perimeter at the summit. The trouble with that plan, though, had to do with the enemy Observation Post he and his team had found. It was just one of many since he knew the NVA had been keeping a closer eye on the Relay Station, and that meant they also had to be watching on from other tunnels and hidden observation posts in between him and the mountain top outpost. And once the cry went out that an American soldier was in the tunnel system and was trying to escape, if they'd failed to trap him inside before he found a way out, then they'd likely assume he'd be heading back up in that direction. The money bet on this gamble would be that's where they'd likely concentrate their search efforts.

The Relay Station was literally within the enemy's gun sights, and if they couldn't catch him before he reached the outpost's perimeter, then they'd have a sniper or two ready and eager to take him out before he made it across the clearing leading up to the outpost. Why send a squad in harm's way when a well-aimed bullet would do? Aim, squeeze the trigger, and pow! Game over.

No, if anything, he'd juke anyone trailing him. He'd fake going one way and then go another. Instead of going up the mountain he would make a sloppy looking false trail for them to take before carefully making his way down the mountain.

The Team's designated extraction site, the exfil point on the west side of the Nui Ba Den where elements of the 11th ACR would've been waiting to pick up his team, was no longer in play. After the explosion had collapsed the tunnel, and he and Norse had been trapped, Harry would've gotten on the radio and called in the contact. The call for immediate assistance would've gone out long ago, the QRF would've already arrived on site, and they would've tried to dig both he and the New Guy out of the collapsed tunnel. Hopefully, they would have reached the new guy and got him Medevaced.

He knew they would have tried for him, too, that is, until they reached that damn block or blocks of heavy stone blocking the tunnel. And since there was no way to get heavy machinery up to that side of the mountain, nowhere to set it down without it sliding and tumbling a thousand feet or more, or without the Viet Cong and NVA circling in like sharks for an attack during any rescue attempt, then the rest of the team and the QRF would've been lifted off the mountain. Like it or not, by now, the consensus would be that he'd been killed in the explosion or the tunnel collapse, and was entombed in the Nui Ba Den. That meant he'd officially be listed as, Missing in Action- presumed dead.

Dead men too, though, sometimes do tell tales! And he'd be happy to tell his once he safely made his way back to Camp Mackie, but there were still a few hurdles to move beyond, and getting out of the belly of the beast was the biggest one.

Oh, but once he made it out of the tunnel, if he wasn't immediately tracked down and killed or captured, then he'd slip into the jungle, hunker down, and wait out the night. In the thin creamsicle light of predawn he'd make his way west to the Tay Ninh Basecamp.

He knew he'd need to be careful and hide from any NVA or Viet Cong patrols, and that when he got within shooting distance of the basecamp, he'd ditch the pith helmet and poncho before approaching the perimeter bunker line.

Even so, he wouldn't show himself until the sun was well into the morning sky since the VC and NVA usually attacked at pre-dawn or shortly afterwards. Thomas didn't want to be mistaken for an enemy sapper. No, he'd wait it out, and when he figured those soldiers on guard duty were finally up and well awake, and weren't rubbing sleep from their eyes, or scratching their asses, he'd stand, raise his hands high above his head, and slowly start walking forward towards the perimeter's barbed wire. As he went, he knew that he'd have to be calling out over and over again in his most unthreatening tone he could muster that he was an American coming in, and for everyone to hold their fire, and not shoot him. Hopefully, those on the perimeter bunker would hear him.

Inside the wire he'd surely be hustled to a Command Post under guard where he'd tell them who he was and explain all that had transpired. After his identity was confirmed, he'd be given something to eat and drink, and later, someone would see that he got on the next helicopter or fixed wing aircraft back to Camp Mackie and Romeo Company.

Being the hero in his own *Ain't I Wonderful* story he envisioned that he'd be welcomed with excited grins, bear hugs, and one too many slaps on the back. He'd be given something cold to drink while he was put through a second debriefing by Lieutenant Marquardt and Sergeant Cantu, with Captain Robison, and SFC Kozak admirably watching on, especially when he handed them the NVA soldier's diary and the notes he made to it.

He'd be updated on the status of PFC Norse and learn that the new guy had survived the blast and was doing well. Better than well, actually. He'd request to visit him at the hospital in Long Binh and the request would immediately be approved. Of course, it would. This was his mind's eye, best-case scenario, and he was writing a better ending.

After the debriefing, he'd take a long, overdue shower, put on a clean set of jungle fatigues, and meet with Harry and the rest of the members of his team, and over a few beers apologize for fucking up the mission. He'd thank them and then he'd call it an early night, go back to his bunk, pull out paper and pen and write two quick letters home. The first letter would be to his mother telling her that he was fine and that the telegram she'd likely already received from the Army was wrong, and not to worry. There'd been a mix-up with the whole Missing-in-action thing.

Mama,
Never mind what you heard earlier from the Army. I just got separated from my unit is all, but I managed to find them again. No big thing. All's good.

Love,

Darrell

The second letter would be to his Uncle Dave. It too would be brief and would simply read:

Hey Uncle Dave,

You were right about the scut work. When I get home, the beers are on me!"

Take care,

D

That's how he played it out in his mind as he crept his way towards the entrance to the tunnel. He was counting on that happening with maybe a few minor variations once he got free of the mountain, but what he didn't count on was a lone NVA soldier sitting to the left side of the tunnel guarding the entrance or that the soldier would be on a field phone talking with someone. Had the cry gone out that an American was in their tunnel complex? Would the guard or guards now be on high alert and waiting for him?

The best and most well-thought-out plans always worked until they didn't.

Chapter 18

The rhythmic squeaks from the overburdened bicycle wheels gave way to muted laughter. The laughter was immediately followed by a harsh rebuke from someone yelling at those doing the laughing. NCOs were the same in any and every army the world over and the command brought the recurrent metal against metal noise once more to the forefront of the clumsily awkward calm.

From where Lieutenant Plantagenet was hugging the ground he was as low as he could get without cutting off the buttons on his jungle fatigues and down behind what he now realized was a pathetically thin brush. His up close and way too personal view of the section of trail in front of him was troubling. What he could see of it through the sparse leaves, branches, and brush was empty, and then it wasn't.

A lone NVA soldier armed with an AK-47 at the ready quietly passed by Hernandez and Plantagenet with purpose. Like any good Pointman he carefully shifted his gaze left and right in a working cadence scanning for threats as he walked. Fortunately, for the two Americans the enemy soldier had turned his head to the opposite side of the trail away from the two on his approach and slowly brought it back around a few steps beyond them. He moved on and the parade began.

The front tire, rim, and spokes of the first overburdened bicycle came into view along with a brief glimpse of the NVA soldier on the other side of the bike who was pushing it. The porter's eyes and focus were on the trail in front of him where they needed to be to keep from dumping the bulky load of crates and plastic tarp-covered boxes the bicycle was hauling.

A second, just as a heavily burdened bike rolled by the two Americans, followed by a third and fourth. The transport bicycles gave way to five two-man teams of NVA soldiers carrying five foot long, single rail, 122mm Katyusha rockets and shoulder fired SA-7 anti-aircraft missiles on long bamboo poles. The poles would later double as makeshift bi-pod for the rockets.

The rocket launching teams were followed by more porters and transport bicycles and then by a small cluster of soldiers who appeared to be in charge of the line. An obvious looking NCO was overseeing the porters as they went while three other individuals were in a casual, almost happy conversation as they walked. One of the three was a tall, sparsely bearded non-Asian looking man in a black beret carrying a shouldered AK. He was accompanied by two older looking NVA soldiers, who, judging from the pistol belts they wore, their ages, and given that they weren't hauling anything, were field grade North Vietnamese Army officers.

Two of the three were speaking Spanish and Hernandez instantly recognized the westerner's accent and the small Estrella Solitaria flag pined to his collar. It was all too familiar. The man was Cubano.

Hernandez, whose family had fled Cuba to Florida on a small, overcrowded, and leaking boat with 33 other Cubans shortly after the revolution, badly wanted to open up on the Cuban Military Advisor but held his fire. His father and two Uncles had been part of the Alpha 66 operation in mid-April of 1961 to liberate Cuba from Castro's control. During the failed Bay of Pigs invasion, his Uncle Marco was killed while his father, and surviving Uncle Paulo, and a long line of other CIA trained Cuban exiles were taken prisoner and led off to the *Fortaleza de San Carlos de la Cabana* prison in Havana. His father, who had been shot in the left hip in the battle, had been looked after by Paulo on the long walk and the difficult time spent in prison that followed. Because of his wounds that for the most part, were purposely left untreated, his father's health had deteriorated in captivity. By the time his father, Uncle, and the other prisoners were eventually released and returned to the U.S. in a secret deal that cost the Kennedy Administration well over fifty million dollars, Luis barely recognized his haggard, emaciated, and crippled father. The once strong and jovial man he remembered growing up was gone. In the year that followed his father's health declined further and shortly after his forty-eighth birthday he died from complications of the gunshot wound in a Dade County hospital in 1967.

Hernandez bristled as the smug little fucker was laughing at something one of the Vietnamese officers had said, and the A-T-L badly wanted to shut him up with a bullet through his right ear. At this close distance there was no way he would miss. Still, the decision wasn't his to make so he held his fire. Besides, he was smart enough to know that it was all about time and place too. Neither were working now in his favor. He stayed down, gritted his teeth, and waited.

The parade wasn't over. More bicycles and porters followed but when the line of enemy soldiers and their bicycles loaded down with war materials, supplies, weapons, and ammunition suddenly stopped on the trail, the two prone Lurps were confronted with a true test of nerves.

For the line of soldiers on the trail this wasn't a rest break because those steering the bicycles hadn't set them down. It appeared to only be a temporary delay, a momentary hold up.

Because the NVA porters guiding the bicycles were utilizing a three-foot-long, bamboo pole extensions on the handlebars from the left side, and because the seat areas and tops of the frames were stacked three to four feet higher with their heavy loads, the two Lurps laying on the jungle floor in their camouflaged jungle fatigues, face paint, and floppy boonie caps, for the moment, went unnoticed.

"*On the rifle range they taught me to hit targets at 500-yards with the open iron sites of my rifle. Proper sight alignment, steady breath, and a slow squeeze of the trigger, and bang! Target down.*" thought the lieutenant. His mind was racing, and his palms were sweaty. "*But this? My God, it's bayonet distance! Not that aiming would even factor into the deadly equation at this short distance where even a blind man could easily hit center mass. All I have to do is lift my M-16 off the ground and fire a short three-round burst through the spokes and the NVA soldier guiding the bike would fall like a dropped watermelon."*

Any moral and ethical considerations of killing the enemy soldier now took a back seat to the reality of war. *When someone shoots at me, I'll damn well shoot back with better aim*, thought the lieutenant. But any further internal dialogue was cut off when the enemy soldier, turned bicycle porter, lowered a modified kickstand, turned, and tilted the handlebars to hold the tentative balance of the load, and then came around of the other side of the bike, holding the bike and cargo steady as he went. The bicycle porter was a short, stocky older man with strong legs necessary to haul the cargo through the jungle. Because he was hauling freight, his SKS rifle was stuffed into the rope webbing that was used to tie down the wooden crates and sackcloth boxes and bags. He could get to the weapon if he had to, and that's what the Lurps, and especially the two out front, were dreading.

The firefight would begin once the enemy soldier turned around and spotted the two Americans. When he did, he would be the first to die. For the moment, he was clueless to his demise as he reached down and grabbed the knotted, loose end of the spider webbed roping across the load of freight and cinched it tighter.

Satisfied that the load was secure and wasn't going anywhere, the porter tied off the rope end and started to make his way back around the bike when he suddenly stopped. He tensed, stood up straight, and then nervously took a look around him.

Plantagenet's mouth went dry, and he was struggling to swallow. Both he and Hernandez were both about to shoot him when the enemy soldier faced his cargo load, hiked his right leg up, and let out a loud and sustained rolling fart.

Dropping the leg back down the NVA soldier/porter made his way back around to the far side of the bike, grabbed the bamboo extension on the handlebars, readjusted the front wheel, and then used his right boot to push up the spring-loaded kickstand.

Once again balancing the bike and its heavy load, he patiently waited until the order came for the line of soldiers to continue on with their jungle journey. When it came he followed the other bicycles in front of him. The transport bikes gave way to twenty more armed NVA soldiers before the parade had moved on to find a new audience. Soon the jungle was growing quiet again as the noise from the squeaking bicycle wheels diminished in the distance.

Hernandez started to rise only to have the lieutenant wave him back down. From where he was the A-T-L could see that two stragglers, trailing the parade, were now hurrying to keep up with the others. When these NVA soldiers too had moved on and melted into the jungle around a bend in the trail and the lieutenant could no longer see them, Hernandez motioned for the L-T to get back to the original task at hand. He also nodded his thanks.

There were still Claymores to set up and maybe now more reason and credence to do so. The two set up the three anti-personnel mines and Hernandez daisy-chained them together.

Unwinding the charging line from the Claymores back to the hide-site, the A-T-L plugged the thin wire into the charging device. Turning to his Team Leader, Hernandez sighed heavily, and shrugged at all that had just happened. There was no explaining it. They had heard stories about some Lurps hiding a foot or so off a trail that had been pissed on by unsuspecting Viet Cong or NVA soldiers relieving themselves and thought they were bullshit war stories, at least, until now.

"That was close," said Carey.

"Too close," said Hernandez.

Carey gave a half smile at the absurdity of it all, shook his head slowly, and then got back to what needed to be done.

"Johnny," he said to Bowman, the Rear Scout. "Set out another Claymore facing the way they went."

Bowman nodded and went to work while Carey set another in the direction the parade had started their show. A sixth and final anti-personnel mine was set up behind the team's hide-site giving Team Nine-One a ring of steel around their position if a fight came.

"Get me the TOC," he said to his RTO when he came back to the hide-site.

"Any idea who the foreigner was with the NVA?" Carey asked his A-T-L.

"Uh-huh, he's FAR," said Hernandez, bitterly, spitting out the last word.

"He's what?"

"FAR, *Fuerzas Armadas Revolucionarias,* one of Castro 's guys."

"Castro, as in Fidel?"

"As in a *chingalito*! I wanted to shoot that sonofabitch sooooo fucking bad!"

"Glad you didn't. We can't afford to lose you, *Hermano*," said Carey. "Oh, and *chin go lito* is what?"

"*Chingalito*. Little fucker."

"How about I just say, 'possible' Cuban National?"

Hernandez shrugged. "Make sure to tell them that he has a shitty beard, too. My Tia has a better mustache than he has."

Carey called in the enemy sighting, the NVA numbers, and reported the 'possible' Cuban national that was with the fighters. He passed along their direction of movement and all that they observed was being transported to the Romeo Company TOC just as soon as Pettit had them on the radio.

"Way to hang in there, lieutenant," said the Team Leader to the still obviously shaken officer. "If you and Hernandez fired, then we all would've been in a world of hurt."

“He did good,” said the A-T-L.

Plantagenet gave a nervous nod. If he and the A-T-L had fired, they both would've been killed.

"I...I thought he'd spotted us," he said, quietly. The lieutenant was still a little rattled. He kept squeezing the pistol grip and stock of his M-16 over and over to keep his hands from shaking.

"To be honest, so did I."

"He...he farted!"

"Yeah, he did, and I suspect that's something you'll never see in a John Wayne movie. But if you did, it might've made 'em seem a hell of a lot more real!"

Chapter 19

It sounded like a one-sided conversation. Whoever was on the other end of the field phone with the guard at the entrance was only getting short, and subservient responses from the soldier manning the site.

When Thomas heard what sounded like a field telephone being set back in its cradle with a decided 'click,' and the guard casually began kibitzing outside of the tunnel's entrance, he felt a whole lot better about his chances of escape. Safe to say, the call hadn't gone out that he was inside the mountain, and better still, it appeared to only be the one man guarding the entrance, one man likely with a Mosin-Nagent rifle or an AK-47. Taking a knife to a gunfight wasn't his best option, so he settled on a better way to take the guard out. He pulled out two of the three baseball grenades from the canteen pouch he carried them in and placed one in the palm of each hand.

Hugging the near wall, he crept forward and quietly slipped out of the entrance.

"So whad'ya think, you goat roper?" he said to the NVA soldier who was reaching up and leaning over to reattach the camouflage cover to the tunnel's entrance after the arrival of the latest squad of enemy soldiers. "One or two?"

The startled guard spun around in a near panic and as he did Thomas hit him with alternating roundhouses. The first strike caught the guard just above the right ear and staggered him, only he didn't fall. The second strike slammed into the soldier's left temple. The impacts from the two lead-based grenades had the desired sap-like effect. The guard keeled over with a face plant into the dirt knocking over his rifle as he fell. He wasn't dead, but he was out, and would be for a while.

"Two," said the Texan.

Placing the grenades back into the canteen pouch Thomas flexed and then rubbed his now sore hands as he took a quick look around. There was much to be done and no time to waste. Reaching down he grabbed the bulky looking Soviet made field phone, tore off the wires, and tossed it down the mountain into a rockslide area just below the tunnel entrance. The radio bounced off several large rocks, cracked and tumbled, and finally broke apart into three pieces before coming to rest against the base of a chest-high boulder. Next, he grabbed the camouflage cover that was used to conceal the tunnel's entrance, wrenched it away from its bamboo frame, and tossed it down the mountain as well. The woven cover caught some air and fluttered in the wind like a loose kite. It drifted up in the slight wind and came to rest high up in the limbs of a tree just down the hillside.

Turning back to the tunnel the Texan reached up and grabbed onto the radio's commo wire that was attached to mounts high up on the wall and pulled it loose. Wrapping the wire tight around his right hand a few times in a balled-up fist, he used both hands to yank on the line as hard as he could. Several wall mounts flew out of the wall, the wire stretched to the breaking point, and finally ripped free from somewhere further back in the dark tunnel.

Balling up the broken line, he flung it, too, down the mountain in the opposite direction of the field phone.

"*Thank you, very mush...Elvis has left the building*," he said to the semi-conscious guard.

Snatching up the soldier's assault rifle, he stripped off the man's chest vest that held three additional magazines for the weapon and slipped it over his left shoulder. Checking over the Chinese assault rifle, he released the magazine, drew back the slide, and ejected the round in the chamber. Making sure it was empty, he then shoved the slide forward and did a dry fire. He smiled at the audible 'click.' He finally had a more viable weapon to fight with than his knife.

The Texan picked the ejected rifle round up off the ground, blew off a few specks of dirt, reinserted the bullet back into the magazine, and locked and loaded the magazine into the assault rifle. The four, 30-round banana-shaped magazines offered him a better fighting chance in his getaway. But unlike Roy Rogers' pistols that never seemed to run out of ammunition in a Hollywood shootout, in an actual firefight the 120-rounds could be used up in a matter of minutes on automatic fire. Still, he was grateful to have the AK as he did another quick scan of the immediate area trying to get his bearings.

Surprisingly, or maybe not so much so, given the descent inside the mountain tunnel system, the exit tunnel opening wasn't all that far up from the base of the Nui Ba Den, two football fields, end to end, at best. Looking back up and around the jungle covered beast he tried but couldn't pinpoint where he'd entered the mountain chasing after the NVA soldier or see anything that looked all that familiar, let alone see the Relay Station on the summit of the mountain. The tunnel entrance was well hidden. Since he wasn't going up to the Relay Station, he turned his focus back on where he was. To his right was a small path that seemed to be leading towards the east side of the Nui Ba Den. More than that it was the route the NVA soldiers that had passed by him in the storage chamber had taken up from the jungle. It was also likely to be busy given the tunnel entrance and the North Vietnamese Army's troop build-up inside the mountain.

There was thin brush with a serious drop off to his left, so he ruled it out, which left the rockslide area directly below him. The rockslide area, some of the scree fields that Lieutenant Marquardt had warned about in the mission briefing, and where he'd tossed the NVA field telephone and commo wire, was problematic. Anyone looking at it was bound to see him if he took it, and the large, open field of broken and loose rock would slow him down as well, but trying to go around it would take too much time and that was time he didn't have. He needed to make his run, but before that he one more play to make.

Finding what looked to be the right spot on the right side of the tunnel he started a short climb kicking and scuffing up enough rock and dirt to scar it up just enough to look convincing. He even kicked over a few good size stones and pulled on a few branches to what looked to be a direction of movement before he carefully made his way back towards the edge of the open area below the tunnel's entrance.

"It's now or never," he muttered. Taking a deep breath, he started working his way down through the field of scree. The rockslide run wasn't a run at all. It was a slow and careful go over Mother Nature's own minefield of ankle breaking, sharp, and shattered loose rock and rubble, but then it had to be. This wasn't the time to sprain or break an ankle, twist a knee, or trip and do a header, and there was more.

The long stretch of rock covered ground made for an array of heat reflective surfaces and that made him uneasy for a few reasons. Growing up in Texas he knew that rattlesnakes tended to like hot, rocky surfaces like roads or pads in the morning and late afternoons, something Staff Sergeant Shintaku reminded others about one early morning when one of the FNGs hurried into the Platoon hootch saying that Specialist Warren had just killed a cobra in the shower area.

"Said it was just lying on the floor!"

"Snakes do that," said the Training NCO, nonchalantly. "They like to warm themselves generally in the morning or at dusk. The heat raises their body temperatures, speeds up their metabolism, and makes it easier for them to digest the birds, mice, rats, other snakes or whatever else they ate. Rocky surfaces and concrete tend to hold heat."

That bit of wisdom, and the fact that it was shortly after sunrise, nervously had some in the hootch looking around them at the concrete floor. It also triggered an immediate discussion about snakes, especially after Thomas turned and asked Shintaku just how many types, kinds, and number of deadly snakes they might encounter in Vietnam.

"Thirty-seven," said the Training NCO, just as nonchalantly as he spoke earlier.

"Thirty-seven?" said Harry Li, climbing up to his bunk and pausing on the ladder as his eyes searched the concrete floor.

"Uh-huh, everything from a dozen or so pit vipers, common cobras, and even an eighteen-to-twenty-foot-long King Cobra, not to mention a handful or so of Kraits that could kill a bull elephant."

"We don't have snakes in Hawaii," Li said, nervously searching the floor of the hootch.

"And good too that the snakes will generally crawl off and try to escape from you every chance they get, well, unless you corner them. Then all bets are off, so don't corner them."

"What's a Krait?"

"A black and white banded sucker about three feet long. Some GIs call them '*Mister Two-Step'* since that is about as far as you'll get before you keel over after being bit. It takes longer than that, but not much."

Shintaku's impromptu discourse made a lasting impression on the Texan as well as the others in the hootch when they had heard it. During his nine months in Vietnam, and especially on patrol, he had only seen the backs and tails of several mud brown snakes that might've been Cobras, but they were too busy hurrying away for him to get a better look, not that he was anxious to get an up close up and personal introduction.

"*So, no, I don't need to get bitten by any one of the Heinz 57-variety of snakes, let alone a Krait, a King Cobra, or even a common Cobra that were far too common in places like this. Common Cobra? Seriously?*" he said to himself laughing at the absurdity of the name and how natural peril in the jungle could be so reduced to sound like the everyday normal.

Well into the rockslide field Thomas noticed there were several large, bowl-like depressions just up ahead of him. When he reached the first one, he could see that it was actually an old crater hole, long weathered and partially covered over by the many broken rocks and dwarf brush that had struggled to push up through it. Maybe it all wasn't just a giant rock slide after all, and when he came to a head bobbing halt in front of a brush and a squat and rusting cylindrical green-grey case, he realized the slide area had more than a little help. In the waning light of the setting sun, he could barely make out the faded Japanese markings on the World War Two bomb, but its origin was clear as was its size. It had to be a good 100-pounds or more.

Giving the undetonated bomb a wide berth, he bypassed a few other fresher-looking craters and shattered rock areas in case there were more modern ordnance to bump into. They were impact areas from heavy bombs and artillery rounds from the look of it. It wasn't a stretch to think that one invading army or another had been pounding the bejesus out of the mountain trying to turn it into gravel in the hopes of getting the Vietnamese inside to surrender, only it hadn't worked. Ever.

"*Tough little sumbitches*," he said, begrudgingly, just before he stepped onto what looked to be several reasonably looking flat rocks only to have them give and buckle. His left foot dropped down hard a few inches between the splintered rocks and one of the sharp edges stabbed into his left heel. The cut was deep and bleeding. Of course, it was. He was wearing sandals.

Looking it over he could see that it wasn't a life-threatening cut. It was just a little nasty looking and annoying. With no time to bandage it all he could do at the moment was swear, and keep going, so he did both.

While the *Ho Chi Minh* sandals were good for the tunnels and the wetlands, they left something to be desired in places like this. Careful as he was working his way down the scree, especially after getting cut, he still managed to stub, scrape, and even cut a few toes as he went, making him regret and even appreciate the jungle boots he'd left behind in the mountain.

He could survive the cuts, stubs, and scrapes, only if he could survive not getting shot before he reached the cover of the jungle below. From the tunnel's entrance to where he was, it'd be an easy shot with a bolt-action rifle, not to mention an automatic weapon. No real need to aim all that much when you just prayed and sprayed at a target that was well within range. Fortunately, no rifle or machine gun fire came at him.

The rocks that gave way when he stepped on them as he by-passed the old bomb gave him an idea and then quickly dismissed it. He'd thought about taking out one of the grenades from the canteen storage pouch, pulling the pin, and carefully setting the grenade beneath one of the rocks. Placed carefully and just right, the rock would hold the pressure on the spoon and keep it in place until someone or something large triggered it with a nudge.

If anyone tracked him down the rockslide area, then they too would most likely skirt the old bomb, follow the same route he'd taken, and BOOM! The boobytrap might not kill anyone following, given the size of some of the larger rocks around it but it would certainly wound a few and that meant others would have to help carry the wounded back to safety. It also meant anyone else tracking him would now be moving more cautiously and a whole lot slower.

The trouble was if the rock or rocks around it shifted while he was setting the boobytrap, or the spoon slipped while he was placing the grenade, or as he was stepping away, then he'd be the one needing to be helped off the mountain, or left to bleed out on the rocks.

No big fan of boobytraps, he nixed the plan, knowing too that the mountain didn't need yet one more piece of unexploded ordnance lying around after this latest war ended.

He moved on until he reached the other side of the natural obstacle course below and then broke into the brush. He was almost off the back of the beast, and it was time to put some distance between him and the NVA tunnel system, so he picked up his pace. He needed time to make good his getaway.

He was certain that once the NVA going into or out of the tunnel found the unconscious or dazed guard, or the other injured soldier in the chamber, they'd alert their people in and on the Nui Ba Den to look out for a lone American that would be making his way up to the Relay Station or down towards the road that led to the Tay Ninh Basecamp just eight miles away. Those were the only two practical options, so he knew they would cover those expected avenues of approach, and they would catch or kill him.

He had a weapon, two grenades, and a vague, working notion on how to do an end around to get to the basecamp. Now all he had to do was make it work.

He picked up his pace. He needed to get deeper into the flatland jungle.

Chapter 20

After calling in the enemy sighting to the Romeo Company TOC and receiving a '*Wait One*' response, Team Nine-One watched and waited for the next parade to show.

The '*Wait One*' reply meant that what they'd called in was immediately being passed along to the BIG-TOC and that Camp Mackie's command, the *Higher-highers*, would assess this new information and formulate a follow up plan.

The reply came back a short time later in the form of a question. The Higher-highers wanted to know how Carey knew the westerner with the enemy unit was a Cuban national.

"Be advised my Alpha Tango Lima is also a Cubano and he recognized the very distinct Spanish accent, a Cuban flag pin, as well as the man's scraggly-ass mustache and beard confirming it."

The Team Leader's report drew a *hell yeah* nod from Hernandez and another '*Wait One*' response from the TOC. Minds were spinning, and action was being planned. Whether the Higher-highers would send out gunship teams to intercept the parade or order it hit with artillery fire from the nearest Fire Support Base, the Lurp Team was out of the equation, which Carey suspected would be why they would inevitably receive a 'Charlie Mike' response to continue the mission.

When it finally came Carey acknowledged the command and handed the handset back to his RTO. An additional follow up order came for the team to remain in place to see if there was return traffic at their location as an artillery H&I- harassment and interdiction fire mission was being readied in the direction the column had been moving. The calculated distance was one kilometer, a thousand meters. The calculated distance to the target could be off but then so could be the artillery strike without an eyes-on Forward Observer.

"Everybody down," said Carey in hushed tones to the team members.

The fire mission that the Higher-highers were coordinating with a Battalion Fire Direction Center at a nearby Fire Support Base came moments later and when the cannon fire slammed into the jungle a mile or so well ahead of the team and then ceased, the Lurps were advised to be ready to ambush anyone coming back down the trail, *if* they came back down the trail. *If* being the operative word. The hidden trail system beneath the double canopy often took many twists and turns. Without eyes on the parade then the direction of travel wasn't a given, so the artillery barrage that was falling might very well be on target or simply brutally tilling innocent ground.

Nine-One waited in place and a half hour later when no enemy soldiers or bicycles and porters came fleeing back down the trail, Carey suspected they probably wouldn't be coming. The ambush posture was relaxed as the wait in the remainder of the day proved uneventful and had passed quietly. The sun that began slipping over the unseen horizon brought in ever darkening shadows in the rainforest. Night would soon fall with a heavy, black curtain, and moving in the dark for the Lurps presented too many problems and possibilities for that curtain to become a shroud.

To play it safe Carey had Pettit call in the team's present location as their R-O-N position, figuring that pre-dawn and sunrise would offer several more Intel gathering opportunities should a next parade or two start rolling by. Because it was an active trail and because their hide-site was good enough to remain unobserved by the previous enemy line there would be no need to move.

Back at Camp Mackie in the Ranger Company's underground and heavily fortified Tactical Operations Center's bunker, Sergeant Cantu would log it in and then circle the team's position on the TOC's situational wall map.

The A-T-L assigned the three shifts for the dinner meal to the other team members. As always, he and Carey would eat last. Any privilege that came with rank also came with responsibilities. His people ate first while they provided security. Hernandez didn't complain and was, in fact, of the same mindset. After they too had finished their rations, they would assign the guard duty shift rotations for the long night ahead.

Carey would keep it simple.

"Same as last night," he said. "Check your watches and sync the times. Stay alert, stay a Lurp, and stay alive."

The words soon proved prophetic as night fell and a convincing reason why no enemy soldiers had fled back down the trail after the artillery strike had revealed itself. The distinct hacks of wood being chopped and the faint, and the occasional, but recognizable glow of flashlights less than 100-yards away through the jungle offered up one answer. The parade had called a halt. Those eating stopped, lowered their food and themselves to the ground and took up their rifles.

“I’m thinking bunker complex or base camp,” said Hernandez, scooting to Carey. The Team leader agreed.

“And another reason to stay hunkered down till morning.”

Unlike previous nights, Carey changed the guard shifts to two-man teams and the night proved longer and more unsettling. At a little before three in the morning rain began to fall. It wasn't a heavy storm or downpour, but it was steady enough to properly soak the six Lurps where they lay on the ground or were sleeping against their rucksacks. The veteran Lurps on the team, not on guard duty, woke to the rain, sighed, grumbled, and took it in frustrated stride. Readjusting the small sections of green or camouflaged cloth or green towels covering their faces they went back to sleep. The tag-along officer, who awoke to the rain dripping down the back of his neck from a bare and drooping limb in a tree above him, tried to find some way to remain dry or at least less wet, and failed.

Like the others, he too was soaked and miserable. Unlike the others, though, he couldn't get back to sleep. When he and Bowman's guard watch was over, Bowman went back to sleep while he sat up with his rifle in his lap with those who had taken over the watch. With the NVA settling down and nothing to actually see, he listened to the pelting rain that sounded like a marching band with bad timing from their snare drums. By his watch, it was a little after four in the morning when the rain finally stopped, and he only had the occasional drops of rainwater plopping down on him. His struggling eyelids grew too heavy to keep open and finally closed. His body was deprived of good sleep, so he took any sleep he could get.

The sleep he found before first light, though, wouldn't be enough to sustain him or make him feel 'chipper.' The morning would find him with bags under his eyes, a bit slower to react than he knew he needed to be, in dire need of a shower and a shave, and with an infected thumb that made it difficult to grab anything with the hand without wincing. Treatment would come later when Doc Moore snapped his fingers twice to get everyone's attention. Pointing to his right ear he pointed he pointed out to the trail. Further back down the trail a new parade was beginning. There were more enemy troops working their way towards the hidden base camp.

Grabbing up their weapons and lowering themselves down in the hide site, the six Lurps watched as a steady line of NVA soldiers casually trooped by their position. There was a reason why the 70 enemy soldiers that they'd counted were being casual as a short time after they had moved on, the sound of them settling into the jungle base camp could be heard. There was a new round of wood being chopped and the smell of wood smoke moving its way closer to the Rangers.

Carey got on the radio and called in the latest activity. His voice was barely above a whisper, and it was only Pettit, the RTO, who was close enough to hear what he was saying. When he was done talking he looked around at the others as he was waiting for a response. When it finally came a few minutes later, he nodded at the reply, ended the radio call with a 'Niner-One. Out,' and handed the radio's handset back to Pettit.

"Prepare to move out," whispered Carey to the others. "We go in five mikes."

"What's up?" asked Hernandez.

"There's a Scout helicopter and gunship on their way to check out the base camp from the air. The Higher-highers need to confirm our sighting."

"What? They don't believe us?"

Carey shrugged. He didn't know but it didn't matter. "Once they confirm what we already know I suspect there's going to be one big wake-up call, so I've requested an early extraction."

"Extraction?"

"Same pickup zone just a day early," said Carey. "Let's pull in the Claymores. I want us out of here before the shooting starts."

It was a good call. Hernandez knew that once the two helicopters engaged the NVA in the base camp they'd take overwhelming return fire. That's when the gunship pilot, after making a few targeted runs, would call for and direct artillery fire which meant the team would be Danger Close.

After the anti-personnel mines were retrieved and stowed away, the Lurps shouldered their rucksacks and quietly crept away following a new compass heading.

They were two hundred yards on when they heard the small, three-man Scout helicopter buzzing in low over the tree tops. Carey called for a halt and had the others set up a temporary defensive position. Pulling out his map, he found their location on the grid squares and then double checked the coordinates just to be sure.

"Louie?" he whispered to his A-T-L trying to get his attention. When he had it, he added, "Check your map and tell me if you agree with where I think we are."

Hernandez nodded, pulled out his map, located where the team had crossed the sprayed Dead Zone and then traced the line of travel they had taken to the ambush site and night halt location with his right index finger. From there he followed the map grid over to where he determined they were now.

"I'd say we're right about here," he said, the A-T-L pointing to the edge of a grid on his map.

Carey leaned in and confirmed the location. "Yep, me too," he replied and called in the team's present location. "I want them to know exactly where we are before the shooting starts."

He called in their present position and line of travel and had the team up and moving again.

Back over the enemy basecamp the small Scout helicopter immediately began taking heavy machinegun fire. The fight had begun. Behind them, through the jungle, the Lurps could hear the low bird's machine gunner tearing into the enemy fighting positions but the far greater return gunfire from the well-entrenched NVA had the low bird peeling away with a few new holes. As the Scout helicopter made room for the Cobra gunship to take over the fight the attack helicopter began hitting the NVA with rockets and ripping minigun fire.

"We need to keep moving," said Carey. "It's about to get loud."

Given the enemy numbers and the heavy machinegun fire, he knew that the gunship pilot would soon be calling the Battalion Fire Direction Center, the FDC at the Fire Support Base, for a fire mission.

Team Nine-One reported that they were 500 yards on when the first 105mm artillery round, a marking round, roared over the double canopy treetops and exploded above the trees east of the occupied enemy bunker complex. The round had Carey and the others looking over their shoulders and while they couldn't see much through the double canopy they knew what was coming next.

The marking round was off target and the gunship pilot was adjusting the fire. When the next round came it slammed into the jungle and exploded with a hellacious impact as the sound of secondary explosions filled the morning. The round was on target. With 600 yards putting them out of Danger Close range Carey pushed the team further on.

The adjusted round was followed by a 'Fire for effect' call by the gunship pilot and four miles away the artillery battery of three 105mm Howitzer cannons on the Fire Support Base responded. Lieutenant Plantagenet stopped worrying about his thumb as the cannon fire slammed into the hidden jungle bunker complex in a deadly systematic dance. The ground rumbled and shrapnel was blowing through the trees, but stopped short of the Lurps.

Even before the Cease Fire order was given and the cannon fire stopped, Carey had the team moving away towards their extraction site. It wasn't an Escape and Evade run, but it would be if they lingered. Behind them the cannon fire, and the secondary explosions, continued. The team's head start was well assured.

"Guess they believe us now," said Hernandez, as Carey and the others, especially the tag-along lieutenant, nodded. Had the two helicopters not found the occupied enemy basecamp then the call for an early extraction would not have been justified, and Carey and the others would have had a lot of explaining to do.

Now though, a recon platoon or an infantry grunt company from the Fire Support Base would be sent in to take over the fight. Nine-One's job was over.

Their exfil would be at another island-like grassland clearing a kilometer away. By the Team Leader's watch, there was time to reach the Pickup Zone with time to spare if they kept moving. Carey had taken point with Bowman bringing up the rear. They moved on with a quickened but still quiet pace and when they were within what he figured was less than a hundred meters from the clearing, the Team Leader took a cautious detour to the site from the south before working the team back up to the Pick-up zone.

They covered the six-tenths of a mile in less than record time, as this wasn't a foot race but a well-executed run. Just inside the tree line facing the clearing where the helicopter would touch down, Carey used hand signals to put the others in place to see if the Viet Cong or NVA had spotters monitoring the clearing. Six sets of eyes scoured the tree line surrounding the clearing while well-tuned ears took in the sounds of the rainforest for anything out of the ordinary. This wasn't the time to get sloppy or let down their guard.

The caution proved its purpose when Doc Moore spotted several Mouse Deer foraging on the east side of the clearing. The reddish/brown deer with silver rumps were only slightly taller than rabbits, and with a slight breeze blowing behind them, the deer hadn't caught the scent of the Lurps. That the deer weren't spooked and with no sight or sound of enemy soldiers nearby, the Landing Zone was looking secure. There were nods of relief all around, a few smiles, and some wincing pain from the tag-along officer who was adjusting the straps on his rucksack and was having trouble closing the hand. His thumb had turned an ugly red and purple from an infection from the splinter.

"Let's take a look at that, L-T," Doc Moore said, studying the thumb as he reached into his Aid Bag for a roll of gauze and tape. "This will help, but I want you to get that checked out at the Aid Station when we get back."

Plantagenet nodded. "Well, at least it ain't the plague," he said, trying to laugh it off.

The medic, though, didn't laugh. "Hopefully not, sir," he said, taping off the bandage. "I know there was one reported case of a GI here in III Corps that had died from the Bubonic plague a while back. However, this looks more like a bad infection."

"Jesus, Doc, I was kidding."

"I wasn't, sir. This jungle is a petri dish with all kinds of deadly microorganisms. Let me know if the thumb gets worse."

In the distance the faint sound of a helicopter began growing louder as Pettit tilted his head into the radio's handset listening to the incoming radio call. The extraction helicopter was in-bound.

"Copy, Valhalla Rising. Longboat Niner-One ready for the school bus," he replied into the handset in a low voice.

"Pop smoke!" came the pilot's command.

"Roger that," said Pettit. To his Team Leader he said, "Huey's on their way in. They want us to pop smoke."

Carey nodded and gave the order. "Get ready to run!" he whispered.

The team members silently took up their rucksacks and weapons and readied to move as Carey pulled a yellow smoke grenade from his web gear and handed it to the lieutenant.

“You up for the toss, sir?”

Plantagenet nodded and said he was.

"Good, then this one's all yours, L-T. Toss it into the pickup zone so we can all get the hell out of here," the Sergeant said to the officer. "Hopefully, it won't sink."

The lieutenant nodded, took the smoke grenade, and then moving in a crouch, he warily stepped from the bulrushes a few feet out into the clearing.

As the rest of members of the team covered him, the clearing, and the jungle around them, Lieutenant Plantagenet pulled the pin and lobbed the smoke grenade out onto the open grassland. The spoon handle on the smoke grenade sprung away in the throw and triggered the mousetrap-like ignitor to the fuse on the small canister.

He was more than a little relieved to see that it hadn't sunk into a bog but had landed on glistening, wet ground instead. As he took a knee and covered his sector of fire the cloud of swirling yellow smoke began to sputter and tumble out and rise into the sky.

"Smoke out," Pettit said into the radio.

"Got lemon!" came the response from the in-bound Huey.

"Confirm lemon."

"Valhalla Relay on short final."

"Niner-one copy."

The helicopter roared in low over the trees and touched down in front of the yellow smoke. Carey gave the order and the six Lurps raced towards the Huey's open cargo bay as the helicopter crew chief and door gunner covered their run. Leaning out of the cargo bay SFC Kozak was helping to pull the tired Lurps inside.

The exfiltration took less than a minute, with all safely aboard, and no incoming enemy fire. The helicopter roared off and steadily climbed through the sky until the jungle was 2,500 feet below and the extraction site was growing more distant behind them.

The tired and grubby looking Lurps were grinning, nodding, and pleased with themselves. There hadn't been a firefight and the new lieutenant who, prior to the mission, had thought he'd wanted one, was thankful for that. That it was a successful reconnaissance mission was enough.

Over the last four days he'd experienced the hardships of the mission, had seen the enemy close up, too close up for that matter, and had better understood why these Rangers were so proud of their berets and 75th Infantry scrolls. He'd been humbled a little too and hoped to high heaven that he hadn't been too much of a burden as a tag-along. For his own selfish reasons, he wanted a good review. He wanted to be the new Ranger Platoon Leader, and he wanted them to know he too could do the job that was being asked of them.

It was Hernandez who offered an unexpected assessment.

"You done good, L-T," he yelled over the noise of the open helicopter bay giving him a thumb's up. "At least the bamboo stalk you stepped on didn't blow the fuck up!"

When Plantagenet turned to the Assistant Team Leader, he got a quiet nod from Carey as well.

"Get that thumb checked out at the Aid Station when we get home, L-T," the Team Leader said.

Plantagenet nodded thinking he'd maybe find a sewing kit for his pants while he was at it.

He was thinking too that the aluminum flooring on the cargo bay was surprisingly cold against his butt, and that if this was his biggest worry at the moment, then he was in the right place, with the right people.

Lieutenant Richard Plantagenet had found a home.

Chapter 21

The flight time of the Pan Am DC-6 from Saigon to Bangkok took just over an hour. As the chartered plane that was filled with wide grins, surging hormones, and hopeful expectations taxied to the designated parking area on the tarmac, a rolling staircase was being pushed out to the plane's main cabin door. Inside the plane, and well before the door had opened, many of the smiling GIs were already out of their seats and gathering in what little bit of luggage they'd brought with them from the overhead luggage shelf. The mostly young soldiers didn't need much for their five-day R&Rs, other than a pocketful of spending money, a shaving kit, and what little more they'd tossed in the ubiquitous black AWOL bags.

Upon entering the airport's main terminal, the GIs were given an R&R welcome talk and a reminder on how to behave in the host country, what not to do, and when they needed to report back for the return flight.

The NCO doing the final briefing offered one last advisory warning. "If you get caught by the Thai Police, using, or trying to buy drugs, you will be arrested and tossed into a hell-hole prison of your worst imaginings. If that happens, we won't be able to bail you out." As an afterthought and in an oddly more congenial tone, he added, "Enjoy your stay in Bangkok."

With the GIs unleashed upon the city, most were hurrying to exchange their U.S. dollars for Thai Baht before making their way out of the terminal and hopping into buses, cabs, or brightly colored three-wheeled Tuk-tuk motor scooter-like taxis to get to the city proper. After checking into their hotels from an approved list, many of them would make their way towards Si Lom Road and the Patpong Night Market District in the Bang Rak neighborhood. R&R stories about Patpong were lusty and legendary regarding its notorious partying nightlife, of which maybe half were true, but all were believed. Considered to be the city's primary red-light 'entertainment' center it catered to the *farangs* or visiting foreigners, especially the soldiers on R&R. Thousands of GIs over the years who had ventured into Patpong discovered that it more than lived up to its hedonistic reputation. It was rumored that GIs who had visited the Red-Light District would never think of ping pong balls in quite the same way again.

But Bangkok was more than Patpong, and the Thai Capitol, known to the locals as Krung Thep, 'The City of Angels,' was bustling with activity. There were many odd, interesting, and unusual things for first time visitors to see, with the kind of street commerce that was mind-boggling to most of the young American servicemen. There were important shrines and temple grounds to visit, ruins of the ancient capital of Ayutthaya just outside of the city to photograph and explore, custom tailor-made suits to be fitted and purchased, wooden elephants and Thai fighting swords to buy, Muay Thai fights to attend, and some tasty and exotic food to eat and enjoy. More than that, there would be the pleasure-seeking carnival nightlife they would revel in until they nearly drunkenly dropped, staggered back to their hotels, passed out, and started anew the following day. R&Rs were an exercise in excess with little rest and a personal discovery of relaxation, and the young men were eagerly looking forward to the exercise.

Unlike the other new arrivals, *The Brick* was in no hurry. He was going to take his time to savor and appreciate each and every minute of his long-awaited R&R. While the younger GIs hurried, he strolled. At the airport's Currency Exchange counter, he traded in $400 for Thai Baht and got a wad of colorful bills in return.

After a scotch neat in the airport bar, he caught a taxi into the heart of the city. The young bulls would run to the cow pasture while an older bull would take his time.

"Where to, GI?" asked the affable driver.

"A good hotel along Si Lom Road," he said. "Someplace nice with a view."

The 'good hotel' and 'someplace nice' the driver delivered him to, was the Siam Grande Palace, an old, but wonderfully maintained Colonial-style, stately six-storied affair that was proudly perched along the bank of the Chao Phraya River. The hotel's balcony view rooms, and especially its rooftop bar, overlooked the ancient and iridescent Wat Arun Buddhist Temple across the river. During the day the view of the Wat was impressive and something to appreciate while at night, lit up, and visually stunning, it became postcard perfect.

The Chao Phraya River that flowed from the country's central plains and eventually out into the Gulf of Thailand, also served as the city's main thoroughfare. Dragon tail boats, powered by roaring car engines kicking up rooster tails, sped up and down the river passing the much slower and many boat taxis and other commercial craft on the flowing Mississippi-like muddied water.

Climbing out of the taxi at the entrance of the hotel, Poplawski paid the fare and thanked the taxi driver with a nod and a good tip.

After checking in at the hotel desk and being handed his room key, Poplawski made his way across the air-conditioned lobby to a set of elevators while appreciating the genuine luxury of the placid setting. When the elevator door opened on the fifth floor, he ambled down a broad hallway and found his suite four doors down. Unlocking the door, he did a brief inspection of the hotel room from the tiled entryway and gave a more than satisfied nod to its polished teak furnishings, embroidered silk wall hangings, and its expansive view. Impressed with his lodging, he unpacked his AWOL bag, which was short work as it carried only a change of civilian clothes, socks, underwear, a shower kit, and a dog-eared copy of Ed McBain's 87th Precinct novel, *Hail, Hail, The Gang's All Here*.

Climbing out of his uniform, he hung it in the closet, grabbed his shaving kit, and opted for a long awaited, honest to God, actual shower, complete with a working shower nozzle, and an endless, steady stream of clean, hot water. The complimentary bar of lime smelling soap and set of fluffy cotton towels, matching hand towels, and washcloths the hotel provided only added to the feeling of opulence for this glorious, and all too often taken for granted activity. With the temperature outside hovering in the mid-90s and the humidity that felt like Mother Nature was weeping, the shower was a welcomed necessity. Back in Vietnam a shower happened under several repurposed 55-gallon fuel or defoliant barrels on a nearly even slab of not so clean concrete. The barrels were filled with lukewarm water you washed with, but didn't gargle, let alone drink. That is, if there was water, and if the nozzle wasn't dripping rust-colored sludge. The Army's thin and grating O-D green towels left a little to be desired too when it came to absorbency. Any shower at Camp Mackie was brief and outpost basic. During the monsoon season the heavy rains, at times, took the place of the indoor showers.

This shower was as much an event as it was a simple cleansing. Reaching behind the shower curtain he turned the water on to just below the HOT setting and let the shower run until it reached what he considered the right temperature. Testing the water temperature with his left hand he happily stepped inside. With a bowed head and hunched shoulders, he stood under the stream of soothing hot water for five wonderfully medicinal minutes before he went to work scrubbing every crack, crevice, and inch of his body with the hotel soap and washcloth. When he thought he was sufficiently clean, he turned off the shower stared up at the nozzle, and gave a deeply gratified, '*aahhhhhhh*!'

Drying himself off with one of the amazingly soft towels, he ambled over to the bed, peeled back the bed spread, and climbed in between the two spotlessly clean and fresh smelling sheets.

It was time for a tactical nap.

The nap was time sensitive and necessary because Bangkok during the high heat of day was frenzied chaos combined with sweat dripping pores for those navigating it. In the evening, though, when the temperature dropped to something more civil, the city transformed itself into a setting that celebrated both street commerce and life. There were crowded night markets, small but busy stalls on narrow streets and gloriously aromatic alleys that cooked up an interesting array of street food, any and every kind of open shop, storefront display, bar, and tourist entertainment delight imaginable, even a few that only this city itself could imagine. The Thais were a gracious people with an extraordinary culture. They had time and the talent to be unique and resourceful.

Leaning over to the nightstand he picked up the phone and called down to the Front Desk for a 9 p.m. wake-up call. Next, he set the alarm on the nightstand clock radio for the same time as a backup. Once done he leaned his head back against the duck down feather pillow and closed his eyes. His time in the army and especially in combat, had taught him how to sleep anywhere and at any time when the opportunity presented itself, since a soldier never knew when he would get another chance to do it, again. In his air-conditioned hotel room, on a firm mattress, with a comfortable pillow, between clean sheets, and after a relaxing shower, finding sleep became so much easier than he'd remembered. He was snoring within minutes.

In his odd *I can't explain how I do it* habit of waking up just prior to any alarm he had ever set, at five minutes to nine, he instantly came awake, staring and blinking at the ceiling, and then the clock radio. He yawned, stretched, and turned off the alarm that had been programmed to wake him. The unnecessary wake-up call from the Front Desk came a moment later. Climbing out of bed he shaved, brushed his teeth, and applied deodorant to his armpits before slapping on some Old Spice cologne to his face and neck.

As his one set of civilian clothes consisted of one pair of Lee jeans, a few tee-shirts and boxer shorts, one maroon long sleeve, western snap buttoned, long sleeve shirt and pair of Army low quarter dress shoes, he figured he'd supplement what he didn't have with short sleeve shirts, slacks, and more comfortable shoes he'd pick up in one of the many market stalls.

Once dressed, he tucked $700 U.S. in the left front pocket of his jeans and then shoved the $400 in Thai Baht in his right pocket. He then stuffed a pack of Marlboro cigarettes in his shirt pocket and his flip-top Zippo lighter into the coin pocket of his jeans. Checking himself out in the mirror, he shrugged and decided that it was as good as it was going to get.

"Yeah well, money in your pocket makes up for a whole lot of less than pretty," he laughed and grabbed his room key. It was time to head out.

Dropping the key off at the hotel's front desk, he hailed one of the many three-wheeled open cab Tuk-tuks at curbside and headed off into the warm Bangkok night towards the adult Disneyland that was Patpong.

There was money to spend and now only four more days to do it.

Fifteen roller coaster minutes later, in the laughably harrowing drive across town, where the Tuk-Tuk driver had seemed to play Dodgeball and Chicken against taxis and much bigger trucks, and had taken several corners teetering on two wheels, he was dropped off in front of the infamous, Red Light district. Paying the driver, he added in a tip, and stepped inside the very, very busy quarter.

In reality, the Patpong District was two long, brightly lit and neon gaudy, parallel side streets with little to no vehicle traffic. They were the infamous Patpong 1 and Patpong 2. The streets, no more than glorified high-troughed alleys really, were crammed and packed with open bars, massage parlors, dance clubs with bikini-clad Go-Go dancers and waitresses, small eateries, vendors selling knock offs of famous brand everything's, and a host of other loud and garish adult entertainments that would even make Las Vegas blush. The music coming from every bar, club, or adult attraction sounded like a bomb run of radios were being dropped on the district and were sending wave after blasting wave of Top 40 Pop, Soul, and Country/Western songs and raucous laughter out from the crowded establishments. Ambling on Poplawski was hit with musical fragments of each song and found himself humming to Tina Turner's take on Proud Mary that kept his big wheels turning as he walked.

Patpong was crowded with GIs and other *farangs*, many accompanied by smiling, young, scantily clad Thai women that worked the many bars and clubs in the district. The revealing tops and short dresses, coy glances or seductive smiles provided visual stimuli to the predominantly male clientele as the women cozied up to the visitors that were buying their time, their drinks, and especially the expensive *'champagne cocktails.'* Poplawski knew that the 'cocktails' were little more than ginger ale at $25 a pop with the women getting a cut of each drink sold, but that was all just part of the quid pro o-so-quo of the entertainment district.

While many GIs would take in the city's sights during the day, their nights would be spent trying to find something more friendly and sensual to take their minds off the stark brutality of the war they'd just left behind.

The Brick was no different. He took in the debauched atmosphere like a wide-eyed grinning fourteen-year-old who'd just discovered a Playboy magazine on his father's nightstand.

"Pretty Girl Naked Show?" said a smiling female hawker, sidling up to Poplawski from his right and pulling his elbow and arm into her warm, soft bosom while slowly stroking his broad chest over the left pocket of his shirt.

She was strategically dressed in a short mini-skirt, flowery peasant blouse with a low scoop neck and no bra and white go-go boots. She had Cher-like straight black hair, candy apple red lipstick, large gold-colored hoop earrings, and a pretty face hiding behind a little too much make-up. If she was a day over 18, thought Poplawski, then it wasn't by much.

"No, I'm good," he said smiling, while she tugged at him a little tighter.

"Come. You see. You like!" she said, trying to steer him towards a curtained doorway. "You be happy!"

Her smile was radiant with an unspoken promise of something more convincing on offer.

Beyond the curtain, *Let's Live for Today* by the Grass Roots was loudly driving the pulse of the entertainment inside and, of course, the hard sell.

Poplawski begged off, one more time.

"Maybe later," he said. "You are very pretty, but I'm really hungry, and I need to find something to eat first. I'll come back."

"You no come back," she said, pouting.

"No, I mean it. I'll come back."

"Pinky promise?" said the young woman holding out the crook of her little finger.

Poplawski locked the little finger of his right hand with hers.

"Promise," he said and shook on it with his little finger and hers interlocked and their thumbs pressed together to seal the deal. She chuckled as they shook semi-hands.

She went up on the balls of her shoes and dropped down on her heels. Her shoulders slumped, and her bottom lip went out.

"You promise, but I think you lie!" she said, with her bottom lip pushed out as she released his arm and gave him a playful slap on his left shoulder. "You no come back."

"Yeah, you're right. I lied about coming back for the show," admitted Poplawski, laughing. "But I am not lying when I say that you are very pretty."

"Then you come back for me!" she said, grabbing his arm again with a lusty grin. "You bar fine me."

"What's a bar fine?"

"You pay bar manager for me, and she let me go with you all night."

"All night? Naw, I'm too old. For that you need a younger man to be your boyfriend."

"I have a young man boyfriend. He no work. He lazy."

"Then he is stupid if he loses you, yes?"

"Yes," agreed the young woman, reappraising the American GI. "Then you come back later, no cover charge, if you sit with me. You buy me drink and who knows, maybe I kick my boyfriend out and teach you to love me better?"

"Who knows?" laughed Poplawski with a non-committal shrug as he moved back into the flow of the bustling crowd as the song, *All Day and All of the Night* by The Kinks seemed to have announced the hours and activities of the club as well as the District.

There were many attractive young girls in Patpong, Lady Boys too, and other hustlers vying for the attention of his wallet. Right now, though, and working from his mental checklist, his initial preference was for some decent Thai food before he settled into the city's very active nightlife distractions.

Ah, Bangkok, living for the day and all of the night.

His first day of R&R was proving to be promising.

Chapter 22

With both the Bangkok flight and hotel paid for by Uncle Sam, a young GI could have a good time in the city with a few hundred dollars. For a not-so-young GI in his early 30's like Poplawski, the $1,100 insured that besides finding a better hotel of his own choosing, there would also be enough to cover all of the grand merriment and revelry he was so planning on doing on his R&R, with plenty left over for a tailor-made sports coat and a pairs of slacks, a few nice dress shirts, a silk tie or two, a custom pair of better shoes, and maybe even a brand new, $250 Rolex watch or, in the very least, a cheap $25 knock-off that had Japanese movements and had spelled Rolex correctly.

Now, though, he just wanted something good to eat. One block away from Patpong he was drawn to a little sidewalk Mom & Pop eatery by the '*come hither*' savory aroma and wafting smoke from some wonderfully flavored pork, tangy shrimp, and lime juice drenched chicken grilling over a bed of burning charcoal. A stooped and bent old woman was tending a sizzling wok perched over a gas burner that held some delectable looking noodles and a colorful assortment of onions, garlic, carrots, cilantro, broccoli, and thin, red chili peppers while an old man, who was probably her husband, was doing the grilling. If the food was half as good as it smelled, then he wouldn't be disappointed that he'd taken a seat at one of the three small tables.

Setting the cooked meat and shrimp aside the old man presented Poplawski with a single page, laminated menu and welcomed him with his gnarled hands on his thin chest in the traditional wai Thai prayer-like posture greeting with a *Sawadee Krab* and bowed head, Poplawski slapped his hands together, nodded and added a *Sawatdee krab* response along with a grin and a follow up order for beer.

"Chang beer?" asked the old man, recommending the local brew.

Poplawski nodded. Chang was a good Thai beer, and it would do just fine.

"*Chai*," he said, using the Thai word for yes. Besides the Thai greeting, he also memorized the Thai word, *mai chai*, meaning no or no thank you, figuring those two words and a lot of pointing would carry him through his time in the city.

The old man gave Poplawski a wide smile and left him to pore over the menu that consisted of four pictured main dishes and a small number of appetizers.

When the beer came it was chilled and very much appreciated. Taking a quick sip, he ordered an appetizer of grilled chicken on bamboo skewers that came with a spicy blend of coconut and peanut sauce and a small dipping dish of chopped up cucumbers and hot peppers in a sweet rice wine mix. For his main course he smiled and thumped the picture of *Pad kee mao*, Drunken Noodles.

When she heard the American's order, the old woman smiled, too. There was money to be made with this big American.

Poplawski had almost finished the first beer as the chicken skewers were served, so he held up the near empty glass pointing to it and to the empty skewers to silently call for another round of each. By the time his dinner was served he was on his third beer.

The dish was piled high and steaming with an aroma that had his mouth salivating like a lawn sprinkler. The mound of Drunken Noodles were broad rice noodles, flavored with ginger, garlic, onions, fish sauce, and chicken in rice wine and mixed with fresh basil and baby corn. The rising aroma held down by the pressing humidity lingered wonderfully near his nostrils and worked its magic.

He dug into the Drunken Noodles wielding his chopsticks like a happy weed whacker before ordering a fourth beer midway through the meal. When he finished his dinner with a satisfied belch, the old woman gave him a smiling thumbs-up.

"Excellent!" Poplawski said, returning the gesture and meaning it.

Leaning back in his chair the Ranger First Sergeant took in the busy street life and marveled at its flowing chaos. The old man was at his side again, this time pointing to a picture of a dessert on the flip side of the laminated menu.

"You want?" asked the old man, pointing to the picture of a plate of Mango sticky rice.

"You bet! *Chai*!" he said happily nodding, and then before the old man went to retrieve the desert he added, "Oh, and one more Chang!"

The old woman smiled again.

The beer and the dessert arrived together. The plate of mango sticky rice came complete with a small purple and white orchid flower that brought yet one more a grin to the American's face.

"Truly a feast of perfection in taste and presentation," Poplawski said, after taking a first bite and closing his eyes with a loud enough, *Mmm Mmm* moan of edible joy for both the old man and old woman to hear.

The small mound of sweet rice in coconut milk, sugar, and topped with toasted sesame seeds was surrounded by tiny, cut cubes of fresh honey mango, but not for long. Poplawski finished the dessert off in possibly record time.

He paid his bill, and even if the old woman that took his money didn't understand what the American had said about how good the food was or how nice and pleasing it looked, she understood his tone, smile, and the more than generous tip.

Comfortably satiated, he made a mental note to visit the sidewalk cafe again on the second night of his R&R as he strolled over to a nearby outdoor night market to walk off some of the meal and seek out another local specialty. Eight stalls into the market he found what he was looking for. After sampling a free shot of the merchandise that went down with not so much a warm glow as it was a slow burn with a fishy aftertaste, *The Brick* Poplawski gave a nod to the seller. The nod signaled for the show to begin. It was now time to take his role in the Three Act haggling play that followed.

Act One- the vendor started high with the asking price saying it was the best he could do. Act Two- the stern-faced Poplawski, looking violated, shook his head in disgust and countered with a much lower offer, and finally Act Three- after a wail, woe, and pained expression that came with a lower selling price, Poplawski raised his previous offer. The seller reluctantly gave in to the give and take script of the street theater negotiations, and the two finally reached an agreed upon price for the large bottle of Snake Wine.

That the vendor had initially asked for $20 U.S. dollars for the Snake Wine and that the haggling had brought it down to $12 was actually a win-win for both of them since the seller was ready to let it go for $6.

This particular batch was locally produced and came in clear liter bottles. The rice wine, which was seasoned with herbs, ginseng, and some grain alcohol, also came with three to four small, but highly venomous snakes coiled and intertwined inside the bottle to add the alleged aphrodisiac prowess to the mix. For a better show and selling point, a small Cobra inside the bottle that Poplawski had purchased had toothpicks holding the snake's flared hood up and in place, as though poised to strike. The reptiles, that were the wine's primary ingredient, were purported to infuse the drink with stimulating qualities for men of any age.

"Make your *lungkh* stand up like flagpole!" laughed the seller, while Poplawski grunted as he studied the snakes through the amber colored liquor and tapped on the bottle just to make sure that the snakes weren't just holding their breaths, biding their time, and only playing dead. Because he didn't know all that much of the Thai language, he guessed that the Thai word, *Lungkh* that sounded like loon to him meant, *pecker* as the vendor was cupping his crotch and smiling as he said it.

Poplawski had heard about Snake Wine from Billy Mezza, who assured him that it would greatly enhance a man's sexual performance, if it didn't kill him in the process. He was told that live snakes, and the more dangerous, the better, were often dropped into the alcohol mix to better steep the wine with its near magical powers.

"Just make sure you buy a good brand of Snake Wine and not some cheap Mama-san bathtub mix," Mezza said, when he cautioned him back at the Safe House in Saigon.

"The venom proteins need adequate time to break down, usually a month or thereabouts. Also, and I don't know if this is bullshit or not, but that since snakes hibernate, it's possible one of the snakes inside the bottle might even still be alive in a recent batch of the brew."

"Alive?"

"Uh-huh. One story making the rounds is that one of the snakes latched onto the drinker's lower lip as he was taking a swig, so no drinking directly out of the bottle, either."

"Some story, so what's a good brand?"

"Preferably one with a clean bottle that ain't chipped, and has an actual printed label," said his friend. "Oh, and it's 80 to 90 Proof, so there's a kick..."

"Whoa!"

"Uh-huh and tastes like crap, by the way, but hey, when in Rome..."

"Well, who can argue with those fine selling points?"

So that it wouldn't frighten others if they caught a glimpse of the snakes through the glass bottle as he walked around the night market and the city's streets of Bangkok, the vendor tossed the bottle in a small brown cloth, shoulder bag for an easier carry.

From the night market to a street-side bar where he sneaked in two shots of Snake Wine from the cloth bag in between two Salty Dogs, Walter, *'The Brick,' as in wall, just don't ever fucking call me Walter,'* Poplawski, was pushing a happy buzz. Feeling better than he had in a long while, he started making his way back to Patpong in wobbly search of The Bangkok Social Center that Billy Mezza's SOG brothers had recommended.

His R&R, he granted, was off to a good start.

It took a little scouting, but he finally found the Social Center halfway down the second, very busy *trok* or alley of the infamous district, inside a small passageway that led out to Surawong Road. Unlike the many massage parlors, Go-Go Bars, loud bars, countless clubs, and assorted vendors that crowded the alley, the Bangkok Social Center was set back away from the busy passageway in a surprisingly somewhat more quiet and secluded setting. Other than a small brass plaque attached to the wall next to a teak and polished brass door that identified the four-storied center, there was nothing more to suggest what the center was, or what took place inside.

The door was manned by what Poplawski took to be a former Muay Thai light heavyweight kickboxer outfitted in a black suit, black tie, a crisp white shirt, highly polished black shoes, scarred knuckles, and a slightly bent nose. The doorman smiled with a nod to the *farang* he recognized as a fellow warrior and opened the door for the GI. As he passed the doorman Poplawski slipped him a U.S. $5 bill and received a thankful nod in return.

Through the doorway was a slate tiled foyer that was lined with red satin wallpaper and gold trim that gave way to a check-in concierge counter just to the left of the entrance. The counter was the gateway to the establishment proper. A large mirror was on the wall behind the counter while an open doorway peeked through heavy maroon curtains. Poplawski deduced the mirror was likely two-way and that the curtains hid the social center's office.

To the right of the counter a highly polished hallway led to a dimly lit lounge and what, at first glance, appeared to be a well-stocked bar. Discreet nooks, partially out of view, showed a dozen or so customers that were enjoying the intimate company of some very attractive hostesses. Slow jazz was softly being played through speakers mounted on the walls. To the left of the counter was a second hallway leading to restrooms and an elevator along the back wall.

With a prayer-like *wai* greeting, head bow, and *Sawatdee krab*, accompanied by a warm smile, the attractive young woman behind the counter welcomed the visitor to the Center as she pointed to a sign on a waist high stand that listed its services, along with their corresponding prices. A notice at the bottom of the sign in large, bold block print in English, Japanese, and Thai announced that there was a $50 cover charge to enter the Center. Poplawski suspected that the high cover charge was there to keep out the riff raff, or at least the riff raff without money. A second Muay Thai light heavyweight in a dark suit, standing at his assigned post nearby, was waiting to toss out on their ears anyone entering the Social Center without paying the entry fee, confirmed it.

Poplawski smiled back at the hostess with a *Sawadee Ka* as he pulled out his thick roll of baht bills.

"Seems reasonable to me! Here you go, young lady," he said, peeling off what he figured was the exchange rate fee of the colorful script.

As the young woman took the money and tried to hand him back a few of the bills, Poplawski shook his head and waved it off. The young woman behind the counter smiled again and thanked him for the tip while his eyes settled on the sign that announced the center's services. The sign showed that the lounge, bar, and restaurant were on the main floor, with saunas, steam bath, and massage rooms on the second floor, while guest rooms for casual or all-night stays with '*Extra Services'* could be found on the two upper floors. He was still going over the sign when a comely looking, early forty-something woman pushed through the curtains behind the desk, sauntered around the reception desk, and greeted him with a pleased look that oozed sensuality. Here was the house manager and Madam, and she was a looker.

"Hello and welcome! How may we enter-tang you, sir?" said the Madam. She spoke with semi-broken Old School British English made more charming by her sultry Thai accent and the slight mispronunciation of the word, *entertain*.

"How about with something interesting that'll keep me grinning long after I leave your wonderful establishment and city?"

"I believe we do have that something," said the Madam, laughing and guiding him towards the lounge. "Two somethings, if you wish your visit to be more memorable!"

"Two?"

Poplawski hesitated because he wouldn't have minded spending some serious time with the Madam for it to be truly memorable. She was attractive, stylish, and wonderfully inviting enough to make even Quasimodo enjoy his hump. Her round face was framed by an expensive Page Boy Flip hairdo held firmly in place by a can or two of hairspray, and she smelled faintly of rare, exotic flowers. Poplawski guessed that her perfume had to be $120 an ounce and not a baht less. She wore a seductive smile over ruby red lipstick, and her makeup, eyeliner, and eyeshadow were expertly applied for ambush. It was all highlighted and enhanced by gold and pearl earrings with a matching necklace, and a form fitting black dress that displayed deep and tactical cleavage.

With the alcohol buzz he already had going for him, Poplawski was sorely tempted to lean in and yell, *Hellllooooo* just to see if there was a pleasant echo, but figured that might get him bounced out the door. So instead, like most men that came into the Center and were greeted by her, he gave her a goofy smile and an awkward nod of joyful appreciation as she hooked one arm and bosom into his arm and led him over to several attractive late twenty-somethings seated on a settee in a nearby alcove just to the left of the lounge.

"May I suggest a two hour visit with extra services, yes?"

"Well, I'd like to think they don't call us servicemen for nothing, so yes, you may."

She rattled off something in Thai that brought the two women eagerly up and towards the ruggedly good looking American GI, made even more appealing after he pulled out his bankroll of dollars and agreed to pay the $200 the Madam had requested, for what she assured him would be a most memorable visit.

"This is Silly," she said, introducing the first young woman who gave the American the traditional wai greeting.

"Silly?"

"Yes, you know, like the Wilson Pickett song, *Mustang Silly.*"

"Ah yes, like the song," echoed Poplawski, mispronouncing the name Sally as well.

"Her name is Silly, too," said the Madam, introducing the second woman who greeted him traditionally as well.

"Well then, silly me!" Poplawski said, and handed over the agreed upon fee. The Madam counted the money and when she was satisfied it was all there, she smiled again, patted his shoulder, and nodded to the women who took over where she had left off.

Silly #1 was dressed in a tight fitting, short black dress and three-inch heels that brought her smile up almost parallel to his. A string of pearls with matching earrings highlighted a pretty face.

Silly #2 was also in a short, form-fitting dress, only hers was hot pink with a broad white belt. No pearls here, just faux diamond-studded earrings, matching pendant, and a well-practiced smile that promised fulfillment of any desire.

"Silly is good, I think. Now you no forget their names and they no forget yours, but you laugh, and have a very good time," said the Madam. With a nod from the Madam the receptionist handed her a room key that she, in turn, handed over to Silly #1 before the two women led him towards the elevator. Poplawski, though, stopped a few steps on and turned back to the Madam.

"Can we get a bottle of Champagne and three glasses?"

The Madam nodded and then held out an open palm as the two women waited until Poplawski fished out his thick roll of Thai Baht and peeled off enough of the bills until she laughed and told him to stop.

"That is enough," she said. "Thank you."

Poplawski winked. "You're welcome."

The dollar to baht exchange rate was well in favor of any GI's budget, and he figured the tab to be a little under $40. It was expensive for the time, but not the setting, and still fell well within his R&R budget.

A young waitress delivered the champagne and three long-stemmed glasses to the trio as they waited by the elevator. Silly #1 took the glasses while Silly #2 took the Champagne bottle and the cheerful party rode the small elevator up to the Fourth floor, ambled down a dimly lit hallway, and found the room at the end of the hall.

When Silly#1 unlocked and opened the door, Poplawski was not all that surprised to find a small, but spotlessly clean room that had the same gaudy red wallpaper and gold trim as the foyer.

The bulk of the room was taken up by a King sized, heart-shaped bed, a small bedside end table, and a settee. An open closet held only a comfortable-looking monogrammed bathrobe on a wooden coat hanger and a pair of slippers on the tiled floor. Through the open doorway of the bathroom, he could see a small open shower area and a bathtub that was the size of a hot tub.

Fresh rose petals littered the bed and added an element of pretend romance to what Poplawski suspected was actually going to be more like an innovative wrestling workout.

"Well now, this will do just fine!" he said, grinning, as Silly #1 led him over to the bed while Silly #2 closed the door behind them.

Popping the cork on the bottle of champagne she began filling the glasses.

What the room lacked with air conditioning it made up with pleasantly cool air circulating from an overhead teak paddled ceiling fan.

Setting the brown cloth shoulder bag with the Snake Wine on the nightstand, Poplawski turned back and smiled as Silly #1 began undressing while helping him to do the same. Meanwhile, Silly #2 had started the bath and was testing the temperature of the water with a hand before she poured the bubble bath into the large tub.

As Poplawski was undressing, Silly #1 said something in Thai to Silly #2, who left the bath water running, chuckled, nodded, and left the room.

"No worry! She come back for good fun. First, we take bath!" said Silly #1, assuring him all was well and on schedule.

Out of her high heels Silly #1 came up to his chin and out of her dress she showed wonderfully curvy caramel colored skin and a fit body. Her lipstick was as red as the wallpapered walls, and as she leaned in, Poplawski caught the fragrance of a floral bouquet. After they finished undressing, a giggling Silly #1 led him to the big tub.

When Silly #2 returned to the room, she came back carrying a large, modified bamboo wicker basket with an attached sling and rope that she set down beside the bed. Spying the two in the tub and happily humming as she undressed, she joined Poplawski and Silly #1 with flutes of champagne in the tub for some scrubbing playtime fun.

Poplawski was thinking that any bath that came after this one in the Bangkok Social Center would never be able to measure up to what he was now experiencing.

When the bath time play ended, the Champagne bottle had been emptied, and some new games were about to commence, the two Sillies dried him off with soft cotton towels before escorting him back to the king-sized bed.

"You lay down there," said Silly #1, smiling as she leaned over and patted the center of the bed as Silly #2 set a large laundry-size wicker basket on the foot of the bed, and the two women then discussed the best way to set it up and proceed.

"Yes, Ma'am," said Poplawski to the playful ladies.

The wicker basket had a padded opening in its center and was fitted with a sling-like harness attached to specially designed loops on its reinforced rim. Standing, Silly #1 straddled Poplawski as she secured the rope to the sling harness and handed the end of the rope to Silly #2. Silly #2 turned off the ceiling fan, and then reaching up she secured the other end of the rope to several supports built into the fan's wooden paddles.

Poplawski's excitement was growing, as was his taste for the Snake Wine. He'd only heard about the famed Thai Basket Trick and his mind was whirling with erotic possibilities.

The two giggling women were joyful engineers as they pulled on the rope and tested the basket that was now resting just above the prone American soldier. Pleased with their engineering and social engineering skills, the two women took their starting positions.

Buzzed as he was, Poplawski decided that maybe he needed a little more of the Snake Wine to help enhance what was about to happen. Reaching over to the nightstand, he grabbed the bag, unscrewed the top of the bottle inside, and took a questionably healthy big gulp.

The alcohol level in the bottle was dropping and the remaining wine sloshed around in the jar making it appear that one of the undulating venomous snakes was rising to the surface to bite him. Remembering Billy Mezza's cautionary snake story, Poplawski quickly screwed the top back on the bottle. He wasn't certain if the two Thai women would be frightened by the snakes in the bottle, but decided not to chance it, so he closed the shoulder bag tight around the neck of the bottle.

Wincing at the wine's fishy aftertaste, he started to feel a twinge down below, and immediately forgave the unusual flavor.

"Happy! Happy! Happy!" he said, chuckling.

"Happy good," said Silly #1, climbing into the wicker basket, laughing, and giving him the okay sign that all was ready.

Well, almost.

As Silly #1 worked herself into the starting position Silly #2 used the dimmer switch to lower the light in the room and then flipped the switch for the ceiling fan to the ON position. She was back in bed and soon at play as the basket slowly began to spin, as did the excitement in Poplawski's mind.

"Wait! Wait!" he said, wanting to get into what he thought was a better working angle.

Taking hold of the reinforced edges of the wicker basket with both hands, he pulled himself up so he could shift his body weight to where he thought it might be put to better use. He was almost where he wanted to be, but not quite.

"No, no, no, no!" said Silly #1 as he reached up to pull on the basket a second time.

"No, it's okay, sweetie. It's okay. I'll guide this bird in!" said Poplawski, pulling on the basket a second time as he shifted his body beneath it with considerably more effort and strength.

Any twirling festivity and sensual innovation came to an immediate halt by a loud, horrendous crack as Poplawski's second muscling pull brought Silly #1 in the wicker basket, the twirling paddle fan and wiring, and a large section of the ceiling and loose plaster crashing down onto the bed.

Drunk as he was his fighting instincts were still in reasonably working order. In the microsecond before the ceiling and everything with it came crashing down he managed to shove both of the women off the bed and out of the way with him following. But as they all tumbled and fell, one of the three's flailing arms bumped against the nightstand and knocked over the cloth bag holding the bottle of Snake Wine.

The large glass bottle shattered as it hit the tiled floor and sent the dead snakes scattering from the bag and sliding across the room. The toothpick-flared cobra landed just inches in front of Silly #2 after she had bounced off the bed and ended up upside down facing the snake. The petrified naked woman let out a bone-chilling scream at the sight of a cobra and the perceived imminent threat. Jumping to her feet she raced out of the room and down the hallway naked and wide-eyed screaming and crying as she ran.

When Silly #1 fell off the bed still inside the basket, the left cheek of her rump was pricked by a small shard of broken glass. Believing she'd just been bitten by one of the deadly snakes, she grabbed her bleeding butt cheek, let out a loud piercing cry that very possibly shattered fine crystal champagne glasses on the outskirts of Prague, and ran sobbing to the bathroom to check on her puncture wound and dying fate.

The terrible noise and clamor from the collapsing ceiling, aided by the piercing screams and cries of the two women brought other curious ladies and patrons out into the hallway as well as an angry looking bouncer who was barreling towards the open doorway of the American's room. The bouncer was soon followed by the Center's none-too-happy looking Madam. A short time later two Thai Policemen arrived on scene with guns drawn, alternately aimed at the dangerous looking long dead snakes and the drunk GI covered in plaster dust and torn bits of ceiling insulation.

The show was over and all that was left was counting up the box office receipts in the crowded room.

After a considerable amount of shouting by the two crying Sillies, and haggling over an abacus by the Madam, and after the Policemen had finished counting out the U.S. dollars and Thai Baht in his jeans, it was agreed that, in lieu of going to jail, the crestfallen American would pay $250 to repair the damage to the room and a $200 fine for the disorderly disturbance call. In addition, he would also pay the two Sillies $100 each, as consolation for any physical or emotional pain they had suffered by his careless and negligent actions.

There would be no bartering, so Poplawski shelled out the money. Given the Tuk-tuk ride, the street food dinner, the Snake Wine purchase, assorted drinks, and tips that left him with just under $100 to cover the Tuk-tuk ride back to his hotel, his one-day stay at the hotel, and a little left over for another Tuk-tuk to get him to the R&R Center in the morning. He figured that when he got to the airport he might have enough left over for a cup of coffee or a beer but wasn't counting on it.

Because one or two young GIs were always overstaying their R&Rs in Bangkok, there usually were a few open seats on the return flight to the war zone the following morning. At the R&R departure desk, a hung-over Poplawski asked if he could get one of those empty seats for a plane ride back to Vietnam.

"You...you want to leave your R&R four days early?" asked the much-perplexed NCO that was working the desk.

"Yeah, I'm good," said Poplawski. "Burned through $1,100 pretty damn quickly."

"$1,100!"

Poplawski shrugged. "Made for one interesting night, though."

"And you're not on the run from the Thai police or trying to skip out on any unpaid hotel bill or bar tabs? We can check, you know."

"No, scout's honor, all's good," said Poplawski, crossing his heart and then adjusting his Ranger beret and winking at a good-looking stewardess walking by. The stewardess returned his smile and walked on. "But you can check if you want. No problem. Go ahead."

The NCO checked and when Poplawski's name didn't appear on the MP's or Thai Police overnight incident reports, he gave a confused shrug and called the Ranger back to the R&R desk.

"Okay sergeant," said the bewildered NCO. "It's your call. I'll get you on the next flight out."

The plane departed Bangkok at 11 a.m. and after a short flight he was back at the Tan Son Nhut airport in Saigon. From Saigon he made his way up to Bien Hoa where he checked into the military airfield terminal hoping to find a flight back to Camp Mackie. Luck was with him, and likely the luck that somehow eluded him on his ill-fated R&R, and he found an outbound helicopter that agreed to give him a lift.

The pilot, a captain, whose name tag read: Scott, saw Poplawski's AWOL bag and commented on it.

"Leave or R&R?"

"R&R," said Poplawski. "Bangkok.

The helicopter pilot broke into a grin as did his crew chief overhearing the conversation. "Bangkok! Wow! I've only heard the stories about Patpong. Did you get there?”

“I did.”

The Pilot’s smile widened. “Whoa Ranger, why do I bet you tore that place up and then some?"

"Goes without saying,” Poplawski said, wanly, so he didn’t.

Chapter 23

His map and compass were his lifelines. Studying the mission map under the red glow of his flashlight and taking a compass reading, Sergeant Darrell Thomas looked around, glanced back at the mountain, and ballparked his current location. Doing the math, he figured the Tay Ninh Basecamp was eight miles away, nine maybe. Tops.

Standing just inside the edge of the rainforest and facing the dirt road that ran from Tay Ninh City, skirted the mountain, and then went further north to the Cambodian border, the Texan contemplated his next move. The road was empty. Of course, it was. These days, there was no traffic, and seldom was.

It wasn't much of a roadway either and calling it such would mess with the mindset of anyone who had a working understanding of what a country or city road should be. In some places the jungle paralleling the roadway had been bulldozed 100-yards back so that previous ambush sites and potential ambush sites could be made ineffective, or at least less effective. The jungle, on the other hand, had other notions, and was slowly creeping its way towards the battered road again as brush and small trees began to sprout and spring up in random clumps while creeping vines worked to reclaim its stolen ground.

The route was rutted, heavily potholed, and long absent of any repair work. There were more than a few large craters too, courtesy of Soviet anti-tank mines and the military vehicles they'd targeted. In the rain the road became a slick, slip-and-slide with deep pockets of orange mud, while in the scorching heat, and with anything resembling a slight breeze, it became a stirred-up dust bowl where only a spiraling dust devil could dance undisturbed.

It was also a toll road for the Viet Cong and NVA that patrolled and monitored it. The toll it exacted over the years of fighting was steep, so much so that the U.S. Army had established a series of Fire Support Bases along its route through the jungle covered countryside to better protect and safeguard the province.

The line of Fire Support Bases with their artillery batteries of 105mm and 155mm cannons, light and heavy mortars, machine guns, and determined grunts had sent thousands of Viet Cong guerilla and main force North Vietnamese Army soldiers to their ancestors in bloodied bits, either in support of the infantry units in the surrounding jungle or in repeated direct assaults on the small outposts. The fights were never one sided and Americans and South Vietnamese Army soldiers who defended the bases, the road, and jungle area had also paid dearly.

After the sanctioned incursion into Cambodia that began at the end of April in 1970 and a second go in the following year the Offensive had succeeded in pushing back the tide of any major Viet Cong and North Vietnamese Army operations in the province. The tide, however, was slowly turning again.

With U.S. and allied units withdrawing from South Vietnam and Fire Support Bases being shut down and abandoned, the Viet Cong and North Vietnamese Army units were regrouping and once again moving larger numbers of soldiers and war-making materials south.

The border area provinces, like Tay Ninh, Binh Long, and Phuoc Long, were beginning to feel the effects of the resurgence. The enemy units weren't back in full force yet, but they soon would be, and in overwhelming numbers. Thomas was still very much behind enemy lines.

Eight, nine miles is do-able, he thought, bouncing his strategies and plans off himself while looking at his map again, plotting possible routes, and voicing his own inner suspicions. *That's what? An easy fifteen to eighteen minutes a mile? I could make it in no time using the road. No trouble at all. Piece of cake!*

The thing he also knew about talking to himself was that tiny voice in the back of his brain that could also hold a decent counter argument to any of his best-laid plans.

"*Uh-uh, dumbass, no road,*" said the tiny voice, *"Follow it and you'll probably be captured or killed in no time. Hey, remember that time at that amateur rodeo event in Belton, after a few shots and beers, and a little goading and laughing reassurance from one or two of your compadres, you figured, what the hell, you'd give it a try. So, how'd that work out for you, pardner?*

Thomas snickered, recalling the memory. *"Two seconds out of the chute, I got tossed off the back of the bull faster than a used car salesman with a smoked down Marlboro could zero in on an old man, with a much younger big chested platinum blonde honey on his arm, kicking the tires of a drop-top Caddy! Not to mention that the pissed off bull damn near stomped the piss out of me for even pretending I could ever earn a belt buckle."*

"Yep," said the tiny voice recalling the memory enough to unconsciously have the Texan rubbing his left shoulder which had hurt for a good week afterwards. *"That's how I remember it too. So, your plan is..."*

"*To stay in the tree line of the jungle and parallel the road?"*

"*Good call, Ace! Go for it!*"

Thumbing his red-filtered flashlight back to life, he took one more compass heading and married it up with his map and the road to get his bearings, just to be sure. The basecamp in Tay Ninh was big, acres upon acres, small town big, complete with a main runway, several smaller flight lines, hundreds of hootches and buildings, artillery emplacements, mortar pits, and enough bunkers and fighting positions for a Division and then some, all wrapped in enough barbed wire, he suspected, to surround Dallas! Even if he was off by five or six football fields with where he thought he was on the map, he could still bump into it, if he could manage to avoid any enemy search parties or patrols along the way.

He moved on knowing it hadn't hurt his getaway by wearing an NVA pith helmet, the East German camouflage poncho, and carrying the AK. He was still of a mind that at a distance and even closer, say at a quick glance, any VC or NVA soldier might easily mistake him for one of them. It had worked inside the mountain in the storage chamber so he didn't see any reason why it might not fool a few others now. Still, he was reluctant to chance being seen. He'd remain hidden and keep an eye out for anything out of the ordinary, which in a war zone, in a jungle older than recorded history, left a lot of room for imagination.

Editing the earlier scenario that played out in his head on how when he got close to the basecamp, he'd dump the pith helmet, poncho, and the assault rifle, he was now thinking that maybe he'd hold onto the AK. That he wouldn't give up until he absolutely had to.

There was rain in the air, and he could smell it. It was coming and when it did the helmet and poncho would offer him a better chance at staying a little warmer and dryer than without them. Wet and cold as he was likely to be throughout the night, he welcomed the rain, and hoped that it would start to fall hard, heavy, and soon.

The rain, and any wind that accompanied it, would blow down leaves or branches, and cover much of the sign he'd made moving through the jungle. It would also reduce the noise of his getaway. And there would be noise because anytime anyone moved through the bush at night in the dark, Viet Cong and NVA included, they were bound to bump into low hanging tree limbs, snap old and thin, dry branches, or get clawed at by the prickly underbrush and stalled or momentarily hung up by more than a few *wait-a-minute* vines while crying out, swearing, or uttering other oaths.

It helped that soldiers in any and every army tended to get careless in the rain too, not exactly letting down their guard, but more like lowering their heads in a downpour and getting lost in better, if not, dryer thoughts. That, too, would aid his getaway.

A half-mile into his trek he came to a small clearing and went around it. On the far side of the open area, he glanced back at the mountain. The sun was down behind the Nui Ba Den and night hadn't just fallen, it collapsed. In what meager light there was from the waning moon that had shown through the broken clouds, the outline of the mountain was visible as only a dark, hulking mass in silhouette.

He was hoping to find the Nui Ba Den dark and quiet, but any hope that showed on his face and shoulders slumped and fell when he saw a few flashlights bobbing and blinking back towards the tunnel entrance. The number of the bobbing flashlights were growing. The hunters were coming out of the mountain and fanning out looking for him and the way he went. The alert had gone out and the frantic search was on for the American *Ghost soldier*.

Thomas' heart was racing as he watched the bobbing flashlights, gambling that they hadn't yet found which way he went. The bulk of the flashlights in the search party seemed to be heading up the side of the mountain where he set the false trail while several others were spreading out from it on both sides of the tunnel opening in the most likely routes someone fleeing might take. Two, though, were working their way down towards the rockslide.

"Uh-uh! No, no, no," he muttered. "Go back up to your buddies. Do it, damn it! DO IT!"

The plea fell on the Black Virgin's deaf or indifferent ears. The two bobbing flashlights were milling around the top of the rockslide area for far longer than he wanted. He couldn't see what those few soldiers were doing, but he heard what one had done. One of the searchers just above the rockslide area fired a single round from his assault rifle into the air telling the others that they'd found the way he'd taken.

He was well aware that the Viet Cong and NVA had often used a single shot from a rifle as a signal to bring others to the location where the shot had been fired. Judging from the way the other flashlights were hurriedly bobbing their way towards the one who'd fired the round and began bunching up like frenzied ants, the posse would soon be tracking his run. Neither the single signal shot nor the bobbing flashlights would arouse much attention back up on the Relay Station. It would be noted in an overnight report and maybe written off by everyone except those tracking him.

A good tracker would pick up signs in daylight; a better one would be able to follow it in the dark. Thomas hoped for the former and went back to hoping even more for the rain to hurry up and start falling to help throw off a good or better tracker.

On dry ground he knew they'd quickly bridge the time and distance gap to zero in on him. First though, they would have to work their way down through the ankle twisting, ordnance driven rockslide area like he had done, and that would buy him some more precious time.

The time, though, sped up when he saw several flashlights to the northwest of the mountain showed a smaller, second line of pursuers working their way through the jungle and looking to block the route west of the basecamp. Those on the mountain had radioed their counterparts below to search for him.

"Shit! Shit! Shit!" Thomas swore, as the NVA began spreading a wider net.

The net was tightening, but not yet closed. Since he was not that far from the road, he tried another ploy. Busting brush, he ran back out to the road and crossed it at an angle, purposely leaving as many sandal prints and noticeable scrapes and scuff marks as he could for the searchers to find. He was kicking himself for not setting the boobytrap back up on the rockslide, but took some solace knowing the scree would slow them down considerably anyway.

On the other side of the road, he ran west towards the basecamp as fast as he could go for two hundred huffing and puffing yards before he stopped well short of the enemy soldiers that were searching the jungle. Tossing an M-16 magazine onto the road he raised the AK-47 skyward he fired off a single shot.

"Rally here, boys!" he whispered, rolling the verbal dice.

To help throw the search party off a little more he took another one of his M-16 magazines out of an ammo pouch and flung it on the road further west, where it bounced, tumbled, and skidded to a stop. The NVA would have no problem spotting it. The brass and copper jacketed 5.56mm rounds pushing out of the gunmetal colored magazine would stand out, if not completely in the dark, then certainly in the morning and the more reflective light of day.

That would be fine by me, thought the Texan as he turned back around and carefully slipped back into the jungle. Leaving as little sign as possible, he headed in the opposite direction.

He felt that move might buy him a little more time. While the searchers would blanket the road to Tay Ninh, he'd be moving well away from it. Who knows, he thought, the signal rifle shots and bobbing flashlights had to have attracted some attention from the Relay Station, so maybe they'd call for a helicopter Pink Team to come and check it out at first light? Then again, maybe they'd treat it as just another night on the back of the grumbling beast.

With his eyes trained on his compass again the Texan figured that the best route, or at least one around the net the searchers were casting, was a few miles out of the way and to the south. It might take a little longer to reach the Tay Ninh Basecamp, but it was a safer option.

Four hundred paces on by his reckoning he stopped at the edge of the jungle near the road one more time. When he was reasonably sure no one was waiting to shoot him, he made his way back across the road, cleared the open space, and then slowed his pace as he went back into the jungle.

There was a tactical line of old and long abandoned grunt Fire Support Bases that were still shown on the map. The nearest one from the quick glance at the map earlier showed that it was Fire Support Base Grant or Ike. The name didn't matter. The location did.

The flight path for the helicopters out of Cambodia and into the Tay Ninh Basecamp often used the road as a visual guide, so maybe he wouldn't have a long trek back, after all. Maybe one of the gunships, low birds, or Hueys using it would spot him and bring him out.

It was worth a shot and, hopefully, one that wouldn't get him shot.

Thomas knew that some people liked to think that war was a game of chess, but he often thought that it was as simple as checkers at times. You just had to position yourself to stay a jump or two ahead of your opponent. The NVA wouldn't expect him to head towards the abandoned fire support base, so it seemed like a good working plan, and this time the tiny voice inside his head didn't disagree. And, if no helicopter spotted him at the old outpost the following day, then he'd begin working his way to the south before turning back to the west and Tay Ninh.

He hadn't wanted to move through the night because of the many potential hazards and pitfalls it presented, but there wasn't a choice. He didn't need the flashlight paralleling the road, but once he stepped back into the dark jungle it would become useful again. The red filter lens on his flashlight was ten times more effective in reducing the likelihood that anyone nearby would spot it over a clear lens in the dark. It also gave him just enough light to avoid any obstacles.

Shouldering the AK-47 he reached up and grabbed the flashlight from his shoulder harness and thumbed the ON switch. The red filtered light came on, flickered briefly, and went out. He tried turning it on again and got the same result.

"Oh, are you kidding me!" he said, thumbing it off and on with no effect before he began banging the flashlight against the palm of his freehand a few times and trying to get it to work.

Nothing.

Unscrewing the battery housing, he slid out the batteries, wiped off the positive and negative ends as best he could, and then shoved them back inside the housing, and screwed the cap shut tight.

He thumbed the ON switch.

Still nothing.

The batteries were dead.

"*Well now, Mrs. Kennedy, other than that, what do think of convertibles?*" he muttered and slowly shook his head with a short, less than humorous chuckle, remembering that he'd read somewhere how government contracts all too often were awarded to the lowest bidders. Maybe when he got home, *if* he got home, he'd write to his congressman to complain about the process, but then realized that a politician's usefulness often went to his campaign benefactors and supporters with the civilian companies doing the bidding. His Uncle Dave was less than kind about what he thought of politicians.

"Naw, best you go on and hold onto that," he'd heard his Uncle say to an election volunteer, who was handing out campaign flyers in front of a convenience store where he and his Uncle had stopped to buy a six-pack after a long day.

When the over eager volunteer asked Uncle Dave which political party he belonged to his Uncle just grinned. "Hookers always love parties. To them it's generally all about smiling, lying, and hustling the money," Uncle Dave said. "My take is you just gotta vote for the one that ain't trying to lift your wallet while their trying to fuck you!"

The appalled campaign worker was about to get one more take on politics from his Uncle.

"Of course, you should never confuse them with actual hard-working streetwalkers who tend to be more honest about what they're doing and why. Now, what say you excuse us while we attend to our better buying needs?"

A gust of cool air came ahead of the rain that was chasing it and the breeze felt good. A short time later what started with a few drops dripping down from the canopied-covered trees overhead soon turned into pelting rain that pooled and spread out across the jungle floor.

Lifting his face to the sky and the rain, Darrell Thomas breathed in some relief that came with the cool wash.

"Good luck in finding me now, you little peckerheads!"

He latched the handle of the flashlight on his LBE harness, grabbed the AK that he had slung over his shoulder, and moved on through the darkness. He no longer had a vantage point to see what the search party was up to, but what he still had was time, distance, and heaven-sent rain.

The tiny voice was back.

"This ain't enough rain for a boarding pass on an Ark," said the voice, *"and since Noah already has his jackass quota, what say you quit treading water, and get swimming?"*

Chapter 24

The mood at Romeo Company was somber.

Two teams had taken heavy hits in one day and five of their people were gone; one dead, one missing and likely dead, and three others seriously wounded. With less than sixty people, the Ranger Company was small by company-sized standards, so everyone knew or had some interaction with the dead, missing, or wounded Lurps. Some were close friends, former teammates, or had gone through training with at least one of them, so the loss was personal and all of them now were harboring a more visceral, gut level understanding of the consequences of being a Lurp.

Since Romeo Company became operational there had been a dozen Purple Hearts previously awarded to team members that had been grazed by bullets, concussed by explosions, or hit with shrapnel. Those Lurps had been patched up, healed, and had returned to duty. There were no Purple Hearts for the twisted or broken ankles or wrists, torn ligaments in knees, or sprained backs from having to leap out of hovering helicopters high above the ground with heavy rucksacks, and none for assorted cuts, let alone for malaria, hearing losses, or snakebites. Up until now those were all just occupational hazards associated with the job, but these harder, deadlier hits, and personal losses cast an ominous and angry cloud over the company.

The needle on the emotional scale hadn't stopped there.

By the time the news of the losses had filtered down to those latest graduates soon to be divided between the two platoons and moved into the respective hootches, it had been plumped up and fattened by gossip and rumor. The most prominent take being that one of the team members, Norse, who only had graduated from the Lurp training class less than a month before, had lost his arm and was paralyzed from the neck down, and his Team Leader, said a rumor monger, "had been crushed beneath a huge, fucking rock, and buried in the mountain!"

"No shit?" said another graduate overhearing the one doing the talking.

"Uh-huh, and another team leader got fucked up, his Assistant Team Leader was killed, and their RTO got his legs blown off."

"Jesus!"

"Five just in one day!"

The talk and rumors continued throughout the evening, with the end result being that one of the trainees decided to transfer out of the company.

"Ain't worth the risk," he said, deciding to toss in the towel. "I'll take my chances with a hundred-man grunt company. Better odds."

Some stared blankly at that, and some heads nodded as they took in the news and the rumors, while all were lost in thought and rethinking their options. Of the thirty-one volunteers they'd started off with in the Lurp training cycle only seven remained, one of which now was quitting the company.

They would inform Staff Sergeant Shintaku in the morning, but later that evening they'd already begun packing their duffle bags.

With Captain Robison and SFC Kozak down in Long Binh at the Evacuation Hospital looking in on the three wounded Lurps, Lieutenant Marquardt was left in charge of the Ranger Company. Inside the Company TOC Sergeant Cantu and Specialist-4 Taras were monitoring the bank of radios and keeping the commo logs while Lieutenant Marquardt and Staff Sergeant Shintaku were studying the enlarged wall map of their Area of Operations with keen focus on the Nui Ba Den.

"Any chance Sergeant Thomas survived the explosion?" Marquardt asked Shintaku, voicing a Hail Mary outside hope that defied the odds and situation.

Shintaku shrugged. "Maybe, sir," he said, not really believing it himself, given the explosion and tunnel collapse caused by the boobytrap, but not wanting to dismiss it entirely. "If he survived the blast and the cave in, then he still could be alive, if there was an air pocket. According to the Engineers, it happens sometimes in cave-ins."

"No way to get the Engineers back up there with equipment to find out for sure or to recover the body?"

"Too steep a location. Nowhere to safely bring it in."

"What about a generator and jackhammer?"

"From what the Engineers said, the tunnel's too unstable, and too many hidden enemy gun positions in the immediate area looking to shoot down any helicopters that get close."

While their eyes never left the wall-map they were monitoring, Taras was taking it all in.

Marquardt let out an exasperated sigh, frustrated that there wasn't anything more to be done to try for a better outcome.

The training NCO, though, offered something more.

"They did say that if Sergeant Thomas was far enough into the tunnel before the boobytrap exploded and wasn't caught in the collapse, then maybe he somehow, might've reached a cave or chamber inside the mountain. God knows, Charlie has Swiss-cheesed the hell out of that mountain, sir, so, I don't know, maybe?"

Hope was better than despair and easier to navigate. But hope had a shelf life, and the clock was ticking.

Chapter 25

It wasn't what he wanted or was hoping to find upon his return to Romeo Company after the abbreviated R&R, but there it was.

The war was front and center again and staring back at him with an ugly sneer. After being briefed by SFC Kozak on all that had happened during his absence, a stern-faced Poplawski immediately resumed his responsibilities as the Ranger Company's First Sergeant. There were things to set in motion, things that needed, and had to be done.

Several new tasks were added to his list of responsibilities; arranging a memorial service for Specialist Warren, looking in on the three seriously wounded Lurps at the Evacuation Hospital, and getting their personal effects identified, sorted, and then packed up so they could be sent to their home addresses of record. In addition, there were witness statements needed for After Action Reports from the surviving team members, not for assigning blame, but for determining a better outcome and course of action for others in the field as Lessons Learned.

Teams were still rotating in and out of the field on patrols and while none had suffered the casualties that Nine-Three and Nine-Four had, the losses that weighed heavily on the minds of the young Lurps had also affected Romeo Company's cadre.

What was weighing on Poplawski's mind and teetering like a teetering wall of sandbags was the thought of one of his people trapped inside a tunnel. Like so many others in the company who'd hoped, prayed, or angrily thought that more could have and should have been done to find him and get him out, the First Sergeant too wanted to lead a team of engineers and volunteers back up to the Nui Ba Den. Within minutes of hearing the bad news, he quickly started devising a rescue plan, and when he had what he thought was enough to get it done, he waited until Captain Robison returned from the Evacuation Hospital in Long Binh to present it to him.

Thinking that his First Sergeant had somehow learned of what had happened to the two teams while on his R&R, Robison was both surprised and quietly pleased to have him back.

"Sir! The X.O. filled me in on all that had happened. I've contacted the Chaplain about a memorial service. I'm working on the After-Action Reports with the X.O. and after we get the intel on the debriefing, we'll get it all sorted. Also, I'm drawing up some medal recommendations for your approval."

"Good. Glad to have you back. I've got a condolence letter to write to Warren's family and I'd like you to write up something for an impact award so we can see that they get it."

"Yes sir, also I have a tentative plan for a rescue mission on the mountain I'd like you to look at. I know the Engineer First Sergeant. He's a good guy, so I'm thinking I can probably get him to agree to sling load a shovel scoop excavator so his people can start peeling away layers of the mountain and shovel out dirt and heavy stone to find Sergeant Thomas," said the First Sergeant.

The Ranger captain started to interrupt him, but Poplawski was on a roll. "We can use our own people to secure the site while the Engineers do their thing. If Sergeant Thomas is in an air pocket, then we'll bring him out, tired, happy, and alive. If not, then we'll at least bring out his body. We can't leave him up there. Let me get on this, sir. I'll see to it and get it done."

The Company Commander was slowly shaking his head even before Poplawski had finished talking.

"We're not going back up the mountain," Robison replied. "I understand your frustration, Top. I get it. I truly do, but it's not going to happen. The BIG-TOC, specifically Colonel Becker, has already turned down my repeated requests."

"Goddamnit, sir. They just can't leave him there!" Poplawski's tone changed, and he was raising his voice more than he should have. This offended him. "They can't and we can't!"

The Company Commander sat up straight, glared back at his First Sergeant for a long moment, and then let out a heavy sigh. Poplawski was right and the Commanding Officer understood and shared both his anger and frustration.

"Believe me, we tried to find him and get him out shortly after it happened. One of the tunnel experts from the Engineers came in with us on the QRF. He said that when the boobytrap exploded, it sealed the tunnel shut."

"Sealed it?"

The captain nodded. "And not just with dirt and debris, but heavy rock and giant granite slabs. I needed to see it for myself, so I went in and almost got trapped too when more of the tunnel came down. I barely made it back out."

"An excavator could make short work of it..."

The captain slowly shook his head, one more time.

"They say there's no way they can get the heavy equipment needed up on the side of the mountain to do it, and any explosive charge they'd use would just bring more of the mountain down on Sergeant Thomas, if he somehow managed to survive the initial explosion and somehow managed to find an air pocket. The Higher-highers said they'd have any of the Pink Teams coming out of Cambodia in this area go by the mountain for the next week to search for any sign of him. They also have the Relay Station monitoring NVA radio traffic to see if there's any mention of an American POW. For now, like it or not, it's the best any of us can do."

The conversation stalled for a moment with the implications of that reality. The Nui Ba Den was Thomas' tomb.

For once, Poplawski didn't have an immediate comeback.

He'd been in the Army long enough to know that combat dictated the situational plan of action and always had. He also knew the decision by Camp Mackie's Higher-highers not to further pursue rescue operations obviously hadn't sat well with the Company Commander.

The Lurp Team Leader would be carried as *Missing in Action-Presumed Dead.*

The First Sergeant didn't like that his rescue plan was shot down. The decision gnawed at him. He was pissed off angry and it showed, but then so was the Ranger Company Commander. Both he and Robison were testy with each other because the thought of one of their people Missing-In-Action grated on them. The one consolation was that Poplawski knew that Captain Robison felt the same way he did, maybe even worse because he was the one that had to write the condolence letter to Thomas's next of kin.

Unlike some officers he'd served under, Poplawski knew that Robison was a true professional, not the bullshit, fake rah-rah kind of leader who might've said all the right things, but never put any weight behind the words, let alone action. Robison was someone that actually gave a damn about those under his command, but his decision still rankled the First Sergeant.

The Military had always promoted the mission over the men. It had indoctrinated leaders with that directive to push for the successful outcome in combat. Like it or not, depending upon how many had been killed or wounded, the mission came first and the casualties to the military became *acceptable losses*.

But to those who led the men, served along them, and interacted with them on a daily basis, the *acceptable losses* were individual and personal, the faces and names of the fallen well-remembered long after the last shot in the war was heard, and the memorial service for the fallen Ranger that took place a day later confirmed it.

The Memorial was a Fallen Soldier's Cross and consisted of an upturned rifle with a mounted bayonet firmly stuck in place in the hard-packed, orange ground. A black Ranger beret with a 75th Infantry Sua Sponte crest had been draped over the rifle butt while a pair of spit-polished Jungle boots were placed in front of the rifle. As Thomas was listed as Missing-in-Action there would only be one Soldier's Cross in place.

The Fallen Soldier's Cross that had been set up in the formation area of the Ranger Company's compound and was the focus of the memorial service that paid solemn tribute to Specialist-4 Warren. The Company's officers and NCOs, and those Lurp/Rangers that weren't out on patrol and were in the basecamp, stood in formation during the service to honor their fallen comrade. The First Sergeant, who was staring at the black beret on the rifle butt and the sunlight that had been reflecting off the metal crest, was lost in his thoughts until the Army Chaplain began his brief sermon and referred to Warren as Specialist Jonas Warren.

Poplawski's focus was brought back from the beret and upturned rifle to the Chaplain at the mention of Warren's actual first name. That threw him off for a bit. First names often didn't matter in the Army. You were a rank and your last name, or maybe a nickname to your buddies; *Moose*, *Red*, *Poncho*, *Doc*, *Pineapple*, or a *Baby-san*, or a variation of a name; a *Mac*, a *Tommy* or *Johnny*, or even something like being called *The Brick* by a few close friends. But you were seldom referred to by your full name other than in a formal ceremony or memorial service where there was need for proper recognition.

The Chaplain gave what Poplawski thought was a heartfelt sermon, although not much in the way of a personal eulogy, since he figured the Chaplain likely hadn't known Warren or any other of the wounded or missing Rangers all that well. The Chaplain had stopped by the Ranger Company from time to time and spoke with a few of those of his faith, and perhaps briefly to others before he moved on to the next unit. Still, his words carried genuine sincerity along with the religious overtones. However, it was the Ranger Company Commander's words that followed that had carried a more honest tenor and tone that those standing in formation could better relate to.

"Rangers lead the way," began Captain Robison, pausing as he took a moment to take in the faces of those in the formation before he continued. "To some it's just a motto or catchphrase, while those of us who've earned the right to wear this scroll know the cost of those words and of leading the way.

"Specialist Warren voluntarily took point on that patrol knowing the risks and dangers involved because he was proud to be a Lurp/Ranger, proud of this black beret," Robison said, pointing to the beret on the upturned rifle. "And proud to be part of Romeo Company. That he charged the enemy rather than retreat, and that he saved the lives of his teammates in the process, showed the courage and commitment he had to his team and to Romeo Company. His loss is ours, yours, and mine, and it is something we'll all carry with us now and all throughout our lives, just as we'll carry the memory of his courage, for leading the way when it mattered the most.

"Remember Specialist Jonas Warren, remember too, Sergeant Darrell Thomas, Sergeant Thomas Wade, Specialist Leon Hagar, and PFC Peter Norse, and remember why you wear that hard-earned red, black, and white scroll. You wear it for them, for yourselves, and the men next to you. You are Romeo Company, you are 75th Infantry Rangers, and part of its legacy and you continue to lead the way." Captain Robison turned and gave a nod to Lieutenant Marquardt.

"ATTENTION TO ORDERS!" barked the Company's Executive Officer as he read the medal award citation as Lieutenant Plantagenet walked towards the Ranger Captain carrying a small, rectangular dark blue box.

Plantagenet opened the military medal presentation box, and the Company Commander removed the small gold star medal with a smaller silver star embedded in its center, and adorned with a red, white, and blue ribbon.

"For Gallantry in action, the Silver Star is posthumously awarded to Specialist-4 Jonas Warren..."

The Executive Officer then read in detail why Warren had earned the nation's third highest award for exceptional combat valor, and when he had finished reading the official citation, Captain Robison gently laid the medal on the beret on the butt of the rifle.

The two officers returned to their previous positions in the formation before the captain gave a nod to his First Sergeant who called the company to attention. The second command that soon followed was loud, sharp, and purposely elongated as would be those that came afterwards.

"PRE...SENT...ARMS!"

Those in formation stood tall and held their salutes in place until the next command came.

"OR...DER...ARMS!"

The hand salutes were lowered and the final command releasing the soldiers from the ceremony rang out across the compound.

"DISMISSED!"

Those in attendance fell out and returned to their hootches or to whatever else they were doing prior to the memorial service. Some, like Carey, Doc Moore, Cantu, Shintaku, and Hernandez glanced back at the upturned rifle and glistening boots that had stood sentinel to the realities of the war and the kind of war they had chosen to be part of. The upturned down rifle with its bayonet pressed into the ground was also pressed into the memories and psyche of those in attendance as well, and when they remembered it, they might pause a moment or even shudder when they did.

Back in the Orderly Room, where the three officers and the First Sergeant and Sergeant Kozak had gathered, the Company Commander held an impromptu staff meeting.

"I've been called down to MAC-V for a briefing, so tomorrow the First Sergeant and I will fly down to Saigon at 0-800 hours. After that, we will check in on our people at the Evacuation hospital in Long Binh," said Captain Robison. "We should be back late in the day. Until then, First Lieutenant Marquardt will oversee the Company in my absence."

Heads turned to the First Lieutenant and Marquardt nodded back.

"We have two teams in the field and a third getting ready to go out. And what?" asked the captain, turning to Marquardt. "One of those teams will need an exfil?"

"Yes, sir. Team Nine-Five," said Marquardt.

"Nine-Five," echoed Captain Robison. Turning to his second lieutenant he said, "Lieutenant Plantagenet?"

"Yes, sir?"

"Since there's a break in the training cycle, I want you and Staff Sergeant Shintaku to run the insertion and extraction for both teams."

"Yes, sir," said both the junior officer and the veteran NCO in tandem.

"Good, and while you're at it, see if you get Staff Sergeant Shintaku to reenlist. In fact, let's all tag-team him. We need more, good, young NCOs like him. He's a *Shake n Bake*, right?"

"Yes, sir, I believe he is one of those NCO *90-day wonders,*" said Poplawski. "I think we have three in the company."

Shake and Bakes or the NCO *90-day wonders,* at least the Infantry trained variety, were the slang term for those enlisted soldiers that had graduated from the three-month long Non-Commissioned Officers Infantry Candidate School at Fort Benning, Georgia. While 90-days referred to the approximate length of the course, the term, *Shake-n-Bake* came from a highly advertised and popular stateside seasonings and flavored coating mix in a ready-to-bake oven bag designed for chopped chicken and pork chops. Just open the box and bag, toss in fresh chicken parts or pork chops, and shake vigorously. Then set the bag on a tray in an oven for 30-minutes or so, and presto-change-o, the now wonderfully delicious chicken or pork was ready to eat. Some claimed the product met the hype, others not so much so.

Because of the *Shake n Bake* course, it wasn't uncommon to have a pimply-faced, beanpole skinny 19 or 20-year-old wearing sergeant or staff sergeant chevrons, showing up in Vietnam at the Replacement Stations looking like it was his first day in killer Kindergarten, all eager and ready to be assigned to combat units so they could lead the troops.

Having the rank and desire didn't necessarily mean having the actual skill set and experience it took to lead others in combat. However, Shintaku and the other two *90-day wonder Shake-and-Bakes* in the Ranger Company had proven themselves capable of leading small Ranger Lurp teams behind the lines and leading them well.

Captain Robison eyed Marquardt, Plantagenet, and Kozak. "Any questions?" he asked.

"Yes, sir," said Lieutenant Marquardt.

"What is it, Ryan?"

"How long do you want to keep the memorial in place? When should we take it down?"

Robison was considering the question as he stared back out the Orderly Room's screen door at the Fallen Soldier's Cross and then realized that the answer was staring back at him.

"Let's leave it in place until sunset," he said. "And let's set up an Honor Guard in one-hour shifts with the five of us. I'll start, followed by Lieutenant's Marquardt and Plantagenet, First Sergeant Poplawski, and SFC Kozak. LBE, weapons and your cleanest set of jungle fatigues. Any questions?"

The Ranger Company Commander looked to his officers and Senior NCOs for their reaction to the unplanned guard shifts. Heads nodded and nobody complained. "Some may think it's a show, but I want any and every one that passes by our compound to see what the cost is to what we do. This is our chosen profession, and it will be honored, if not by anyone else, then at least by us."

Chapter 26

The abandoned fire support base was little more than a military ghost town, a battle-worn and battered outpost that had created its share of ghosts that now stood in ruins.

The standard practice and policy was to dismantle, remove, or to destroy as much reusable materials on the outpost as possible in order to deny the enemy anything that might prove useful or advantageous. What remained of this particular fire support base wasn't much. Two hundred yards across the once bulldozed open ground that served as No-Man's Land from the jungle's edge to the defined defensive perimeter, Thomas took in the busted perimeter, collapsed bunkers, broken fighting positions, and scattered debris that still littered the area. GIs often inadvertently dropped, discarded, or left behind various broken bits of equipment that no longer worked or that they didn't want to carry. Along with a number of unwanted tins of C-rations that seemingly nobody felt eager to eat, there were other remnants of their time occupying the distant outpost as well.

Most of the eight-foot-high dirt berm that had served as a perimeter wall and had linked the bunkers and fighting positions together had been ploughed down and ploughed under. The protective rows and multiple strands of ankle high, tanglefoot, and chest high barbed wire that had ringed the fire support base had mostly been removed and what fence posts or strung wire that proved too difficult to be taken down and hauled away were few and left rusting in place.

Inside the perimeter where the battery of howitzer cannons once roared and the mortar pits thumped out round after round of high explosive ordnance, the gun emplacement sites and pits now stood vacant and empty. Scorched and heavily rusted, overturned shit burn barrels, and empty olive drab colored C-ration cans and sun-faded cases, broken ammo boxes and cans, and other scraps of garbage were strewn over the ground. Shell holes and craters from countless enemy mortar and rockets pitted the enclosure and showed the price of its purpose when it existed.

Its strategic value, however, had long since passed.

Aware that the Viet Cong and NVA had often gone into the deserted U.S. military sites rummaging through and pilfering sandbags, shell canisters, and other useful items or dropped military gear after the units occupying them had moved out, Thomas took a cautious knee inside the edge of the rain forest and watched the old fire support base for a good while from just inside the tree line.

Before he would venture out across the deadly open ground to check out the abandoned base, he needed to be sure there were no nasty surprises waiting for him.

The rain was letting up, but there were angry storm clouds coming in from the east out of the South China Sea that would either dump more rain over the province or sweep their way into neighboring Cambodia. The waning moon that showed itself in glimpses through the breaks in the clouds only accented the shadows in the old camp with unnerving shifting light that made it appear to be spectral apparitions.

Moving in behind a vine covered fallen log for better cover and beneath the tall trees and tropical foliage, Thomas took a seat and kept watch on the abandoned fire support base. The wait proved judicial because as he was scanning the deserted base his eyes caught the flickering glow of a small fire just inside one of the remaining partially collapsed bunkers on the northern side of the camp's broken perimeter.

Given the angle, the dull glow wouldn't be visible from the air, and it was barely visible from ground level, but it was definitely a light source, a small fire from the look of it. Careful as they were, whoever was using the bunker, and he had a good idea who they were, they were out of the rain, warm, and relatively safe inside. The Texan watched on.

He hadn't seen the NVA soldier coming out of the bunker, but he did notice him in the thin light as the dark figure briefly looked around the empty base, and then walked around to the near side of the sandbagged shelter. Because the bunkers didn't have indoor plumbing, he leaned his assault rifle against a waist-high wall of sandbags, unbuttoned the fly on his trousers, and took a piss. When he'd finished, he buttoned his trousers, grabbed up his rifle, and went back inside the bunker.

Down behind his rifle and using the log as a shooting bench, it would've been an easy shot had he taken it. In the dark and blending in with the surrounding underbrush and jungle in the rain, he was pretty sure he hadn't been seen, so there was no need to give away his position.

He remained sighted in on the bunker opening ready to fire in case he somehow had been spotted, and the NVA soldier or any of his buddies came back out guns blazing.

They hadn't.

The Texan was cold, wet, and had been looking forward to getting out of the rain and the jungle for a bit but now knew he would remain where he was a little while longer. Besides, who knew how many other dug out fighting positions and bunkers were occupied? He wasn't in a hurry to find out.

It also had him wondering if the NVA search party back on the mountain had hedged their bet by reasoning that if the American Lurp wasn't going up towards the Relay Station or trying for the Tay Ninh Basecamp, then he might very well head towards the nearest Fire Support Base, abandoned or not. The soldier or soldiers in the bunker might've been sent as a blocking force for the search party that would be closing in behind him come daybreak. If so, then they'd made a good call. On the other hand, it could've only been a work party to retrieve anything useful they could find.

Darrell Thomas' time in the Army had taught him patience since most of his time in uniform held to the principle of '*Hurry up and wait.*' His time as a Lurp had taught him to be even more patient, so he sat back against the base of a good-sized tree for support, thankful for the many leaves and branches above and around him that made for a good, semi-working umbrella. The borrowed poncho and pith helmet kept away most of the rest of the rain that had found its way down through the trees. Pulling out the C-ration can of Turkey Loaf he had saved, he began opening it with his P-38 can opener as he kept watch on the empty No-Man's Land and the abandoned base, and specifically on the occupied bunker.

With no other lights visible in and around the abandoned base, and no more flashlights bobbing from either of the search parties trailing him, Darrell Thomas realized he was safe for the time being, or at least until dawn when those searching for him might, once again, picked up his trail. He also realized that when a GI is really, really hungry, a C-ration can of Turkey loaf, the same size and shape of a small can of tuna, even with a dead mosquito or two and a little bit of dirt wasn't half bad. He ate with gusto!

Safe for the moment in his hiding place, he wasn't out of the proverbial and actual woods yet, but he was out of immediate human danger.

"*Yep, ready and raring to go, so long as it ain't far and I find that damn unicorn*" he said to himself. Considering the circumstances, all was okay for the moment. Not great, not good, but okay. The thick brush and jungle around him offered more than adequate concealment, and unless someone accidentally stumbled over him, then there wasn't much chance of him being found out.

Removing the pith helmet, he pulled off the poncho and began spreading it over him as a makeshift tarp as he settled in beneath it for the night. The poncho was only so big, so there would be no stretching out for comfort. Leaning back, he hugged his knees and the assault rifle into his chest, lowered his head, and tried to get some sleep sitting up. It was no difference really than any of the hours sleeping in a Deuce-and-a-half truck or any of the cattle car-like trucks the Army had provided during Basic and Advanced training after a long day at the distant rifle ranges or training areas. On the plus side there were no potholes to jostle and jar him awake. On the downside there was the wet ground and several small, but steady streams of rainwater trickling down on him from small troughs and folds in the wrinkled poncho. Tilting the AK's rifle barrel up to use as a tent pole, the plastic poncho sent the rainwater streaming down in another direction. That, at least, eliminated the momentarily shivering.

It occurred to him that maybe not all the shivering was from the rain. *'Might coulda been all that had happened up until now, and a little to do with the foreboding threat of things that just might happen come the morning,'* he thought, and then philosophically offered a 'fuck it' as he hugged himself tighter. When sleep came, it came with more than a little exhaustion.

It was a string of heavy whumps, one quickly hitting after another, that brought him up and out from beneath the makeshift shelter, ready to fight. Nervously gripping the AK and looking around in near panic, it took a moment for him to realize the whumps were from the impact of the mortar rounds on the mountain. The rain had stopped, and in the pale light of dawn he could see that the NVA were attacking the Relay Station outpost atop the Nui Ba Den.

Prior to being in the Army, and especially before serving in combat in Vietnam, and thanks to Hollywood pyrotechnic special effects, he once believed that when incoming mortar and rocket rounds hit, they exploded in a hellish fire and roiling maelstrom much like burning napalm. Well, at least on the silver screen that was the case since it made for a better visual effect, a better show. In real life and death explosions, though, from the enemy mortar and rocket attacks he'd witnessed, there were only brief flashes of light and the more insidious and concussive waves of searing heat, flying splintered pieces of blistering hot shrapnel, and broken and shattered pieces of whatever and whoever else they'd hit. The brief flashes of light upon impact and deep bass *whumps* that shook the small mountaintop base reverberated over the countryside.

The show was building its audience. Three NVA soldiers emerged from their bunker on the not so abandoned Fire Support Base and were also taking in the attack at the top of the mountain in the dull grey morning.

But just as quickly as the attack on the Relay Station had begun, it ended, and a new act was about to take the stage.

Retaliatory strikes on the attackers, or at least, in and around the area where the mortars had been launched, soon followed. Artillery generally was the counter response, but Thomas could hear a helicopter Pink Team coming in behind him over the jungle from the northwest.

The Light Observation Scout Helicopter, the *Loach*, with its three-man crew, was taking the lead. It came in low over the tops of the trees and the jungle leading to the mountain, searching for those that'd fired the mortars. The small helicopter was playing its role as dangling bait for the Cobra gunship lazily circling high above it.

As the *Loach* searched the relatively flat rainforest covered countryside before rising up to the side of the Black Virgin Mountain it was met by a stream of green tracers from concealed enemy .51-caliber gun emplacement well entrenched inside the mountain. The enemy gunners were trying to track and lead the helicopter's flight path to bring it down with heavy gunfire that would leave holes the size of softballs. But like a well-schooled matador, the *Loach* pilot swerved away from the stream of incoming fire at the last moment and banked in a tight turn to give its machine gunner better return fire on the NVA's heavy gun position.

"Ole!" cheered Thomas, under his breath.

The small helicopter peeled away as the Cobra gunship swooped down with rockets and automatic grenade fire on target. Thomas suddenly felt relieved that he hadn't tried to make his way up to the Relay Station. In his get-up in the poor light, he'd easily be little more than a target of opportunity for either of the two helicopters.

Behind him, to the southeast he heard a second Pink Team, likely flying a first light mission and looking for prey, change its course for the mountain ready to assist the other team in contact. The flight path for the second team of helicopters would bring it over, or very close to, the abandoned Fire Support Base.

If he was going to make it out of the jungle alive then this might be his best chance, so he took it!

With the small helicopter coming in low over the forlorn base a jubilated Thomas came out from where he was hiding and into the open No-Man's Land, waving his rifle and free hand over his head. That drew the attention of the scout helicopter's machine gunner who opened up on him.

"Oh shit!" Thomas cried, diving out of the line of fire to avoid being hit by the full six-round burst. The dive and tumble saved him from the first five rounds from the Loach's scout machine gun while the sixth caught him across his upper left deltoid and punched deep into the shoulder. The jolt from the copper jacketed bullet that hit him like a sledgehammer left a deep and burning wound in its place.

"You dumb shit!" he yelled, crying, and cursing at himself as he crawled behind the cover of the fallen tree and chided himself for the foolish move he'd just made. With the pith helmet, AK-47, and poncho, he'd been mistaken for an NVA soldier. No wonder the 60-gunner opened up on him!

"I would've opened up on me, too!" he said, bringing a hand up to try to stem the flow of blood. Direct pressure both helped and hurt at the same time.

He also knew that he must have looked the same to the three NVA soldiers in the abandoned fire support base since they were now firing on the small helicopter to protect him. The low bird took several hits from the ground fire but was still airborne as it veered away, and the sleek and more deadly Cobra gunship took over the fight. The gunship was making a steep run on the three enemy soldiers who wisely and hastily retreated back inside the protection of the bunker just as the attack helicopter hit it with several 70mm rocket fire.

The rockets slammed into the sandbag-layered bunker with little damaging effect but offered the Ranger a way out. As long as the NVA remained hidden inside, then the helicopter's ordnance wouldn't have much impact on them where they were, and this he could use to his now shaky advantage.

Machine gun fire from the smaller of the two helicopters that roared back into play kept up the attack on the bunker's opening as the Cobra gunship circled around in a wide arc for a second run.

As the *Loach* got out of the way of the gunship the low bird came buzzing back over his position looking to finish what they'd started, the Texan tossed away the NVA helmet and the East German poncho and set aside the AK-47 and got to his feet again. This would either be his salvation or his deadly mistake. Rising up from behind the fallen log he held both arms high over his head in surrender, praying the Scout helicopter's 60-gunner would hold his fire long enough to recognize him as a friendly. The Ranger Sergeant held up his bleeding left arm up as high as he could muster with his blood-covered right hand to show that he wasn't a threat. It took all the teeth-gritting strength he had just to raise the painfully damaged arm.

It was an agonizing, butt-clenching wait as the small three-man helicopter slowed its air speed and turned just enough to give its machine gunner a better aim. With the machine gun hanging from an overhead bungee cord, the 60-gunner once again sighted in on Thomas. He was a fraction of a second from blowing him away when he jerked up from behind the weapon with a stunned look on his face. Thomas could see him yelling something into a radio headset to the Pilot and the Observer in the front seats of the helicopter as he began pointing at him. The Pilot turned the *Loach* forward so he and the Observer could get a better look at the bleeding soldier to their front.

With his hands and arms still held high up over his head, blood spilling down from the ugly wound, and his knees shaking, Thomas did his best not to make any sudden moves. If they didn't recognize him as a friendly, then he hoped like Hell they wouldn't see him as a threat. With the gunship rolling in on the bunker and buying time for the *Loach,* Thomas just stood there in the open watching as the helicopter buzzed to a low hover from where he was standing. The low bird Pilot and the enlisted Observer were clearly visible in the cockpit through the front fishbowl bubble of the aircraft before it swung back to the left and the 60-gunner, who was now leaning out of the back part of the aircraft.

"COME ON! COME ON!" he yelled, waving Thomas on. "MOVE IT! LET'S GO!"

Thomas didn't need a written invitation. He ran with all the speed he could muster over the uneven ground and jumped in the back of the small helicopter. With the help of the 60-gunner who was hauling him in and holding on tight to his LBE web gear to keep him from falling out, Thomas was pulled safely inside the now cramped space. The *Loach* was airborne in an instant and took off over the abandoned base, the surrounding tree tops, and quickly gained some serious altitude.

The wounded Texan was giddy and laughing and slapping the 60-gunner on the back and giving him a bloodied thumbs-up.

"WHO ARE YOU? WHAT'S YOUR NAME?" yelled the machine gunner over the rush of the wind and mechanical noise of the helicopter. "YOU THE MISSING LURP?"

Thomas had to lean in so the crewman could hear him. "Yeah, I am. My name's Thomas, Darrell, Sergeant. Romeo Company Ranger!" he said, and then grinned like a mad man. Disheveled and dirty as he was, he must have looked like one as well. Struggling with his good arm, he pulled the small bandage from his First Aid pouch and began treating his gunshot wound. "Got separated from my team in the mountain…"

"In the mountain?"

"Yeah, the Black Virgin. Been escaping and evading the NVA for a while now, a day or two maybe."

The 60-gunner just stared at Thomas, unsure what to make of him, although he was certain of one thing.

"I'm...I'm sorry, man!" he said, looking hang dogged and more than a little distressed staring at the wound he'd inflicted. "I...I didn't mean to shoot you. I thought you were a gook!"

"No, no! You didn't shoot me, they did," lied the Texan. He motioned towards the gauze bandage. "Can you tie this off?"

The 60-gunner nodded and took over tying off the bandage while Thomas was holding pressure on the wound. Even with the bandage in place and secured, some blood was seeping through the gauze. The bandage, though, had stemmed a heavier flow.

The guilty look on the machine gunner's face said he wasn't so sure about Thomas' take on the event, so the wounded Lurp gave it again with a little more emphasis.

"Two of those NVA were trying to bring down your bird while the third one was aiming at me. I barely had time to get out of the way. If you guys hadn't landed and picked me up, they would've killed me for sure. You guys saved my ass!"

His account was plausible and there was relief showing on the 60-gunner's face with Thomas' version of the incident, and that worked for the both of them.

"Can you let my Unit back at Camp Mackie know I'm alive?" Thomas said. "I'm a team leader for Team Niner-Four. R Company Ranger-75th Infantry, MAC-V. I say again, I'm a team leader for Team Niner-Four from the Ranger Company at Camp Mackie. Can you call it in?"

The 60-gunner nodded and relayed the message through the comms in his flight helmet to the pilot.

The 60-gunner listened to the Pilot's response, nodded even though the pilot and Observer couldn't see the gunner or the wounded Lurp.

"Mister Bennet's calling it in!"

"We're going to Mackie?"

"No, we're taking you to a Field Hospital," said the 60-gunner. "How are you feeling?"

"Like a happy pig wallowing in shit!"

"We're going to get you to the hospital. You're going to be okay."

Thomas gave a tired nod. His arm and shoulder were hurting like hell and feeling heavy and useless. His stomach was growling from the lack of any real food, and he was dirty, disheveled, and smelled like he'd done laps in a cesspool. The Field Hospital was sounding like a pretty good choice about now.

The Pink Team, the two-ship small Scout helicopter and the sleek Cobra gunship now had a new flight plan and mission, and they were racing towards it.

Chapter 27

The rescue helicopter had barely touched down on the heli-pad at the Evacuation Hospital in Long Binh before the trauma team rushed out to retrieve the wounded soldier.

Even as they were laying him on the gurney and wheeling him into triage, a team of trauma surgeons, nurses, and medics hurriedly went to work in a whirlwind of coordinated activity. Someone was cutting away his dirty uniform and sandals and someone else was slapping on a blood pressure cuff to his non-injured arm, while a third someone began swabbing an alcohol wipe on the back of his good hand and inserting an IV needle and cannula into the best vein they could find. The hectic activity and the shifting movement of the gurney as they were rolling him in had loosened the tape holding the needle in place.

“Tape that down,” said someone behind a mask while someone else added two more strips of adhesive tape.

As the gurney came to a halt inside the Evacuation Hospital a surgical doctor carefully started cutting away the bloodied field bandage and removing the sticky mess to get a better look at the gunshot wound. The blood soaked bandage was sticking to the raw trench-like shoulder wound, and as it was peeled away the pain that came with the unmasking felt like needles jabbing him in the eyes and had him groaning.

"Let's get him 10-mgs of morphine," said a doctor ordering up the drug. The delivery was swift, and Thomas felt a needle going into his left hip as the doctor was saying something else to somebody about a ‘through and through GSW,’ and using other medical code and speak that Thomas didn't quite understand. While the surgical masks they were all wearing muffled some of their speech, they didn't hinder the working dialogue. The morphine was quick to take effect.

The Texan's attention shifted again as a nurse made note of the dirt and blood-matted gash on the back of his head that had the doctor checking the wound as well as his eyes and ears.

"We'll need to debride that head wound too and get some antibiotics started," said the doctor. "Shave around it and give me something good to work with."

Someone else had called out another small wound.

"Laceration to the left heel," he said, and brought someone leaning in for a closer inspection.

Meanwhile, another one of the someones was getting ready to pull a sheet over his near naked body after the numerous scrapes and discolored bruises on his legs, back and arms were examined and charted.

Someone with a clipboard was asking him for his name and unit as a Radiologist and tech were preparing him for X-rays in this seemingly chaotic, but well-rehearsed ballet that both mystified and impressed the weary Texan.

"Soldier, we need your name, serial number, and unit?"

"What?"

"Your name, rank, serial number, and unit?"

"It's Thomas, Darrell, NMI, Sergeant. Romeo Company-Ranger. Camp Mackie," he said, in a near casual tone and then rattled off his service number. The shot of morphine was flowing over him like a warm, comfortable wave. He was feeling faint from the blood loss and talkative. "Ain't much of a base, really. Smells like burning shit most of the time. We use JP-4 or kerosene and wooden paddles. Smells nice here, though. Whoa! She has pretty eyes!"

Thomas smiled and someone else behind mask chuckled as that last bit was enough to let the doctors, nurses, and medics know that the morphine was working just fine. Even so, the lead doctor ordered someone to monitor his breathing in case there was an adverse reaction to the drug. He'd be sleepy, have a loss of appetite, and most likely be constipated by morning but those side effects wouldn't be life threatening.

After the portable X-Rays were taken and the surgical team had something to work with, they began cleaning out the wound before closing off whatever was bleeding, removing shell and bone fragments, along with pieces of his jungle fatigues that had entered the wound with the bullet.

The lead surgeon, who was assisted by several Nurses, began a fasciotomy, meticulously taking his time to stop the bleeding before he began cutting and trimming away the jagged, necrotic flaps and edges of torn skin and muscle.

The 7.62mm machine gun round that had punched and sliced deep into the soldier's upper arm and shoulder left an ugly wound. He couldn't see the expression on the surgeon's face behind the facemask, but judging from what his eyes were doing, there was cause for concern.

The morphine left him with an odd, almost out of body sensation like he was passing an accident scene on the side of a highway, staring out a passenger window and gawking at the mess, only to see that he was the one trapped in the wreckage. The pain from the wound, he knew, was following. For now, thanks to the morphine, it was still a distance away, held up in the temporary traffic, and not honking its horn

There was more medical poking and probing from a myriad of angles and when the medical team had finally finished the urgent work ninety minutes later, and when they were satisfied with all that had been done for the time being, a nurse started applying a bandage to the wound that would hold the shoulder and arm in place against his chest. Zoned out as he was with the morphine, Thomas noticed that the wound hadn't been closed.

"No stitches?"

The Nurse smiled. "Not to worry," she said. "We need to check and clean the wound over the next few days. If all goes well, then we'll get you sewn up good as new. For now, though, you just need to rest."

"Looks like you've been banged around a bit out there, Sergeant," said the lead surgeon coming back to check in on him as he removed his mask and bloodied rubber gloves.

Thomas figured the 'there' being the jungle far beyond Long Binh. He nodded.

"Muscle damage, a fractured shoulder, and a concussion to go along with the head injury. By the way, how did you get that head injury? Did you hit your head when you got shot?"

"No, sir. Boobytrap."

"Boobytrap?" said the surgeon, a little bewildered by the timeline. "The pilot told one of our people that you got shot in a firefight today."

"Uh-huh. Yes sir, I was. The bullet knocked me on my ass. The boobytrap was from a tunnel that blew up yesterday. Got trapped inside after the explosion and everything collapsed."

“Yesterday?”

“Coulda been the day before .Watch got broke, lost track of time. Dug my way out, though. Got shot this morning. I guess the same boys that didn't like me wandering around their hidden tunnel complex decided I needed a little more schooling."

Thomas managed a small laugh while both the surgeon and nurse, along with several others nearby who'd overheard him, briefly paused what they were doing and quietly stared at him.

"Get some rest," said the surgeon. "We'll look in on you later."

Rest, real rest, wasn't just what the Doctor ordered, but was something Darrell Thomas definitely needed. His left arm and shoulder felt heavy and useless. On the helicopter flight to Long Binh the arm, shoulder, and the left side of his neck seized up in terrible pain and began to spasm and ache more than he thought he could handle. His fingers and hands had grown cold and numb and when he leaned his head back against the back wall of the small helicopter and was breathing through clenched teeth, the bump to the head injury only added to the overall misery.

Leaning back into the hospital pillow, the blood loss, morphine, and spent adrenaline were all having their say with him. He was lightheaded, woozy, and his body gave way to a much welcomed, drug induced slumber.

He slept until well into the afternoon when the drug started to wear off and he awoke as the pain receptacles in his brain were more than hinting at a vengeful return. The gunshot shoulder wound was pulsating and the pain, like the beat of a drum, was growing louder behind his eyes as it thumped on.

Before he had to ask for something to relieve the pain, a smiling brunette showed up carrying a cup of water and a small, white paper cup that contained a single white pill.

"Something for the pain," the Nurse said, handing him the pill cup and the cup of water. She wore the silver bar rank of a first lieutenant but didn't look to be all that much older than he was. Her name tag read: Colasurdo.

"Thank you, Ma'am."

"You're welcome," said the Nurse. "I'll check in on you later to see how you're doing."

Thomas gave a slight chin up nod as she left to attend the other patients on the ward. Up until then he hadn't noticed the others in the dozen or so beds around him. The soothing medication, combined with profound fatigue, had helped him, for the time being, escape all that had happened and allowed him to sleep, again. His face and upper body that had started to contort in pain once again began to ease up and relax. Lowering his head back into the pillow he took in a number of the beds around him that were filled with other combat casualties; some who looked to be having a tougher go at it than he was having.

Across the aisle in the hospital bed directly across from him, another young soldier had bandages covering the lower half of his face where his jaw should've been. Although his eyes were red and swollen, they had long since been cried out. A round disk that had been surgically implanted in his throat allowed him to breathe with raspy breaths. Next to him a blond-haired soldier not much older than him was staring forlornly at where his left arm was missing at the elbow. Somewhere down the ward an unseen patient was crying in deep, mournful sobs.

“Jesus Christ! Give him fucking something, will you!” shouted another wounded soldier as nurses and medics raced to the crying patient.

Thomas turned his eyes to the ceiling and blew out a slow, steady breath. Hell here, was spotlessly clean, antiseptic, and something on a level perhaps only Dante could have imagined or say a combat surgical ward medic or nurse could prior to his or her next assigned shift. What showed here would never be used on a Recruiting poster. Thomas leaned back into his pillow.

Later, when Lieutenant Colasurdo returned she was carrying a small, soap-filled plastic tub.

"Let's get you cleaned up a bit," she said, setting the plastic tub on a small nightstand next to the bed and retrieving a sponge from the soapy mix. Squeezing out the excess water from the sponge, she methodically began to wash away some of the dirt, sweat, and grime from the face, ears, and neck of the injured Lurp. She worked around the bandage covering his head injury and was talking all the while she was working.

"I heard one of the doctor's say that you're a Lurp. What exactly is that? Special Forces or something?"

"Ranger, Ma'am. Lurp's the job we do."

"Lurp?"

"Long range reconnaissance patrol. Five-to-six-man teams, mostly, and mostly those who need their heads examined."

"But they said you were out there alone fighting the Viet Cong when they picked you up, but that didn't sound right to me. Is that true?"

She had moved on to his left arm and the dried blood that had spilled down from the wound when he was shot. The soapy water changed its hue and color with each new squeeze in the small tub.

"No Ma'am," Thomas said, correcting her. "Only an idiot would go out alone. And it wasn't the VC. They were NVA regulars, a bunch of them."

Colasurdo stopped what she was doing, reared back, and stared at him, momentarily confused. "But the helicopter pilot call that came in said you were all by yourself out there?"

"Like I said, Ma'am, only an idiot," he said with a lopsided grin. "Actually, I got separated from my team when I got caught in an explosion in a tunnel."

"I'm going to crank up your bed to make it easier for me to get to your back. When I do, I'll need you to lean forward. Can you do that for me?"

"I'll try," he said.

The nurse raised the back of the hospital bed and as she did Thomas used his good arm on the bed frame to help shift his weight forward. Colasurdo assisted him with a hand on his lower back and it took a little doing.

"Sorry, the whole left side of my body feels like dead weight," he said, apologizing for his slow movement.

"It'll get better."

With the pain blocking pill working its magic and him feeling only some minor discomfort, other than a few sore, bruised, and strained muscles, several small cuts, and a plague of mosquito and bug bites, he almost felt human, again. Thomas leaned forward as the Nurse reached behind the open hospital gown to get to his back.

Once the back and stomach had been cleaned, she washed his chest, the shoulder area around the bandage, and his stomach.

"Can I ask a favor of you, Ma'am?"

"A favor?"

Thomas nodded. "Yes, Ma'am," he said.

"Well," she said, smiling, "I won't promise you anything, but you can go ahead and ask."

"One of the guys on my team, PFC Norse, was badly injured. Is there any way for you to check to see if he made it here?"

The requests some patients made were generally flirtatious or ribald in nature, so she was momentarily thrown off by what he was asking. His request changed the Nurse's light-hearted, suspicious demeanor, to something more profound, and she was genuinely touched.

"You said his name is Norse?"

"Yes Ma'am, PFC Norse from R Company, Ranger, MAC-V."

“What’s his first name?”

“New Guy,” Thomas said with an embarrassed shrug.

"I'll check and see if I can find out for you. So, where are you from, Sergeant? Where do you call home?"

"Eh, Athens, Texas, home of the best, fried pickles you'll ever find!" he said, trying to get his mind, both of them, off what all was happening elsewhere.

"Fried pickles?"

"Yes, Ma'am, a little bit of heaven with a Shiner Bock or a long-necked Pearl."

Not sure what a Shiner Bock or a long-necked Pearl was but assuming they were beers, she smiled anyway. She kept him talking as she was cleaning his thighs and legs and pretended she hadn't noticed his growing erection.

"So, is that anywhere near Dallas?"

"Oh Lord, no," he said, slightly embarrassed and happy that she'd moved down to his feet and toes quelling another Texas uprising.

"Where you from, L-T?"

"Jersey City, New Jersey, home to Frank Sinatra, Hoagies, and the Statue of Liberty."

"Statue of Liberty?"

"Uh-huh."

"I thought that was in New York?"

"Nope! Liberty island is actually in Jersey City waters. Manhattan just appropriated it. So, how did you get the cut on your heel? Didn't the jungle boots protect your feet?"

She was cleaning away the dirt and grime between his toes and was careful with the jagged cut on his heel.

"It was from the Ho Chi Minh sandals I was wearing. They're lousy for sharp rocks, thorns, and anything that stings or bites, but they're good for mileage, especially when you're trying to run from some North Vietnamese soldiers who are chasing your ass.... eh, sorry

Ma'am. I mean, when someone's chasing after you through the jungle all night and trying to turn you into a soup strainer with chunks."

The Ward Nurse just stared at the young, good-looking soldier with a funny, almost sad smile.

"You hungry?" she asked, holding the tub of dirty water, and getting ready to leave. "Can I get you something to eat?"

The prospect of eating real food brightened his spirits considerably. "Oh, Good Lord, yes! That'd be great," he said, very much appreciating an actual meal. "I didn't have much to eat when I got stuck inside the tunnel in the mountain after the explosion."

"The mountain?"

"Yeah, the Black Virgin Mountain, the Nui Ba Den. We were chasing after an NVA soldier looking to snatch him up and followed him into the tunnel. Norse accidentally triggered a boobytrap and the blast caused a cave-in. Later when I came to, I tried going back for Norse, but the tunnel was blocked behind me, so I just kept digging my way forward until I reached a hidden cave system inside. Took me awhile to stumble out of the beast."

“Inside the mountain?”

Yes, Ma’am! Pretty elaborate funhouse too, I’ll tell ya! Caverns and caves all connected by tunnels and not one damn exit sign. I only had a few small cans of C-rations on me while I was hiding from the NVA,” Thomas chuckled. “Thought my growling stomach might give me away."

The Nurse stared blankly at him for another troubled moment before she resumed her professional bedside manner.

"How about I also get you something to drink? Besides water, we also have apple juice, Coke, and orange Fanta."

"Coke, please."

"No problem," Lieutenant Colasurdo said smiling as she gathered up the small, plastic wash basin, sponge, and towel and started to leave. "I'll see if I can find you some ice to go along with it."

The Nurse returned carrying a clean and folded hospital gown beneath a food tray. She set the food tray on the end table next to the bed and placed the hospital gown on the bunk. A soft drink and a cup of ice sat perched next to a covered plate and silverware. Lifting the cover he found a neat array of meatloaf, mashed potatoes, steamed carrots, and a small square of lime Jell-O.

"Recovery Ward food, I'm afraid," she said, apologizing.

"Trust me, Ma'am, it's fine. Thank you."

"You'll be transferred to the surgical ward in the morning, and in three to four days, depending on how your GSW looks, they'll close it up."

"GSW's, I take it, are gunshot wounds?"

"They are, but that doesn't look like one on the back of your head, judging by the depth of the wound. Did you get hit by shrapnel?"

"Naw, a chunk of rock, I suspect."

"From the explosion inside the tunnel?"

"Yes, Ma'am, it rang my bell pretty good. After that when I came to, I was playing Hide and Seek, mostly Hide from the NVA in and out of the mountain. Fortunately, the helicopter got to me before the folks that were chasing after me did."

"And that's when you got shot?"

"I guess I was a little slow to duck. Dirty as I was, I'm glad the Loach gunner recognized me when he did, but I suppose it was pretty easy..."

"Easy how?"

"I was the one pissing myself."

Thomas chuckled and Colasurdo chuckled along with him even as she was shaking her head. "Your war is a lot different from my war, Sergeant."

"Yes Ma'am, it is," Thomas said, as he was looking around the other patients in the ward and involuntarily shuddered. "But from what I see here, yours looks a whole hell of a lot worse. This is your everyday, I take it."

"It is."

"Then, no thank you, I'll take my jungle over this every time. I appreciate what you folks do here. Pretty sure we all do."

"You're welcome. I'll be back for the tray."

After he'd finished eating, he placed the tray on the nightstand, pulled off the old hospital gown, and almost managed to slip into the new one. The gown hung off his injured arm and shoulder.

"Close enough," he said to himself, easing back into the hospital bed. With the medication and full stomach, he welcomed the sleep that followed. There was better refuge there.

Somewhere around two in the morning Lieutenant Colasurdo nudged him awake in the darkened ward.

"Medication," she said, handing him another paper cup with a pill and a small cup of water.

Thomas wasn't sure if he said thanks or simply grunted it as he took the pill and washed it down with the water. He nodded and handed her back the small cup.

Taking his vital signs, she noted them on his hospital chart, and then smiled again.

"Get some sleep, sergeant," she said.

Groggy as he was, he said he would and smiled as he watched her walk away. Leaning back on the pillow, he closed his eyes and with the help of the soothing pain medication, he was asleep before the Nurse had finished her rounds.

The pain pill swept the hospital ward, the war, and his pain back into the recesses of his mind. It would all return again, and the waking would bring him back to the nightmare that was the ward when the next round of medication would serve up another very much appreciated temporary escape in small, white paper cups.

Chapter 28

Shortly after breakfast and well after a team of Doctors and Nurses on duty had conducted their morning rounds, and any pain medication was delivered to the patients, a nurse and a tall, heavy-set black medic showed up with a wheelchair at his bedside.

"You're changing wards, Sergeant," said the nurse. Back to the medic she said, "On three."

With legs bent and feet planted they shifted Thomas from the bed onto the wheelchair. While the medic got ready to push, the nurse readied the I-V drip on the rolling stand it was attached to.

"You're in good hands," she said and turned the task over to the medic. The medic's name tag read: Hanon. His rank showed he was a Specialist-5.

"You ready to roll, Sarge?"

"Good-to-go."

"Then you hold onto the rolling I-V stand, and I'll push. Let's do this."

With the wounded Lurp holding onto the tall metal stand for the I-V drip bag and tube that fed into his good arm and Hanon rolling the wheelchair down the ward's center aisle, it was a short ride to the nurse's Duty Station where they stopped.

"V-S-I ward transfer," he said to another nurse who was working behind the nurses' station.

"Patient's name?"

"Thomas, first name, Darrell, Sergeant," Thomas said, all the while as he was looking around for Lieutenant Colasurdo, the friendly Nurse, from the night before, only she was nowhere to be found.

The nurse behind the desk pulled an opened manila envelope from a records divider that she handed to the medic that he, in turn, handed to Thomas who placed it in his lap.

"Your patient chart."

Thomas turned to the nurse behind the desk and said, "Excuse me, Ma'am, is Lieutenant Colasurdo around? I wanted to thank her for looking after me like she did?"

The nurse, a stern-faced Captain, shook her head.

"Her next scheduled shift begins at 0-700 tomorrow," she said.

"Ah, then would you thank her for me?"

“I will,” she said, appreciating the gesture. Her face actually brightened. “You're that Special Forces Sergeant, right?"

"No Ma'am, a Lurp."

"I don't know what that is?" the Duty Nurse said, confused and looking to Specialist Hanon for clarification. Hanon shrugged. He didn't know either.

"Ranger, Ma'am." He was about to tell her what Lurps did but cut it short since both the nurse and the medic were looking at him like he was crazy. Instead, he just said, "and someone who appreciates what all you do here, so thank you."

The compliment drew an appreciative smile.

"You're welcome," she said. "Oh, and when she reports for her shift, I'll let her know. That was kind of you."

Thomas nodded and Specialist Hanon wheeled him out of the ward and down a opened covered walkway.

Halfway to the new ward, Hanon started to chuckle.

"So, did you mean any of that or were you just looking to try to get laid?"

The Texan looked up to the medic and grinned sheepishly.

"I'm wounded, Doc. I ain't dead," he said, laughing. "I haven't seen a good-looking woman in months outside a Playboy magazine fold-out, so I'm just happy to see one that ain't folded in thirds."

"Dude, you're funny! Where you from?"

"A small town in East Texas... Athens. You?"

"A small town in Illinois... Chicago," laughed the medic. "Good sports teams, lousy winters that are almost as cold as my First Sergeant's heart...well, almost. You like an honest to God cowboy or something?"

"Naw, I ain't that tough, but that's what most people seem to think whenever I mention where I'm from. Hard to change their minds, at times."

"Tell me about it! I'm black but I don't have any rhythm, can't dance worth a hoot, and I want to be a veterinarian!"

"Veterinarian?"

“Uh-huh, because truth be told, I just like animals, people not so much at times.”

“I get it. So, what exactly does V-S-I stand for?”

“Very Seriously Injuries.”

"Ah,” he said. “And as for the compliment, I meant it. The jungle don’t scare me as much as this place does. What you got here is every momma’s nightmare, so yeah, seriously, I appreciate what you do."

"Well then, you're welcome," said the medic. "By the way, that nurse who took care of you last night, Lieutenant Colasurdo, her first name is Teresa. I'll let her know what you said."

"Thanks."

"No problem. I'll tell her The Lone Ranger said howdy. Yo, here we are."

Hanon pushed him through a series of double swinging doors and wheeled him into the new ward. At the Nurses’ station Hanon handed the manila envelope with the patient chart to the officer behind the desk. "Thomas, Darrell, Sergeant," he said to the Nurse who nodded.

She directed the medic to an empty bed at the far end of the ward where Hanon helped Thomas get settled.

"Catch ya later, Lone Star!"

"You too, Doctor Doolittle. Hey, man, thanks."

“All part of what we god-like medics do, so you’re welcome.”

Just like the Recovery Ward he found himself surrounded by other critically wounded or injured GIs, only here there were considerably more beds. He counted thirty beds in all with the beds equally divided along the walls of the long, thin ward and separated by a wide aisle. The two sides of the Recovery Ward were only a prelude to the reality of the weekly casualty count that lingered here.

Thomas avoided looking around the ward and settled back in the new bed. The breakfast and latest round of medication left him drowsy and struggling to stay awake. It was a losing battle and sleep soon won over.

A sharp cry brought him immediately out of his sleep and had him reaching for a rifle that wasn't there. At the far end of the well-lighted and antiseptic smelling hospital ward just up from the Nurse's Duty Station, two medics were beginning the grim task of changing bandages and cleaning out the soldiers' wounds. As the medics worked their respective sides of the center aisle the moans, cries, and some swearing grew in frequency. One of the medics was Specialist Hanon.

Both were pushing small carts stocked with what they needed to carry out the task. Some of the more badly injured GIs moaned or cried out during the cleanings, either from the bandages clinging to raw wounds and angry flesh, or the realization of how their lives had been drastically changed because of their wounds. There was more than just physical pain in play here. By the time Hanon wheeled up to his bed, the more trepidation and anxiety the Texan felt. Hanon gave him a nod as he moved his cart in between Thomas' bed and the one to his left.

"I'm not going to lie, Lone Star, this might hurt a bit, “ he said, by way of apology, “but we have to keep that wound clean to keep from becoming infected."

"Figured it was something like that, Doc," Thomas said, staring at the cart. "Looks like you got everything you need."

The young Ranger’s voice was calm and almost casual given what was about to happen. It was his darting eyes that gave him away.

The top tray of his pushcart held an array of tape, bandages, several plastic tubs, containers of a clear fluid, and what looked to be a turkey baster.

Hanon pulled a pair of scissors from his top left pocket, and then carefully cut away the tape that held the bandage on Thomas' arm and shoulder. With that done he slowly began peeling back the layers of gauze to get to the wound so he could begin the cleaning process. The last thin layer of the bloodied gauze was stuck on an irritated ridge of flesh in the open wound like a giant blood and discharge stained Band Aid.

"This might sting some," the medic said after pulling away the last gummed up bit. The nearly dried, blood-soaked gauze ripped at a painful part of the wound and Thomas winced as it was peeled away. Instead of swearing, he managed to find a chuckle.

"Oh, good Lord," he said, taking a deep breath as the medic dropped the dirty bandage on the bottom tray of the cart.

"Sorry about that," Hanon said. "But this will actually help."

Reaching back to the cart he brought out a small container of a clear liquid, clean towel, and what looked to be a turkey baster. With the bandage removed and dumped in a second pail on the bottom shelf on the cart, Hanon filled the turkey baster from the fluid in the container.

"Hydrogen peroxide mix," he said, placing the towel beneath the wounded arm and then systematically began squeezing out the solution in the baster directly into the wound. The hydrogen peroxide fizzed, bubbled over, and then calmed. What it didn't do was hurt.

As the medic was working Thomas asked him why they hadn't stitched up the wound earlier. He remembered something of what the doctor who'd initially worked on him a few days earlier had said about an infection, but with the morphine he was given at the time, the memory was fuzzy.

"Sepsis."

"What?"

"Sepsis. It's when an infection overrides your immune system," he said. "If that happens then it shuts down your organs and induces heart failure. Bottom line, you flat line and die."

"That happen a lot?"

The medic shook his head. "Not as much when the wounds are kept clean," he said. "And not on my watch. They cleaned out the dirt and debris from your wound when they brought you in. They even removed the dead tissue around it to open it up and give it a better chance at healing. The bacteria from the jungle you 11-Bravo Infantry types seem to spend so much time in, combined with the high Southeast Asian heat tends to fill a wound with staphylococcus..."

"Staff-da-what?"

"Staphylococcus, nasty ass germs and pus, if we didn't do this. Without the cleanings, gangrene would set in, and you'd lose the arm or a good portion of it. So, we'll clean it twice a day to keep that from happening. You should be good."

"Good! I'm hoping to get back to my team."

Hanon stopped what he was doing, leaned back, and eyed him sideways in disdain and a second questioning look that said that maybe the doctors forgot to notice a more troubling brain injury.

"Dude, you serious?"

"Yeah."

"So, nobody told you?"

"Told me, what?"

"With your wounds you're not going anywhere except for maybe Camp Zama, Japan, or Letterman General Military Hospital stateside. Your days in Nam are over, my man. Besides the gunshot wound, you also have a fractured left clavicle, most likely from the impact of the bullet that hit you. That'll need to mend too, and that's all before you start a whole lot of physical therapy it's gonna take to get that shoulder and arm working properly again. Now, let's take a look at your head wound for that dumbass thing you just said about wanting to stay here in the Nam."

So that others nearby might not hear him the medic leaned in and added, "This is a VSI ward- Very Serious Injury. Be thankful you're going home, some of these guys in here maybe won't be."

The medic then inspected the head injury, found it in better shape than he'd expected to find, and left it alone.

"Looks good for now," he said. "I'm thinking we'll hold off on that one until tomorrow morning and slap on a new bandage on your shoulder instead."

"SHAMMING, I SEE!" came the all too familiar booming voice of First Sergeant Poplawski from down the center aisle of the hospital ward. Poplawski was joined by the Romeo Company's Commanding Officer, Captain Robison.

The medic turned to see who was making all the noise and was surprised and uneasy to find an intimidating looking NCO and black officer in their starched jungle fatigues, spit shine boots, and black berets. A just as surprised and uneasy Thomas started to sit up in bed at some sort of position of attention.

"N...no, First Sergeant, I'm...."

Poplawski's loud voice drew a frown and rebuke from the senior nurse at the Duty Station and a gesture from the Ranger Captain that he would calm his First Sergeant. Poplawski too held his hands palms out and opened in a placating gesture back to the nurses at the Nurses' station and mouthed the word, *'sorry.'*

To Thomas, in a more conversational tone, he said, "I'm just busting your chops, young Buck Sergeant," while pointing to the bandage that was being applied to the gunshot and the head injury. "You okay?"

"They say I will be, Top. Sir," Thomas said, acknowledging the captain.

"Glad to see you, Sergeant Thomas," said Captain Robison. "You had us worried for a few days."

Hanon was uncomfortable and a little intimidated by the two *Lifer* hardcore Rangers. He quickly finished with the new bandage, and quietly dismissed himself from the small reunion as he moved on to the final bed in line. He may not have been happy to see them, but Thomas was.

"We thought we lost you. But now we learn you may receive two Purple Hearts for two wounds in as many days."

Thomas listened and nodded sheepishly, and then got to what was really more important on his mind that he needed to get out.

"PFC Norse and I got stuck inside the mountain after the explosion. I couldn't reach him. Did they get him out? Is...is he...?"

Thomas dreaded asking but he very much needed to know.

"He's alive. Specialist Li and one of the other members of your team got him out," said the captain. "He was flown out to Japan yesterday. He's busted up some, but he'll make it."

Thomas breathed a sigh of relief and then lowered his gaze.

"He only got hurt because I screwed up, Captain. It's my fault he's wounded. I shouldn't have chased after that NVA soldier inside the tunnel. I should have shot him instead, but I wanted to bring back a POW. Norse followed me in."

"Specialist Li says he heard you yell at him not to follow."

"He was just trying to help, sir. I'm the Team Leader, so it's my fault."

Thomas' response earned a quiet nod from the Company Commander and something more.

"No, Sergeant," said the officer. "That's on me. I'm the one who screwed up. I'm the one that offered a three-day in-country R&R for every POW brought in. I set the rules of play in motion. I'm just glad the two of you made it out."

"I figured if we snatched him up then we could get off the mountain with some good Intel," said Thomas and then went on to tell of all that had happened inside the mountain, his escape and running evasion. The hospital bed was a confessional of sorts with absolution coming in the form of a gift.

"We're told that they'll be Medevacing you to Japan as well, so the First Sergeant and I wanted to be sure you had this," Captain Robison said, reaching inside his cargo pants pocket and retrieving a black

Ranger beret. The officer handed the Ranger beret to the wounded Team Leader.

"Thank you, sir. First Sergeant," Thomas said, genuinely moved. He wasn't sure what to expect, an ass chewing maybe, but not this.

"When we get back to the Company, we'll pack your personal items up and make sure they're sent to your home address," said the captain.

Thomas nodded, again. "Much appreciated, sir. Oh, and if you find out where they put my things when they brought me in here, there's a notebook in one of the pockets you need to look at."

"Notebook?"

"Yes sir, a small notebook-like diary I took from the NVA soldier when I finally caught up to him after the explosion."

"You caught him?" said the First Sergeant.

"More like catch and release. He was pretty messed up from the explosion and cave in, too, but I pulled him into a cave after the explosion and left him for his buddies to find before I took off. The notebook's mostly his stuff, but I made some drawings and notes on what all I stumbled across. There were generators, some well lighted tunnels, storage chambers, water cisterns, ammo caches, stairways, and everything but a burger joint. The Nui Ba Den's like an angry ant-farm in there, sir. It really is."

"That's in the notebook?"

"Yes sir if you can make sense of my chicken scratch. I figured if I couldn't bring back a POW then I might as well bring something back that might be of some Intel value. A few of the pages might be smeared with some dirt and blood, and maybe some peanut butter."

"Peanut butter?"

"Yes, sir. I only had some C-ration crackers and peanut butter and a can of Turkey loaf on me when I got stuck inside the mountain."

Thomas told more of the extensive tunnel system in the Nui Ba Den, more of what he'd found, and how he avoided capture. He left out the part about being hit by Friendly Fire. When he was done both the First Sergeant and the captain were quietly staring at him.

"I wrote as much down as I could."

"In the notebook?" said the surprised and now impressed captain. The First Sergeant was impressed as well and the look on his face showed it. Poplawski hated tunnels.

"Yes, sir. As best and as much as I could. I made rough estimates on a few things, like the sizes and numbers of the storehouses, connecting tunnels, and distances between them. My step count was for shit at times, so there's that. It did get better, though, once I finally found a way out of the mountain. I tried to marry up the hidden entrance with my mission map and wrote down the approximate coordinates in the notebook. The map should still be in the right cargo pocket of my fatigues that they cut off me."

"Not to worry. We'll find the notebook and the map, Sergeant Thomas," Captain Robison said. "You done good, Ranger. Get some rest. We'll stop back in a few days to check in on you before they fly you out."

"Yes, sir," said Thomas. "And if Norse is still in Japan when I get there, I'll make a point of finding him. I'm just glad he's still alive."

"Too early to convince you to re-enlist, I suppose?" asked Poplawski.

Thomas laughed as best he could, given that the laughter sent a jolt of eye stabbing pain from his chest to his shoulder. He managed to laugh, anyway.

"Way too soon, First Sergeant, but even if I get out of the Army, I'll always be proud to have been a Lurp with Romeo company."

"Get some rest, sergeant," said Captain Robison. "We'll see you again, soon."

The hospital visit ended with all three feeling a little better or perhaps, relieved that some good had come out of the patrol. Robison would sleep better at night knowing that one of his people was no longer Missing in Action, but alive and soon to be on his way home. The map and the NVA soldier's diary with Thomas' notes, once they were recovered, translated, pored over, and analyzed, might even provide some valuable intelligence material or at least a better understanding of the inner workings of the puzzle that was the Nui Ba Den to the Higher-highers, even if they didn't always understand or appreciate what went into getting it. If they didn't, Robison did.

"I don't know about his time in grade as a PFC, but let's see if we can get Norse promoted to Spec-4, if we can," Robison said to Poplawski on their way out of the ward.

"Yes, sir," said Poplawski. "I think if we put him in for, say, an ARCOM with a V device that would better help the cause. I'm thinking a Bronze Star write-up for Sergeant Thomas?"

"Good call so let's get it done," said the Ranger captain.

An ARCOM was the Army Commendation Medal, with a V device meant it was for valor, for the badly wounded PFC it was for assisting his Team Leader in the capture of a POW. The award would no doubt be approved, as would the promotion at the U.S. Army Military facility in Japan.

The medal requests he made for Wade and Hagar had already been approved and the medal ceremonies would follow them to Camp Zama, Japan, too, if not there then certainly stateside at Letterman General Army Hospital or Walter Reed. The approvals came too late for Robison to personally present them so he would make a point of using whatever influence he had to push the medal requests through MAC-V Command. He wanted to personally present the Bronze Star to Thomas, as well as other medals to a few others for their recent actions during both firefights for several reasons. Firstly, because he'd been in the Army long enough to know that far too many others with more rank had received higher awards for a hell of a lot less. Secondly, there was a unscheduled time factor involved.

All four of the wounded Lurps had tough roads ahead of them with their recoveries. There would be more surgeries, more physical therapy, and they would heal, but it would be a long, slow, and painful process for each of them, and there would be scars and not all of them would be visible. The medals were warranted, and they would be small consolations and remedies.

"You didn't tell Sergeant Thomas about our meeting with MAC-V and their decision to deactivate the company, Captain?" said the First Sergeant as they followed a sign towards the Hospital's Admin office to retrieve the notebook and map.

"No, I think for morale purposes we'll keep that under our hat for a while. Need to Know basis. When we get back to Mackie, we'll let our two Lieutenants and SFC Kozak know what's happening. We still have, what, 50-days?"

"Barely."

"With no more access to new personnel, which means we'll be shutting down the selection training, too, and make do with who we have."

"We're down a few team leaders, sir."

Robison grunted, nodded. "We are, so I'll look to you and SFC Kozak for recommendations. Wouldn't hurt us to maybe conduct some heavy team operations," said the Captain, offering another viable option.

Poplawski nodded. Heavy teams consisted of ten team members or more with more than just reconnaissance in mind. He was thinking targeted raids and ambushes on the off-ramps into their A-O along the Ho Chi Minh Trail. He wouldn't mind getting back out the field for a few missions either. There was time for that but little more. Shutting down the unit would take the bulk of the time they had left.

"We'll need to take a look at our TO&E while we're at it too to see what we have on the books to turn in, and maybe get rid of whatever we've, eh, *borrowed* as well."

Poplawski was amused by that last part of the Captain's comment. Romeo Company had indeed *borrowed* more than a few items that they would need to get rid of before the unit was disbanded. Generally, with most units in Vietnam just before an annual Inspector-General's inventory, any and everything that wasn't officially on a unit' books would be loaded into whatever vehicles that had been *'borrowed'* and driven around the base or camp until the I-G auditors were done with their inspection. However, since Romeo Company was being disbanded the probability of an I-G team would show up for their inventory was low.

The I-G inspection teams would go over a unit's TO&E, the Army's Table of Organization and Equipment which was the game plan that outlined what each unit was assigned to operate. For Captain Robison that meant everything he had signed for. The list of items and equipment was long and covered everything from the weapons assigned to Romeo company to the radios in the TOC and what each team carried in the field to the jeep, truck, and flatbed mules in their small motor pool, as well as to the desks, typewriters, and any and everything of military value that the Army had issued to the unit.

What wasn't on the Ranger Company's TO&E were a *borrowed* jeep and one *borrowed* three-quarter ton truck that the Company had appropriated from another unit and had the original unit's markings painted over with Company R's markings to hide the fact that they'd both been stolen.

Also, not on the TO&E were several *borrowed* M-60 machine guns, 4 crates of 7.72 linked rounds for the machineguns, two *borrowed* M-14 rifles that were converted into sniper rifles, two *borrowed* Starlight night vision scopes, four *borrowed* M-79 grenade launchers, and 10 captured Soviet bloc AK-47 assault rifles, 9 SKS rifles, three Makarov pistols, and one RPG.

In the coming month they knew that the paint on the unit ID markings of the *borrowed* jeep and three-quarter ton truck could and would need to be scraped away and the vehicles driven to separate locations on the camp and left to be found. The bulk of the *extra* weapons and equipment could be easily passed along to other nearby combat units that would turn a blind eye to the offerings since additional firepower in the field was always appreciated, especially by recon units. Generally, the standard issue for a grunt platoon was one M-60 machine gun. In a firefight an additional M-60 or two could help make for a much better outcome.

Poplawski had an idea as well about some of the captured enemy weapons and offered it while they walked.

"You know, sir, several of the SKS rifles would make good war trophies to some folks," he said, outlining his idea. "I'm thinking maybe we get a few 'thank you' plaques made and say, present them to some worthy types, like the approving authority for the awards and decorations at MAC-V. I'm thinking that might help expedite the medal requests for our people. Maybe while we're at it present one to the Camp Mackie Commander, too?"

"Brigadier General Reese?"

"Yes, sir. He, at least, appreciates what we do."

"And Colonel Becker, the Assistant Base Commander? Do we give him one too?"

"No sir, fuck him. He never liked us anyway, especially after the sheepskin seat cover incident. His driver told one of our guys he's still whining about it. Makes me wish PFC Wexler had a bigger bladder."

The Ranger Company Commander chuckled. "One of these days you're going to have to learn how to stop holding things in, come out of that shell on yours, and let out your true feelings?"

"Thank you, sir. I'm trying my best to get over being a fucking wall flower, but it doesn't seem to be taking," said Poplawski.

"God help us all," said the Captain's chuckling and the chuckling turned into a belly laugh.

"So, any idea which Ranger Company you think will be the last one to go, sir?"

The Ranger officer shrugged. "The 1st CAV's Hotel Company Rangers, I suspect," he said. "Vietnamization is changing the playing field and who'll do the scrimmaging, all I know is that it won't be us. "

"Don't know what in the hell they're thinking, sir," grumbled Poplawski. "Lurp patrols have done some good out there."

"They have and they are," agreed the officer and that got him thinking about what else was on his mind with the deactivation order other than the TO&E. "While we're at it, let's make sure we get a number of the others in the Company some official recognition before we're shut down."

"Roger that, captain," agreed Poplawski.

"Maybe try to get some of those who still have time left on their tours better transfers or stateside duty stations, and some early outs for those with under 90-days left in service."

"I'm sure they'll appreciate it, sir. We have some stellar people, well, give or take maybe a few shitheads."

Robison chuckled. "But good Lurps?"

Poplawski reluctantly agreed. "True. So, what assignments do you want me to find for them, the shitheads?"

"We'll let Command sort that out because, I suspect, they'll somehow find a way to manage, seeing how they'll either end up in jail or in Congress."

"Romeo Company did some good, sir. We still are."

"A shame MAC-V doesn't see it that way."

"50 days," muttered Poplawski.

"And then Romeo Company is disbanded."

Neither said anything more for a good while as they made their way to Admin Office to track down the missing NVA diary and team map. Their minds were elsewhere, a lot had happened, and a lot more needed to happen.

They still had 50 days and there was much to be done.

Coming soon.

Sweet Sorrow

Book III and the final installment of the Chasing Romeo Lurp Jungle War Series.

CPSIA information can be obtained
at www.ICGtesting.com
Printed in the USA
BVHW090837180222
629431BV00006B/50

9 781647 199067